Praise for The Blackhart Legacy

'De Jager's fantasy world is enthralling and immersive, many fathoms deep . . . wonderful'
M. R. Carey

'One action-packed story! Full of battles, weapons, mythical creatures and, of course, magic – it's guaranteed to keep you on the edge of your seat from start to finish'
Guardian

'The intriguing plot – set across human and Fae worlds – is interspersed with twists and traitors that you're not likely to see coming, and will keep you reading'
SciFiNow

'A juicy mystery, elusive leads, scattered clues and no little excitement as Kit and Dante venture ever nearer to

Judged

While writing her debut novel, *Banished*, Liz de Jager fostered her love of YA and genre fiction by developing the popular *My Favourite Books* review blog. This ran for seven years and enabled her to gain a unique insight into the publishing industry. She grew up in South Africa and now lives and works in the UK with her husband, Mark. *Judged* is her third novel.

You can find out more about Liz here:
www.lizdejager.co.uk

Or follow her on Twitter:
@LizUK

By Liz de Jager

Banished
Vowed
Judged

LIZ DE JAGER

Judged

The Blackhart Legacy: Book Three

TOR

First published 2016 by Tor
an imprint of Pan Macmillan
20 New Wharf Road, London N1 9RR
Associated companies throughout the world
www.panmacmillan.com

ISBN 978-1-4472-4770-8

1 3 5 7 9 8 6 4 2

A CIP catalogue record for this book is available from the British Library.

Typeset by Palimpsest Book Production Ltd, Falkirk, Stirlingshire
Printed and bound by CPI Group (UK) Ltd, Croydon, CR0 4YY

Visit www.panmacmillan.com to read more about all our books
and to buy them. You will also find features, author interviews and
news of any author events, and you can sign up for e-newsletters
so that you're always first to hear about our new releases.

T DEJA
18738650
(Fantasy)

This book, the final one in the trilogy, is dedicated to my parents. Mum, Dad, you raised me to never give up and to believe in myself. You taught me that stories matter. Thank you. I miss you every day.

Acknowledgements

A book is written by one person, the writer. But it's the invisible people in the background who make it all happen so that the writer can hold that finished product of their hard work in their grubby paws and say: 'I wrote this.'

A debt I don't think I can ever repay goes to my agent, Juliet Mushens, who kicks my butt, has my back, and can talk kissing, fights, the effects of magic on technology and how impossible it is to run in high heels on wet grass when running away from ogres . . . she's pretty damn special. Juliet believed in me and in Kit and these books when I had no idea what I was doing. She's been my champion from the beginning, and I would not be here today if it wasn't for her.

Huge thanks to my editor Bella Pagan at Pan Macmillan, who, when we first met to talk about the book, leaned closer to me and told me how much she loved the world and wanted to know everything about it. I think I fell in love with her a little that day. Bella handled me well, she taught me what was expected of me and she had so much patience for a noob. I appreciate it all and I hope I've made her proud. By Bella's side was her assistant, Louise Buckley, who has never failed to be warm, encouraging and genuinely lovely to me whenever we meet up. Thank you for the tweets and emails of encouragement! Naturally, epic hugs of thanks have to go to the Pan Mac art department. I mean, look at my stunning covers! They're so recognizable and gorgeous. I still can't believe my words are contained between these covers.

Over at Pan Mac South Africa I have to send all the hugs to my publicist there, Tarryn Talbot-Da Costa, who, even though she was thousands of miles away, sent me emails and encouraged me to stay in touch. I can't thank you enough for looking after both me and Mark when we visited in May 2015, Tarryn; your hard work is much appreciated. And to all the press, authors and bloggers I met at events whilst in South Africa: I can't begin to express how pleased I was to meet you all. You are my people – thank you for your support!

My experience at Pan Macmillan as one of their authors has been great. The editorial department and my copy-editors and proofreaders were all genuinely amazing and helped me work hard on the trilogy. I appreciate every single one of you. I grumbled, I moaned, but I know you guys did your best and that made me want to do my best, so thank you for all your hard work.

Now onto everyone else. My friends Sarah Bryars, Sharon Jones, Zoe Marriott, Tanya Byrne, Karen Mahoney, Tiffany Trent, Nazia Khatun, Nick Coveney, Edward Partidge, Jenni Nock (from the top of my head, there are so very many more) and all of Team Mushens, the UK YA community (writers, readers, bloggers): you guys are incredible. Your support has meant the world to me. You cheered me on, you kept me on track, you listened and you gave advice and it kept me going.

Of course I have to thank my crazy massive extended family in South Africa too, but especially my oldest sister, Elize, and her husband, Shayne: I love you guys so much. Your support over the years has been amazing because you never stopped believing in me. A girl couldn't ask for anything more from her siblings. Huge hugs have to go to Michelle Kirshenbaum (Penguin Girl), who introduced me to my first ever Cornelia Funke book all those many years ago and is sort of to blame for me wanting to write even more than I did before. I love you so much, my friend. Thank you for believing in me and for all your unfailing support.

I could go on and on much like a dreaded Oscar speech here; but I won't, because you'd prefer to read the final instalment of the trilogy, I'm sure. But there is one more thank-you I need to write down, because I don't think he realizes how much he means to me.

The final thanks go to my husband, Mark. An amazing writer in his own right, he has had infinite patience with me as I wrote the trilogy; as I stressed, had sleepless nights and cried about plots not making sense and characters misbehaving. He sat with me, brainstormed with me and helped me choreograph fight sequences so that they read 'true'. He stopped the house from exploding around us both as I filled it with more books and paper and research, and through all this he kept me sane. Sweetpea, you are my touchstone and the one person I know will always be there for me. You are my man, my Jacopo. I hope I can do as good a job for you as you did for me when you go through all of this yourself!

The trouble is not in dying for a friend,
but in finding a friend worth dying for.

Mark Twain

Prologue

The Otherwhere, Alba – The Fae Lands

Thorn stared down at the corpse of the great antlered elk at his feet. After a glance around the small glade to ensure he was unobserved, he placed his bow by his side and crouched by the head of the beast, resting a hand on the antler. He took a moment to mourn the passing of the majestic creature felled by disease rather than old age or a hunter's arrow.

The soft velvet covering the growth felt unnaturally brittle to his touch. Leaning closer, he ran a gentle hand up to one of the tines and, gripping the point between his fingers, he gave a firm twist. The tip of the antler broke off and crumbled to dust in his palm.

Wiping his hands clean against his thighs, he picked up his bow once more, ensured his quiver was settled against his back, and stood to move around the animal's body.

The clearing itself showed no sign of any animal or bird activity. What was more telling was that the beast had not been butchered by any of the goblins that inhabited the wilder parts of the forest. The elk had also been dead for at least a week and nothing had tried to eat it. Apparently not even Winter, wrapping her dark cloak over the land, could convince the various foxes, wolves, crows and ravens to dine on the red elk.

The giant red elk were rare in the Otherwhere and were truly the undisputed giants of the forest. He'd been taught they were completely extinct in the Frontier, in the human lands – there they had been hunted for their succulent meat and pelts thousands of years ago – and now they only survived in the forests of the Otherwhere.

As much as he regretted the creature's passing, finding the dead elk had not been a surprise.

It had taken him weeks to pinpoint the discomfort he'd felt, which had settled into his bones. Acting on instinct, he'd eventually taken his bow and escaped into the ancient forest with his tutor (and jailer) Odalis's hounds by his side. He'd been gone a week now, by his estimation. He'd walked from sunup till sundown, tracking the source of the dissonance that thrummed so deeply within him.

The sense of discord had been keeping him awake at night, a continual distracting background noise to all he did. He'd trekked for days, following the discordant tone and its feeling of wrongness. Then, as he'd neared the clearing with the dead elk, the hum of the tone had changed – becoming louder until it dominated all else. But when he'd knelt by the creature's lifeless body, all sound had ceased and in its wake the silence was deafening.

A rustle from nearby drew his attention and two of the hounds loped towards him. Behind them he recognized the shape of the Fae high king's forester, Crow. Like Thorn, he was dressed for moving swiftly and quietly through the forest; he bore a longbow in one hand, a long curving knife at his side and a quiver of arrows fletched with white feathers on his back.

'Guardian.' Crow's lip twisted at Thorn's honorary title. His gaze swept the glade, across Thorn, and came to rest on the corpse of the bloated animal. 'You found him.'

'I did.'

'There is more. Come.'

He beckoned Thorn to follow him. The dogs jumped up at Thorn and, once he'd acknowledged them by patting their sleek heads, they spun off into the forest ahead of the two Fae, tails held high.

Thorn followed the forester for what felt like an age. The forest grew more and more dense, the light disappearing almost completely under the heavy canopy. The air felt damp and thick with ancient magics. The denizens here were primitive and not all of them were friendly towards the Sidhe sons of Alba.

Crow moved swiftly ahead of him, occasionally making sure Thorn was keeping up, but he gave the young prince no quarter, setting a punishing pace.

The forest was so very old that it almost seemed to have developed a life of its own. Thorn couldn't help imagining it as one unique living and breathing entity – and like every living entity it had to have a heart. Thorn suspected this was what Crow wanted to show him. If the heart of the wood was sick, the rest of the organism would also suffer.

'Look up.'

Thorn frowned at the curt instruction but obeyed, his jaw dropping open at the sight of an enormous tree stretching to the heavens. He struggled to take it in at first, then turned back to where Crow stood patiently waiting for him.

'This is what we are allowed to see – above ground,' Crow said. 'Come, she is ready to meet you.'

3

'She?'

'I call her *she*. She seems to like it.'

Crow pressed a hand against the bark and gestured for Thorn to do the same. It felt warm beneath his touch and Thorn almost pulled his hand away in surprise. He leaned against the trunk and closed his eyes, breathing in deeply. The air here was pleasant and smelled of warm, lazy summer days and rich earth. For all the tranquillity, Thorn could sense something bruised, something darker. The undertone of decay.

Crow watched him with an intent look and when the forester gave him a nod, Thorn steadied his heartbeat and allowed his consciousness to shift and sink into the heart of the forest.

He was disorientated for only a moment, then she was there. A majestically tall figure behind his closed eyes. She reached for him imperiously and he allowed her to drag him deeper into the wider stream of power that made up her pulse. His consciousness was flung upwards, and suddenly he was seeing the vast primeval forest from her dizzying upper heights. The forest was vast and sweeping, stretching from horizon to horizon.

She pulled at him once he'd taken in the endless forests, and he scrambled to bring all of himself present. He thought that she would leave it at that, but instead she plunged his consciousness ever downwards and then flung it outwards. He realized that he was not only to see the forest from above, but to experience it from below as well.

She pushed him through the intricate root system at disorientating speeds; he sagged heavily against her bark, unaware of Crow steadying him. He let her push him ahead of her and he now saw the reason for her urgency. As

4

tremendous as the forest appeared from above, the root system was even more intricate and impressive. It was also where he found the cancerous growths. They grew thick and black on the roots of the trees, ugly pustules that suffocated and killed their hosts.

There were so many, hundreds of thousands of them, spread throughout the entire forest. The trees were dying, suffocating from below. And as they were dying, the animals living off them were also being poisoned, and so the sickness spread wide. He saw wooded groves lying dead or dying and felt the ache of their loss in his bones.

If the dark forest died, the heart of the Otherwhere would die. The death of the forest meant the death of the Otherwhere, and what happens in the Otherwhere happens in the Frontier. Fleeting images of a desolate wasteland, skeletal buildings and savage packs of humans and animals preying on one another came unbidden. The vision was so vividly powerful that Thorn struggled to disengage from it, ultimately dipping himself further into the magic surrounding him in an attempt to escape it.

A sense of her approval came over him and he realized she'd meant for him to see this, to understand fully that it wasn't just the Otherwhere at stake. She pulled him from his reverie and led him back into the clearing, her presence fading gradually as she sank into the leylines once more.

Thorn moved away from Crow's steadying embrace and sat down heavily on the ground beside her trunk. He opened his eyes with difficulty, fully expecting still to see roots before his eyes – but instead he found the forester watching him curiously.

'She showed you the disease?'

'It's everywhere,' Thorn acknowledged. 'The infection is everywhere.'

'I have walked this forest all my life, boy. I sense the ebb and flow of its magic and it no longer feels stable. Nura and the other foresters are reporting that there are more remote parts of the forest that can no longer sustain those that dwell within. And the disease is spreading rapidly.'

'The roots of the Otherwhere bind the realms together and the Veil sustains the magic within the Otherwhere. In turn the Veil is fed by the power in the goddess.' Thorn closed his eyes. 'The root of all of this is the goddess's power failing. Our world is coming apart, Crow, and I don't know what to do to fix it. I'm not . . . I'm just not up to the task. I know *nothing*. What if I'm not able to save the Otherwhere? The worlds would die.'

'Nothing lasts forever, boy.' Crow put a hand on Thorn's shoulder. 'And there is time yet. It's not in our nature merely to accept our destruction.'

Thorn stood and moved away from the forester, pacing the small clearing. 'Imagine what would happen to the Frontier if the Veil between the Fae and human lands came apart entirely? We'd have packs of redcaps and ogres roaming their cities, picking off solitary humans, and then they'd become brazen enough to attack whole city blocks. The carnage, once the human authorities caught wind of what was going on, would be impossible to determine. If humans then found their way into the Otherwhere, into Alba, there would be a full-scale war – and in a war between humans and Fae, neither side would win.'

Crow cast a thoughtful eye over the younger noble Fae, before speaking once more. 'We will do what we can to ensure the safety of our worlds, Guardian. As long as we are alive, we can fight; and if we fight there is a chance we might succeed.'

Chapter One

A month is not long enough to recover.

The speedbag hums under my steady rhythmic onslaught. I break from it. Pick up the rope and start skipping, varying my speeds as I watch the clock. I skip for ten minutes before I jog over to the wooden man and flow into a series of blocks and blows.

Kick.

Block.

Punch.

Duck.

Punch.

Kick.

I do this until I realize my exercise playlist has cycled over for the second time. I'm the only one down here in the Garretts' gym, and if the playlist is repeating itself, it means I've been down here for at least three hours. Although I'm tired, I'm still carrying residual anxiety that makes me feel tense.

It doesn't help knowing that I'm not up to full speed or fighting fitness and that this is mostly due to cuts and bruises not healing the way they should. And that in turn is down to me being unable to sleep for more than two or three hours at a time, if I'm lucky.

I've gulped down half a bottle of water when I jump, realizing someone's watching me from the doorway. I turn, readying for a fight, but find myself staring at Dante. He's propped himself against the closed door with a thoughtful expression on his face.

'Creeping much?' I say, and my voice shakes only slightly as I recover from the shock of his sudden appearance.

'I've called your name twice and you didn't hear me,' he points out evenly and walks over to hand me a fresh towel.

I take it and wipe my face and neck before tossing it aside.

'You gonna come train with me?'

'No. I got tired just watching you and I'm worried that if I spar with you, you'll just punch me out.' His smile smooths the bite in his tone. 'Besides, you've been down here for hours ignoring us. Come upstairs, we've ordered pizza. We're doing a movie night *and* Leo's here, kicking Aiden's butt on Xbox – so you have to come and save him from being completely annihilated.'

'Leo is a deviant Xbox fanatic. There is nothing I can do to save Aiden. He's on his own.'

'But you'll come up and hang out with us?' He leans a little forward and drops his voice, making it drip with schmaltzy sexy allure. 'Pizza, Kit. Real pizza. Not even the frozen stuff, but homemade pizza as made by the Italian restaurant around the corner.'

I grin at his antics and push his face away. 'Fine. But I'm not sharing with any of you.' I'm hungry and pizza fixes all ills. Or at least, it goes a long way to fixing all ills. I grab my towels and the remote, turning the music off before switching off the lights in the gym. I follow Dante down the passage to the showers.

'Aiden said that if you needed any T-shirts, he's left some in the bathroom for you.'

'Yeah, I got some blood on my T-shirt and I didn't bring too many changes of clothes for the weekend.'

'You got "some blood" on your T-shirt? Huh, I'll pretend to take that story at face-value but when you're ready to tell me the truth, you know where to find me.' His gaze settles heavily on my face. 'You know you can talk to me, right? We're still partners, still friends.'

I nod and duck my head so he can't see my face properly because I really don't need his kindness or concerned looks right now. I don't deserve them.

'Take your time. The pizza place will have their hands full as the guys ordered seven pizzas, all large.'

In the end I have a long shower and change into yoga pants and one of Aiden's softest, oldest rock T-shirts.

I ignore my face in the mirror as I swiftly finger-comb my hair, smearing product into it and despairing that it's getting long again. I don't see my too-pale face or how my eyes are stark and a little too big and wild. No, I ignore any signs of that and instead I practise smiling and looking like a nice person rather than someone who would fail their mission. Someone who would leave small children trapped in faerie, having the life leached out of them to keep a goddess alive.

There is a lot of noise. Aiden and Leo are playing Mortal Kombat on the Xbox in the main lounge off the kitchen. There's more shouting, swearing and the occasional punch going on there than on the screen. Shaun, Aiden's older brother, is talking to someone on the phone, possibly his dad, and Dante's flipping through a newspaper, waiting for the kettle to boil.

He looks up when I walk in.

'You look better.'

'Thereby implying I didn't look okay before?'

'Yes.'

'You're a terrible flirt.'

'So Aiden keeps telling me.'

I laugh outright at that because Dante looks so very disgruntled. 'I'd love some coffee, if you're okay with the stink of it?'

'Machine or instant?'

'Instant is fine.' I pull myself onto the counter and watch Aiden trying to kick Leo off the couch while they play. 'They act like they're three.'

'I think they are. They bring the worst out in one another.'

Dante comes to stand close to me. I lean against him and we stay like that for a few seconds, watching Leo and Aiden. I skim the newspaper he left on the counter. The headline shouts about the unseasonably cold conditions, with meteorologists struggling to make sense of the shifting weather patterns. I follow the article onto page five, where there are quotes by scientists on high-pressure cells, low-pressure cells, climate change and the risk of flooding. There are so many similarities to when Olga manifested in dragon form – over a year ago now – with the power of her shape-shifting disrupting the world's balance.

'What are you thinking?' Dante asks.

'That the weather is just as up the creek as when Black-hart Manor was attacked by the dragon.'

He sips his tea, watching me over the rim with a steady

expression, before guessing my own thoughts. 'Do you think this is Thorn's doing?'

'I really don't know. But it would make sense if it was down to him.' And here we are, openly talking about what we saw in the Otherwhere a month ago – for the first time. That day we ran for our lives, leaving Thorn behind to tear our attackers apart after his own change into dragon form. 'But Thorn shifted in the Otherwhere, so I'm not sure why that would affect us on the human side. And it's probably been over a month, so why would the weather only start responding now?' I frown. 'Do *you* really think Thorn is behind the weather, then?' We stare at one another for a few long silent moments. I drink my coffee, barely tasting its black bitter twist on my tongue, before speaking again. 'It could just be nature, you know. Getting her freak on.'

'You don't really think that, do you?'

I think for a bit and hold up a finger. 'Let's "what-if" this. The Veil between the Fae realm and our own is permeable. Magic trickles through in places, we know that, and it's been happening for hundreds of years. And when Thorn shifted into a dragon, he used magic and no doubt tapped into the songlines to fuel the transformation too.'

'And the songlines criss-cross the earth, carrying magical energies on both sides of the Veil . . .' he prompts me.

'Which means it's likely that his shift affected not just our world,' I continue, 'but the Otherwhere too. When Olga manifested as a dragon here, destroying the Manor, the weather started going weird almost immediately. If Thorn's shift has done the same, why are we only seeing the weather patterns changing now?'

'I can only imagine the amount of energy it took to shift shape like that.' Dante pauses to trace the newspaper headline mentioning the bad weather with a finger. 'Maybe the type of energy he used is different. Perhaps with him being the guardian of the realms the power shift was more controlled and it took this long to hit us.'

I recall the draw of power I felt as we ran from Thorn into the forest, leaving him behind, at his own insistence. 'It could be.'

We hear shouting and glance towards the lounge. Aiden's jumped up and is crowing his excitement about a spectacular knockout in the game, but Leo isn't taking it so well.

Dante looks away from the fighting boys with a shake of his head. 'Have you tried contacting Thorn?'

I nod, fingering Thorn's gift to me – the silver and obsidian pendant. It's replaced the Blackhart antler for everyday wear, unless I go out on a job. I just couldn't bear to lose my connection to him.

'Yes. I've not been able to reach him using this at all. I get the sense he's there, that he's aware of me peripherally, but it's as if he's just not really present or listening to me.'

'But he's okay?'

I pull back a bit. 'Yes, of course. Why wouldn't he be?'

'He did a crazy thing, Kit. He turned into a dragon. And then set the *forest on fire* to protect us. He went up against a small army to keep you safe.'

My expression must have shifted because Dante suddenly has his hands on my shoulders.

'Oh, hell. I'm sorry. I'm being an idiot. I didn't think that you'd . . .'

'No, no, it's fine. I'm okay, sorry.' I take a moment before looking up at him, not liking the genuine concern I'm seeing in his eyes. 'It's just . . . I'd *know* if he wasn't okay.'

'You would?'

I nod, and I mean it. But it's not something I've given much thought to, this feeling of knowing that Thorn is okay, just not *present* or accessible. I've not had any shared dreams with him either and it's been over a month. I didn't realize how much I'd come to rely on the occasional contact, the little chats we'd had, the small touches.

Dante sighs under his breath and reaches up to brush hair from my forehead.

'You need to talk things out, Kit. I'm worried about you.'

'I'm fine. I promise.' I smile at him and know he can hear the lie. I sense the smile isn't reaching my eyes so I stretch my mouth wider, forcing myself to look happy. It's always worked in the past, this pretending to be okay. If you pretend hard enough, you start believing you're okay. I'm good at this.

'Kit.' He's next to me, so close I can feel his magic brush up against mine. 'You're lying. You're not fine. Neither am I. I look like crap and so do you. We –' he gestures between us – 'are not okay.'

Dante's hair's no longer neat and tidy and his glasses have gone missing somewhere. There are dark circles under his eyes and he looks like the type of boy you'd cross the street to avoid, even in broad daylight. After he'd come back from the Otherwhere, he did a few weeks at HMDSDI, the Spooks' HQ, helping his fellow agents with an ongoing investigation. He also tidied up the Child Thief paperwork as much as he could, before putting in for a month's leave. Aiden forced him to move into the massive Garrett mansion and has been keeping an eye on him – reporting to me that Dante has been spending a lot of time in the gym, doing insane amounts of workouts and going over his martial arts katas. He'd disappear for hours, doing Parkour runs around the city, returning just to sleep for a few hours before repeating the behaviour all over again. And now, when Dante's not working himself to exhaustion in the gym, he's having long conversations with his adopted parents in Bristol – leaving him miserable. It's why Aiden asked me to spend the weekend, to see if being around Dante would help him chill out a little. But he's comforting me. Looking up into the Fae's shadowed eyes and seeing my own pain mirrored there, I have to hold back tears. We were both trying to forget leaving the kids behind with Brixi, what we'd learned about the goddess, but there were some things you just couldn't turn your back on.

'Okay. We're not fine. What do we do? How do we fix it?'

'I thought you'd know. You *are* the expert.'

I snort. 'Yeah, not so much.'

Our conversation is interrupted by a delivery of a mountain of pizza boxes and ice cream. At the sight of the food, Aiden commits suicide in the game, but he's not fast enough to beat Leo, who just tosses the controller to the side, flips himself over the couch and into the kitchen.

There's nothing about Leo that I don't like. It's easy to see how he can fit in so seamlessly with the werewolves and be Aiden's best mate, whilst not really being part of their world at all.

'Hey,' he says, passing me a plate, as if he doesn't know the Garretts never use plates for pizza. 'We're going out later. You wanna come along?'

'Is it the Glow thing?' I'm reluctant to be involved, mostly because of sheer stubbornness. The fact that Uncle Andrew effectively handed the Glow drug case to the wolves, bypassing me, still smarted. Yes, I was working on the Child

Thief case at the time, but I could still easily have looked into who was distributing the drugs that were being given away *for free* across London clubs and illegal raves. When Glow was *my* case, I made some progress – tracking down the Fae, Lady Morika and her small team, as they set up a deal to further distribute Glow in the Frontier using one of the Jericho gang. I sent Morika back to face the Sun King's judgement for her part in the distribution of drugs in the Frontier, and yet it seems that I'd hardly made a dent. Then I was put on the Child Thief case. But that case is closed, no matter how much I wish it wasn't, and my hands are tied in this respect too – and I know Shaun and his older brother Connor have been working on more Glow leads, and without Uncle Andrew's permission I can't interfere or help as officially it's no longer my case.

'No, not a Glow thing. It's a new club opening and I got us on the guest list.' He looks at me, eyebrows raised expectantly. 'The DJ is supposed to be really good.'

'One of your dad's?'

'Not this time: a friend of his, from France. Kit, come out with us. You've not danced in ages.' He watches my expression as he sneaks a slice from my pizza onto his plate. 'Come on, it will be fun.'

I wrap some mozzarella around my finger as I consider the offer. Leo's father owns a number of nightclubs so, with Leo's help, the wolves have a direct line into what's going on in the clubbing world to track Glow distribution. And Leo's been collecting rumours and tips for the boys to run down. But he's promising tonight isn't to do with Glow. Four weeks ago I'd have been all over this because I love dancing, but right now? After everything that's happened? It is the last thing I want to do.

'I'm sorry, Leo. I'm not in the mood for people or crowds.'

'Bad excuse, Blackhart,' Aiden grumbles next to me. 'Dante's coming along, right?' When Dante nods, Aiden turns back to me, draping his arms around Dante and Leo, pulling them in close. 'Come on, come out with your best bros. We'll make sure you have fun. F.U.N. Right? No one will mess with you, I promise.' He winks at me and gives me a pleading look.

'You play a good game, Garrett, but no. You won't change my mind.'

'We promise not to get into any trouble,' he continues, looking hopeful. 'There'll be no fights. None. No bleeding, no flirting, just dancing and having fun.'

'I like how you put bleeding and flirting in the same sentence, like there's no separation.' I laugh at Aiden. 'But no, come on. You didn't mention this when you picked me up earlier. I don't have clothes to wear out. I just want to chill out at home.'

Surprisingly it's Leo who comes to my rescue. 'Yeah, that's fine. But next time? These guys are idiots and only behave when you're around.'

After we've eaten, Leo checks his phone and his dad's confirmed they're on the list, but a frown mars his usually smooth forehead.

'My dad's not happy about us going to this and would prefer us not to go.'

'Cos it's not one of his clubs?' Aiden asks as he removes the pizza boxes.

'No, it's Glow. There's more of it getting into clubs and it's spreading. More kids are using and no one will say where it's coming from. The cops are desperate for leads and no one is talking.'

Shaun grunts in response. 'Connor and I have been going nuts getting anyone to give us anything but nothing. Nothing is working – not money, not threats. Connor's in a grump like you cannot believe.'

'Even worse a grump than when I superglued his hand to the remote when he fell asleep?'

Shaun tosses a used napkin at Aiden before pushing away from the counter and loading the dishwasher with Leo and Dante's plates. 'About ten times worse.'

Aiden squints at his older brother. 'Shaun, you guys said this was under control.'

'We thought it was, okay? Things aren't as easy as we thought.'

'So, maybe tonight's not just a party. Let's see what we can find out. Someone must know who's dealing.' Aiden stares hard at Shaun, who seems reluctant enough, but he nods. Aiden turns back to me. 'You sure you don't want to come along, Kit?'

'I'm not . . .' I sigh and scrub my face. 'You know I'm off the case, Aide. I can't do this.'

Leo heads to the lounge to grab his keys. 'I'm going home, I need to change. I'll see you guys at the club. I'll text you the address.'

Shaun pulls a face and I appreciate that he's trying to play down the sombre tone that's crept into the evening. 'As the responsible adult in this venture, let me just say I'm not spending the whole night keeping you guys out of trouble. Aiden! Listen to me. Are we clear? No fights. I will leave your werewolf ass behind for the police to sort out.'

Aiden seems unperturbed by Shaun's glare. 'Fine. Just so we're clear: I'll keep an eye on *Leo*. He likes to mack on girls who've got boyfriends. I have to keep pulling his ass out of the fire.'

Leo gasps his denial as he heads towards the massive front door.

'Shut up, Garrett. Or next time three of your exes team up against you, I'm not helping.'

Chapter Two

I'm downstairs scrolling through Netflix when Aiden comes down from changing. He flops down on the couch and pulls me into a tight hug against his lean body. It's a new thing this, him being hands-on with me, and when I called him on it he just shrugged and said, 'Why can't I cuddle against my friend who looks like she needs it? Do you hate it? Do you want me to stop?' and I had to agree that it wasn't entirely unpleasant. I can't shake the feeling that he thinks his proximity to me will help ease that band of anxiety across my chest that makes my heart thump too fast and with too much pain at really odd times.

Aiden presses his nose into my hair and takes a deep breath. 'Blackhart. I've missed you.'

'You've seen me every day, Aiden, since we got back from, you know . . .' my hand stirs the air lightly before dropping back to my lap.

'Being chased out of the Otherwhere by some ogres? Yeah, that's not what I meant, and you know it. I'm talking about you not being here, Kit. I watch you and I see a girl going through the motions of being present but you, the stuff that makes you *you*, is gone.'

I don't speak for a while. 'It's just hard for me, this time.

Harder than before. Leaving it all behind, coming back here. There's so much that the last case left unresolved – Brixi, the kids.'

'Thorn,' he prompts softly and I nod, not even fighting against the tears forming in my eyes.

'Thorn. Yes.'

We ignore how small my voice sounds and sit in silence staring at the list of movies on the screen in front of us. There's more, but I try not to think about it. Nosebleeds have become a regular thing now too and even just acknowledging them to myself is enough to freak me out. So I don't, employing the age-old *if I ignore it, it will go away* tactic that I'm pretty sure my family invented.

The silence is marred by music coming from the floor above, where it sounds like a herd of buffalo are dancing. I glance up at the ceiling; the light is swaying dangerously.

'Shaun,' Aiden offers, following my gaze. 'He has the grace of a flailing hippo.'

I laugh because it's true. I've seen Shaun dance. It gets ugly really fast.

Aiden shifts against me and clears his throat. 'Kit, listen. Can I talk to you about something?'

'As long as it's not asking me about borrowing my car, we're okay.' I locate the search box on the screen and put the remote down. 'Okay, ask away.'

'This thing with Dante.'

'You like him?'

'I think so.'

'Does he like you?'

'I think so.'

'You know he's my friend too. If you break his heart, I'll have to hurt you loads. And I've been trained how to

22

hurt werewolves. You taught me how. Don't make me use silver on you.'

Aiden's laughter makes me grin as he replies. 'That's it? No dire warnings, no crying because you're a little bit in love with him?'

'I was never in love with him, Aide. He's sweet and he reminds me a little of Thorn. But other than that, there was never anything more.'

'Oh, well, that's okay then.'

'You wanted me to make more of it?'

I look up at him and what I see in his eyes makes me pause because I've become so used to Aiden falling in and out of love with boys and girls, it's never occurred to me that he would one day actually like someone for real. 'Okay, so, are you telling me you *like him* like him?'

'Yes. I think so.'

I worry at my lower lip and frown at him. There's so much that can go wrong if things go south with them. And I don't even want to think about the rule that Fae and humans must not be together, which has kept me and Thorn apart. Does this mean werewolf and Fae relationships and even same-sex relationships fall under the same taboo?

'Kit.' Aiden's voice is very quiet, but it still stops me and I stare at him. 'I'm not asking him to marry me, okay? I don't even know him all that well. And, yes, he's attractive and when he does the whole magic thing I sort of forget how to behave like a sane person. But it's more than physical, Kit. This is serious. This isn't me being dumb about someone because of hormones or the thrill of the chase. This is actual deep stuff and I don't want to screw this up by being stupid around him.'

I feel like the wind's taken out of my sails and I stare at him.

'Oh, no,' I breathe because I get it. 'We are screwed if you're going to go soft on me and all emotional.'

He laughs and leans his forehead against mine. 'I know.'

'This is a little crazy. Do you know if he's interested back?'

'Oh, I know it's crazy, but I think so. He's not said or done anything, you know, to say otherwise. I flirt like crazy and he flirts back and it's really good. Being around him makes me and my wolf feel happy. I would just like the luxury of liking someone where I don't have to hide who I am – and maybe he likes me back a little. Who knows?'

'Just be careful, Aiden. I don't think I can fix you guys if you break one another.'

He rumbles something against me and hugs me closer. 'I love you, Blackhart.'

'I love you too, wolf boy.'

He makes a little satisfied noise and kisses the top of my head and it makes me laugh. I fall asleep like that, leaning against him, and for maybe half an hour there are no nightmares or monsters stalking my dreams.

The Otherwhere, Alba, the Citadel

'My liege?'

Aelfric, High King of Alba, one of the most powerful men of the Otherwhere, peered expectantly over the glasses perched on the tip of his nose, fork paused halfway to his mouth. It was the one thing upon which he insisted: an undisturbed lunch served within the privacy of his chambers. No one would dare disturb him – except, of course, his lieutenant and left-hand man.

'You're interrupting, Oswald.'

Oswald schooled his features to look deferential and apologetic. The obvious show fooled no one, least of all Aelfric, who sat back in his chair with the air of someone greatly put upon.

'Speak, man. Or are you here to watch me eat?'

'Sire, I have come from meeting with one of our . . .' Oswald's mouth twists around the word. '. . . Informants.'

Aelfric pursed his lips. 'Which one was this, again?'

'The fire pixie, sire. You personally vetted her as an informant.'

'Ah, yes.' Then. 'No. I don't remember her. What did she have to say for herself?'

'She's found the boy, sire.'

Aelfric paused thoughtfully, head tilted to the side slightly as he considered Oswald's words. 'Which boy would this be?'

'Eadric's son.'

'Well, now. That's a thing.'

'Indeed.'

'And where did our enterprising pixie find my traitor brother's illegitimate son?'

'Eadric did marry the prin—' Oswald stopped mid-sentence at Aelfric's dark look. He cleared his throat. 'He's with the Blackhart girl. They were spotted together several times in the past few weeks.'

Aelfric pretended not to notice Oswald's wary gaze or how the man took a step back when he rose from his chair.

'Does the boy know of his lineage?'

'We aren't certain.' Oswald turned to face him as Aelfric moved towards the windows. 'What would you have me do, sire?'

'The Blackhart girl, does she know who he is?'

'That's not clear either, but it would be wise to assume that she does. And if she does, the boy would know too.'

'Kill them both.'

If Oswald had any quibbles or questions, Aelfric would never know. The man did as he was told and always had done. It was why Aelfric paid him so well.

Oswald bowed briefly before slipping from the king's chambers through a hidden door. Only a handful of people even knew of its existence and the king liked it that way.

Aelfric seated himself once more, but the food no longer appealed. He felt a cold, hard rush of anger and allowed his magic to run free, overturning the laden table onto the floor. The crash as it fell brought guards and a young page running.

'I'm done. Clean this up.'

Aelfric waited until his staff had hastily set the room to rights before he entered the adjoining private audience room. He saved it for his more clandestine gatherings – outside the remit of his privy council.

'I need you to escalate the spread of the drug,' Aelfric told the lone waiting Sidhe. 'I don't care how you do it. Flood the Frontier with the stuff. Use everyone we have at our disposal. I no longer care about being careful or working to a slow or steady timescale. Do it now. I want the Frontier under my control by the New Year.'

'It's going to be a risk, your majesty. The Veil isn't strong enough to handle the flow of magic as I take more Fae and components for the drug across. We risk it tearing entirely—'

The man's voice broke when Aelfric grabbed his face, his fingers hooking and digging into the curve of his jaw.

'Don't for a moment believe I care what you think, Zane. I've given you an instruction and you will follow it. Is that clear?'

Zane, the Sun King's chamberlain and chief confidant, could only nod, his eyes very large above the steel grip of the High King of Alba's hand.

'Good. That's good.' Aelfric dropped his hand and smoothed the smaller man's jacket.

'Now, what does your Sun King want from me? What little favour this time?'

Aelfric listened to Zane prattling on, pleading the Sun King's case. But his mind was occupied by the extensive preparations for the upcoming Midwinter Ball. It would be a fine time, he thought, to reveal the Fae's existence to the humans and extend his hand in friendship to the governments of the world. Christmas was such an emotional time for humans, who believed so wholeheartedly in magic and miracles. It was time to remind them that magic and monsters were just as real as fairy tales made them seem.

Chapter Three

I spend Saturday morning catching up on paperwork and the coursework my tutor Lan has sent along. She's spoken to Uncle Andrew, and it has been agreed that all in-person classes are to be suspended for the rest of the year. But both Kyle and I have to continue doing our lessons remotely and independently, sending them on to Lan for marking. I am so far behind on any coursework that even if I spend every day for a month doing it, I'll still not catch up.

I work for as long as I can, but by the time lunch comes round I just can't ignore the growing headache at the base of my skull. I only saw Aiden and Dante briefly at breakfast earlier. Their night out at the club has given them no new clues as to who is handing out Glow to kids, and Aiden excused himself to go for a long run around Hyde Park after breakfast.

I am due to meet them for an hour's worth of training in the gym downstairs, but the thought of being active makes my stomach roll.

I head upstairs instead and stand in the shower for ages, letting cooling water soothe my aching head. The headaches usually go hand in hand with nosebleeds. More worries to add to my growing list of *Things Wrong with Kit*.

I think I doze off in the shower because when I wake up the water's not that warm any more. I hastily dry myself off and shiver in the cool air. With the towel wrapped around me, I walk back into my room and find Aiden stretched out on my bed, flicking through my sketchpad. I hesitate and he lowers it to stare at me.

'You don't look so good.'

'Get off my bed, Aiden. I'm just tired and my head hurts. Nothing serious.'

I walk past him and grab my backpack, pulling out my toiletry bag to try to find the painkillers I'm always reluctant to use.

The migraine is threatening to flare into a full-blown roaring nightmare and my hands can't stop shaking.

'I'm worried about you,' he says, watching me, 'and I don't like it. I'm not built for worrying.'

'I'm fine.' I look down at him and smile. 'Seriously. I'm just tired. I haven't been sleeping well.'

'I can tell you're lying, Kit.'

'No, you can't.'

He stands to tower over me. I hate it when he does that.

'Lying.' He drops hands to my shoulders. 'Come on, tell me what's going on.'

I step out of his reach and pop two of the tablets onto my palm and reach for the water bottle next to my bed. 'No, really. I'm just tired. My head hurts a little.' I swallow the pills and sit on the bed. 'I'm going to have a nap. Call me for dinner?'

I worry that he's going to insist on talking but he moves towards the door. He turns back, one hand on the handle.

'I thought we were friends.' He says the words so softly that for a second I'm not sure I heard him right.

'That's a dumb thing to say. Of course we're friends.'

'Then why do you push me away? Why don't you tell me what's going on with you?' He walks back to stand in front of me and I notice the strain around his mouth. It makes me feel guilty.

'What's there to tell, Aide? I'm worried about Thorn and the way we left him in the Otherwhere. And I left those kids behind too, when it was *my job* to get them to safety.' I can see the image of the room with the goddess and those kids all too vividly in my mind. 'Every time I fall asleep I dream about them, and the fact we ran away, leaving Thorn to fight for us. I dream about what those kids are going through. The fact that they're being used as batteries to feed an ancient goddess. It's sick and twisted and weird and we did nothing to help.'

'There was nothing we could do, and you know that.'

'But those kids, Aide. I promised I'd bring them back.'

'Sometimes things are taken out of our hands and we just have to find a way to live with it, you know.'

'No. We always have choices to make and I ran. I ran to save my life.'

'You ran because running meant you would live to fight another day. And your uncle and my dad now know about the goddess and they're searching for a way to help her – and those kids.' He touches my cheek lightly. 'You're not alone, okay? Get some sleep. I'll call you for dinner. We're doing movies and chilling out tonight. I promise. Nothing strenuous.'

I nod and watch him leave, pulling the door shut behind him. I change into sleep-shorts and a vest and crawl into bed, letting the pills work their magic.

Chapter Four

I clatter downstairs just before seven after an unexpectedly restful sleep. I'm about to head into the kitchen when I catch movement from the corner of my eye; I check the large lounge area.

The Fae stands in the middle of the room, tall, broad-shouldered and dressed in elaborate courtier's clothes. His overcoat is red and gold, but the sash around his waist is black, matching his slim trousers.

'Lady Blackhart,' Strachan says, gloved hand resting formally on the hilt of his sword as he executes a light bow. He looks so different to the combat-ready Fae who helped me stake out a North London warehouse just a few weeks ago when we took on Morika and her cronies. Strach's gaze sweeps over my sweatpants and out of shape jumper before coming to rest on my face. 'You look . . . interesting.' His lips twist and I realize that of course he can't lie and tell me I look good when I don't. It's one of the few things with which faeries tend to have a problem, although they seem to have no issues with twisting the truth.

'Strachan,' I say, my voice wavering as I feel genuine concern. As the youngest son to the heir to Alba's throne, a formal visit from Strachan was a pretty big deal. 'Aiden didn't tell me you were here.'

He gestures nonchalantly, dismissing my concern. 'I've only just arrived. Aiden will be back at any minute. He had to attend to something. I think he's escorting *a rúnsearc* from the house.'

I struggle for a moment to translate the unfamiliar word and the way he pronounced it: *uh-ROON-shark*. And when I do, I can't help but smile and blush. The word is Irish and translates as something close to *secret beloved*.

He must mean Dante, I realize, and feel a chill tinge my amusement. Aiden must be hiding him from Strachan. Aiden knows that by being obvious about trying to hide a lover, he'll attract less attention from Strachan, as Strachan knows of his amorous reputation.

Even so, with Dante's father a traitor to Aelfric's kingdom of Alba, having him around is asking for trouble. We have no idea how the scions of Alba would react to finding Dante in our protection. It just isn't a chance we can take.

'What are you doing here?' I keep my voice as level as possible and smile prettily. I don't for one second think Strach believes my game.

There's a definite tremble to my hands when I take the envelope Strachan hands me in reply. Envelopes like this never mean anything good. Not ever. And Strachan looks very serious.

The envelope bears the crest of Dina, High Queen of Alba and Thorn's mother, and it contains a lavishly produced invitation – to a Midwinter Ball at the Prince Regent's Palace. And it's only three weeks away.

'It's an invitation to a ball,' I blurt out, relief flooding over me. 'Strach, I thought this was something serious!'

'It is. It's very serious.' He frowns at me and I compose my face to match his stern expression but it doesn't last.

'I thought someone had died or something.' I stare down at the invitation clutched in my hand. Then I shake my head and hold it out to him. 'Come on, *me* going to a ball? Thanks, seriously, but no thank you.'

He crosses his arms and regards me with an expression that would make lesser mortals cry, but I've been around the sons of Alba enough times and they don't intimidate me.

'No one turns down an invitation issued by the House of Alba.'

'I'm really not someone you'd want there.'

I am being rude, I know, but being in Alba around Thorn's family would break me. I still carry a residue of the anger I felt towards them for what I feel to be a betrayal of Thorn. I have to guard against bad behaviour around them, but it's especially Aelfric, with his self-satisfied expression, who tries my manners and sanity.

'I think you're making a mistake, Kit.' Strach drops his formal demeanour and looks pleadingly at me.

'Strach. It's not my thing.'

Strachan, when he speaks after a brief silence, looks supremely uncomfortable.

'Not everyone in Alba has ulterior motives, Blackhart. Sometimes an invitation is merely an invitation. The ball is a way for us to show you that not everything is about life or death, fight or flight.' He smiles lightly and taps the card against my arm. 'Besides, there is a good chance Thorn will attend. Come, walk me to the door. I have business in the City before I return to Alba.'

I fall in beside him and lead him to the front door of

the Garrett mansion. 'Thank you for visiting,' I tell him and my smile is as honest as I can make it.

He takes my offered right hand – and stares at the gold band on my finger for a moment. 'I did not think my grandmother would part with it.' His gaze was unexpectedly intense, belying the light tone.

'The ring? I think Dina just felt so guilty about how badly I was hurt, after fighting Istvan and his sister, that she gave me Thorn's ring to make up for it.'

'This is not Thorn's ring, Blackhart. This is my grandmother's ring that was gifted to her by her mother. It is a family heirloom – as is the ring she gave Thorn. They are a pair.'

'Oh.' I stare at it, then at him, completely nonplussed. I pull my hand from his and open the front door.

It's dark outside, but I see a movement in the shadows by the front door and a Fae warrior I don't recognize moves forward. He's taller than Strach and built like a tank. One of Dina's Stormborn, then – her personal guard. The newcomer gives me a polite nod before speaking.

'My prince? Are you ready?'

'Thank you Elisior, let's go. Kit, it was good to see you. Think about what I said before you respond to the invitation.'

I nod and watch them walk along the pavement before darkness completely swallows them.

Chapter Five

Five minutes after Strachan has left, Dante lightly bounces down the stairs and Aiden reappears behind him looking tense.

'Which one was he?' Dante asks.

'That was Strachan. Aelfric's oldest son's youngest son.' I consider my explanation when I see his confused expression. 'I really should show you their family tree one day. Even I can't keep them all straight. But he's a good guy. Aiden and I ran a job with him about two months ago.'

'The guy's arrogant but he's a good fighter,' Aiden adds. 'What did he want?'

'He dropped off this.' I hand Aiden the invitation. 'The annual Midwinter Ball is happening and I've been invited.'

Aiden looks impressed and passes it to Dante, who scowls at it unhappily before dropping it on the kitchen counter.

'You going?'

'Not if I can help it. I've had enough of the House of Alba to last me a very long time.' I swipe my fingers over the paper. 'But he mentioned that Thorn might be there.'

'Did he say anything else about Thorn?'

I mutely shake my head and Aiden nods. 'Well, that's okay. So we know Thorn's okay, that he made it back out of the clearing. That he's in touch with his family. Strachan wouldn't lie about something like that.'

'I don't think he would, no.' I draw a deep breath and let my anxiety smooth out a little. If Thorn is to attend the ball, it means he's fine. The fact that I left him behind in the Otherwhere and ran for my life, while he fought off wild Fae and ogres hangs heavily on my shoulders. None of my attempts to reach him through the little sliver of mirror he gave me has worked.

Aiden rummages through the kitchen drawers and comes up with a handful of take-away menus. 'What food do you want? I'm happy with whatever.'

I'm wondering why I'm not hungry, which is unusual for me, when Aiden's mobile rings.

'Leo! Yeah, we're just about to order dinner. Wanna come over?'

While we're debating the choices Aiden suddenly heads past us to the lounge. 'Guys, check this out.'

He turns on the TV and flicks to the news. He has the phone cradled against his ear and he's still talking to Leo while beckoning us over impatiently.

Dante moves the coffee-table books to the side and we both grab seats on the solid wooden table in front of the TV.

'I'm reporting from the burned-out remains of Icon, a recently opened nightclub in London's West End.'

Aiden pauses the newscaster mid-sentence.

'We've got the channel,' he tells Leo. 'Speak in a bit.' He hangs up and comes to sit next to me. 'This is where we were last night.'

'And you let it burn down? Without telling me?' I nudge him but he looks unhappy.

'No, we left this morning and it was fine. Leo's just heard about it too. Apparently there was a fire and the whole place burned down. It happened after the club shut.'

'This isn't good,' Dante mutters. 'Did Leo say anything else?'

'Just that his dad's talking to one of the investors. Apparently the guy is seriously pissed off. He spent a lot of money on getting Icon up to scratch and now this has happened.'

'Did someone have a grudge against him?'

Aiden shrugs at Dante's question. 'I'm pretty sure that as a club owner and property developer in London you can't *not* have people have grudges against you. It comes with the territory.'

'But no other clubs are being burned down,' Dante points out, and I have to agree with this. This was weird, and from Aiden's expression he thought so too. We watch the rest of the story unfold. No one apparently got hurt but it was a close call, as the manager and some of the bar staff were cleaning up when the fire started. The fire brigade was called and they battled the fire and saved the surrounding buildings from catching fire but unfortunately Icon was a mess.

On the TV the reporter points to a huddled group of staff, who look soot stained and dazed as she covers the arson and police investigation.

Aiden's phone rings again and he answers, muting the TV.

'Hold on, let me put you on speaker phone.' He fiddles with the touch screen. 'It's Leo. We're all here, Leo. Tell us what's going on.'

'Hey, guys. So, my dad's been talking to the owner and one of the main investors on and off today. Turns out a bunch of guys came into Icon last night . . . no, this morning, after we left, but the doorman and his crew tossed them out when they caught them dealing. And by dealing I mean these guys were handing out baggies of free stuff to everyone who wanted any. And they weren't even being circumspect.'

'So because they were tossed out, they burned down the club in retaliation?' Dante asks.

Leo sighs a little before he answers. 'It's a theory.'

'Did the doorman see what they were dealing?'

'I'll give you one guess, Kit. Go on. But I bet you won't get it. Never ever.'

'Glow.'

'Wow. It's like you knew all along.'

I roll my eyes at Leo's sarcasm. 'Do we know what these guys looked like?'

'Nondescript Caucasian dudes, in their twenties and thirties, wearing leather jackets, jeans, shirts. Hung with.gold chains. Basically: your quintessential douche-bag drug dealer. There's a reason Hollywood portrays these guys this way.'

I scrub at my face and fight the tiredness. I've had some decent sleep brought on by the migraine pills but listening to Leo makes me weary. A part of me wants nothing more than to launch out into the night, question people and talk to them about Glow, but it's not something I can do. And, honestly, it's not something I'm interested in doing all that much either, even if the short-term impulse is there. The case was taken away from me. It belongs to the wolves now; my uncle Andrew made a big song and dance about giving it over to them.

And, yes, it still smarts.

'Cheers, Leo. I'll ring Connor and Shaun and tell them about this. If you hear anything more, give me a call, okay?

Or get your dad to ring Connor directly and they can figure out what to do next.'

'I will do, guys. Stay safe.'

Dante stands up as Aiden turns the TV off.

'That's *it*?' he says. 'You guys are just going to sit here and do nothing?'

'Hey, I'm still on the case,' Aiden mutters. 'Without knowing what Connor and Shaun are up to, I can't just go and do my own thing.'

'I'm talking about Kit.'

I sit up with a jerk at the mention of my name. 'What?'

'You. You're sitting here, *moping*, when this crap is happening out there.'

'I am not moping, Dante.'

'You are. You've done nothing in days except sit at home and here, you've been training and not really here. You've not even spoken to your family since you got here yesterday. Crap is happening out there and you . . . you're just shutting down.'

I blink at him. 'What do you want me to do?'

He growls in frustration. 'I don't know. Something! Anything. I'm not used to you being this passive and *still*. It's freaking me out. Kit, people are taking faerie drugs, a nightclub burned down and you're just sitting here looking a little bored.'

'I'm . . .' *Too tired even to think about this.* '. . . not ignoring any of this, Dante. I can't just rush off and investigate and make a mess of things.'

'Why not?'

'There are rules.'

He snorts. 'Yeah, and you're so good at following rules.'

I frown up at him. 'What is your problem, Dante?'

'My problem is the both of you just *sitting* here. When we should be out there doing things, getting to the bottom of this.'

Aiden moves closer to Dante. 'Dante, you don't know . . .'

Dante holds up a hand and Aiden snaps his mouth shut at the peremptory gesture. 'No. You're right, Aide, I don't know. So maybe you should stop hiding things and tell me what the hell *is* going on here. Why are the both of you dragging your feet on this? There are drugs out there, being given out for free to unsuspecting people. People have died in the past and now they've gone and burned down a night-club. What next? More burnings? People being shot or stabbed for denying dealers access to clubs?'

Aiden is staring into the middle distance, and I can tell that he's doing his utmost to calm down, so as not to shift in front of Dante.

'Remember when we were given the Child Thief case by Suola?' I ask Dante. His gaze moves to me and he nods. 'You remember the vow we took?'

Again he nods.

'In this instance, Uncle Andrew took on the Glow case. He delegated it to me first time round. I was partially successful and we sent one of the main dealers back to the Otherwhere to be judged. Then you and I were given the Child Thief case and Andrew took the rest of the Glow thing away from me. Remember the fight I had with Aiden about that?'

'It wasn't really a fight,' Aiden offers, sounding stiff. 'There wasn't even any blood.'

'The wolves are running the Glow case now,' I say, ignoring Aiden's interruption. 'I can't just walk in and start doing stuff, unless Andrew gives me the go-ahead or Aiden's brother Connor invites me onto the case.'

'That's such bullsh—' Dante starts, but I shake my head.

'No, those are the rules, Dante. Do you just pick up another Spook's case and run with it? Is that how police work works in general? Anyone can just start investigating a crime and asking questions?'

'Well, no, but . . .'

'And it's the same thing with us. We have a lot of rules; some can be bent and twisted, yes, but there has to be a clear line of command when it comes to running any of the jobs we get given . . .'

'Okay, so, I understand, but I still don't necessarily agree with it.'

Aiden leaves the room and I watch his back for a second before looking at Dante. 'You don't have to agree with it,' I tell him. 'That's just the way things are – and until I get called to be part of the case, there is nothing I can do about it.'

'What about me?' he counters. 'What if *I* decide to interfere?'

'Then that is your prerogative. I can't stop you.'

He crosses his arms over his chest and frowns at me. 'I really don't like this. It feels like we've been sidelined.'

'We have,' I answer. 'But right now we can't change that. Let's order some food instead. I was told no drama tonight and right now there's loads of drama happening right here. My headache is coming back.'

'I vote Chinese too,' Aiden says as he we join him in the kitchen, where he rifles through the drawer of take-away menus. 'Choose what you want.' He sits down at the counter and flips his phone on, his thumb flying over the touch screen. 'I'm sending Connor a message about all this. He needs to talk to your uncle Andrew. This is getting to be a joke now. We have to get things sorted out.'

The call comes just after midnight. Dante sits up with a jerk from where he's fallen asleep, with his head on my lap. Aiden answers the phone.

'What?' he says groggily, blinking at the movie we've managed to not stay awake to watch. 'Yes, she's right here.'

The number on the display as he passes the phone to me tells me nothing, apart from the fact that it's somewhere abroad, possibly America.

'This is Kit Blackhart.'

'Kit, it's Megan.'

A million scenarios cavort through my mind, none of them good.

'Are you okay? Is Andrew okay? Is it the boys?'

'I'm fine, everything is fine, I promise.' There's genuine amusement in her voice, even if the connection's not so great. It hisses and crackles and what she says next is completely lost in the static.

'Megan, I can't hear you. The phone's breaking up.'

'Uch . . .' Static breaks her voice up and a loud whine makes me wince. '. . . Instead,' she mutters. 'Hold on.'

There's the sound of something thudding, her groaning a curse, the sound of footsteps on metal, and then the noise of traffic intensifies.

'Is this better?'

'Yes, what did you do?'

'I climbed out on the fire escape. I'm now on the roof of the building. The signal in my room is atrocious.'

'As much as I love hearing from you, Megan, why are you calling me at one in the morning, on Aiden's mobile?'

'Because I can't get through on yours. Kit, what's going on? Dad's been blowing up my phone with texts and calls all day. He's been trying to get hold of you and you've not answered at the house or on your phone, at all.'

I frown, trying to remember the last time I saw my mobile.

'I'm staying over at the Garretts' for a few days. My phone is probably somewhere in my backpack. I've not checked it since I got here.'

'Kit.' Her tone is exasperated. 'Dad's going nuts because you've not called.'

'Why should I call him? I'm fine.'

She makes a noise that's not very ladylike and I laugh soundlessly. 'The spoiled brat act doesn't suit you, just so you know.'

'It's not an act,' I counter.

'I refuse to believe you're behaving like this on purpose. Kit, I have to tell you something.' Her voice dips. 'Glow. It's hit the US hard, especially the big cities like New York, Los Angeles, New Orleans, Washington, Chicago, Houston. They're targeting students and people in their twenties. It's not just in clubs here, okay? I found some in my friend Katie's bag. She got it from a friend at a coffee shop on campus.'

'Oh *crap*, Meg.'

'I know. Connor and Dad've been talking and Dad's been a ball of stress about this for weeks. He's been in and out of meetings with some law enforcement guys who are in the know about the, uh, *other* world shenanigans we face.'

'Is this why he's been trying to get in touch with me?'

'I think so, but also to just check in. We've not really heard much from you, sparky.'

'Get him to call me on Aiden's phone. I'll go and find my phone in the meantime and put it on charge.'

'Okay. Stay safe, Kit.'

'I miss you, Meg. You be careful too. Don't . . .' I close my eyes. 'Don't do any jobs by yourself, okay? Not if they're spreading drugs around like sweets.'

'Not much of a choice. With only me and my dad here, we've got to do what's necessary. Can't have crap like this happen on our watch. It's what we do, right?'

'Do me a favour, Meg. Call your dad and get him to put me back on the Glow case. Let me work with the wolves on this.'

'Kit, no.' There's a crackling noise and I grumble in annoyance as it robs me from hearing the rest of her words. '. . . worried about you.'

'No, listen. The phone is breaking up again. I'm fine, seriously – just get him to give me a call. There's so much trouble happening all over the show, I can't sit on the sidelines, even if your dad thinks I'm incapable of handling myself.'

There's a silence on the line and for a moment I worry we've been cut off. But then Megan's talking again.

'I'm not sure what you're talking about, but I'm on my way over to the house now so I'll get him to call you.'

'Okay. Be safe, Megan.'

I hand the phone back to Aiden and he looks at me curiously.

'That sounded intense.'

'Glow's hit the USA too. Not just clubs but the univer-sities and the big cities. In a big way.'

'What are they doing about it?'

'I don't know. Uncle Andrew will probably call soon. I'm just gonna go and find my phone, put it on charge.'

I'm halfway up the stairs when I hear Aiden behind me.

'Call Andrew right now,' is all he says before he hands his mobile to me and jogs up the stairs ahead of me. I frown at his retreating form but dial my uncle's number anyway. I glance back downstairs as I hold the phone to my ear and see Dante watching me from the lounge.

'Andrew Blackhart speaking.'

'Hey, Uncle Andrew. It's Kit. I've just talked to Megan . . .'

'Now isn't the best time, Kit. I'm glad to hear from you, though. Are you all right?'

'Uh, yeah, I'm okay. I was . . .'

A howl forces me to pull the phone from my ear and I squint as the sound echoes up out of the speaker.

'Should I call back?' I ask after a few seconds, once the howl has died down.

'No, now is as good a time as any. Just hold on.' There are what sounds like gunshots and then rapid footsteps. 'Okay, just give me a minute.' Another pause, then Andrew's back on the phone to me. 'Kit? I've only got a few minutes. I'm putting you back on the drugs case. I think Megan must have told you that things have escalated dramatically here. I've been putting together teams to try to figure the mess out, but these Glow guys move fast. They hit the cities, hand the drugs out at colleges and clubs, then disappear. This past week alone we've had reports from seventeen schools and campuses about the drug. It's in the news here and things are getting very fraught. The authorities are at a loss because no one can finger any of the dealers. They have some kind of glamour working so no one can describe them accurately, but everyone says the same thing.'

'And what is that?'

'The reports all talk about five guys. Caucasian. Leather jackets, gold chains, jeans.'

'Like movie villains.'

'Exactly.'

'So, I'm okay to be with Aiden on this again?'

'Yes, we need everyone to be . . . excuse me a moment.' There's a grunting noise and then a muffled curse. 'Sergeant Aaron, would you kindly get that goblin under control? Thank you.' Back to me. 'Sorry, about that, Kit. But yes, back to working with the wolves. I'll put the paperwork through from my side. You're officially part of their team.'

'I'm not entirely . . .'

'I've got to go, Kit. I'll see you at Christmas. You get your invitation to the Midwinter Ball? Talk to Megan about clothes, it's a family affair and we always all attend. Speak later.'

And as he hangs up there's another howl in the background. Dante stares at me from where he's come over to listen.

'That sounded weird. And I thought I was used to weird by now.'

'It was weird.' I dredge up a grin that I don't really feel. 'But Andrew's reassigned me to the Glow case, with the wolves. So, yay.'

'Yeah, yay. I'm sorry I was a dick earlier. I'm just frustrated by stuff not making sense.'

I consider him and can't help but feel a little bad for him. I'd been a mess and taken it out on both him and Aiden by acting the diva. 'No, you were right, I was moping.

Having Andrew giving the case to the wolves and then not putting me back on it when we got back from the Other-where – it really hurt. I know he told me I needed rest, but it felt as if I'd failed with the whole Child Thief case. And then when he had me kicking my heels and not doing anything else serious, it felt like punishment, you know? I sort of felt they didn't trust me – after I screwed up by not bringing the kids home.'

'Kit.' Dante looks as if he wants to say more but then the phone in my hand starts ringing. I answer on reflex.

'Kit? It's Connor. Is Aiden there?'

'Yeah, hold on. He's in his room.' I turn and head up the stairs and along the first-floor passage to Aiden's room. He pulls it open before I can even knock and beckons us in.

He takes the phone from me after glancing at the name on the screen. 'Con? What's up, dude?'

I crawl onto Aiden's bed as he speaks to his brother and pick up the topmost book of a small pile he has resting on the nightstand. The books are an eclectic mix of folklore, poetry and medieval ballads – along with a few well-thumbed Punisher comics that I think my cousin Kyle must have let him borrow.

'Yeah, we can get there in about an hour or so. Sure. Do I ask for anyone or . . . ?' Aiden watches me snoop around his stuff with an amused look on his face. Dante's not come further into the room at all and hovers by the door instead, looking a little uncomfortable. 'Yeah, we'll call you when we know more. When are you guys thinking of getting back home? No, the place isn't a pigsty, Con, bloody hell. Mum won't freak out, I promise. Fine, don't get killed. See you soon.'

I flip myself back off the bed with a dramatic little bounce and look at him. 'I'm back on the team. What are we doing?'

'We're going to Croydon. Someone hosted an illegal rave. A kid has died and others have been injured. Come on.'

Chapter Six

The drive down to Croydon takes a while. I've never been there but I know the area is a well-known crime hot spot, as well as boasting a vibrant night life. As one of the largest business districts in outer London, Croydon isn't the most attractive of places. Its tall buildings and unsightly squat car parks are broken up by even uglier 1970s office blocks. The address Connor had sent us is on the prettily named Cherry Orchard Road, but the place itself is a large disused industrial building and as ugly as sin. We park a few blocks away and although the rave itself had been broken up, there are still hundreds of people standing around outside.

There is also a formidable police presence, which isn't all that surprising. A group of teens no older than us are standing in a huddle and Aiden takes the lead as we walk towards them.

'Hey,' he says, casually, nodding at everyone in greeting. 'What happened? We heard about the party, we get here and this is what we find.'

'Bro, it's a mess.' One boy shakes his head. He's got eyeliner smeared under his eyes and too much glitter down the side of his face. He leans against a girl, her arms wrapped around his waist. Looking at the group, I realize they all look shell-shocked. 'We got here about an hour before the police showed up. Everything was going so well and we were all just partying hard.'

'How did the cops even know it was going on? What happened?' Aiden's voice held just enough annoyance to trigger a response.

'Good question,' Eyeliner Boy says, hugging the girl closer. 'People were being stupid, I guess.'

'Yeah.' One of the other boys pipes up as he inhales smoke from his cigarette. 'We were supposed to be casual about this, not turn up in big groups.'

The girl, dainty but fierce in leather and lace, snorts her annoyance. 'It's what alerted the cops, for sure.'

'So, what? They busted the rave?' I shake my head when the smoker offers me his cigarette. 'Did someone get hurt?'

'Yeah.' Cigarette Boy scowls through the smoke, jerking his chin to where the response vehicles are parked, lights swirling. 'One kid OD'd and some others were taken to hospital.'

'So, I guess we head back to the West End, then,' the girl says. 'Tonight sucks.'

'I know, babe, I'm sorry.' Eyeliner Boy hugs her and kisses the top of her messy head. 'We should have stayed at the other club.'

'Why are there so many cops here?' Dante asks, moving forward and staring out over the crowd.

'There were guys in there giving drugs away for free. And obviously people were taking it. When were you last at an illegal rave? Everything goes.'

Dante snorts. 'Yeah, believe me, I know.' He scratches

his jaw where the stubble's taken over. 'Do you guys know what they were dealing? Is it still going around?'

And somehow the way he lowers his voice makes all of us conspirators. I don't know how he does it but we all move a little closer to one another and share a *look*.

'I'm asking for a friend, of course.' Dante grins at them in a way that leaves no doubt as to his *real* intentions. 'He told me about this stuff that he took a few weeks ago. Made him see bloody faeries.'

'No, mate. I have no idea what the stuff was – but there were at least three guys handing out baggies.' Eyeliner Boy shoots a look at his watch. 'We're outta here. We're heading back to Game in Soho if you guys want to tag along? We've got space in the van.'

'No, we're good, cheers.' Aiden gestures behind us. 'We drove too, anyway. Faster than the bus.'

'Too straight, mate. Have a good night.'

We say our farewells and they head away from the milling crowd.

'Let's keep on checking. If all else fails I'll pull the Spook ID out and talk to some of the police,' suggests Dante. By mutual agreement we arrange to meet back at the car in about an hour and split up.

I pull my jacket closer and lift the collar because it's become really cold out. I attach myself to various groups and chat to them about what happened in the club. And slowly but surely a picture starts to form. Too many people turned up for the rave – and with only one entrance and one exit, the crowd became too obvious for the local constabulary to ignore. Reinforcements were called in and people started panicking when the cops turned up. Some even started throwing things out of the windows and a few club-goers outside actually started attacking police vehicles. Things got messy when one of the kids the police had cornered, obviously high, went into some kind of violent fit. The paramedics reached him, but were too late to help and he died there. Everyone else who'd obviously been under the influence was carted off en masse to a local hospital. And the police started taking statements and arresting those they considered suspicious or who already had arrest records.

I find it strange that so many people stayed after the rave had so obviously been shut down. But, as one girl told me, most people had no real way to get home once public transport had pretty much stopped running, and the buses weren't reliable at all. They'd just wait until the early-morning train services started.

I'm the last one to arrive back at the car and I gratefully accept a styrofoam cup of something black and bitter from Aiden, before he sinks into the back of the Cayenne. The interior of the car is quiet for a few seconds before Dante speaks.

'This is a mess.'

'I know,' I sigh, looking out at the crowd. 'This is the kind of place where we would've hung out before, Aide. This could've been us.'

'We know better, Kit.'

'No, she's right.' Dante looks at me, then back to Aiden. 'This could've been me three years ago. The crap I did.' His voice trails off. 'We've got to stop people distributing this stuff. More are going to die.'

Aiden watches a girl in a pair of stiletto heels walk past, leaning heavily on a friend. 'I found out which hospital took in the others kids. I managed to talk to one of the bouncers.'

'Did he know who was distributing the drugs?'

'He's seen them before. He knows the one guy well.' He twists in his seat to look at me. 'We met him when we did the raid with Strachan on the warehouse in Catford. Our good friend Marko.'

'That means the Jericho Gang is still involved.' I remember the map my cousin Kyle showed me once, and the reach of the Jericho Gang's territory. 'Okay, let's go to the hospital.'

As we drive, I fill Dante in on the raid we'd pulled off with Strachan, how we thought we'd shut down one of the main Fae Glow distributors in the south-east. But if Marko is still involved, maybe he has a new supplier. The University Hospital is less than a ten-minute drive from the site of the rave, so it feels as if we're parking far too soon with no real plan as to how to get to the kids who've been brought in.

'How do we do this?' I ask Dante.

'We lie, and cheat, and steal,' he says, smiling.

While Aiden asks after the kids at the A&E reception, Dante and I head down one of the corridors. I'm not fond of hospitals at all. There's something about the sterile smell of them that makes me feel unwell. Dante looks pale in the bad lighting overhead and there's a damp sheen of perspiration on his forehead. We slow our pace when a nurse exits a staff-only room and hurries away from us. Dante moves hastily to catch the door before it slams shut all the way. He pulls out a slender pocket knife and pushes it into the lock, jimmying it so that it closes but doesn't lock. Then he pulls me into the dark room and closes the door behind us. We stay quiet for a few seconds, listening to the nurse's footfalls fade away. I fumble for the switch and the storage room behind us is lit up.

'Jackpot,' he mutters and investigates the stacked shelves. He's soon enough passing me back a neat little stack of clothes. 'These should fit.'

I shake out the nurse's tunic and trousers and ask, 'What about you?' in a low voice. 'You'd better be changing too.'

He holds up a dark blue tunic and trousers. 'Get changed. You better not peek.'

I glare my indignation at him and he chuckles. The room is cold and I change quickly into the tunic and trousers.

When we're both in our disguises and we've neatly stacked our clothes so they're easy to grab on our way out, Dante also takes an official-looking clipboard and pen from a shelf and we leave the small room.

My phone vibrates and there's a message from Aiden: *Can't get past main desk. A girl under light sedation on 2nd floor. Overheard nurse mention.*

I reply with a quick *Okay we're in*, sliding the phone back into the elasticated waistband of my trousers.

Walking side-by-side with Dante, I'm amazed that we don't attract more looks. But it just goes to show how people don't pay attention if you look as if you fit. Then I spot a pass card on an unmanned nurse's station and quickly swipe it and clip it to my tunic. Soon we've on the second floor without anyone interrupting. We slow our pace just past an empty trolley because we see a police officer stationed outside a door. Without a moment's hesitation I walk towards the officer and flash my pass card. He glances at it, then at me, dismissing me as staff and therefore not a threat before standing aside and I'm in.

There's a girl lying on the bed hooked up to various

beeping monitors, and I locate her folder of medical notes while keeping a wary eye on her.

I quickly take photos of her paperwork using my phone and don't even try to make sense of the medical jargon. But a few words stand out.

Hallucinations

Possible drug intake to include MDMA/LSD variant

Patient is a danger to herself and restraints have been used

I glance at the girl and notice the fabric straps tying her to the bed by her wrists and ankles. I make sure I stay far away from the equipment, in case my magic manages to interfere with the machines. I don't want to trigger any alarms in doing so but I know my time is limited. Looking down at the girl makes my heart clench in my chest. She's my age but she somehow looks both younger and older. Her cheeks are sunken and there are dark circles beneath her eyes.

'Jane?' I whisper, leaning close. 'Can you hear me?'

For a second there's no response but then her eyelids flutter open and she stares fuzzily around the room.

'Who . . . ?' Her voice sounds scratchy and I find a plastic cup with a straw by the side of the bed. I hold it for her so she can take a few sips. 'Thanks,' she manages. 'Who're you?'

'I'm here to find out who sold you the stuff you took tonight.'

'Din' sell it. Free.'

'Jane. We're trying to stop these guys. Someone died tonight.'

She sighs a little, her eyes dull, pulling desolately on the restraints on her arm. 'Where am I?'

'In hospital. You got sick at the rave. An ambulance brought you here.'

'Parents know?'

'I would assume so. You're a minor so they would've called your parents or your guardian, at least.'

She breathes a swearword and her eyes drift shut. 'Raves are fun,' she whispers, 'but tonight wasn't.' She coughs and I give her another sip of water.

'Jane. What were the drugs you took?'

'Glow. Love that stuff. It makes me see things, pretty things.'

'You've taken it before?'

'Yes. At other raves.'

'Are they the same people every time, handing out the stuff? Glow, I mean?'

'They host the raves, right? You pay at the door. Then if you're good you get given some of the stuff for free. After, you pay for more.'

'So, do you know who runs them?'

I press the straw to her lips again and she drinks.

'Marko's boss. We don't know who he is. Marko always just calls him *the boss*.'

'So, this guy Marko? He hands out the Glow?'

'Yes. He's got a team.' She frowns at me. 'You're not the fuzz, are you?'

'No, no, I'm not.'

'Oh, that's okay, then.' She seems to sink deeper into the pillow. 'So tired. You don't have any Glow with you?'

I shake my head. 'Do you have extra?'

'They only hand out two pills. You take one at a time. I don't know where my other one is . . . maybe in my clothes? It's all you need to see *everything*.' She yawns widely and struggles feebly against the restraints holding her. Confusion creases her brow. 'Why did they do this? I'm not dangerous.'

'I don't know, Jane. Maybe they're worried you'll hurt yourself.' There are voices from outside the door and I realize I've been in here for quite a while. 'You rest, Jane. And stop going to raves. They're not good for you.'

'Yeah, okay, can I sleep now?'

I watch as she sinks into slumber and feel genuine fear for her. She barely makes a dent in the bedding she's lying on, her body is so slight. I move away from the bed and look around the small room. There's a small closet and I pull the door open to have a look. Her clothes are in there I make short work of rifling through the tiny top that seems far too flimsy to wear on a night as cold as this. There's nothing in her jeans either, but when I pull the belt away from the loops I spot the small clear plastic baggie containing one small round pill that looks like it's made from crushed malachite, that she's hidden beneath the buckle. So as not to get my own fingerprints on it, I take the baggie out with the tips of my nails and pop it into an unused plastic cup – which I fold so that it fits in my pocket. I quietly leave the room and pull the door shut behind me.

'She's sleeping. Someone else will be around to check on her soon,' I tell the policeman and he just nods. I see no sign of Dante at all so I choose a direction, and head back the way I came.

He's waiting for me on the stairs looking unwell, and we head back down to the ground floor and the closet where we left our clothes. We change hastily and I wipe down the pass card I'd taken and leave it there too.

We exit the hospital through the main doors and find Aiden lurking outside, talking to a group of smokers near the entrance.

Chapter Seven

'They had her tied up,' I say, not for the first time, once we're home. I'm sitting at my laptop, downloading the photos I took of Jane's medical records. 'Like she was dangerous.'

Aiden leans forward to see the screen.

'There's not a lot of info here,' he says, skimming the pages. 'But what it says is bad enough. The fact that they're mentioning LSD and MDMA means they'll have the SOCA – the Serious Organized Crime Agency – guys in as part of this investigation. I know my dad reached out to them when we took over the case, but they've been playing their cards close to their chest. Maybe we could try again.'

'I feel a little out of my depth here,' I admit and stare at the screen. 'I'm better at fighting monsters and drawing spells than the official side of things.'

'It's why you've got me,' Dante says as he walks into the dining room. 'I speak the language. Okay, so I called in a favour from one of the tech support guys at the Spooks' HQ. He tracked down this Marko guy and I have his address. How about we go now?'

'Where does he live?'

'Whitechapel.' Dante smirks at Aiden before opening his

hand and showing Aiden's car keys resting in his palm. 'And I'm driving.'

It's almost four in the morning when we pull up outside Marko's building in Whitechapel. The ringing doorbell is answered by a sleepy-looking guy with a week-old scruff on his jaw. He stares at us blearily for a few minutes but Aiden's there talking fast, looking earnest and asking for Marko. He talks a good spiel, says he's just come from Game in Soho and needs to talk to him immediately about a business proposition. The guy looks as if he's zoned out completely but he grins at Aiden the whole time and by time Aiden's finished he has Marko's schedule for the next three days, the guy's name (Louie) and Marko's mobile number. We head back towards the car as Aiden rings Marko's mobile to find out where he is. We're guessing he's a night owl. The conversation is brief but it seems friendly, especially when Aiden lets Louie's name drop, as if they're friends.

Both Dante and I stare at him, a bit open-mouthed.

'What?' he asks, shimmying so that he can get the phone back into his jeans pocket. 'Hey, no judging. I use what I've got to get what I want.'

I lift my hands up in protest. 'Not hearing any complaints from me, at all, Aide. I just wasn't aware that you could turn on the charm to *that* extent. I always thought you were more the "dangle them by one foot from the roof" kinda guy.'

'There's a time and place for everything, Kit,' he says rather primly, but the way he jiggles his eyebrow at me makes me laugh. He checks his phone. 'We need to get to Covent Garden.'

Dante turns back to the steering wheel and starts the Cayenne.

I watch late night/early morning London slide by the window as we head back into the West End. Jane's face is firmly lodged in my mind and I wonder if she'll recover. The fact that Marko and his people have been actually staging raves and she's taken Glow more than once is really terrifying. I wonder if they've been changing the compound, too. Otherwise, why would some, like the boy who'd died, react so aggressively to the drug compared to Jane?

'. . . me, Kit?'

I blink at Aiden's voice and focus on him.

'Sorry, what?'

'I'm checking that you're okay. You've gone very quiet. How's your head?'

'Oh.' I move my thumb over my eyebrow. 'Fine. The painkillers and sleep helped a lot.'

'You're getting them more often?' Dante's eyes meet mine in the rear-view mirror. 'Have you been to see a doctor?'

I shrug. 'I've always had them. My nan had them. She told me my mum had them. Sometimes migraines are just hereditary.'

'That's utter rubbish. If these migraines are happening more often, you should be seeing someone.'

'It's probably just stress and lack of sleep, *Dad*. I'm fine, seriously.' I kick the back of Dante's seat. 'Besides, you can't talk. You need to concentrate on driving your boyfriend's car.'

'Yeah. Don't scratch my baby or crash her,' Aiden chips in.

'Also, I'm not your boyfriend,' Dante shoots back easily

and for a second there's a breathlessness in the car that I attribute to how still Aiden's gone, but then he laughs softly.

'Not *yet*, Alexander. Give me time.'

Dante gives him a surprised look. 'I like that you're making this a challenge, Aide.'

'Oh my God, your awkward flirting is killing me,' I mutter and fling my arm dramatically over my eyes. 'How did I ever think you guys were smooth?'

And that's all the journey needed to erupt into a full-blown conversation about smooth moves, bad dates and conquests. I grin to myself and sit back, letting their one-upmanship roll over me. By the time we hit the West End my stomach hurts from laughing so much at them both and they've both forgotten to pester me about the migraines that have become the bane of my existence.

Dante parks near Covent Garden and leads the way to the Island club, which I never would have found because it's down too many winding side-streets.

The place isn't as big as Milton's, but it is busy. Aiden scans the crowd with a quick glance, his gaze snagging on a booth in the corner.

'There are Fae here,' he says. 'Also another were, but not sure what type.'

'Will they be an issue?' I glance around but my sight shows me nothing but a lot of energy being generated by the people on the dance floor.

'Not sure. Let's go get something to drink and then we try to find our friend Marko.'

I take the lead and weave my way across the floor. The music is good but not, I think wryly, as good as Torsten's music had been at Milton's. At the bar, I get lucky and am served quickly – an alcopop for me and beer for the boys.

'I thought you didn't drink,' Dante says, looking at the alcopop.

'I don't. It lets me blend in.'

Aiden looks up from his phone. 'Marko's earlier text says he's at a table near the back, in the VIP area.'

'Listen, Aide, he might remember me,' I say, hanging back. 'He saw me when we busted Morika and her merry band of faerie followers the last time.'

'Ah, but Strach's boys hit him with a memory spell so he may *not* remember you at all.' Aiden peers over my head towards the VIP area. 'He definitely won't recognize me. Unless I turn wolf on him.'

I nod when I remember that big wolf's paw pressing Marko into the concrete floor of the warehouse two months ago. 'Yeah, okay, let's do this.'

We push our way back through the dancing crowd and Aiden casually jabs a guy in the gut who tries to grind up against me. By the time we get to the other side of the dance floor we're all three a little out of breath and there's a high colour on Dante's cheeks.

'You okay?'

'Yeah,' he says, giving a weird little shiver like he's shaking off water. 'There are a lot of hungry, desperate people out there. If I don't concentrate on you and Aiden, I can hear everything they want.'

Aiden looks as worried as I feel, and I nudge Dante lightly. 'You want to wait elsewhere if your senses are giving you trouble? Outside, maybe?'

'No, I think I'm okay. I have to figure out how they work. Now's as good a time as any. Let's find this Marko guy and take him and his buddies down.'

The VIP area is guarded by a large, heavily tattooed,

tank of a guy, wearing a wife-beater and black jeans. He looks about as friendly as a bulldog with a flea infestation. As we near he lifts the tablet from the table next to him.

'Names?'

'Ah, we're not on there, I think. We're here to meet Marko.' Aiden doesn't smile or turn on the charm. Instead his eyes scan the tables behind the tank. 'He said he'd be here.'

The man scowls. 'Yeah, he left about ten minutes ago. And because you're not on my list, you can't go back there. Feel free to take off.' With that he puts a hand against Aiden's chest and pushes him lightly, increasing the pressure when Aiden doesn't budge. Before Aiden can react, Dante's there, pulling Aiden away. I give the tank a stink-eye as I follow the boys.

Chapter Eight

'Punching that guy is not a smart idea,' I tell Aiden as we sit down at the tiny table they've managed to secure. 'We should check around, see what else we can see.'

He grunts and takes an aggressive gulp of his beer. 'Where the hell did that Marko guy go? When we spoke he said he'd be around for at least another hour and now he's not answering his phone.'

'People change their minds, Aide. Calm down.' Dante's between us and has an arm wrapped around both our shoulders. I realize that he's mostly stopping Aiden from standing up and decking the tank in charge of VIP security, if only to feel the satisfaction of some kind of action. 'There's still a chance we'll figure something out.'

I shrug out from under Dante's arm and glance over the dance floor as if I'm looking for someone. I focus my sight, seeing if I can spot the faeries Aiden mentioned when we walked in. Their energy spikes differently from humans' and if I concentrate it's easy enough to spot, even in a place as brimful of energy as this. I don't often do this, allow my magic to flow from me, surfing the stream of energies pulsing around us. It feels incredible, as if you're being drawn along a strong welcoming tide that envelops, heals and soothes all tiredness from you. But it is dangerous to do this without an anchor to pull you back. I've read a few accounts where magicians have escaped into the expelled energies during a ritual and lost their minds, becoming nothing more than broken shells of their previous selves. The trick is never to get wholly sucked into the energy you're connecting with – be it directly from the songlines which channel the earth's magical energy or during a ritual where energy has been raised through chanting or a suitable sacrifice. But it's hard to pull back. The temptation is always to open yourself further, for longer, to just keep absorbing.

With this in mind I curl my nails into the palm of my hand and squeeze tight. Using the pain I'm inflicting on myself as an anchor, I let my magic surge forward, tracking the Fae that are present. Two are dancing, one's buying a drink at the bar and the last one . . .

I find her easily enough. She's crowding a human girl with pale hair and dark eyes against the wall near the VIP area. The faerie looks as if she's taken her outfit tips from Marilyn Manson himself. She's bleached bone pale with enormous gold eyes that reflect the club's light in a crazy way. And because of the way she's dressed, presenting this persona, there's no alarm in the human girl's expression when the faerie presses kisses to her neck, or when the faerie whispers something to her and it makes the human girl blush and nod.

I narrow my focus and my sight brings them into sharp focus. The faerie has something in her hand and when she opens her palm, the girl looks absolutely thrilled, nodding enthusiastically, reaching for whatever it is.

'We've got one,' I say over my shoulder, knowing that Aiden would hear me even over his conversation with Dante.

'Watch my back but don't interfere. Unless there's more than five of them. Then come in swinging.'

I push my way through the dancing crowd with little finesse, provoking a few angry glares. The faerie and the girl are still there, talking quietly and intimately, but the second I'm within six feet of them, the faerie lifts her head and looks directly at me with those unearthly golden eyes and a smile on her carnelian lips.

'Blackhart.'

Her teeth, I realize, look very sharp against the fullness of her lips, especially the canines. I hesitate for a second because this is not the look Fae usually go for.

'You have me at a disadvantage,' I say, keeping my tone civil.

'Good. You have no right to interfere with me. I have a token from my liege.' At that she shows me her slender wrist and sure enough, the small silver token on a delicate bracelet glints up at me.

'I'm not here to send you back. I'm here to ask you about the Glow.'

The human girl turns slowly to look at me; her pupils are blown wide from whatever she's taken. I assume it's Glow, possibly even something else. I remember Aiden's words to me a month ago, asking me how things can go so badly for some humans that they'd go out of their way to smear, ingest and inject themselves with all kinds of substances merely to forget. I had no answer then and I still have no answer, but looking at this very pretty dainty girl with the dark eyes and too much mascara and eyeliner, I sense a deep-seated sadness in her and I have to resist the urge to just hold her tight.

I glance back at the faerie. 'Did she take the tablet you gave her?'

'I don't know what you're talking about.' She looks down at the girl, and leans down for another soft kiss. 'I found her like this.'

'We need to talk,' I tell her, stepping closer. 'Please, don't make this difficult. I don't want a scene. Just come with me.'

'And if I don't?' Her gaze moves past me and I sense the solid muscle of both Dante and Aiden behind me and I grin at her.

'I can ask my friends to help me.'

Before she can move, the human girl sways on her heels and moves towards me.

'Look,' she whispers, staring at Dante, her voice breathy and awestruck. 'He's so pretty. Is he real?' Then her gaze turns to me and she dimples a smile. 'You're all so beautiful, but he's extra beautiful. Just look.' With that she moves to stand before Dante, peering up at him. 'Can you see his antlers? They're wide, huge, rising all the way to the sky. Is he magic, Dorya? Is he one of you?'

Dorya, obviously the faerie, shakes her head pityingly and lets out a little put-upon sigh. 'Humans are so easily distracted,' she mutters, then stares at me. 'But not you.'

'I really think we should talk. Away from the crowd.' And just to make it clear, I press further. 'Privately.'

My hand rests lightly on her wrist, the gold band of my ring brushing lightly against the skin there.

Dorya tilts her head to the side a little and I will the magic in the ring to help convince her. I keep the touch of my magic light and brief, but even so the result is her taking a moment to consider my request before inclining her head in a queenly fashion.

Dante falls in behind me and we trail Dorya through the side exit and into the narrow alleyway behind the nightclub. I lead Dorya further into the alleyway, away from the smokers around the door, and am grateful for Dante's bulk blocking us so we can talk privately.

She slouches against the wall and her skin looks luminous in the dim lighting. 'Tell me, Blackhart, why exactly do you care what these humans do with their spare time?'

'I care because *these humans* you're referring to are dying because of a drug, Dorya, that you seem to have no qualms about handing over. And I'm pretty sure you know this, but in case you don't, it is still illegal to distribute the stuff in the first place. In both realms. I don't care whether your token is from the Sun King or Suola, you *are* breaking the law. And because of that, I can actually send you back to be judged by your Court.'

'You're prepared to risk that?' Her gaze flicks to Dante, who's remained very quiet throughout. 'It could be a diplomatic debacle.'

'I don't see it that way.' I smile and it's the kind of expression Aiden's told me will get me beaten up one day. 'You break our laws – I have permission to send you back. Simple.' I look over my shoulder at Dante; he's clearly read my intention. 'Or, we can have a nice talk and you tell me what I want. My friend here has some skill with magic.' He steps closer and there's something dangerous in his demeanour, as if he's going to enjoy how the next few moments play out. I look at her and let my smile grow wide.

She doesn't actually back up, but she straightens to frown at me.

'Blackhart, don't do this.'

'What? We're having a friendly discussion.'

Her eyes rest on Dante, where he's opening and closing his hands by his side. Every time he flicks open his hand a ball of blue swirling energy appears. When he shuts his hands it disappears. He does this a few times, and it's an impressive display of magic for a Fae in the Frontier. Dorya watches, then actually focuses properly on him.

'Kami,' she says, and there's something like awe in her voice. 'You have a *kami* working for you. Voluntarily? How did you . . . what have you promised him?'

'Dante is a friend,' I say, and watch him shake his hands, letting blue fire drip from his fingers like water. The magic hits the ground at his feet and spreads like wildfire. But unlike wildfire it doesn't burn out of control. Instead it circles him, blue flames shooting into the air on an 'up' gesture from him, blazing happily in the darkened alleyway.

He's clearly been practising this and I feel a stupid amount of pride at the little display and grin at him in approval.

Dorya's still eyeing Dante and I wonder if she's sorting through the various stories she's heard about kami, or Japanese nature spirits, in her head. About how their powers can cut off a Fae's magic from the Otherwhere completely. And how adept they can become at draining other Fae to the point of mortal death – whilst themselves growing stronger. None of these stories could be disproven and Dante remains an unknown quantity, a weapon in my arsenal, and I have no qualms about directing him right at my target.

Dorya's smile is now less predatory and a little sickly. 'And if I do tell you what you want to know?'

'We can come to some agreement, where you may remain in the Frontier.'

'With a Blackhart as an ally?'

'Let's not push my generosity.'

Chapter Nine

We've had maybe four hours' sleep in the past twenty-four hours. I feel wrecked and the boys both look pretty near to breaking point. We head home hardly talking, each of us busy with our own thoughts. My mind flicks between Jane in hospital and the information Dorya gave us. Her drugs came from an old 'knocker', a type of mining goblin. They frequent the deeper parts of mines all around the world (says the handy phone app Kyle made me). This particular knocker, he goes by the name Antone Pensa, does the occasional bit of business from the Fae Hold in North London. He's been in the human world for such a long time that he apparently no longer presents as Fae and looks mostly wholly human. Interestingly, Dorya's take on Marko was less than flattering. She didn't like him or any of his crew.

He seems to have a problem with the Fae, so whenever they are working the same club, she usually lets him know, as a courtesy. Invariably she's the one to leave, to move on to another club. But tonight Marko and his little crew were the ones who opted to go elsewhere. Dorya knew that Marko has steady access to Glow and that he runs raves, especially down in Brighton and on the Kent coast – his speciality, apparently. Other than that, she didn't know much more about Marko or the boss who runs the Jericho Gang at all.

On our way back to the house I ring the North London Hold. When I ask to speak with the Lady Mar, I'm told she's not at home but would be the following day. The voice on the line sounds young, pre-teen and friendly. So I tell him who I am and that I'd like to meet with Mar as soon as possible. My name seems to startle him a little, but within minutes I've got my appointment. The young voice tells me his name is Laurent and he is Lady Mar's grandson. We say our goodbyes and hang up.

Back at the Garretts' I give each of the guys a brief hug before heading to bed. I need a few more hours' sleep and another shot of painkillers to get rid of the lingering sore head. The good thing about the painkillers? They make me drowsy. The bad thing about the painkillers? They make me drowsy – even when I'm awake. And the drowsiness doesn't help the accompanying nausea either.

The house is quiet and once I've showered and pulled the covers up over my head, sleep takes me.

I sit down for breakfast around midday, after a few hours of bad dreams and tossing and turning. I let the mirror pendant on my necklace dangle from my fingers. Dante carries over our plates of sandwiches before taking a seat opposite.

'Someone moved my necklace.'

'Where from?'

'It was on my bedside table but when I went to put it on, I found it on the floor.'

'I've not touched your stuff.'

'I didn't say you did. Maybe Aiden?'

'He wouldn't touch your things either, Kit.' Dante

wrinkles his nose and drops his voice low, trying for humour. 'It's girl stuff.'

I run my finger across the surface of the black mirror contemplatively and look up at him from beneath raised brows.

'I'm going to try to sing it awake,' I say, and my voice wavers only slightly.

'Are you sure you want to do that now? You don't look so good. Will it be a strain if it works?'

I move my shoulders in a half-shrug. 'I don't know, mostly because it's not really worked before. Why would today be different?'

'Okay. But have something to eat first, maybe. Give your magic something to riff on that's not just caffeine based.'

I nod and pick at my sandwiches. 'You'll make someone a good wife,' I tell him.

'Husband.'

'Whatever.'

But he's smiling at me, digging into his own food. He gets up and pours us each a cup of hot chocolate from the pan on the stovetop. I pull it closer and inhale the smell of the chocolate deeply and sigh with contentment.

'You are my favourite, Dante Alexander. Ever.'

'You like me because I feed you, no other reason.'

'Eh, sometimes you even manage to fight like you were trained properly.'

I get a little push for my sass but he chuckles. When we've cleaned up after lunch, he gestures towards the pendant.

'Okay, do your thing. Let's see if we can find your boyfriend.'

I roll my eyes at the boyfriend thing but I pull the necklace closer and run my fingers over the surface. I close my eyes and recall the lullaby Thorn sang those long months ago. I know the tune well; it's settled beneath my skin.

I hum it when I'm alone and I tap the rhythm on my knee when I watch TV or when I'm thinking. I know I do this because Kyle's told me and I've caught Aiden frowning and shushing me. I hum the refrain, reaching for a small sliver of my magic and start singing the tune, my voice nowhere near as clear as Thorn's or as pure. But I put a lot of strong will into the tune and I hope that makes up for my lack of musical talent.

I have very little hope that Thorn will reply. These scrying mirrors seem to have a will of their own and the other times I've tried since he gave me the pendant only ever met with static.

'Kit!' The voice is so loud – and right in my ear – that I startle and almost drop the pendant. But Dante's there, his hands covering mine, and his eyes are wide with fright. I realize he's never actually seen the mirrors and how they work.

'Thorn?' I nod at Dante to show him I'm okay, and I open my hands so I can look into the depths of the black mirror.

'Kit.' This time Thorn's face is there, although slightly fuzzy, and I exhale in relief. 'Are you all right?' he says.

I cup the disc between my hands. 'I'm fine. I've been trying to find you since we came back – and all I've ever managed to see is a bit of mist and trees until now.'

'. . . been fluctuations and not safe to reply until now. I'm well, as is Crow.'

'I was *worried*. We all were. We'd not heard from you after what happened.'

I am not imagining his tense expression or the way his mouth narrows to a flat line. 'It has been an interesting few weeks. Someone is with you?'

I drag Dante closer so that he can also look down into the mirror. I'm pretty sure all Thorn is seeing of us are our nostrils so I angle the disc a little to help with the view.

'Dante's here. We're at Aiden's house.'

'Thorn.' Dante sketches a little salute and Thorn smiles at him and there's definitely relief in his eyes.

'It's good to see you are both well and together. Where is the wolf?'

'Out shopping for supplies,' Dante replies off-handedly, scowling at his cousin. 'Thorn, what's going *on* with you? We left you in that clearing and you turn into a bloody great big *fire-breathing dragon*. And then we hear *nothing* – until now. This is not how we operate!'

I bite my lips because this is what I am desperate to yell too but, really, I don't want to be that girl. The girl who loses her mind if the boy she fancies doesn't bother calling. Or, you know, use a magical mirror to communicate with her.

Thorn looks taken aback by his cousin's outburst but then his expression softens and he hangs his head in apology. 'It didn't even occur to me to get in touch,' he says, and I can hear the truth of it in his voice. 'I am not used to others, to *friends*, caring about my well-being. I am well, as you can see.'

'Well, you've a bunch of people who care a lot right now, so you should –' Dante's scowl deepens – 'definitely check in more to let us know you're not lying dead in a ravine somewhere. And even if you were, I'm sure you could still find a way to let us know – you strike me as the stubborn type.'

I can't help it. I burst out laughing and pat Dante's shoulder and I really want to hug him hard. 'Yes, Thorn. What Dante said. No more hiding from us. We are interested in knowing you are okay. And alive.'

Thorn's smiling now too and the tight worry lines around his eyes ease a little. He says something but it's lost in a burst of static. His face becomes blurry for a second before it refocuses.

'It may be difficult to stay in touch as often as I'd like,' he says. 'Crow and I are due to travel soon. The Veil . . . there are things happening in the Otherwhere that are . . . a cause for concern.'

'There are things happening here that are cause for concern too,' I point out. 'The weather here is weird, Thorn. Even worse than when Olga manifested as a dragon.' I wait a beat for that to register with him. 'We think that whatever is happening in the Otherwhere is being reflected in the Frontier.'

'As above, so below,' Thorn mutters, and I only hear it because I'm leaning closer to the mirror, because the damn thing keeps flickering with the weird static. 'It is only strange weather that you're experiencing?'

Dante and I share a look and he mouths 'only' at me questioningly – and suddenly I'm worried by the implication that there could be and should, possibly, be more things happening.

'Isn't it *enough*? It is freezing out, like tundra cold. There are freakish storms all over the world in places that never get storms and there's snow, Thorn. Snow in Jordan. Where it never snows at this time of year. And it's on TV and in the newspapers, because the meteorologists are unable to make head or tail of it.'

There's movement in the mirror and Thorn's sitting back, showing some of the room behind him. The term Spartan comes to mind and I wonder what kind of life he leads in that tower, where he's undergoing his training.

'I wasn't aware that matters had gone this far in your world,' he says, sounding weary. 'I should have checked earlier, I'm sorry. You're right, Kit, I should have thought about it sooner.' He shuffles a bit in his chair and leans closer to the mirror; there's another burst of interference before it settles. When he speaks, his voice is low and quiet with worry. 'The Veil is collapsing and it means . . . actually, it means a great many things. Crow and I, we're hoping to find something to help stop the Veil from crumbling further.'

'The kids?' I ask, sitting closer still. 'The goddess? Is she okay – surely she's being fed enough so that her power can sustain the Veil? Are the kids okay?'

'Brixi has not spoken to me since we left the ruined palace, but there's more to this trouble with the Veil than merely the goddess's powers failing.' Thorn looks up and suddenly seems so very tired. 'The great forest is infected with a blight. Parts of it are failing. And along with the Veil, the forest forms the Otherwhere's biggest defence. The forest constrains the magic the Veil generates. Together, the goddess, the Veil and the forest prevent raw magic from seeping into your world and other worlds.'

'When you say raw magic,' Dante prompts him, 'what exactly do you mean?'

'Raw magic is what the songlines are made of. The closer to the source of the magic you are, the more dangerous it can be. There hasn't been real magic in the human world for centuries. Occasionally something would happen, a node would burst or a creature would get through without permission and go on a rampage. For humans to experience raw magic, uncontrolled magic, would mean . . . it would mean being consumed by it entirely. A rare handful of humans have the ability to deal with magic in the first place, others would merely become magic's pawns.'

'You make it sound like magic can be an infection, turning people into zombies.'

Thorn's gaze narrows as he stares at Dante. 'If you call it an infection you make it sound as if it has a will of its own. Magic is the essence of life. It enhances what is already within you. It's a neutral power within us all that can be directed to manifest in order to do what we want it to do. That is how sorcerers use magic – they harness the ability they're born with. Wizards learn spells and incantations and *mimic* this ability.'

I let this sink in. I think about my own magic and ability and I wonder exactly what I am, as I seem to be a mix of both. I notice that Dante's expression is thoughtful as he too digests the information Thorn's sharing.

'Is there anything you need us to do this side?' I ask him and Dante's grip tightens on my shoulder. 'Anything that may help you figure out how to make things better?'

'Nothing that immediately comes to mind, but I'll be sure to be in touch.' His hand drifts towards his eyebrow to rub the curve there in a gesture that is so familiar it makes me ache. But then he smiles lightly and looks at me and his eyes seem so very blue in that moment. 'Thank you, for offering. Both of you.'

I swallow against the knot in my throat. 'Yeah, okay. Just don't wait so long to get in touch, okay?'

'I won't. I promise.' His gaze shifts to Dante. 'Cousin, may I speak to Kit in private for a few moments?'

Dante nods without question and leaves the kitchen.

'Kit.'

'Thorn.' I grin at his little eye roll when I use the same serious tone he's using.

'I feel I need to apologize. For being a bad friend. For not thinking about contacting you. For letting you worry when there was no reason for you to be concerned.'

'For the guardian of the realms you're really a bit of an idiot, aren't you?'

'Yes. I think so.' He sits closer to the mirror and it distorts completely before it refocuses, the static giving a soft whine to his words before his voice stabilizes. 'Kit, everything I said before, the last time we were together – I was serious. I think we stand a chance, you and I, of being together, of getting to know one another when the world isn't breaking. I'm going to do my utmost to make that happen, by fixing whatever is broken. We deserve to know one another. To see where this –' he gestures between us – 'goes, don't you think?'

I bite my lips against the upswell of tears and nod. 'Yes, I'd like that, very much. I mean, it's fun fighting by your side, but it's all we seem to do. And I think sometimes it would be nice to just sit down and talk, like normal people do.'

He does a little shocked moue and it makes me laugh. 'Like *normal people* do? Kit . . . are we so very abnormal?'

'*Yes*.' I try for a light tone but it falls flat; instead, I just feel incredibly sad. 'We're not normal, not at all. And, yes, we deserve better and more. Let's fix this latest problem and then figure out the rest. Does that sound like a plan?'

'It does indeed.' He looks to the side and I hear voices in the background. 'I have to go. Be safe, little Blackhart. Don't pick fights you can't win. I'd be loath to lose you.'

I touch the small disc with reluctant fingers. 'I'll do my best. Stay in touch, Thorn.'

The mirror gives a last high-pitched static blast before turning black and I take a shuddering breath. Wow, okay. I didn't expect that to hit me so hard. I wipe a stray tear from my cheek

'You okay, kiddo?' Dante's back at my side within moments. His eyes search my face and there's real concern there.

I open my mouth to tell him I'm fine, but instead what comes out is a real sob and to my horror the sob is the trigger for more tears to start falling down my face. Without a word he pulls me out of the chair, wraps both arms around me and holds me tight.

Chapter Ten

It's about an hour later when my phone starts to ring. I don't recognize the number at all.

'This is Kit,' I say, my voice wary.

'Blackhart, this is Detective Shen. I need you and your Spook to come down and meet me.'

'Why?' The question is out before I can help it. There's no reason for Shen to contact me at all. 'We've not been near Brixton, the estate or Tia's parents since you escorted us away the last time.'

'I'm aware of that. Write down this address.' Her tone tells me exactly how little patience she has with me. 'How long will it take you to get here?'

I flash the address at Aiden and mouth 'How long?' at him, knowing that he'd have heard most of the conversation anyway, because of crazy werewolf hearing.

'Tell her about forty minutes, maybe longer, depending on traffic.'

Before I can reply to her she's talking again. 'I heard. Get here, as soon as you can. Faster if possible.'

'Do you want to tell me what this is about?'

Previously I'd just heard impatience in her tone; the way she suddenly hesitates now worries me. 'Not over the phone.'

'Fine, we'll see you soon.'

I hang up and look at the two boys. 'Well. I have no idea what to think about that. Why would she call us?'

'Maybe she needs you to hunt a ghost? Or slay a demon?' Aiden says, pulling his hoodie on over his Henley T-shirt. 'Get a jacket. You're gonna freeze out there.'

We hustle, putting on scarves, hats and gloves before we head back out, via the basement where Aiden's car's parked.

'When she said, "Get here faster," do you think we can pretend we're the Sweeney?' Aiden asks as he guns the Cayenne out of the garage, startling a tiny elderly lady walking her equally diminutive chihuahua along the mews.

'No,' Dante says decisively. 'I don't think she meant that at all. Just . . . don't drive like you stole the car. I'm sure whatever it is will wait till we get there.'

I listen to them banter and Google the address. It's somewhere past Shakespeare's Globe on the South Bank. There's nothing there I recognize from previous jobs I've worked. I wonder if it has something to do with the Child Thief case, but following that line of thought makes me feel very uncomfortable.

Detective Shen is waiting for us when we pull up to an unremarkable building near the river and the Tate. There are unmarked police cars, 'police do not cross' tape is being strung along the road and a number of serious-looking people are earnestly checking the scene. I feel young and out of my element as I slide out of the car, immediately shivering in the cold air. We shake hands, and Dante introduces Aiden. Shen's dressed warmly against the chill and she looks less than pleased to have us around; or maybe she's just cold.

'I expect you to share whatever thoughts you have on what I'm about to show you – is that clear? I'm laying my neck on the line here calling you in but, as it involves you to a certain extent, I had no choice.'

I nod, feeling nervous as hell. Her serious expression and ominous words sit heavily on me. 'What about if we can't help at all? Or what if whatever this is is more Blackhart than cop-stuff?' I ask her. 'What do we do with that?'

Shen's eyes go flinty and she suppresses a sigh. 'You're more like your uncle Jamie than I anticipated.'

I'm sure she means it as an insult but I pointedly grin at her to show her I'm taking that as a compliment. Behind me Aiden mutters under his breath but it's Dante who takes the lead.

'You rang us, Detective Shen.'

'I did. I'm starting to doubt my sanity, though.' She continues, after an unimpressed pause, 'A body was found this morning. I need you to tell me if you can . . . I don't even know. Sense something? If you can tell what happened? The body is of a small child. Be prepared.'

I feel a numbness stealing over me at the unreality of the situation as we're handed wrapped overalls and booties by a crime scene technician. I swim in mine, Aiden looks as if he's going to do a Hulk impression, and Dante somehow makes even the protective gear look stylish. I hate him a little. But Shen doesn't let us linger, hastily donning her own gear before turning to lead us towards a white incident tent.

'The call came two hours ago. Someone saw something in the river, thought it was flotsam. It wasn't.' Shen waved a hand. 'Long story short, we were called. Divers went in, took a look. It's one of the kids that went missing from the estate – last seen with the goddess, as per your respective reports.'

'Tia?' I ask her and I don't know how I know I'm right. Shen's mouth tightens even more and her nod is brief.

'I brought you here as a matter of professional courtesy. I know that in theory, Agent Alexander, you're on holiday – but as you were part of the investigation with Ms Black-hart, I thought it prudent to have you both here.'

'What about me?' Aiden asks her as we loiter outside the tent.

'You, Mr Garrett, can be the hot yet ultimately useless friend who gets underfoot.'

There's a beat of silence before Aiden speaks again. 'Wait, you think I'm hot?' he says, just as Shen ushers us into the tent.

'Give us a moment,' she says to the four men and women made anonymous by their protective overalls. They leave without question and the silence in the tent is unnerving. My hands start shaking as we walk over to the tiny covered figure lying on a cold-looking table.

Dante has his notebook out and is making notes as Shen talks. Aiden looks as if he's trying not to go wolf in anger at the presence of the small body. And as I stare down into Tia's unblinking gaze, I can't think about anything else.

She's small for her age. A tiny thing with a cute button nose set in a smooth thin oval face, gangly little limbs and crazy corkscrew curls that were once full of life and bounce. Nothing about her looks out of the ordinary. She's just a cute girl who should be tucked up in bed dreaming about normal stuff little girls dream about. She shouldn't be lying here, on the table, in this tent, not breathing.

I curl my fists by my side. There's a smell in the tent of damp and unpleasant things that's oppressive and I fight to stay standing.

I breathe through my mouth and I really need to get a grip, because I can feel myself starting to panic. My magic's thrumming wildly under my skin and my heart's beating loudly in my ears.

Dante slants me a curious look before going back to what Shen's saying, nodding and writing notes.

Tia's dead.

I left her behind in the Otherwhere, alive, and now she's back here in the Frontier, no longer alive.

There's a police investigation happening right now and I can't freak out like a civilian weakling because I'm not.

The shift happens so unexpectedly, between one blink of an eye to the next, that I'm taken unaware. The room around me vanishes and the smell of magic is thick and heavy in the air. In my vision, I'm suddenly flat on my back, with the water of the river closing over my head.

Chapter Eleven

'Get her outside, right now, and stop her from bleeding everywhere.' Shen's voice is cold as I come to.

I gasp for air as the vision loses its grip. I clutch vaguely at the chest I'm pressed against.

One moment we're in the tent and the next we're outside and the air is fresher, but I can still smell the river.

'Dammit, Kit, what the hell?' Aiden spins me so I'm suddenly upright again. I sway dangerously, my head swimming from the motion and from the power of what I've just experienced.

His hands cup my face and he tilts my head a little so that all I can see are his angry eyebrows and the dim grey skies above. 'I thought you said the nosebleed the other day wasn't anything to worry about.'

There are tissues being thrust in my face and I'm on autopilot, pinching my nose to staunch the flow. This time the accompanying headache is heavy and thick, and it spreads within seconds, making my vision go completely weird.

'Why didn't you say something about this to me earlier?' Dante mutters to Aiden. 'She's had these before?'

'I think so. She had one in the car on the way over the other day. Didn't think anything of it.'

'How can you not know it's a thing? She's your *friend*.'

'*I didn't know*. She didn't say anything about it before. So just stop shouting at me!'

'Stop telling me I'm shouting because I'm *not* shouting.'

'You're both totally shouting.' I clear my throat and push away from them both. 'Also, is this your first fight, because it's kinda cute.'

Before either of them could turn their bickering on me, Detective Shen steps out of the tent, looking grim. 'What's going *on* with you?' Her voice is sharp but I have trouble focusing on her. 'You look like hell. What was that fainting episode back there? Since when are you a diva, Blackhart? If I'd known, I wouldn't have called you to the crime scene. That's as sterile an environment as we could make it and now there's blood everywhere.'

I try to speak but Dante steps between me and Shen.

'Detective Shen.' There's something accusatory in Dante's voice that stops her short and she blinks at his tone. 'I'm sure Kit didn't start her nosebleed on purpose. I would also remind you that not all of us are veteran police officers, and seeing the dead body of a small child is a shock to the system. If you can let us regroup, I think we may have some insight into what happened to Tia.'

I don't know who's more surprised by his calm and deliberate words, me or Detective Shen.

'I shouldn't have called you. You shouldn't be part of this. What was I *thinking*?' she mutters, but then her eyes find mine and she relaxes slightly. 'Are you okay?'

'Fine, thanks. Just a nosebleed.'

'Do you sniff drugs? Because that eats away at the nasal cavity and . . .'

'I don't sniff drugs. And I never will. Or smoke. Or inject. Trust me. My life is screwed up enough as it is – I don't need chemicals to help me along.' I grimace at the tissues in my hand but shove them into my pocket rather than my bag. 'Sorry about back there.' I find Aiden's gaze. 'I had a weird turn, like time slipped away from me.'

Detective Shen drags a hand through her fringe and takes a steadying breath. 'You are in agreement, though, that the child we found in the river is Tia?'

I nod. 'From the photos I've seen in her room, that is definitely Tia.'

'It's not a bit of tree that's been glamoured to look like her?' Detective Shen looks at me intently. 'Because I've been on a case where that's happened.'

'No, it's her. It's really her.' I rub my aching head but manage to keep my voice steady when I speak next. 'She didn't die in the river. You'll find no water in her lungs, so she didn't drown. I don't know how she died but it was fast and peaceful. You'll also find that she's been well fed and that she is probably in a very healthy state.'

Shen's expression is one of surprise. 'We've already determined that she didn't drown.'

'Good. That's good. Her death wasn't planned. She was looked after by someone who'd gone to a lot of trouble to do so.'

'How do you know that?'

'Her hair, her clothes, her hands. The person who had her made sure she stayed healthy.' I stare at her and shrug. 'And yet here she is, no longer alive.'

Shen watches me for a few minutes longer before shaking

her head. 'You are very much like Jamie. Thank you, Blackhart. You have been of some assistance.' She sighs and turns back to the river. One of the technicians approaches and they speak in hushed tones. She gives a nod and within moments everyone heads back into the tent. Everyone except Shen. 'I need to ask you this: can you give your whereabouts for the past twenty-four hours?'

It shouldn't come as a surprise, but it does, that she asks us to give alibis. We give her all the information we can before she nods her thanks, but only after warning us not to go on sudden holidays or leave the country. She also warns us away from visiting Tia's estate again and we solemnly swear that we won't go near it or any of the parents of the missing children. Or their friends. After a final searing glare she dismisses us and heads back to her team.

We're halfway to the car when Aiden turns to look at me.

'What?'

'You know exactly what.'

I try to ignore the eyebrows and concerned scowl but in the end I give in. 'I'm sorry. Usually I can control the start of my visions, when I'm actively trying to *see* what happened.' I draw a heavy breath and wince as my nose aches in the frigid air. 'Things went a bit weird in the tent and I couldn't even fight it. The vision just took me.'

'What does that mean, Kit? Try to be clear so we lesser mortals can understand.'

I'm aware that Dante's standing protectively by my side and I give him a grateful look before continuing: 'I know who sent Tia here.'

'*Who?*' Dante's a fraction of a second faster than Aiden.

'Brixi. Brixi left Tia in the river.'

'So he's actually *killing* the kids now? Is that what we're expecting? Will there be more kids being left behind for us to find?'

'No, I don't think so. Something went wrong. That's why he brought Tia back.'

'He didn't bring her back, Kit. He dumped her body in the river.'

Behind my eyes I replay the vision that hit me in the tent – and see again the reverence in Brixi's ritualistic gestures as he lays the small body down in the wooden craft. The small silver coin he places in her mouth before pushing the boat into the river. He then wades back to shore, with its soaring trees and thick undergrowth. He turns to watch the coracle float down the misty river and moves his hands in a ceremonial goodbye. His expression is haunted and sad.

'He didn't bring her back here, to the Frontier.' I frown as I walk ahead of them a little. 'He was in the Otherwhere when he put her in the river. There should be a little boat too, like an old-time kind of boat. A coracle.'

'How did she get here from there, then?' Aiden's voice is harsh and Dante shoots him an annoyed look before replying.

'Someone could have brought her here.'

I close my eyes and remember what I saw: the flat pebbled shore and the wide rushing river. The impenetrable thick forest. The way Brixi moves, the slump of his shoulders, the way his head hangs low.

'Thorn said things were changing in the Otherwhere, and I wonder if this is part of it?' I fix them both with a stare. 'If things are going south with the goddess, it could be that she's using up more power to keep the Veil intact and that in turn is putting a strain on everything else. It could mean that she's using up the kids faster. And if that is the case, more of them could die and more could be taken from our world to help sustain her.' I shudder at the thought.

'And then what happens if *those* kids are used up?' Dante hunches his shoulders. 'They take more from our world to feed her? Or everything just stops? I just want to put this out there but I think this whole thing – the way the Veil is being maintained by the goddess and the kids – feels somehow makeshift. How do I put this? It feels like the Fae want the Veil to be strong, but are using the supernatural equivalent of gaffer tape.'

Both Aiden and I stare at him.

'That is a terrifying thought.' Aiden shakes his head. 'I'd rather believe the guys in charge aren't just making it up as they go along.'

'The guys are in charge are the ones stealing children for their energy, so they can act as batteries for the goddess,' I point out. 'How safe does that make you feel?'

Now I'm the focus of both their stares and I add, 'I'm stating a fact. If the goddess's powers are failing completely, Brixi and his handful of left-over Faceless underlings will be stealing more kids.'

'We stop them from doing that,' Aiden's voice is flat and hard. 'No *way* do they do that. Not again.'

'Listen, let's get in the car. I know you're not bothered by the cold, Aide, but Kit's turning blue and I can't feel my toes any more.'

Aiden unlocks the car and we clamber in. I fiddle with the radio as we drive away. The news announces another cold front is due to hit the UK and that heavy snow's been predicted across all of the British Isles. The threat of flooding will also be high once the ice melts. People are being urged to stock up on basics and not to travel long distances if they can help it.

'This is sounding worse and worse,' Aiden mutters, hunching over the steering wheel. 'Give me a minute.' I sit back and listen as Aiden activates speaker-phone on his mobile and has Dante call the pack's farm in Hertfordshire. Aiden instructs the caretaker to be ready for an influx of wolves, in case they need a place to stay if the weather worsens. Then another call comes through.

'This is Aiden's phone,' I answer in my best PA voice and he rolls his eyes at me.

'Kit?'

It takes me longer than I would have liked to place the voice, but when I do I'm genuinely surprised.

'Philippe?' I look at Aiden in surprise and he shrugs – why would Milton's head barman be calling now?

'Is Aiden with you? And the Spook?'

'We're all here,' I tell him and for no reason I suddenly feel tense.

'Philippe. Are you okay, dude?' Aiden indicates and turns down a side road.

There's a muffled noise in the background and a muttered curse. 'No, not really. I need you three to come to Milton's. Miron's asked me to call.'

I look at Aiden, who looks as worried as I do. 'In what capacity are we coming to Milton's? Are we just hanging out or is there something else going on?'

'Something is *definitely* going on. Don't spare the horses. Just get here.'

And then the call is disconnected.

Chapter Twelve

Miron the demon is behind what is left of the bar; Philippe is cleaning up nearby. Dressed in a shredded suit and wearing cuts and bruises as if they are medals, Miron looks like utter hell. Pun intended. There's also a faint stench of sulphur in the air and the residue of recent magic buzzes uncomfortably against me. As Miron watches us approach, picking our way over the debris of broken tables, glitter balls and other bits of furniture, he throws back a shot of something that makes my eyes water even from across the room.

'Miron, you threw a party and you didn't invite us? I'm hurt.' Aiden grins at the demon and shakes the proffered hand. Dante and I get a nod each before Miron moves out from behind the bar.

'Thank you for coming this fast. Let's go and talk in my office.'

'What happened?' I ask the demon, as he leads us up the damaged staircase to his office space.

'A brawl. Humans on Glow are vile and unruly. Just look at the mess.' He sighs in deep annoyance. 'However, there may have been some Fae involved. Possibly some Infernal. Definitely one of the angels.' He waves an elegant hand. 'Everyone fought. I'll have to deep clean the premises.

But the unfortunate taint of magic, alcohol and blood leaves a miasma that just won't come out – no matter how deep you clean. I'll possibly have to remodel it completely.' The nightclub is wrecked; there's not a single table or chair that's survived unscathed. The DJ booth is in pieces too and even one of the chandeliers has somehow been torn from the ceiling. It now lies in a neatly swept-up pile in the middle of the dance floor.

'I'm getting too old for this. Maybe I should retire and let Philippe take over.'

'Please, no,' Philippe calls from below. 'Never get me involved in any of your schemes ever again.'

We follow Miron past the VIP booths and private rooms and into his intact office. He sinks down behind his desk and rubs tiredly at his face. Without asking for permission, Aiden drags the couch over so we can sit in front of him.

'I sent everyone home after we managed to deal with most of the mess. None of the humans were too badly hurt, apart from the three who took Glow and started the fighting.'

'What exactly *happened*, Miron?' I ask him, not entirely sure how three humans could make this much mess.

'And how did they get past your doorman and his team?' Dante asks him, leaning forward. He has his notebook out and his pen is hovering. I bite my lip and don't say anything, but Aiden and I share a look of amusement. Dante and his little notebook really have become one of our favourite things.

'Hysteria.' With great care Miron shrugs out of his suit jacket and I'm shocked to see how much of his shirt is ripped and covered in blood. I must make some sound of distress because he just lifts a calming hand. 'This isn't my blood. And before you ask, I wasn't the cause of said personage to bleed out.'

I mouth 'bleed out' in horror but before I can ask anything, Dante asks, 'What do you mean by "hysteria"?'

'And "bleed out" means "bleed to death" in some circles, Miron,' I point out, but he just frowns at me in annoyance.

'I said personage, not person. No one died here, Kit. Or, if they did, they picked themselves up and walked out of here first with everyone else. Let me show you what happened. It's easier than trying to explain.' From a hidden drawer beneath the desk Miron removes a small remote and, after he presses a sequence of buttons, the wall behind his desk recedes by a foot and a band of TV screens slides down.

'I had the cameras installed maybe a year ago, when my doorman Rorke noticed we were routinely being targeted by some unpleasant Unseelie. Right, here we go. The cameras are manufactured to my specifications – which is why you'll actually be able to see the Fae, Infernal and others that frequent the club.'

Others? What can be more *other* than the creatures he's already mentioned? I try not to dwell on that as we settle in to watch Miron's home movie.

It's just after midnight, according to the timings on the screens, and Milton's is full to bursting. It seems everyone is having the time of their lives. I recognize some of the waiters as they move around with drinks, clearing glasses and bottles from the tables dotted around. They are fully manifesting in their Fae form and I spot a dryad and one is definitely a little Japanese kitsune – if her six tails and cute ears are anything to go by.

'Watch.' Miron taps the screen. 'It starts here.'

He does something on his tablet and the camera zooms in. Initially I don't see anything much apart from people dancing but then I see it and I gasp. A young woman, maybe in her early twenties, is levitating. It's not obvious at first, she just suddenly seems a bit taller than the people around her, then she keeps getting taller until you realize she's not growing but rising into the air. The people around her react with gasps of awe and looks of surprise. Then that changes to incredulity before turning into shock and fear. People stumble away, giving her more room. The woman's expression is ecstatic and she's smiling like a painting of a blissed-out Madonna in the National Gallery. Her arms are flung wide as she starts spinning in slow circles, at least a metre above everyone else's heads.

'People start applauding at this point. They think it's some kind of show we're putting on. But then look.' He taps the screen to reveal another part of the floor.

Another girl moves through the crowd, a lone figure in a pretty floral dress. A guy bumps into her, turns to apologize, then they're suddenly kissing violently. There's no other way to describe it. And no matter how much he tries to push her off, she keeps her arms wound around his neck and it's horrifically intimate, watching her before she releases him. He crumples at her feet and the girl's face is serene and beautiful as she steps over him.

There's a commotion near the bar then and the crowd surges away from two guys throwing wild blows at one another. Then one just steps back, rolls his neck to loosen up, grabs his opponent by the shirt and just tosses him like a sack of potatoes. The guy goes flying across the heads of bystanders and hits one of the columns, where he falls to the floor in a bloody unconscious mess.

And that's all it takes for a proper fight to break out. It starts off as an ordinary brawl, for sure, but it's a riot within moments. The chaos that erupts isn't helped when more Fae start manifesting in their true forms, freaking more people out. Rorke's in the middle of the crowd, along with some of the other staff, directing people to the exits. Everything seems to be calming down a little – which is when the angel steps right off the mezzanine balcony and punches Rorke in the face.

'What happened?' I ask Miron after watching too much of the violence on the screen. 'What triggered this?'

'Glow.' Miron grimaces as he shifts in his chair and I hear his breathing hitch. I recognize that sound and the way he winces slightly. His ribs are hurt for sure, even if he claims he isn't injured. 'I have no idea what they've done to the stuff, because now it's also affecting Fae, the angels *and* the Infernal. My club is no longer neutral territory as the fight contravened every law and bylaw governing neutral areas. I'm going to have my licence revoked and no one will ever come here again.'

'That was a huge fight that escalated pretty fast,' Dante points out, simply ignoring Miron bemoaning his club's potential demise. 'How did everyone get the Glow? And by get it, I mean how did everyone ingest it?'

The answer seems obvious to me, but it's Aiden who answers. 'It was airborne. It would be the fastest way to spread the drug. Unless everyone somehow managed to eat or drink it, which, in a club this big would be very hard to bring off.'

'You're coming to the same conclusion Philippe and I did. We had a bunch of goblins in during the week to adjust the air conditioning throughout the club. We suspect they're the ones who jimmied the vents.'

'Why didn't you or Philippe get affected?'

'I'm not sure we escaped. I think we were both just less affected than others.' He points to himself. 'Demon of a higher order. Phillipe as an acolyte of Dionysus.' When I stare at him he sighs. 'Also known as Bacchus, the god of wine and ritual madness and general insane revels. Don't you learn anything worthwhile these days?'

Dante sits back on the couch, his pen making scritching noises over the page.

'Have you spoken to the police?' I ask Miron, letting his sniping at my education go by without rising to the bait.

'No. This is an in-house matter that I prefer not to share with the human authorities. They'll ask questions I'm not at liberty to answer.' At my raised eyebrows he continues, 'There may have been an ambassador from a foreign country entertaining a few of the Infernal in one of my VIP rooms. Things got messy.'

'I'm sure Detective Shen . . .' I start ·but he interrupts me.

'Is not my friend.' He looks pained. 'It's why I had Philippe call Garrett. We know he's been working with his brothers on the Glow case. Aiden – I spoke with your brother Connor before you arrived. He mentioned that you went to the rave in Croydon the other night, where the boy died.'

I trade a significant look with Aiden before he replies. 'Yeah, we did. There were police everywhere. We found a lead on one of the distributors, we think.'

There's another pause before I speak up again. 'What about the humans that were harmed here? And the ones on Glow?'

'Philippe hit the guy who started the brawl with a memory spell. He shouldn't remember what happened here. We're not too concerned about the other humans who were in the club – their memories will also be affected when they leave here. It's a precaution only,' Miron adds before I can protest. 'I never invoke the blanketing spell unless it's completely necessary. In all the time Milton's has been in business, we've only needed to do so en masse once before in the past.'

Aiden and I share an uncomfortable look.

'The effects of the Glow didn't last long, and Rorke took three other humans to hospital – those most strongly affected. We couldn't just send them home – even I'm not that heartless. The one girl was hovering, for Lilith's sake.'

'Can you send us details of the goblins you employed to fix your air conditioning? And anything else you can think of, and a copy of that video?'

'Already done.' Miron hands me a slender USB stick. 'Everything we have is there. The USB contains the video, copies of the paperwork and contact information.'

I stand to go, but Dante's asking Miron a few more questions behind me. I only partially listen, leaning against the internal window that looks down on the club below. I allow my mind to wander as I consider what we've seen. Listening to Miron, and seeing for myself the evidence of the use of Glow going wrong is a wake-up call. The problem is big and it's getting bigger. And as much as I'd like to try to do everything, especially rescuing the kids in the Otherwhere, I realize my options are limited. I need to focus on the stuff I can fix. That means that Glow takes priority now and if Thorn needs me to help him further down the line with whatever he's into, then that's fine too. Right now, though, I need to throw all my energy into helping Aiden and Dante find the Glow manufacturers – and take them down.

It feels good having come to this decision and I suddenly feel more positive than I have done for weeks. It's the part of a case I like the most. The decision to act.

Chapter Thirteen

'How far do you think we can run before our families notice we've skipped out on them?' Aiden asks as we walk towards his car. 'I've got cash in the back of the car. I reckon we can get to the Bahamas within twelve hours. Leo can help. Hell, he'll probably want to come. He can get us passports too. What do you say?' He drapes an arm over me and Dante and hugs us close. 'Think about it.'

Dante looks down at Aiden with an expression close to consideration and I laugh.

'Hey, the last time I wanted to run away you stopped me,' I tell him. 'What's changed?'

'Everything.' He sighs and opens the car door for me but I get in the back seat instead, leaving Dante to sit in the front next to him. 'I really feel like we're being battered from all sides, and just not getting any kind of break.'

'When is your dad back from Russia?'

'Not sure. In the next week or so. My mum's coming back with him.' Aiden grins at Dante as they buckle themselves in. 'She's going to love you so much. She's an awful cook.'

'Great – I think?' Dante stares out of the window. 'So, what's our play? What do we do next?'

Two pairs of eyes stare back at me from the rear-view mirror and I groan. 'Why must I be the one making decisions?' But I can't help feeling chuffed that both of them defer to me. 'Okay, I think we let Uncle Andrew know about Tia first. I'll drop him an email when we get back to yours and he can liaise with Detective Shen. While I'm doing that, you see what we can get from the USB Miron gave us. The info about the goblins should be helpful.'

'Sounds like a plan. What do we do if the integrity of the Hold is called into question?'

'I honestly don't know.' I worry at my thumbnail. 'We'll have to talk to Jamie or Uncle Andrew if there's any evidence of that.'

'Explain to me about the Holds,' Dante says, twisting in his seat so he can look at both Aiden and me. His hair's a mess and his jaw is dark with stubble. He definitely no longer looks like the neat little government employee and I'll be honest when I say I far prefer the dishevelled look on him.

'The Holds are like Switzerland,' Aiden tells him. 'Neutral. Seelie and Unseelie and the Free Fae can ask a Hold to put them up for a night or a week, as long as they can pay. They are guaranteed safety here in the Frontier. And because each Hold has strong ties to the Otherwhere, through an item or person of power, the faeries prefer to stay there rather than elsewhere in the human world because it doesn't tire them out as much.'

'Are the Holds all over the UK?'

'All over the world, basically. They're everywhere, as long as you know where to look. Some are grand and strong enough to have their own permanent gateways to the Otherwhere.'

'You mentioned payment?'

'Yep. Nothing in life is for free, especially not staying at a Hold. You pay for whatever you need. Some faeries just go to socialize and meet up with friends. Others stay for business with humans.' Aiden grins at me in the mirror. 'Did I miss anything out?'

'No, you pretty much covered what I know.'

Dante digests this, nodding. 'It makes sense that they'd want something like that. How are the Holds run?'

'Their ownership is hereditary. There are some families who've run the Holds for centuries, whilst others occasionally change hands. I'm not entirely sure how it works because I've not really looked into it.' I tap my fingers on my knee and meet his eyes in the mirror. 'But I'm sure we have info on the database somewhere or you can just talk to Kyle, you know? My baby cousin's just a phone call away.'

'Yeah, I think I'll do that.' He smiles at me and I smile back. 'I want to go for a run when we get back, clear my head. Wanna come?'

'Sounds good. I've not stretched my legs for a few days. Aide?'

'No, thanks. This wolf is happy to stay in and make some calls. I need to open the rest of the house in case any of the pack comes round. You guys go run around in the wet and miserable cold.'

I've not run with Dante before. It's far less competitive than running with Aiden. We take the back roads that lead to Kensington Gardens, keeping up a steady pace. It feels good to be out and about, even if it's so cold that our breath mists the air. Very few people are around and it's mid-afternoon. Usually we'd be running past ladies who lunch and families out for strolls in the park. Even the traffic seems dialled down a notch – which is unusual this close to Christmas.

'You good?' Dante asks me as we wait for the lights to change at a junction.

'Yeah, you?'

'I think so. Thanks for coming out with me.'

'I'm totally here to protect you against marauding packs of toddlers and their nannies,' I say, having been privy to an embarrassed confession of this fear as we were leaving the Garretts'. 'It's the only reason you wanted me along.'

He gives a laugh, tugging his beanie further over his ears. 'They are feral. I fear for my life every time I come running.'

We head into the park, where some of the trees are lit up with bright lights, creating a pretty holiday feel. We spot a group of nannies and toddlers, who all perk up when they spot Dante. He mutters something under his breath and raises his hand to them in greeting. They all wave back excitedly.

'You weren't joking,' I gasp, genuinely amused, stretching my legs to keep up with his quickened pace. 'Seriously – why are you so grumpy that they're being nice to you?'

'Oh my God, Kit, they keep bringing me things to eat. And most of them want to introduce me to their daughters.' He grimaces and pulls his beanie down lower as if it could hide him from them.

I'm still laughing at him when I see movement behind him. I straighten in alarm and, acting on instinct, I shove Dante hard out of the way. He stumbles off the path onto the grass just as his attacker takes a swing with his sword. Because I'm straightening and standing in the space Dante occupied, I manage to get right in beneath the attacker's guard. I'm not proud of the knuckle-punch I throw straight into his throat, right beneath his chin, but it takes him down hard and fast. He drops, desperately gasping for air. I step over him, pick up his sword and heft it in my hand. I toss it in the air, spinning it, getting a feel for it. The balance seems okay but the blade itself could be sharper, perhaps. Even so, the point is nice and sharp and I reverse the hilt and tap him against the temple where he lies on the ground, knocking him out completely.

'Stupid move,' I tell him and wonder where Dante's got to, risking a glance to my right. I'm surprised to see Dante engaged in a strangely silent fight against another opponent. The guy is big, bigger certainly than Dante, but not as fast. And speed is crucial when you're fighting an opponent larger than you.

Dante murmurs something and his opponent falters for a moment, staring at him. A warm breeze circles me and I sway towards Dante as he brings his siren power to bear, luring the guy closer. His attacker drops his sword and reaches for Dante's face. Dante wastes no time playing nice. He grabs the guy's extended hand in a powerful wristlock and applies the minimum amount of pressure to his attacker's arm; the guy drops to his knees. Then Dante just knuckle-punches a set of nerves in the side of the guy's neck, knocking him out.

He looks up and his gaze finds mine. He looks as startled and angry by the unexpected attack as I am.

'Who're these guys?' I ask, staring down at my guy, taking in the clothes that look Fae-made.

'I don't know. But there are more of them.' He sounds grimly delighted. I turn to follow his gaze and I feel a surge of adrenalin.

'It's like all our Christmases came at once,' I say ironically. 'I've not been in a fight in weeks. Which would you like? The two really big guys or the other two really big guys?'

'I'm not picky. Ladies' choice.'

I move away from my unconscious opponent and do that ridiculous twirl with the sword that looks like showing off. What I'm really dong is limbering up my wrist and playing for time. This is not an everyday situation, despite our job descriptions, and I'm worried that someone may walk into the middle of this and get hurt. The path is quiet, badly lit and set apart from the rest of the park – so we're unlikely to be disturbed. But the sound of fighting has an unpleasant way of attracting attention. Especially the clear ring of steel against steel.

The four Fae – they are definitely Fae – are spread out in a semicircle before us. They're dressed in loose-fitting dark clothes, and the way they're moving makes me doubt they're wearing much armour. Their faces are also marked up so that there's little that doesn't blend in with the descending darkness. These guys are here for a quick and violent mission – either to kill us both or to take one of us after the other's been subdued. They're not expecting much of a fight, not dressed the way they are.

Dante's not bothered with his attacker's sword and instead has moved some distance from me, creating space in which to fight. He looks far too at ease when he glances at me. I recognize his expression and groan a little. Part of him is looking forward to this.

'Gentlemen,' I say turning back to the four Fae. 'Shall we dance?'

*

I duck and spin away from my opponent. He's like quicksilver, agile and good with his blade. Ridiculously good and I'm starting to panic. I'm okay with my blade, when I go up against goblins and less well-trained wannabe-assassins, but these guys are accomplished. Dante's already felled his first attacker. I heard bone crack and I doubt that guy's going to be getting up in a hurry.

I deflect another parry, barely keeping it together, backing away from the flickering blade. He's already managed to draw first blood, a small nick on my bicep, and it burns like all hell. Behind him, the other attacker seems torn between joining the fray and staying out of it. He edges towards Dante and I won't lie, I'm relieved. My guy is giving me a lot of fight to think about and I'm not sure I can handle another right now. My mind works overtime as I meet his blade with mine, the clash vibrating through my wrists and arms.

There's a flash of annoyance in the eyes staring down at me and I see his resolve hardening. He is toying with me, I suddenly realize, letting me tire myself. Then he can deliver that final blow, walk away and not feel that he's taken a life with ease. The thought jolts me and my magic rips through me in answer. I lift my hand and slap it into his face, directly over his eyes. I accompany the slap with a ball of fluorescent bright white light and sort of *smear* it with intent across his face. And as I do it, working on pure instinct here, I *will* it to start burning.

He falls back in shock, the blade of his sword dropping away from mine, freeing my weapon. As he staggers, I move forwards and ram the butt of the sword straight into his face, breaking his nose, and he drops to the ground, both hands grabbing for his damaged face.

I turn towards Dante, gasping for breath. He's felled his second guy in a move I didn't see, but as I watch he stomps on his final opponent's foot, anchoring him in place. Then with two hands behind the guy's neck, he jerks the guy's face towards his knee and our last attacker goes down too.

Dante stalks towards me. His shoulder's bleeding and his eyes are wide.

'What's this about?' he asks me, his breathing ragged. 'Who've we pissed off now?'

'The list is getting too long for comfort,' I say wearily. 'We have to go, come on. Someone's probably heard the commotion and called the cops.'

'Wait.' He kneels down beside his most recent aggressor and pats him down with a rather worrying degree of expertise. 'Check the other guys' pockets. See if they've anything on them to tell us who they are.'

'Bad guys, that's who.' But I do as he says and come up with a small bag of something. I pocket that to examine when we get back to Aiden's.

'No identification; they don't have anything on them.'

'They're Fae though, right?' Dante asks as he stands, staring at his opponent's unconscious form. He'd ripped the covering from the guy's face and his features look young and elegant and have that sense of *other* that is so familiar to me now. Dante takes a step back, wiping his hands on his hoodie in an unconscious gesture to get his hands clean. 'Why did they come after us?'

'We need to do more running away,' I say clearly. 'Right now. Talking later. Come.'

He lets me grab his hand and pull him into a jog, away from the six unconscious, dead or dying Fae assassins. Halfway through the now-dark park, it starts drizzling and

I start shaking from spent adrenalin. We lengthen our stride and by the time we get to the main road I'm soaked through and feel sick.

Dante flags down a taxi and we bundle into the back. He gives the driver Aiden's address and holds my trembling hand in silence all the way there.

Chapter Fourteen

I don't know how long I'm in the shower, letting the hot water pour over me, but by the time I'm done I've stopped shaking. I use my small first-aid kit to clean the cut on my upper arm and bandage it securely. Neither of the boys noticed the cut in all the rush when we got home and I'm grateful for it. Their fussing would've made me come undone.

I pull on track-pants, one of Aiden's Henley T-shirts and one of my own worn hoodies. And once it feels like I've put enough layers between me and the world out there, I sit down on my bed and take a breath. I touch the smooth skin of my hand, the one that slapped my attacker's face. I can still feel the residual heat from the magic and the slippery way his features shifted beneath my hand. Then I remember the pouch I lifted from one of our attackers and dig that out of my wet hoodie pocket.

It fits neatly into the palm of my hand. The pouch is made of worked leather and has a small drawstring. It looks like the little leather pouches sold at re-enactor stalls, in which you'd keep coins and valuable stones. Opting not to open it, I put it in my pocket and go to find the boys.

Aiden almost had a fit when he let us in earlier and went into full-on mothering mode, especially when Dante stumbled and he caught a glimpse of his pale face. It was really sweet but I had to get clean and needed time to regroup myself, so I left them to it. I now hear them talking in Dante's room so I knock lightly and push the door open.

Dante's had a shower and he's sitting on the edge of the bed, shirtless, with his head bowed. The first thing I focus on is the cut on his shoulder, the other thing I notice is the spread of his tattoo across his skin. He gives me a searching look over his shoulder as I enter, and I smile to show him I'm okay.

'Now that you're both here, how about telling me what exactly happened?' Aiden's retrieved their first-aid kit but looks a bit clueless as to what happens next. I point to the alcohol swabs.

'Use those first. To clean out the cuts.'

'We went to Kensington Park. Ouch, bloody hell, Aide. Are you hurting me more on purpose?' Dante shoots Aiden a venomous glare but endures his clumsy ministrations.

'Can you stop being such a whiner? Kit is a better patient than you are.'

'Kit is a superhero. I'm not.'

'No, you're a bloody faerie, so you should be tougher than a human girl.'

I'm not distracted by their bickering but I smother a grin.

'Who were they? The faeries who attacked you?'

Dante hisses through his teeth. 'Aiden, I swear to God, if you keep hurting me I will . . .'

'What?'

'Punch you. Hard.'

In answer, Aiden just pets Dante's damp hair soothingly before going back to work.

'I don't know who they were. But they were fast and they were trained, really well trained.'

'We beat them, though.' Dante's voice is strained when he speaks and I wince in sympathy as Aiden runs the swab a little too hard over the deep cut on his shoulder.

'That doesn't make me feel any better,' he replies. And while it's true that these guys were skilled, I've seen exceptional – thinking of Strachan and his highly trained squad in action. If we'd come across anyone that good, we'd have been in trouble and probably wouldn't have made it home alive.

'But they were definitely Fae?' Aiden asks me over his shoulder. 'Because that would mean you can take this higher.'

'What do you mean?' Dante asks.

'It was an unprovoked attack,' I explain, 'indicating that it was unsanctioned – and that means if we find out who's behind it, we can take them to the High King's Court and ask for the instigator to be judged.'

Dante winces when Aiden leans too heavily on him so he can get a better look at the cut. 'Okay, so . . . if someone declares they've a grudge against you and I or Aiden here that's okay, but attacking us without – what? The right paperwork? Contravenes some faerie laws?'

'Yes. Sort of. It's weird, okay. But this is how it's been done for a long time.'

Aiden just sighs. 'Faeries, man.'

'I'll send Uncle Andrew another email and tell him what's happened. As the head of the Blackharts he can, you know, demand to know who was trying to kill us.' I take out the small leather pouch and hold it in my hand. 'And of course, there's this.'

They both look up at me and I shrug. 'I took it from one of them. I have no idea what it is.'

Aiden reaches beneath the pillow on Dante's bed and passes me a long-bladed knife. I take it without comment but he seems embarrassed that his macho pillow-hiding habits have been rumbled.

I tug open the pouch strings using the blade. It falls open easily enough, revealing its contents to be a handful of gold coins.

'Okay, so that's a little underwhelming. Give me my knife back.'

'No.' I creep a little closer and, using the point of the knife, I move the coins around a little, flipping them over. There are also a couple of gems mixed in amongst the coins and I roll them around too. 'There's something . . .' I pick up one of the gold pieces and stare at it. The one side is worn almost smooth but the other side reveals a set of runes.

'I recognize these,' I say, holding the coin up between my thumb and forefinger. 'The runes. I've seen them twice before.'

'Can you read them?' Dante asks me.

'No. I don't recognize the . . .' I shrug. 'The style? It's like they're part of the usual alphabet we're familiar with on Viking relics but not quite.'

'But you've seen them before?'

'Yes.' I look up at Aiden. 'The first time I met Thorn, he was fighting these red caps in the forest. One of the goblins had a bandana inscribed with these runes tied around his arm. The goblins I fought on the island also had these runes on their bandanas.'

Aiden's given up trying to administer first aid to Dante and it's not my imagination, but Dante definitely looks relieved. I hold out my hand and Aiden passes the alcohol swabs with something like resignation, and I continue cleaning out the cut over Dante's shoulder.

'So, if the redcaps in the forest were Istvan's servants, that incriminates him? But he's dead. You saw him get sucked through the gateway into the void when you guys were shutting it down.'

I shrug, taking out a new swab. Dante really needed to be more careful during fights. And he seriously needed to start carrying weapons, rather than rely on his fists. 'I saw Istvan get taken on the other side. Then the roof collapsed on top of me.'

'So, what do we think? Istvan's supporters somehow found out about Dante and are using his coinage to fund their activities? It could be possible. But that would mean that they're still active – and I thought Aelfric locked all Istvan's allies in his dungeons or executed them.'

I raise my hands. 'I have no idea what Aelfric's plans were with Istvan's –' My eyes grow wide the same time as Aiden turns to look at me with a similar expression on his face – 'Eadric!' we both say.

'Do you think Eadric's people are behind this?' I address them both. 'Aelfric had him executed for treason after the attempted coup but perhaps his allies knew about Dante and came for him, to steal him as a bargaining chip.'

Dante scowls unhappily. 'I'm not exactly a damsel in distress, ripe for kidnapping.'

Aiden pats his other shoulder in a placatory way and Dante shrugs him off irritably.

'It could be,' Aiden ventures. He then pauses for a moment and lowers his voice, as if he hardly dare frame the thought. 'Or could *Aelfric himself* be trying to kill

Dante?' We are all silent for a long moment, until Dante grumbles and reaches for a discarded shirt:

'Can we not talk about the suddenly expanding list of people trying to kill me for five minutes? I'm getting cold and I'd like to get dressed at some stage tonight.'

I make an 'awwww' face at Dante and he grunts at me, but he keeps still under my ministrations. I lightly dab disinfectant on the cut I've just cleaned and try not to notice how the tattoo vines snake towards my hand. Watching more closely, I press my hand against Dante's skin, just below the cut. I watch, fascinated, as the tattoo spreads and curves back on itself, actually sidling steadily towards my hand. There's magic at work here, but it's a soft buzz that doesn't alarm me or make me want to shield myself. Dante twitches beneath my hand and lets out a muttered curse.

'What the hell, Kit? What are you doing? It feels weird.'

'No, wait.' I push him back into position. 'I'm not doing anything. Your tattoo is moving. Aiden, check this out.'

Aiden leans forward to get a better look and raises his eyebrows in surprise, staring at me. 'Kit, what did you do?'

'I don't know. Seriously, look at this. You try it.'

'I am not a science experiment.' Dante's head hangs low and his words sound slightly slurred to me.

'Stop being such a baby,' Aiden admonishes him and nudges me out of the way. 'Show me again.'

I put my hand on Dante's shoulder once more and the hooked vines resume their creeping movement towards it. Aiden frowns and when I lift my hand away, he presses the palm of his hand against Dante's shoulder. The vines become still, but their colour darkens.

Dante lets out a soft grumbling noise and pulls away from us both. 'Okay, enough with the touching. This is getting weird now.' But neither of us listen because, well, what's happening now is truly strange.

I know Thorn can heal himself pretty fast when he's connected to the songlines. But even then, depending on the severity of his wounds, it would take a few days for the scars to fade and the hurt to go away – and sometimes the scars don't fade all the way away either. I know Aiden heals faster when he shifts into wolf shape. Me? I just get bruised and cut – although if I manage to open myself to the songlines it helps marginally with my healing. But mostly it just assists with general tiredness. This, though, is crazy. The vines are moving beneath Dante's skin, the thorns hooking and tugging at the bruises and cuts. And when they move away, his skin is left completely unblemished.

'Your shoulder,' I tell him, tugging him towards the full-length mirror on the wardrobe. 'Look at it.'

Dante's gaze snags mine in the mirror before he leans towards the mirror. 'How is that possible?' he says in wonder as his fingers touch where the cut had been a mere few minutes ago. He bunches his shoulder muscles, working his arm. 'There's nothing there. Not even any stiffness. And the cut is completely gone.'

'Your face still looks pretty bad,' Aiden offers helpfully, drawing a scowl from Dante.

'I didn't get hit in the face,' he replies, puzzled. Then when Aiden laughs he shoves him hard onto the bed. 'But how's this happening? And what's the tattoo doing?'

'There's colour to it now.' Aiden's come to stand next to me and I move closer to inspect Dante's side. 'I can actually *feel* the vines moving beneath your skin with my magic and I'm not even touching you.'

I shift my sight and stare at Dante. He's covered in a

soft sheen of magic that swirls millimetres above his skin. It's concentrated over the thick lines of the tattoo on his back, and moving with the ebb and flow of it. I drop my gaze when he catches my eyes in the mirror. This was strange and magical and somehow personal.

'I can honestly say that I have never been this closely examined in my life,' Dante tells us, but I sense humour, not annoyance – although there's an edge of alarm.

'We've objectified you, your wounds and your tattoo enough now – you may get dressed.' I wave my hand at him imperiously and give him an apologetic grin. 'Come on, Aide, I need coffee and let's figure out what to feed our hero.'

'Hey, I'm not quite done. I'm pretty sure there are more bruises I've not . . .' Aiden lets out a yelp when Dante shoves him bodily towards me and shuts the door in both our faces.

Chapter Fifteen

'So is Eadric behind this?' Aiden hisses at me when we get to the kitchen. 'Or even worse, Aelfric? Why can't we stay away from these bloody tyrants?'

'I know.' I rub my eyebrow, realize what I'm doing and drop my hand. 'I might ask Thorn if we should tell his mother about Dante. Dina seems less inclined to megalomania than Aelfric.'

'No. We don't know how they'll react if they find out that Dante even exists. I mean, his dad was a traitor.'

'But Thorn is *fine* with Dante.'

'Thorn loves everyone,' Aiden says dismissively, and spots my sharp look. 'Well, no, you he loves. Everyone else he merely likes and tolerates.' I gape at him wordlessly and he laughs. 'Oh yes, I'm sure he often puts his life at risk to save a girl he really doesn't care about.'

'That's not relevant.' I scowl. 'Shut up. This is about Dante, not me. If they wanted me, they could have found me at any time in the past month when I was at home alone. He was definitely the target. Why would anyone send those guys after him, Aide? He's not done anyone any harm.'

'But he is the son of a traitor.'

'So killing him is the best option?'

Aiden shrugs and his expression is suddenly serious. 'Kit, I dunno, okay? I don't know how crazy people think. All I'm grateful for right now is that you're both safe and that you're home. How about emailing your uncle Andrew and catching him up on all of this? He needs to know.'

'Yeah.' I nod and head for the lounge and my chunky laptop. 'Good plan.'

'Hey, Kit?'

'Hey, Aide, what?'

'Thanks for not dying.'

I grin at him and settle on the floor, pulling the computer onto my lap. And when I'm giving Uncle Andrew the details, I realize something. None of our attackers had made a single sound.

It feels weird being by myself in my borrowed car. I've become so used to having people around lately that the unexpected quiet grates on my nerves. Just before turning up Park Lane, I find a radio station that plays rock. I turn the volume up, check the satnav and settle in to the drive to the London Hold. I'm armed with a handful of gems to exchange for information, but I've also brought my sword. It's currently resting on the passenger seat, strategically covered by my leather jacket.

I've left Dante and Aiden to their own devices and we're due to meet later this morning – to try to track down the goblins who 'fixed' Milton's air conditioning system. I'm starting to build a healthy respect for Aiden's computer skills because he dug through layers of data to find the holding company for the firm the goblins had used. Turns out the goblins' company was one of many such companies spread around the UK. Aiden found at least twenty-five other smaller companies installing air conditioning, plumbing, electricals and whatnot. This means that these companies and those in their employ have unfettered access to clubs, business and homes all around the UK. The idea that Glow could spread this widely within days makes me feel ill.

When the guys offered to come with me I declined. I genuinely just wanted time to myself, to find my equilibrium. My emails to Uncle Andrew last night were met with concern and warnings to be careful. He promised to reach out to his contacts to see if he can find out who had arranged the attack.

I pull up outside a large house in North Finchley and double-check the address. The house looks a bit ramshackle. I know the previous house was razed to the ground by Eadric's cronies last year. It was a casualty of his shock-and-awe campaign, designed to gain followers in his bid to overthrow Aelfric. But I did not expect the new Hold to be this . . . dusty-looking pile of stones – unless it was a glamour.

I shift my sight and peer out of the window but no – no glamour at work here. The barred windows and the battered front door seem real enough. The house looks disreputable and out of place amongst its well-kept neighbours. I can actually feel eyes peering at me from behind curtains; can almost see fingers poised over phones to call the police about yet another dodgy person hanging around the neighbour-hood.

As I get out of the car, I glamour the sword so it will pass as an umbrella and shrug into my jacket. A sharp sleet's started to fall and my breath mists the air. It's even colder than it was last night. We've easily hit the double digits in the below freezing scale as the unusual weather continues to worsen.

I'm sure I've been noticed by the Hold and note the chimes dangling beside the large green front door. They drip with protection spells. I ignore them and knock politely. As I mean no harm, the spells shouldn't react to me.

The woman who answers the door is Sidhe, and she's typically tall, straight-backed and slim. She's casually dressed in Frontier-appropriate clothes – jeans and a black blouse. A profusion of bracelets dangle and clink on her arms as she shakes my hand, examining me with her soft grey eyes.

'I am the Keeper here, Lady Blackhart. My name is Mar.'

'Please call me Kit.'

Her grip is firm and brief. 'Please, do come inside.'

A young boy hovers behind her in the small foyer.

'My grandson, Laurent.'

'Lady Blackhart.' Laurent's maybe fourteen and his smile is polite. His curious gaze snags on the sword, its glamour now dissipated. But he swallows whatever question he was about to ask when his grandmother's hand tightens on his shoulder. 'Welcome to the North Hold.'

Mar gestures me into a large room, beautifully decorated after the style of a Moroccan riad – brimful of solid furniture, exotic rugs and huge plants.

The other person present appears to be much older than anyone else I've met before – in either the human world or the Otherwhere. Tiny and wizened, she's far smaller even than Laurent and dressed in a colourful kaftan, with a sash tied around her narrow waist. Her eyes are dark in her wrinkled face, and I get the idea that I've made a really bad impression on her, because she doesn't bother shaking my hand and barely acknowledges me – except for a chin tilt in my direction before shuffling out of the room and disappearing.

'Clotho,' Mar says, watching her go, 'has been unwell since the previous Hold burned down. It sapped a lot of her energy to keep the Fae safe that night. She has still not recovered.'

'I didn't know she'd been there. Did any visitors to the Hold die that night?'

'No, we lost no one, but Clotho's our tie to the Otherwhere, so the toll on her was exceptionally heavy.' Mar smiles stiffly. 'Would you like anything to drink?'

'Tea, please. Camomile, if you have it.' I don't even let my lip curl when I ask for the awful herbal concoction.

Mar nods at Laurent, who leaves us without a word. 'Come, let us sit and you can tell me why you've come to visit.'

I choose a beautiful leather wing-backed chair whilst Mar seats herself on a small loveseat.

'I'm sorry my first visit is family business, Mar. But I'm here to ask you about the knocker, Antone Pensa?'

Mar's interested smile slips a bit. 'Antone? He does visit often, uses one of my private drawing rooms for business meetings. But what is your interest in him?'

'We caught a faerie giving Glow to a human. The faerie said Antone gave her the drugs. Apparently he said that if she didn't distribute the drug, she'd be prevented from staying in the Hold. And for Fae in the Frontier, of course that can mean sickness or even death.'

'That can't be right.' A tiny frown mars her smooth forehead. 'Antone has no power here, none. He can't threaten or deny any faerie the use of the Hold.'

'And yet he did. Do you have any idea where he got the Glow from?'

'No, I'm afraid I haven't. He works as a jeweller. He's

123

always very courteous, paying his account for use of the rooms here on time. I can't believe he's involved in this.'

'Does he live in the Frontier or the Otherwhere? And do you know how to get hold of him?'

Before Mar can answer, Laurent comes in carrying a tray of small cakes and tea. I wait patiently for him to set things out and notice how gracefully he moves. Mar notices me noticing and I smile at her.

'Laurent has been in training to become a page in the High Queen's household,' she comments.

At her words the tips of his ears go bright red. 'Maimeo, she doesn't care. Stop.'

'She cares. And I care. Let your grandmother show some pride in her grandson, Laurent.'

'Your grandmother's right,' I tell him. 'Being chosen to be part of Dina's Court is a big compliment. She's very fastidious.' I make a show of sipping my tea. It's disgusting.

'Come now, we have business to discuss,' Mar addresses her grandson. 'Go and make sure Clotho's comfortable. This odd weather's really bad for her.'

Chapter Sixteen

Once Laurent's left the room, I turn back to Mar. 'If Antone's running businesses in the Frontier, do you have his address?'

'Of course. I'll get it when you're ready to leave.'

I smile my thanks at her. 'And have you heard any rumours about Glow?'

Her expression is one of distaste. 'It's a vile concoction,' she says. 'I've been following the reports in the news. Know that no one in my Hold has sold Glow, or had it in their possession, to my knowledge. The fact that Antone approached a visiting Fae to help spread it angers me greatly. I will ensure that he is not welcome in this or any of the other Holds. We do *not* want to be associated with drugs that harm humans in any shape or form. A stigma like that attached to a Hold . . . it doesn't bear thinking about. And if Fae feel endangered and stop visiting a Hold, we have to shut our doors. And that would be a great loss to our community as a whole. It's understood that the Holds are a place for safety for any of us who come here.'

'Do you have visitors at the moment?' I ask, because the place seems quiet.

'Oh yes, the Hold is full to capacity. We have our regulars. We also have a pooka, whom I think you may have met recently. He mentioned something about an altercation near a canal?'

My eyebrows jump in surprise because yes, I do remember. I was ambushed by two guys whilst out on a jog early one morning. One of my attackers was dragged beneath the water by a monstrous faerie horse and never came up for air again.

'Well, if you could say thanks to him for saving my butt, that would be great.'

'The others are a mixture of businessmen and nobles. Aelfric hosts an annual Midwinter Ball, which is coming up soon. Many Fae have been securing passes to the Frontier, to shop for garments for the occasion. Human fashion is in great demand.'

I smile stiffly and am relieved she doesn't embroider on the Midwinter Ball and those attending. 'Mar, do you know anything about a company called Mosby and Clarke? They specialize in air conditioning?'

'No, I don't, I'm afraid. I could ask around perhaps? Are they involved in the Glow case?'

I hesitate for a moment and wonder if I should trust Mar. So far everything about her seems trustworthy and I like her. She reads *true*.

'We don't know. Last night a club was flooded with Glow. We think the stuff's been spiked with something new because this time it affected humans, Fae, the Infernal and an angel – and we think that the guys from the air conditioning company had something to do with it.'

Mar pales visibly.

'It affected non-humans? Please, tell me what you know.'

I give her a brief breakdown of what we witnessed at Milton's. And I reveal that the only odd activity before the attack was the work done on the air-con vents – by a group of goblins from Mosby and Clarke.

'Like you, I am shocked by the implication that it's affected *others* at the same time as humans. I need to put the word out and warn the other keepers to be aware of its spread.'

I shrug. 'This is the first time we've heard of it affecting non-humans. Perhaps it's a stronger formulation. Or maybe it's because it's been changed to make it airborne?' I stare into space for a few seconds, my mind whirring. 'We just don't have the answers right now – which is one of the reasons I'm visiting you.'

Mar is silent for a few moments. 'It could be that whatever they were trying to accomplish with Glow wasn't happening fast enough. So they changed it.'

I suddenly feel like the dumbest person in the room. 'Trying to accomplish with Glow?' I echo.

'You've not thought about this before? That whoever's sending Glow into the Frontier has an ultimate goal?'

'Apart from getting people addicted to the stuff and making money?'

'Addicted, yes, but for what reason?' Mar toys with her cup, thinking, before speaking again. 'This doesn't feel like money's the motivation, because it's a Fae drug. We don't need human money. We can make our own.' Here she leans over and picks up a leaf that's dropped from the plant in the window. She passes her hand over it and hands it to me and I take it without even thinking about it. In my hand lies a fresh crisp £50 note. I turn it over and, even though I'm using my sight to determine the glamour, it looks and feels very real. I hand it back and when she takes it, it changes back.

'So, if it's not money, what are we looking at?' I ask. 'Just getting people to try it until people either die or become addicted?'

'What are the effects of Glow? What happens when a human ingests it?'

'They see faeries, stripped of their glamour. They experience hallucinations. And now, some humans have been levitating and also seem super-strong.'

'So, the drug changes some humans, warps them. But it also allows them to see supernatural creatures.'

'Yes. And it's not just working on humans any more either.'

'We can't assume that it's not worked on angels or the Infernal before now, just because we've not seen proof.'

'The absence of evidence doesn't mean the evidence of absence,' I quote from one of the books on logic Jamie made me read and smile at Mar when she gives me a thoughtful look. We sit in silence for a few seconds and I drink more of my tea, desperately wishing it was coffee instead, before Mar speaks again.

'It feels like the opening moves in a game of strategy to me. The ultimate aim of the strategy being war.'

Before I can begin to ask her, politely, how she came up with that thought, she leans towards me. 'Think about it,' she says. 'What better way to gain both strategic and tactical advantage over an enemy without sending in an army? You do it by weakening them first, by exposing them to an illness that has no cure, an illness that can be spread easily amongst the populace.'

'Glow is an illness?' I ask, trying to follow her thought processes, but she's like mercury and I feel even more out of my league.

'It maybe didn't start out like that . . . But what if it *can* be used in that way – perhaps as a weapon? It makes sense.' Mar stands up and starts pacing, thinking aloud. 'But why? Why risk the Fae getting sick too, by meddling with a compound that has obviously worked well in the past and we assume only affected humans? If Fae become ill and start dying, it could mean huge losses. It could mean a decimation of the population if Fae addiction becomes widespread too. But to what end? What is the ultimate goal?' She moves to stand beside a beautiful tropical potted plant. 'Come on, Mar. If it were you, why would you introduce something like this into the population? What would you want it to achieve?'

I watch her and consider how Jamie would analyse this if he were here. I think about the books he's made me read, the tactical volumes, but also the more esoteric stuff that I had difficulty applying to the everyday.

'The best thing of all is to take the enemy's country whole and intact; to shatter and destroy it is not ideal. So too, it's better to recapture an army entire than to destroy it . . .' I look at Mar's face and notice her pallor at my hesitant words. 'That's paraphrased from Sun Tzu's *The Art of War*. My uncle made me read it.'

'I know of the sage. What else do you remember reading?'

I frown in concentration, remembering the battered old paperback Jamie had me carry around for months when I first started my training. 'Something about supreme excellence . . . it means breaking the enemy's resistance without actually getting into a fight.'

She nods, satisfied. 'Whoever is behind this just wants to ride in with all the hard work done already and not be challenged. Perhaps they would make a gesture of goodwill and cure those afflicted by Glow, or perhaps they would sell the cure to whoever is prepared to give the aggressor or aggressors what they want.' She clasps her hands in front of her and it looks like she's steadying herself. 'This is how I would do it if it were up to me.'

Mar sits down at last, having given me a lot to consider.

'This is not the kind of conversation I ever thought I'd have with a Hold keeper. You remind me of Jamie.' At her raised eyebrows I explain, 'You sound like a soldier.'

I hold my breath, wondering how badly I've insulted her, but she smiles at me.

'How old do you think I am?'

Oh God. This is the worst question imaginable because what do I say? I know how I hate being judged for how young I am – but trying to guess the age of a faerie could be dangerous.

'I think in human years you look, maybe, in your forties. In faerie years? I have no idea.'

Mar looks pleased. 'I fought my first battle in October 1066. I was made lady because of my deeds. I received lands and titles and returned to the Otherwhere as victorious as any of the princes I rode with. I was ninety-seven.'

'You definitely do not look a day over . . .' I wave my hand helplessly. 'What does this have to do with me asking you about—? Oh! I see. You speak like a soldier because you were one!'

'Yes.' Her expression is reflective. 'I tired of it. For years I rode under Aelfric's banner, fighting his battles, keeping his peace. I asked to be retired.'

'And this is how you were made keeper?'

'Eventually, yes.'

I consider what we've talked about before speaking again.

'So somewhere in the Otherwhere, someone is launching an attack on the Frontier using Glow?'

'That's what I think. And from the sound of things, it seems as if they're escalating the spread of the drug. And if that's the case, maybe the endgame is in sight. You therefore *must* put a stop to this – now.'

Chapter Seventeen

I drive from the Hold after texting the boys the address Mar gave me for Antone. It's a small workshop in Hatton Garden. The area has been London's jewellery district since medieval times, so it makes sense that his office would be there. Now, in addition to rows of jewellery shops, it is home to various media companies and publishers. It is a bustling area of London and it would be the perfect place for someone with Antone's jewellery know-how to disappear.

I'm patient with the daytime London traffic, pondering Mar's theory about Glow being a means to an end – not *the* end. I've not really considered this before, naively assuming I'd find a way to stop the supply and that would be the end of it. But, like most well brought-up people who carry knives and swords on a daily basis, my knowledge of drug cartels is minimal. I need to rectify that.

I park the Audi as close as I can get to the coffee shop near Antone's workshop. The boys are seated near the window and it looks as if they've been up to research because there's a laptop open and papers everywhere. I bring over a hot chocolate and two croissants for myself, rubbing my hands to get them warm. It is so cold out there that the air itself feels like it has teeth. Of course Aiden is dressed in his usual hoodie and a T-shirt – his only concession to the cold is the ridiculous beanie hanging artfully from the back of his head. Dante is more appropriately clothed, but only slightly, and I feel very much the puny human.

'Are we communicating telepathically or are you going to tell us what you found out?' Aiden asks me after a few minutes of me trying to get my shivering under control.

I kick him underneath the table as I draw out my own notebook. Keeping my voice low, I give them an update on the little Mar had to say about Antone – and also her worrying theory on Glow. Then I examine the papers they have spread out in front of them.

'What am I looking at?'

'The paperwork on Mosby and Cole, the air-con fitters. We took the liberty of doing a little digging and it looks like they're actually part of Antone's businesses.'

'Are you *serious*?'

'Yep. The paper trail, if you dig hard enough, leads straight to Mr Antone Pensa himself.'

'Well, that's really very interesting indeed.' I riffle the pages and skim-read addresses, bank account details, names, incorporation certificates. 'Good job, you guys.'

'I did most of the work,' Aiden offers, licking his fingertip so he can collect the pastry crumbs from my plate. 'Dante just sat around and looked pretty.'

I share a look with Dante at Aiden's words and that look can only be described as fond and a little frustrated.

'Right, let's go and talk to Mr Pensa about his little operation – and get his thoughts on threatening faeries into providing unsuspecting humans with Glow.'

We leave the warmth of the coffee shop behind. In the forty minutes I've been in there I've managed to warm up.

But that first step outside, with the cold biting at my exposed face and hands, takes my breath away. I shudder, hunch my shoulders and tilt my chin at Aiden to lead the way to Antone Pensa's nondescript front door. There is a bronze plaque above the buzzer with the name PENSA in an understated copperplate font. I run my thumb over the plaque and, using my sight, I strip the glamour away and frown at the spell layered over it. The thing writhes with energy and it's anchored in the font itself and the name. I can't even begin to tell what the spell entails, but it makes my skin crawl and I take an involuntary step backwards. I'm not keen to figure it out in the least.

Aiden takes the direct approach and beats his fist against the door, hard enough to make it shake. It's anything but subtle and I roll my eyes, knowing that things are about to get out of hand.

Pressing a finger against his lips for quiet, Aiden bends his head a little. From the way he's closed his eyes and angled his head, I know he's listening to the noises inside.

Further down the building, a fire escape door opens and stocky man in a suit exits. He throws a casual look over his shoulder at us but there's something *off* about his tense demeanour.

Aiden's still focused on the sounds behind the door, so I push my bag at Dante without further thought and start moving towards the man. He gives me an alarmed look and then, because he's definitely guilty of *something*, he starts running.

I really hate it when they run. It's just so tiring and there's sweating and invariably crying and blood afterwards. I'm taller than the runner and I'm also faster. He sprints down a side road, and as he turns a corner on to the main road, I trip him from behind. He goes down in a flurry of limbs before I can grab him, and I can't help wincing in sympathy at the *crunch* of his face-plant on the ground.

I lean down and 'help' him up, the small iron blade that I press against his shirt covered by my thumb. I know he can feel the sharp tip resting just beneath his armpit. He has both hands in front of his injured face and mutters something that sounds pretty rude and gross to me, but I just sigh dramatically.

'Uncle Antone,' I say loudly, all big eyes and concern, 'I told you not to run to your meeting. You're not as young as you once were.'

A woman tuts at us but her expression is sympathetic as she steps past, barely breaking her stride. The few onlookers move away too and I have to thank London's population for taking things at face value. I turn Antone back down the side road just as Dante reaches us. He looks pissed off and I beam at him, proud of my catch.

'Look who I caught,' I say, not bothering to hide my glee.

'You ran,' he grinds out and takes position on Antone's other side. At least I assume it's Antone, as he's not said anything much apart from snivelling into his hands and swearing at me. The tang of blood is heavy in the cold air and I try to breathe through my mouth.

'Kit, dammit. You're not listening. You should have left this to me.'

'I caught him, it's okay. Where's Aiden?'

'He went in through the side door that this guy left unlocked.'

Just then the main door swings open and Aiden leans

out to stare at us. He looks flushed and pleased with his own bit of breaking and entering.

'Interesting place Pensa's got here. Come check this out.'

He leads the way up a set of stairs to a heavy metal door. The door is about seven inches thick and propped open by what looks like gold bars. As I walk past I nudge one with the toe of my boot and it doesn't budge. Real gold, not a glamour, then. I push Antone into the workshop ahead of me and stare around the place as he stumbles towards a high stool by the workbench.

Wordlessly, Dante finds a cloth from somewhere and passes it to the faerie, so he can take care of his bleeding face. The place looks like a workshop, unsurprisingly. It's lined with shelves holding tools of all shapes and sizes, also mysterious little boxes and things. I assume it's all part of his jewellery-making equipment.

I step towards Antone Pensa – as he hasn't denied it – and stare at him. 'I hope you're not too badly hurt,' I say, gesturing to his face. 'Sorry, about the . . . blood and stuff. But you shouldn't have run.'

'Mpfine,' he mutters around the cloth in front of his face. When he pulls his hands away, I grimace at the sight of his nose.

'Aide, can you?' I incline my head, feeling ridiculously woozy and lightheaded. What is wrong with me? I've seen blood before. I've bled before. It's never bothered me before, not like this. 'It looks broken.'

Dante pulls a face and pushes Aiden aside. 'My nose was broken a few times a year at the dojo. I can do this. Find me some water so he can clean up properly.'

I look away as Dante does that thing where he aligns the cartilage and then there's a crunching noise, swearing and the smell of more blood in the air. I blindly grope for a chair and sit down heavily, fighting against an unexpected urge to throw up.

'What's so interesting about this place?' I ask Aiden in an attempt to refocus my attention. 'It just looks like a workshop.'

'The fact that it's only a workshop is what makes it interesting.'

'What did you expect, a Bond villain lair?'

'Actually, I did, sort of.' He turns to look at Dante helping Antone. 'Also, he doesn't look much like a goblin, does he?'

I glance at the man in question and I have to agree with Aiden, he really doesn't look like a criminal mastermind at all. He doesn't look like a goblin either. He looks human, maybe on the shortish side, with bow legs. But other than that, whatever glamour he's spelled himself with is impenetrable, because not even my sight can discern his real form.

'So are you Antone Pensa?' I demand, just to clear things up.

He grimaces as Dante casually wipes his now-bloodied hands down the front of Antone's dishevelled suit jacket. 'And if I am?'

'We're here to ask you about distributing a drug in the Frontier,' Dante supplies, and he's doing his sensible, calm voice. It's the Spook voice he tried on me the first time we met. I still don't like it. 'We would like you to tell us where you get it from.'

'Just like that?' Pensa dabs at his nose with his bit of cloth. 'No manipulation? No threats? No torture?'

I open my mouth to scoff at his words, because what does he think we are – actual villains? – when I breathe in a tang of magic and it hits the back of my throat. His blood,

I realize belatedly. His blood holds magic and I've been thoroughly exposed to it. Unlike Dante's magic it's not gradual or pleasant. It roars out at me and all at once, I *see* . . .

Chapter Eighteen

Pensa's words reverberate through the room. Shadows become fluid. Aiden turns from him and glances towards me questioningly. I open my mouth to warn him. Warn him about what?

The words don't come.

My magic shivers and there's the taste of metal in my mouth. I blink and the movement is heavy, dragging at my eyelids. There are voices nearby. I reach out blindly and someone grips my arm. I stare at the bloody hand circling my wrist and I wonder why it's so bony and pale against the rich red of the blood.

I'm only vaguely aware of falling.

I tuck and roll, coming up ready to defend myself, but the action feels peculiar to me. I stare down at myself and I don't recognize the brocade sleeves that almost reach the tips of my buffed fingernails. I register the unusual clothing that presses heavily against me, restrictive and formal. Then I look up and around me. My (our) breath falters. This is not just time that I've run backwards, I realize – I am experiencing this as Pensa. There is no me, there is only him.

The room is made from marble, with thousands of mirrors, and the ornate ceiling drips with blazing crystal chandeliers. Surrounding me are swirling Fae dressed for revelry. I try my utmost to not gape, but it is supremely difficult. The opulence is shocking, the lushness of colour staggering. It is as if I've viewed my life in black and white and I've unexpectedly been allowed a glimpse into the full richness of the colour spectrum.

My gaze drifts across the room. All three faerie Courts are represented, as are the individual families that constitute the twelve houses of the Sidhe. I feel myself recognizing familiar faces and the banners hanging from the glass ceiling show the number of houses in attendance. Once more I look down at my formal clothes but, before I can move, a heavy hand comes to rest on my shoulder.

I know the man. Only a little taller than me, he's dressed in unadorned black and wears no glamour. The fact that he feels no need to do so, when everyone in attendance is suffused with magic, is somehow significant. But I am not sure why.

'Pensa.'

'Lord Zane.'

Those fingers tighten reflectively on my shoulder.

'Come.'

I follow him because I have no choice. He is the reason I have been invited to the Sun King's palace. The celebrations are for one of the high feast days, perhaps Midsummer. The air is redolent with the scent of ripe fruit and spices. Not entirely unpleasant, but I am a simple man and I prefer the fresh mineral smell of cleanly cut stones to any other aroma.

We are making our rapid away across the ballroom. Fae move aside for him and it is a peculiar sensation to be pulled along in his wake, seeing the deference people pay to him. I do not belong here, amidst this throng of exotic Fae. I am not a noble and I have no pretensions to be one as I hurry behind him. It is, I think to myself, as if no one wanted to be noticed by him and I wonder why that would be.

Once we're outside the ballroom he leads me down ever-narrower winding passageways, until we finally come to a set of plainly wrought doors. He gestures and I do not see who controls the doors, but they swing open on silent hinges. Zane sweeps into the room, his boot heels clicking loudly on the uncarpeted floor. The rooms, for there are two that I can see, are large. Their windows face towards the town that's grown up around the Sun Palace and its grounds. And in the distance I can just see the Dark Forest.

'Do you approve of the rooms?'

I frown at him as I'm not sure what he means. I glance around once more and feel at a loss, sure that I am missing some vital clue as to why we're here.

'The rooms, are they adequate for your family?'

'My lord, I am not sure I follow.'

A guarded look crosses his fine features. 'Let me explain.' He shakes the black lace from his cuff and snaps his fingers. For the longest moment nothing happens, but then I make out the distinct noise of a child crying. And as the sound moves closer, so do heavy footsteps.

From the other room, two ogres lumber forth. One holds my son in a bruising grip behind the neck, like one would hold a mongrel about to be drowned. The other holds my wife. Her face is bruised and tears have cut through the grime and blood on her cheeks. I move on instinct, desperate to get to them, but Zane puts out a hand, pushing me back firmly, and I stumble over my feet.

'Stop. Or I will have them killed.'

My wife lets out a low moan of terror and my son renews

his vigorous attempts to break from his captor, squirming and kicking. I'm gratified to see him using the techniques I have taught him – but against an ogre nothing but a length of cold, hard iron would do.

'What is the *meaning* of this?' I turn to look towards my wife and son. 'We have done nothing wrong. You have *no right* to do this. None.'

'You refused my business, Pensa. I do not take kindly to being refused.'

My confusion and fear must be apparent, but even so I feel the need to correct him. 'I'm sure, my lord, that you are mistaken. I would be honoured to create whatever jewels you require, for yourself or for the Sun King.'

Zane's laugh is mocking and a shiver runs down my back. 'Ah, but it's not your jewellery I'm after, my good Pensa. You turned someone away recently who came to you on my behalf. He asked for access to your extensive network of businesses in the Frontier and you declined. Surely you remember that?'

It takes me just a moment to recall. 'Merrick? You're talking about that . . .' My lip curls in disgust. 'That creature has no business being in the Frontier. His touch taints everything.'

'Oh.' Zane seems a little taken aback by my dislike of his servant. 'It's unfortunate that you don't get along, because after tonight you *will* be in business with him. Merrick and another, a human called Caleb Jericho, will work closely with you and you'll ensure they have unfettered access to storage, trucks and warehouses. And if anyone asks you, you will say that Merrick and Mr Jericho are good men and are to be trusted.'

'No. I'm sorry, my lord, but I have spent many years

building up my Frontier businesses and I won't stand by and have people like Merrick and this Jericho abuse them. I won't stand for it.'

'That is a pity. And I thought you loved your family.' Zane stares across at the two ogres and their captives. 'Did you know I was good friends with Lord Istvan? He taught me a great deal. We worked on creating chimera for the circuses that travel the Otherwhere. I am not a boastful man, Pensa, but some of my creations were works of art.' His smile makes me want to rage but I tamp it down as he continues, 'I do believe that there are some Sidhe lords and ladies who would pay handsomely for a boy as beautiful as your son to be crafted into one of my chimera. A beautiful monster. A pet, to be shown at luncheons – perhaps to fight beasts from the northern wastes.' His expression looks distant, as if he's enjoying the imagery he's conjuring for himself.

I strain against the hand on my chest. 'If you harm them I will *kill* you. What kind of man are you, Lord Zane, to stoop so low as to use women and children like this? Where is your honour?'

'I am a realist, Pensa. And I will only hurt them if you displease me.' Zane's hand moves to grasp the back of my neck, pulling me forward so that we are almost nose to nose. 'Now, do we have an accord? Will you work with Merrick? Or do I send your boy to my workshop and your wife to the dungeon, where she will spend the remainder of her days?'

I stare at him, and suddenly understand why no one wanted him to notice them upstairs. His eyes are dark and fathomless, and within their depths I see something twist and curl. I am not a stranger to madness, and seeing that

143

turmoil banked into coals within him, burning slow and heavy, I decide on the wisest option to keep my family alive.

'Yes, damn your rotten heart, Zane, we have an accord.'

When I come back to myself, I find myself propped against Dante's side. He's standing beside me, a reassuring hand on my shoulder. Aiden's seated next to Pensa, and Pensa's expression is one of shocked disbelief. It mirrors Aiden's but for different reasons, I think. The time-slip was unexpected and unwelcome but, even more strangely, this time I wasn't a bystander, but a participant. I draw a deep breath and rub my hands through my hair; the familiar movement grounds and settles me. When I open my eyes, Pensa's gaze has softened slightly.

'How is what you just did possible? You are a human. A Blackhart.'

'What I am, Mr Pensa, is complicated.' I shift under Dante's grip and he lets go of me but stays close. 'You expect us to treat you the same way Zane's treated you, with threats?'

'He made a very persuasive case.'

'You're working for Zane. To keep your family safe.'

'Not just my immediate family, but also my friends and extended family. If I didn't cooperate, he promised his hunters would find them and bring them to his workshop. There he would dissect them and experiment upon them.'

'You believe this?' Aiden asks him, after I've given them a quick run-down of what I experienced and saw first-hand through Pensa's memories. 'You *believed* what that guy was saying?'

'Zane is deranged. In the past I only knew him as Lord Zane, the Sun King's chamberlain. Now? Now I realize that the Sun King does whatever Zane tells him to do. Zane rules the Summer Court in all but name. And he is very good at intimidation and blackmail. No one makes a move against him. He has spies everywhere and he keeps his business dealings very close to his chest.'

'So he's forcing you to work with this crony of his, Merrick? And Caleb Jericho?' I trade a grim look with Aiden.

'Yes. Merrick has access to all my businesses now. I initially thought they wanted to launder money, but then I realized they wanted access to storage space and my distribution network.'

Dante leans closer to him. 'Distribution network?'

'Merrick manufactures the drug somewhere. I don't think they stay in one place too long. He then uses my trucks and delivery systems to move the drugs across the British Isles and Jericho supplies the men and the muscle.'

'How many companies do you have?'

Pensa thinks about it as I remember the amount of paperwork the boys had been looking through earlier. I remember a lot of names.

'Under my direct control, maybe a hundred? Subsidiaries are far more numerous.'

I turn huge eyes on the boys. They both look ill.

'But why were you given some of the drug personally?'

'I asked for it. I was handed a small amount only.' Pensa rubs his hands together. 'I wanted to see if I could somehow cause a stir within the Fae community living in the Frontier. The only way I could think of doing this was to threaten one of the visiting Fae when she stayed at the Hold. I thought she would speak to the Lady Mar, tell her what had happened, what I had done. Mar and I have known one another for a long time. I knew she would not stand for me threatening anyone. It was also a way for me to test if Mar was part of Zane's extended circle. I didn't imagine the Fae would keep quiet about the drug and distribute it instead, using it for her own enjoyment.'

'That really sucked as a plan, mate,' Aiden said, clapping him on the shoulder. 'You really should have just told someone.'

'Not an easy thing. With no one to trust . . .' Pensa's hands flutter in the air between us. 'What else could I do? I had to set it up in such a way that suspicion would fall on me for being *stupid* but not . . . purposely careless.'

'At least we know who the bad guy is,' Dante offers. 'How do we take him down?'

'Zane is not the one.' Pensa's face is apologetic. 'He may be the one giving orders, but he is receiving them too. He's as much a pawn as Merrick.'

'This Merrick guy. Why do you dislike him so much?'

'Merrick is an animal. A beast. He cannot be trusted around humans. He flouts the laws and takes what he wants whenever he wants. He has been judged in the past and sent to prison, but every time he's released, he just goes back to doing whatever he wants.'

'And what does he want?'

'He seeks . . .' Pensa's eyes don't meet mine. 'He specializes in deflowering . . .'

'Holy hell, Batman, that's enough. Really. I don't think we need to know more.' Aiden chokes on air. 'And he prefers humans, does he? What of the laws?'

Pensa's expression says it all. There are no laws for the lawless. I have to close my eyes against the building aching pressure in my head. 'How is that even possible? How is he allowed in the Frontier?'

'Zane – am I right?' Dante asks, and when Pensa nods he swears softly. 'So, I don't think this is why Zane keeps him around. What is so special about Merrick?'

'He's an alchemist of the highest order.'

'Alchemist? Isn't alchemy the transmutation of base metals into gold?' Aiden frowns at our surprised expressions. 'Guys, I do know stuff too, you know? I'm not just the pretty one.' He turns to look at Antone, prompting him with a gentle, 'Alchemy?'

'Certain Fae have always had the ability to transform metals. It is a speciality for some.' My eyes flicker to the bars of gold holding the door open and Pensa nods. 'Gold is easy. Metals are easy. Stones are more difficult to change. But we digress. Alchemists are able to create potent potions which allow Fae who are unable to use glamour to transform themselves.'

'And what does that mean when we're talking about Glow?' Aidan asks.

'It means that Merrick uses a similar recipe, if you will, to the potions he creates for the lesser Fae. The ones who struggle to use glamour in the human world when they come across to the Frontier. The potion is potent and he's distilled it into something even more potent, adding ingredients only found in the Otherwhere. I've tried analysing it . . .' He gestures to his set-up in the corner and I notice it for the first time. It's a compact laboratory and it looks the business. I can only begin to guess what all the equipment is for. '. . . But I've not had much luck.'

I stare down at my hands. At least they've stopped shaking. 'So Merrick's the one making the Glow, using a weird formula that he's probably tinkering with each time he makes a new batch?'

When Pensa nods at my question, I heave a sigh.

'So we set up a meeting with the Jericho gang to hand over more drugs,' I say. 'Then we plant a tracker on the dealers and figure out where they're heading. Is that something you can help with, Mr Pensa?'

He looks reluctant but after a few moments he speaks, his gaze moving between the three of us. 'I can do that. On one condition: you help get my family away from Zane. You get them to safety and I will help you.'

I nod, thinking of Strachan and the guys who helped me bring down Lady Morika the last time. They would revel in something like this. 'I can speak to some people, get it set in motion. We'll make sure that no one knows it was you.'

Antone Pensa is not an impressive man. Nothing about him is impressive, except perhaps the lengths to which he will go to keep his family safe. He watches me for a few moments before agreeing. 'Very well. I will do this. You get my wife and child out in the next twenty-four hours and arrange something similar for my extended family, and I will do what I can to arrange with the dealers I used before to sell me more Glow. After we meet them we can track them, see what they do, and set a trap.'

We shake on it, he and I, and I'm flooded with a sense of his relief.

Finally. Finally there is something that feels concrete and real and true, a way to ensure my family's safety. A way for us to run and be safe.

The relief that courses through me is immense and I lean against the counter for a moment. I withdraw from Antone

Pensa's grip and turn away to gather my thoughts. When I bring my hands back up to rub my face, they come away wet and sticky with blood.

Chapter Nineteen

'I can't believe I'm on another stake-out with you,' Aiden grumbles in my ear. 'The last one was meant to be the last one. And now look.'

I give him the side-eye. He looks so genuinely out of sorts, when I know he really loves all the sneaking around and subterfuge.

'You look hot when you're dressed like a special ops operative,' I tell him, derailing his grump with obvious flattery.

'I can't deny that I look good in black,' he admits, but elbows me in the side, 'and flirting with me won't get you out of my bad books, Blackhart.'

'Shut up, Garrett. Pay attention to the stake-out.'

I peer back out at the warehouses below us.

'Nothing is happening. No one is coming. We've been set up.'

'We don't know that.'

'Pensa could have double-crossed us. He could have told Merrick we got to him.'

'No,' I say, certain of this one thing above all else. 'He wouldn't have done that. His wife and son are now safe. Strachan came through on that, so he will keep his word. Pensa hates Merrick almost as much as he hates Zane.'

There's a crackle from my headset and I hear Dante's voice in my ear: 'Can you guys just stop talking? You're making it hard to concentrate. And if you can't shut up, stop talking over comms.'

Aiden and I share a long-suffering look. Dante really does enjoy the whole covert operations thing far too much for someone who's probably had a week's worth of training with the Spooks.

'He's bossy,' I mutter. 'Thinks he runs us.'

'I know,' Aiden replies. 'It's kinda hot.'

'Seriously?'

'Yes. He gets all focused and determined. And bossy.' Aiden's eyes are a bit dreamy. 'And he smells great.'

'You know I can *still* hear you both,' Dante's voice crackles in the earpiece and I have to hide a grin when Aiden lets out a soft *meep* of surprise.

'It's the truth, though,' Aiden manfully insists, and a girl has to admire his honesty in the face of being caught blatantly talking about his crush.

'You're both distracted. You need to focus. Someone's coming.' Dante's trying his best not to let his amusement show, but there's a hint in his voice that makes Aiden swoon against me like the diva he is.

But someone *is* coming and I don't even need to enhance my sight all that much to see them. Antone and Dante are already in the building and two guys are walking towards the warehouse.

'They're human and they're armed,' I tell both boys using my headset, mostly for Dante's benefit. 'Guns, for sure.'

'How can you tell?' he queries immediately. 'Weapons drawn?'

'Their jackets. They're too bulky to just be padded. Also,

the guy on the right, the taller of the two, keeps touching inside his coat. There's probably an underarm holster on his right side . . . so that makes him a leftie.'

'Okay, let's get ready.' Aiden's smile is all teeth and savage intent. 'Am I wolf or human tonight?'

'Let's start you off human and then, if things go south with them and they make a run for it, you go wolf,' I suggest.

'Okay.' He rolls off the building and flips elegantly mid-air so that he lands in a low crouch. I follow suit, but less dramatically. No mid-air flips, just straight down, my magic cushioning my landing so I don't break my ankles.

We ghost across the open tarmac towards the building, where Antone's waiting to meet his contacts, with Dante as back-up.

All of this is very reminiscent of a few weeks ago, when Strach and I trapped Lady Morika and her little crew of deviant faeries as they were setting up a new deal to supply the Frontier with Glow. That was the first time Aiden and I met Marko too. Only this time I didn't have Strach or any of his Fae special-ops guys with me. It's only me, Aiden and Dante – with the goblin Antone Pensa as bait.

The guys are both in their late thirties; one is clearly the eldest and a smoker. Aiden and I are behind some broken wooden pallets and we should be near-invisible in the shadows to the rear of the warehouse.

Dante's a casual dark shadow near Antone's shoulder. Nothing about his presence should alarm these guys and it would be stranger still if Antone didn't have anyone with him as the deal went down. The two humans stop a few paces away from Antone and they greet one another amicably enough. They shake hands and chat for a few minutes.

Antone makes no attempt to introduce Dante and although the humans take note of him, they don't mention him either. But it doesn't mean that he doesn't make an impression. The blond younger guy keeps shooting looks at him but, perhaps because Dante doesn't seem intimidating, they soon lose interest.

The younger guy's stepped forward, opening his backpack. Dante says something to him and they exchange smiles, standing slightly to the side as Antone inspects the contents.

Satisfied, Antone then removes a flat velvet jewellery box from the inside of his jacket and passes it over as payment.

I hold my breath. We've hidden a small tracker in there, cunningly disguised by Pensa's workmanship and skilful use of glamour.

The older guy pops the lid open and even from my hiding spot I can see the gleam of jewels light up his face. He gives a happy grunt before slipping the velvet box into a jacket pocket. Dante takes the backpack from the blond, using the opportunity to shake hands with his new friend. The guy leans in close to say something and Dante's soft laugh makes the hair at the back of my neck stand up. I tighten my magic shields around me, because even at this distance I can feel the low thrum of Dante bringing his magic into play.

While Antone's chatting to the older guy, his friend and Dante and are standing far too close. The guy looks a little dazed by Dante, who's not doing anything overt but seems *really* present and somehow more vibrant than he was a few minutes ago.

Aiden's hand rests heavily on my shoulder and I nod because I know what's coming next. I've practised this with

Dante endlessly the past twenty-four hours. It's the same move Jamie's drilled into me along with all my other lessons. The tricks of legerdemain, or pick-pocketing, are simple. They're about distraction, self-assurance and speed.

I'm tense as I watch the younger guy duck his head and grin at something Dante says. It's killing me watching this but Dante's so good that I hardly see the move myself. But Aiden sees, his eyes sharp.

'He's got his wallet,' Aiden sighs in my ear. 'We're good.'

Dante makes a show of looking at his watch and the meeting draws to a close. There's a round of goodbyes and the humans stroll from the warehouse. Aiden slips away to make sure they're leaving and I wait until I hear a car start before exiting my hide-out.

Antone gives me a small tight smile as I walk closer.

'That was remarkably easy,' he says. 'Maybe there is something to having a siren on your side in meetings like this.'

Dante rolls his eyes. 'I hardly did anything. That guy was projecting his loneliness so much that an unconscious person would have felt it.'

'Ah, but you distracted him enough to get his wallet,' I point out with a grin as I wiggle my fingers. 'Show me.'

He passes the wallet to me, handling it with care. I flick it open using my nail to prevent any of my own fingerprints transferring onto the leather. Name. Address. Cash. Credit cards. Nice bit of a trail right here, which is handy, along with the dealer's fingerprints. I hand it back to Dante. Should the tracker fail us, we'll have an address to follow up on too.

'Now what?' Antone asks.

'Now we've bought a whole bag of Glow that won't hit

the market and we've put a tracker on those two.' I try not to look too pleased. 'Sadly, you're down some gems . . .'

'It is nothing. My family is safe and in a secure location. I leave to join them this weekend and I have you to thank.' He shakes our hands in turn. 'Thank you, for everything. You have risked yourselves for me. I could have betrayed you and yet you never wavered. I am a generous man, Blackhart. Any time you need the help of the Pensa family, for generations to come, it is yours.'

I nod, bowled over by the intensity of these words, knowing how big a deal it is for a Fae to pledge his loyalty to the Blackharts in this way. I drop his hand and give him a hug, hoping that for once I've done something right.

Chapter Twenty

The boys leave the warehouse in the Cayenne and I follow in the Audi. We opted for two cars in case we needed the extra wheels. My mind's wrapped up with the Jericho Gang and how drug cartels work and I know just the person to call. I ask the car to dial me through to Leo's number.

'Kit? Why are you calling me? Are you guys okay? Is someone bleeding?'

I start laughing. 'Leo, seriously. Can't a girl just ring a boy and chat to him for five minutes?'

There's a pause on the line before Leo replies, 'Is this a trick question?' His voice drops and he sounds worried. 'Is Aiden okay?'

'We're all okay, I swear, Leo. I just need to talk to someone about the Jericho Gang.'

'Hell. You don't beat around the bush, do you? No easing into it. Even Aide's better at this than you are. Okay, I've pulled over. Now, let's talk.'

'Is it okay to speak?' I have no idea how *criminal* Leo's life is and in my mind there are wire-taps all over his house and on his phone. I have too many American police shows to thank for these images.

'Yes. I had the phone and car checked before I came out. I'm on my way to the gym, so we're okay.'

My jaw hangs open for a few seconds, wondering if he's joking – or not. 'Uh, okay. So, what can you tell us about these guys? I mean, Kyle checked them out a while ago but, you know, I'd rather hear from someone who knows rather than just someone who can use the internet.'

There's a small silence on the phone before he speaks again.

'The Jericho Gang . . .' The way he says the words is the same way I've had some Fae say my name: with distaste and a hint of fear. '. . . They are *not* the kind of guys you want to go up against by yourself. They're not sane, most of the time. Their boss is this nut-job called Caleb Jericho. The guy worked his way up from runner to bullyboy to a captain in one of the smaller gangs – one that runs drugs and guns in Northern Ireland. Then, when he became the boss of that, he turned his attention to the Midlands. He runs his business like he ran his soldiers, back during the Troubles. His word is law and he only takes on the most hardcore and proven guys as members. I overheard my dad describing Caleb to a friend once. Caleb suspected someone close to him of being a police informant. But instead of looking into it, Caleb brought this guy in for questioning. He questioned him by torturing his family. He never touched the guy. By the time the guy's parents and wife were cut to pieces, the guy confessed that he had been working with the cops. It didn't matter if it was true or not. And that put the fear of God into everyone in the Jericho Gang. Caleb prides himself on not being a violent man, but when he does mete it out, it's pretty much a given that there's death and gore.'

'I think I'm going to be sick,' I mutter, wiping a hand over my face as I wait for traffic lights to change. 'Why haven't we heard more about this guy?'

'He's never drawn attention to himself or his operation, and his men know better than to get caught in cop raids.' Leo's voice is quiet. 'This guy is bad news, Kit. I think you need to go to the cops with this. Get your uncle Jamie to ring some of his buddies.'

'Surely the cops know about him already. Why haven't they done anything?'

'It's a case of them watching and waiting for him to slip up somehow to give them a reason to go in hard and fast and take his operation down. None of Caleb's men have ever been to jail, Kit. Not one of them.'

'He has good lawyers?'

'He does, but no. Those under suspicion die. They never make it to court or to jail, so they never get the chance to turn on him.'

'The guy sounds charming. A really stellar employer.'

'He is, actually. He runs legitimate businesses and all his employees have private health insurance and other benefits.'

'And the businesses are covers for his illegal operations?'

'No, some are actually what they say they are.' Leo sighs and sounds frustrated. 'Kit, I really think you're in over your head on this one. This isn't what you guys do. Getting involved with Caleb Jericho, even if it means stopping this Glow crap . . . dude, it's not worth it.'

I stare at the road in front, focusing on what Leo's just told me. The Jericho Gang sounds terrifying and dealing with the Fae hasn't necessarily prepared me for real-world gang crime. It makes me want to crawl into bed and pull the duvet over my head. But I can't. There are too many lives at stake – not just human lives but Fae lives too.

'I'll speak to my uncle Andrew,' I tell him. 'Aide can speak to his dad. We'll figure something out.'

'Yeah? You're not going to run off and try to be Hawaii Five-O?'

'We don't have surfboards, Leo.'

'Oh yeah, dammit.' There's a pause, then: 'We should move to Hawaii.'

'Leo, listen. I owe you big time for this. Thanks for talking to me about these guys. When I get home I'll speak to Andrew and Jamie, let them decide how they want to handle this.'

'Good, and be careful, okay? You're my favourite magic human.'

'Good. You're my favourite hipster. Enjoy the gym.'

I hang up, knowing that we have our jobs cut out for us on this. But we've made a tiny bit of progress and, now we know more about the Jericho Gang, we can make a plan.

Chapter Twenty-One

I am not even surprised when I wake up in a dream. Thorn looks up when I push my way through the overhanging ivy. He's sitting in a ruined once-grand room, within the arc of an empty stone window-frame. The room has no roof, apart from a last few sturdy beams. Opulent red flowers cling to them, scenting the balmy night air with something sweet and cloying.

'Kit.' He jumps off the windowsill and moves towards me. 'You're here. I didn't think I'd be able to reach you.'

He sounds as if he's just dialled my number, and it makes me want to laugh. It's strange being here, seeing him again in this in-between place where we've spent so much time in the past. He must sense my hesitation because he peers at me in concern.

'Kit?'

'What are we doing here, Thorn? I thought we were done with these weird meetings out here. You gave me the mirror so you could reach me through that.'

'Ah.' His smile falters. 'I thought we could speak, without the mirror's interference. I've tried getting in touch that way, but something feels wrong. The magic that powers the mirror feels stretched thin. I'd rather not risk having the mirror shatter.' His eyes search my face and I see concern there. 'Would you rather sleep and have me leave?'

'No.' The distance between us is less than a pace but he's never felt further away. What is wrong with me? I should be pleased to see him. Instead I feel annoyed at being brought here, without any warning. 'Thorn, this is getting weird. It *is* weird.' I try not to notice the strong lines of his jaw or how his lashes sweep against his cheeks when he looks down and away from me. He now looks guarded, and a frown appears when he looks back at me.

'I am sorry. I shouldn't have presumed you'd want this.' He makes as if to move away and I'm the one to close the gap, reaching for his hand. 'It isn't fair, bringing you all the way here, but I can't deny that it is good to see you, Black-hart. I *have* missed you.'

'I have missed you too. And this place.' I try to smile and it must soothe him a little because I get a smile in return.

'It is beautiful here.' He gestures and I look out of the empty window across the forest. Heavy black clouds scuttle across the heavens, but it feels warm here. 'Come, there's enough space for us both.'

I follow him wordlessly and climb onto the wide window ledge so I can look down. We're high up, higher than I remember being in the past. I stand and stare down at the abandoned city far below us, and at the massive forest that stretches from horizon to horizon and wonder at the mysteries it holds. I let him tug me down onto the ledge and we sit there, our knees touching. His smile is hesitant, and the way the ambient light catches his eyes as he looks at me makes me feel a little breathless.

'Are you angry with me?'

'I'm just tired, that's all.' But I don't pull back when he cups a hand to my face, a thumb gently tracing the curve of my cheek. 'We've been busy lately and my family's having some issues with how the wolves are running the Glow investigation.' I try not to nestle into the warmth of his palm but I do close my eyes for a few seconds because it feels so good having him touch me. 'And I've been worried about you.' I swallow with difficulty, twisting my fingers together on my lap. 'When we heard nothing. No messengers came, nothing. Worse, I thought you'd been captured and hurt. And I couldn't send you a message directly, because we weren't supposed to be in touch, so I had no way of knowing. None of the messages I tried to send Crow worked. None of the acorns were taken, none of the little spelled boats worked.' I sigh. 'But there was something, an awareness. I could *feel* you somehow – and I couldn't talk to anyone about it because it made me sound crazy. It was this inner certainty that you were out there – *somehow.*'

He's quiet for so long I worry that I've made myself sound unhinged. But then he hunches his shoulders almost defensively. 'For days after the attack, when we last saw each other, I was not myself. You can't imagine the shock I felt when I found I'd finally and for the first time shifted to my dragon shape. It took me a long time to find myself once more. And when I finally returned to the tower, I had to pretend that I'd been camping with the foresters, learning about the Dark Forest. Odalis had me watched for days. Nothing I did escaped her scrutiny and only after two weeks of this, did she marginally relent. But by then I was so exhausted from pretending that everything was normal, I had no energy or thought left for anything but keeping up the charade. I knew you were safe. Crow sent word, and the relief I felt was immense. I didn't care that I was being watched and I threw myself into my studies and practices – *willing* Odalis to leave me alone. She finally did and all I could think of was reaching out to you.' He leans closer and his eyes are intense as he stares into mine. 'I am so sorry I made you worry. You *must* know how dear I hold you. You're the first thing I think about when I wake. The last thing I think about when I fall asleep at night.'

'That's so romantic,' I tell him and grin, but a blush creeps across my face. 'It's ridiculous.'

'But it is the truth, so . . .'

We smile at one another and it's perfect, sitting this high up, far above the world, with the boy I've come to care so much about.

'Why have you brought me here?' I finally ask.

'I wanted to talk to you –' his smile widens and a hint of mischief creeps into his eyes – 'without my cousin being present or the wolf listening in.'

'Well, here I am, so go ahead.'

'You first: I want to know what you're doing. I want to know why you have these hollows in your cheeks. These dark circles beneath those eyes. Have you not been sleeping? Has the wolf not been taking care of you?'

I take his hand and hold it captive in my lap, lacing our fingers together. He feels so vibrantly alive that I hope some of it rubs off on me.

'I've been worried. I've not been eating very well, or sleeping. Mostly I'm worried about the goddess and the children who sustain her power. The girl, Tia – the smallest one of them – was sent back dead, Thorn. What is Brixi *doing* to the children?'

'One of the children . . . are you sure? It was not a changeling? A poorly goblin child sent in her stead?'

'No, it was Tia. There was no glamour. And I saw what Brixi did – he put her in a coracle in the Otherwhere and sent her off down the river. She arrived, dead, in the Frontier.'

For a few seconds Thorn doesn't move, lost in thought.

'How did you see Brixi? What he did?' He asks next.

'I can see back in time. It only happens sometimes. I can see into the past, as if time is spooling backwards.'

'Has this happened before?'

'A few times, usually by accident.'

'This is not a natural human ability.' He frowns lightly. 'You weren't able to do this when we were together a year ago.'

I twist my lips. 'Oh, I know. The first time it happened I thought I was crazy. Trust me on that. It freaks me out every time it happens now and I don't think I'll ever get used to it. Especially because getting these visions makes me sick, too.'

'You've been ill?'

If I thought his gaze had been intense before, it wasn't close to the way he's staring at me now. It feels a little too close to being examined, as if I were some curiosity, and I don't appreciate that at all.

'Nothing serious, I promise. Headaches, a few nose-bleeds.'

'I can send a physician . . . ?'

'I'm fine, Thorn, really. What can you tell me about the children? About Brixi and the goddess? Why did Tia die?'

'I didn't know she had died. I'm so sorry, Kit. Brixi is no longer here – in the palace. He's moved the goddess to a new location, somewhere he told me she'll be safer. And the children are with them, of course. He and the other Faceless removed them all after the attack we witnessed. It was too risky to keep them here.'

'Will he be stealing another child to replace Tia?' The question's been preying on my mind for the longest time. Every time we have the TV or radio on, I keep an ear out – wondering if we'll hear of another child being taken.

'I'm not sure. The pipers have been used to abduct candidates for the goddess – but they have gone into seclusion since one of their own was brought back in disgrace. He's to stand trial by the Unseelie Court and I doubt Brixi would risk using them again.'

'So, he's one child short to feed the goddess power.' I rub my forehead. 'That can't be good, right?'

'It depends on whether the others are strong enough to keep the goddess stable.'

The way he says it makes me shudder. 'She's not stable, though, is she? Things are breaking down here and in the Frontier. There's this really bad weather we're experiencing across the whole world. And it's because she's either waking up, or dying, and it's affecting the way she anchors the Veil.'

'That is the conclusion I've come to as well.'

I close my eyes and try to think past the tiredness I feel. 'So what do we do?'

'You do nothing. The goddess is dying and the Veil is tearing – and it's up to me to come up with the solution.'

'Maybe we need the change,' I say. 'Maybe it's time for things to change drastically.'

'No. Not like this.' His gaze meets mine. 'If the Veil between our worlds failed it would mean the end to your world and mine. Neither is ready to accept the consequences of that.'

We sit in silence for a few moments longer. The air is warm and a soft breeze stirs his untidy blond hair. It's grown so long. He's tried pulling it back in a knot, but long strands have come loose and float around his face. I stare at him for a few seconds more but look away when he catches my thoughtful gaze.

'Ask me. You've wanted to talk about my transformation since we spoke through the mirror. I'm here now. Ask me what you want to know.'

'Am I that obvious?'

'No, I just know you.' His smile is teasing and I duck my head. 'Come. Ask me. I'll tell you anything.'

I don't hesitate at all. 'Explain the dragon thing. Because when you changed – that was *very* unexpected.'

'My mother kept a few truths about my birthright from me. It came as a surprise to me, too.'

'Did it hurt?'

He looks as if he's considering, but then he shakes his head. 'No, not at first. I wasn't aware of the shift. There was just so much rage present, and fear. Fear that you would be hurt, mostly. I had to get you away from there and make sure you were safe. When I turned around and the wild Fae rushed me, my magic came screaming to the surface and it felt like I was on fire. And then I was.'

'I was so frightened for you. I'm relieved you're okay.'

Then he's kissing my hand as he says, 'Me too.' He notices the ring I always wear now and pulls back a little to look at it. 'Where did you get this?'

'Your mother. She gave me this. I thought it was yours.'

'No, don't take it off. My mother gave you *this*?' He

holds up his own right hand to show me the twin to my ring. 'They are a pair.'

'Strachan mentioned that too.' I look at the two rings. Apart from the size difference, they do seem exactly alike.

He returns to lacing our fingers together and his expression is thoughtful. 'It is interesting that she gave this to you. I must ask her about it.'

'Why's that?'

'The two rings are linked. They were made for her grandparents – and the legends say that the rings opened up a connection between them, so they would always know if the other was in danger. Apart, the rings could influence how others reacted to the wearer.'

'I remember your ring trying to influence the way I treated you when I first met you.' I stare at our linked fingers. 'And now I almost do the same thing. I use it to calm people down, make them more amenable to talking to me when they're upset. I've changed so much since that day, Thorn. I sometimes don't even recognize myself.'

'The magics in the rings aren't huge, but the intent behind using them is important.'

I think about this.

'Is that why it feels as if you're around all the time?'

'You can sense me?'

'It's never invasive, it's just this light pressure, and it's a little comforting sometimes.'

'Do you ever remove the ring?'

'No. Most of the time I'm not even aware of it.'

Thorn's smile is a little tense and I resist the urge to comfort him as he looks so serious. 'My mother never fails to surprise me. Giving you a family heirloom in this way is very unusual. Especially because you're human. She would have known it would link us.'

'I don't think she'd have done it if she knew, Thorn. I think she gave me the ring to calm me down when you left. She was very . . .' I search for a word to describe Dina's devastated face as she told me about Thorn leaving her realm, about his training. '. . . "Distraught" doesn't come near her reaction.'

'You know she fought my father? She threatened him with a split household if he sent me away.'

My eyes widen in shock and I shake my head. 'No. She never said.'

'She accused my father of caring more for his kingdom than his children – his family. She threatened to take their children and her Stormborn guard and return to her ancestral home. She was prepared to cut ties with him and with Alba.'

'What did your father do?'

'He pleaded, of course. He promised her whatever she wanted. He brought in the sages and they spoke to her of the prophecies. They went to great lengths to describe the role of the guardian, my training.' He scowled. 'It was very unpleasant.'

'And she still gave in; she agreed to let you go.'

'My father is the High King of Alba. He always has and he always will get what he wants.'

'Somehow I don't think your mother would have let you go without a big fight.'

'My mother is a general first and foremost, Kit, even before she is a queen and a mother. She has seen battle and she will act when she think it's in her best interest.'

His fingers cup my face and he presses a soft, chaste kiss to my mouth.

'My cousin is calling you. I think you should go.'

I swallow against a suddenly dry throat and slowly the dream fractures around me. Then he's gone and I'm lying sprawled on the couch. Dante's clicking his fingers in my face, trying to wake me up.

Chapter Twenty-Two

I shove Dante, hard, and he takes a step back. 'That is the deepest sleep I've ever seen,' he says.

'Ouch,' I say eloquently and gingerly touch my head, which feels thick and heavy with sleep. I let him pull me up into a sitting position.

'Have some water.' Aiden passes me a bottle, the small halo visible on the label. He bought a stock of holy water for me to drink, calling it my juju-juice. 'You stink of magic,' he says conversationally. 'And of Thorn. The whole house reeks.'

Dante looks between us. 'What are you talking about?'

'I've noticed that when Thorn's been piggybacking on Kit's dreams and she wakes up, she smells like him. I could smell him the day you guys used the mirror too. It clung to you too, but at least you didn't carry his scent as much as Kit did. However, I don't suppose you've been snogging him in your dreams.' Aiden's watching me with an expression that tells me he's more than a little concerned. His words are teasing but he looks worried. 'Welcome back to the real world, Blackhart.'

'I hate you,' I mutter and stand up, stretching my aching back. 'What time is it? Why did you let me fall asleep?'

'It's after 3 a.m. We couldn't get you to wake up at all. Dante even suggested trying love's one true kiss but I explained it wouldn't work, because you've already met your Prince Charming.'

'Why are you even talking?' I mutter, pushing past him. 'Just keep quiet. Or I'll shove you off the nearest tall building when we get to one.'

My limbs feel like lead as I try to navigate the furniture, but one of the boys grips me gently before I can fall and land on my face.

'She's just started bleeding,' Aiden tells Dante as if I'm not even there – and I'm not really. I can't seem to escape the clutches of my deep sleep. I sag in Aiden's grip and watch, fascinated, as two drops of red blood splash from my nose onto my Converse. I lean forward to stare at the widening circles of blood and feel myself drawn towards the depth of colour, towards the scent of iron and blood. It's with great difficulty that I lift my head.

'Kit, no. No passing out. Come on. This isn't you.' Aiden is staring at me, his expression very serious. I try to pat his shoulder reassuringly, trying to indicate that I'm fine, but I miss it completely.

I let Aiden lead me back to the sofa and I sit down with a sigh and close my eyes. Someone passes me a wad of tissues and an icepack and I go through the whole ritual of pinching my nose, and waiting it out until my nose stops bleeding. I don't have to open my eyes to feel them watching me.

'What?' I mutter, my tone defensive. 'I'm fine. Just tired.'

Aiden is the one to speak. 'You're seeing the doctor in the morning. These nosebleeds aren't normal . . .'

'I'm not registered with your GP,' I point out, gingerly

moving the icepack away from my face and dabbing at my nose.

'Dr Forster won't care.' Aiden throws me a look. 'He's *my family's* GP.'

'Is he a vet?' I can't help but snark. 'Do werewolves even have GPs?'

Dante looks horrified but Aiden just shrugs. 'Mature. A dog joke.'

'You won't get an appointment that soon,' I point out, pleased that I could still think even if it feels as if my brain is turning to mush.

'Who says anything about seeing him at his surgery?' Aiden thumbs a speed dial number on his mobile and goes into the kitchen to make the call.

'How're you feeling?' Dante's voice is a bit too quiet for my liking when he speaks.

'Eh, I've been better. Sorry about the bleeding. I think you got some on you.'

Dante looks down at his grey T-shirt and shrugs. 'I've had worse.'

I try not to focus on how he's treating me, as if I'm something fragile.

'Why haven't you been to see someone about the nose-bleeds before now? What are you really scared about?'

I'm surprised by his astute question but wonder if he's using his ability to sense my feelings. 'No, that's rude,' I mutter. 'Stop reading me.'

'You're deflecting now.' Dante sits closer, his eyes dark. 'I try never to read you, but I don't need to do that to see you're scared, but you're doing your best to hide it.'

The air's taken on a tint of his magic now and isn't that just the best smell in the world? Blood and magic is a lethal combo and I seem to have become very susceptible to it of late. I let the silence stretch out too long and Dante leans closer.

'Come on, Kit. What are you worried about?'

This isn't something I've even wanted to think about, never mind share with someone else. And yet Dante's possibly the one guy who'd understand this, so I decide to put it out there.

'My magic,' I whisper. 'I'm human, Dante. I shouldn't have magic. If I go and see a doctor they'll do tests and they'll *know* . . .'

'Know what?'

'Know that I'm not normal. That I'm a . . .' The word sticks in my throat and I shake my head. I can't say it. I fight the tears back and blink up at him.

He frowns but catches on quickly. 'You're not a freak, Kit.'

The word reverberates through me and I gasp, feeling as if I've been punched. Hearing the word from someone else makes it real, makes me ache, but I press on because I have to try to explain myself to him. 'What I can do isn't normal. Humans don't have magic.'

'How do you know?'

My mouth opens and I stare at him. 'What?'

'Maybe humanity had magic thousands of years ago. And maybe, when the world split into the Otherwhere and here, mankind lost that ability. What if a spark of magic still lingers within some, like you? From what you've told me, about when your power manifested . . .' His voice trails off and he watches me carefully, choosing his words with deliberate care. 'It had not been a good time. You faced your grandmother's killers with a knife in your hand and your uncle by your side.

You'd just found out what being a Blackhart really meant and what your family did for a living. Something in you reacted to that. You found a well of strength within yourself that few people need to tap into. And I sense you dug deep – because you're not half-hearted about anything. And maybe, that's all it is. You accessed your strength and found that *your* power turned out to be magic.'

I brush the tears from my eyes and stare at him. 'You're ridiculous,' I manage in a whisper, my throat tight. 'You make it sound like the worst promo for a superhero movie ever.'

He gives me a hug and I take a ragged breath, closing my eyes against the tears.

'Anytime, Blackhart.'

'I don't want to see a doctor,' I say, and even to my ears I sound like a petulant three-year-old. 'This isn't something a doctor can help me with, anyway.'

'Tough, because you've got an appointment in an hour.'

Aiden re-emerges, his voice seeming harsh, but I know how little patience he has with introspection. And I've seen that look on his face before – Shaun wears it a lot when dealing with Aiden himself – a look that says he's about three thousand per cent done with Aiden.

'Dr Forster is expecting you and, even if I have to tie you up, I'm taking you to see him.' He crosses his arms across his chest. 'Doc Forster is a good guy, Kit. He has strong ties to the supernatural community and he'll be able to tell us what's going on, okay?'

'Okay, fine, we'll go. But if he does anything *weird* I'm out of there.'

'Weird like how?' Aiden asks me, trying and failing to

hide a look a triumph. 'He's not going to see if a radioactive spider will bite you, Kit.'

'I'll punch his lights out first,' I say, and I mean it. I stand up and touch Dante's shoulder for a brief second, trying to convey my thanks when I don't really have the words. He flushes slightly and I know that, like me, he's a little over-whelmed by our conversation that felt very much like Real Talk.

'You got blood on my shirt again,' Aiden says, and I sense he's trying to lighten the mood. 'You owe me a new wardrobe.'

In my en-suite shower, I lather up and ignore the amount of blood swirling down the drain at my feet and suppress the anxiety threatening to overwhelm me. If this Dr Forster was such a good guy, why hadn't I heard of him before? Still uneasy after I've dressed in blood-free clothes, I head back downstairs.

Aiden drives us to a stately part of town just north of Regent Street. I clamber out of the car and stare up at the impressive facade, knowing I'm delaying.

'Go on,' Aiden prompts. 'We don't have all night.'

Chapter Twenty-Three

The door opens after Aiden's brief knock and a woman lets us in before disappearing into the inner recesses of the house. We follow Aiden into what looks like a waiting room and the heavy silence immediately bugs me. Even Dante seems affected and shifts uneasily between us.

'Is it me or does it feel like we're being watched?' he asks, and I shake my head. I don't feel that at all. I just feel sleepy and uncomfortable. Not two sensations I thought would go hand in hand.

'The walls have been built to absorb sound.' Aiden stretches his long legs out. 'It makes it very difficult to accidentally overhear confidential patient–doctor stuff.'

The door to what I assume is the consultation room, opens and Dr Forster comes out of his office. He shakes Aiden's hand and then each of ours as we're introduced. He looks to be in his late forties and is completely nondescript. Everything about him is calming, and it puts me on edge. I follow him into the room and he shuts the door behind us before taking his seat behind the desk. It feels weird, being around someone who can sit and regard me so thoughtfully without fidgeting. It makes me feel I should fill up the silence but I bite my lip and watch him nervously instead.

'I've only ever dealt with one Blackhart in the past,' he eventually says. 'Andrew.'

'My uncle Andrew. What did he do?'

'He'd become ill after a witch cursed him. He'd also been poisoned and we thought he might die.' He frowns. 'As I recall he fought the spell after we identified the poison and went on to kill the witch. It caused quite a stir. She'd been using her magic to create love potions that actually worked. You could imagine the mess that created. So –' he claps his hands together and I notice that he has beautiful hands – 'what can I do for you today? Aiden mentioned something about regular nosebleeds and migraines.'

I nod, trying to get a grip on my rabbiting heart. It takes some time but I eventually get the story out about the nosebleeds, magic, nightmares and the weird dreams. Dr Forster nods as I speak, writing rapid notes in a folder. I can see my name at the top along with a code and wonder at it. But he encourages me to talk, to tell him about my abilities and what I've done to control them.

I'm not sure how long we're in there, but I share more with him about my magic than I've done with anyone before. He listens intently and I find myself relaxing marginally.

'Have you met other humans with magic?' I ask him after I've finished speaking. 'Or who thought they have magic?'

'I have met some who thought they had abilities. And to a certain extent, some had skills that I've not seen generally displayed in the human populace. But certainly none of them had the kind of abilities you've mentioned to me tonight.'

I close my eyes. 'What do we do next? Do you want to see what I can do?'

Dr Forster considers this, but then shakes his head. 'Not immediately, no. You look ready to bolt from the room and I sense you're not comfortable with any of this.' His smile is gently teasing and I smile back. 'No, I'll just give you a quick general check-up because that's not half as terrifying.'

'Easy for you to say,' I mutter and he laughs with good grace.

I subject myself to being listened to, prodded, my pulse taken and my blood drawn into several different vials – all of them marked up. The last part worries me the most but his smile is calm as he senses my distress.

'Your blood will not have your name on it. It will have a code identifier. I understand the world you live in, Kit, and I understand the importance of making sure your blood stays safe. No one will be able to use it against you in spells.'

'Okay. Why are you drawing my blood, anyway?'

'I'll be asking for certain checks. I'll get a full blood count. That means we'll be able to check on your red and white blood cells, see if they're behaving. There will also be electrolyte testing and a few other things.' His expression is kind. 'Next, I'll be arranging an MRI scan. I want to see how things look inside your head.'

I grimace. 'I don't think that will work.'

'It's non-invasive.'

'No, I mean, the machine itself. The MRI is a giant magnet, right? It probably won't work. I'm not good with or around electronics. Things break after I've been around for maybe five minutes.'

'Interesting.' He makes a further note in his folder. 'But not that unusual.'

I feel my worry increase when he makes more notes.

'Okay, we may have to rethink that, then, but honestly, right now all I'm seeing is a healthy young woman who perhaps needs to eat a bit more healthily and get more rest. It could be that your nosebleeds have to do with anxiety. From what we've been talking about it sounds to me like you are under an unhealthy amount of stress.'

I nod, because it could be true. Really, my life isn't exactly moonlight and roses. But in my heart of hearts, I have the feeling that all my symptoms are tied in with my magic. Humans aren't born equipped to handle magic, and so it's more than likely that my brain is rotting and leaking out of my nose.

'Having said that, I'll send your bloodwork away and we should know in about three days if we have anything serious to talk about. I very much doubt it. In the meantime, I'll be investigating the benefits of using an MRI scanner, or the equivalent thereof. I have a friend who is a powerful psychic and I've used her in the past to help me pinpoint how best to help a patient. I'll contact her in the morning and, depending on your results, I'll ask you to visit her soon. Will that be okay?'

I must look absolutely terrified because he carefully caps the ballpoint pen he's been using and looks at me.

'Kit, let me be clear here. From what you've said you're anxious about your abilities and you feel that your ability to control them is slipping. It's my opinion that the head-aches and the nosebleeds are linked to your magic. You suspect this too, am I correct?' At my nod he continues, 'I feel that perhaps you need a tutor or a guide, to help control your energy. My friend, the psychic, has abilities in this field. She is a strega, from a very old line of witches. She has a great deal of knowledge and I am sure that with her assistance we will be able to help you.' He watches me for a few more seconds. 'And, as you're a Blackhart, my next bit of advice may be met with some amusement, but I'd prescribe some rest, perhaps a holiday. You don't strike me as an overly anxious person – and yet you've reported a lack of ability to sleep for an extended period and I've seen traces of your hypervigilance whilst you've been here. Again, it makes me think that the migraines, the nosebleeds, everything you *feel* is wrong with you, are all interlinked. It's my job to help you fix that – if you will let me help you.'

I take a deep breath. 'You make it sound so simple.'

'Maybe because sometimes it *is* simple.' His expression is gentle. 'Now, I know your friends are dying to drag you off on some other adventures and I can almost hear Aiden complaining about the uncomfortable chairs, so I'm going to let you go. But, Kit, take my card and if anything happens that is out of the ordinary –' his lips twist here – 'I need you to call me. I know you're scared and I would be too, but you're my patient now and I have a great many friends who I can talk to if I'm unable to help you. The supernatural community is large. And, contrary to what the Blackharts may have told you, not everyone is out to get you.'

He says the last bit jokingly but he's given me something to think about. I pull on my jacket and wrap my scarf around my neck.

'Thank you for listening and for not thinking I'm crazy.'

He pulls open the door and Aiden is right there, looking tense and pale.

Dr Forster gives both Dante and Aiden a reassuring smile. 'Call me, if you need anything, Kit. We'll speak soon.'

Without waiting for a response, he closes the door and I look at Aiden.

'What's going on?'

'We have to go, right now. Something's happened.'

I shoot a look at Dante, who's already heading for the corridor. I want to ask what's happened but Aiden's expression tells me that it's something really bad and that he's not going to tell me until we're out of here.

Chapter Twenty-Four

The way Aiden and Dante move, as a unit, frightens me. They're suddenly behaving like two super-anxious body-guards, and I wonder what's happened in the short space of time since I left them. It's only once we're in the car that Aiden breaks the tense silence.

'Connor and Shaun have been kidnapped.' He starts the car with short jerky motions. 'My dad called from St Peters-burg. It's the Jericho Gang.'

'Are they asking for ransom?'

'They're not asking for anything. My dad was sent this.'

I take the phone from him and wince when I see his two older brothers blindfolded and kneeling shirtless on the stone floor in some kind of warehouse. I can't see their faces well, but I recognize the palm-sized Celtic knotwork tattoo of the Hound of Ulster that both Connor and Shaun have inked over their hearts. It alludes to the Garretts' familial connec-tion to Irish folk hero Cu Chulainn – and I know Aiden's due to receive the mark on his twenty-first birthday.

Both Garretts are covered in a network of cuts and bruises. But even kneeling and in obvious discomfort, neither of them looks defeated. It lifts my heart a little.

'Why haven't they healed?' I ask. 'Some of those bruises look bad.'

'Silver. Whoever's torturing them knows about were-wolves. We're guessing their captors are using a mix of silver and wolfsbane – because even if they can't shift, those wounds should look better than they do, even if they're fresh. We can heal most things over a couple of hours, days even. But it's a hell of a struggle when there's silver and wolfsbane involved.' Aiden's gaze meets mine. 'I have to do something. We have to help them.'

'There's no question about that,' I say vehemently. 'Let's just get home first. Then I'll ring Uncle Andrew and let him know what's going on.'

Dante drops a comforting hand on the back of Aiden's neck and I lean sideways in the passenger seat and put my arms around him. He sighs deeply and after a few minutes I let him go. I can't even begin to figure out how the Jericho Gang took both Connor and Shaun. The two oldest Garretts travel extensively for their father, and I know Jonathan Garrett relies on Connor to be his right-hand man when it comes to their businesses in Europe and North America. Shaun is mostly in charge of Aiden, as he handles pack business in London and the UK. But, even so, he's hardly at home. They have one more brother, Cillian, who no one really ever talks about and who I've never met. He's between Shaun and Connor in age and apparently refuses to have anything to do with his family. In a family of werewolves, he was born human.

'Do you think they'll go after my family too?' I ask, as the thought hits me and I turn to Dante in alarm. 'Kyle and Marc are in Devon. I mean, they're alone out at the new build for the Manor and they'll be completely unprepared for attack.'

'It's possible. Ring them now, and tell them to be careful,' Dante says. He's still talking when I see his eyes widen in shock. Then bright lights slide over his face and I feel a terrible impact as we're rammed by a vehicle that wasn't there two seconds earlier. The sound of tearing metal fills the air. The Cayenne spins wildly out of control across both lanes, into any oncoming traffic. Thankfully there's no one around because it's the middle of the night.

I'm flung forward and to the side and reach blindly to prevent myself from head-butting the dashboard. The airbags deploy and I'm punched back in my seat. I find my knife in my boot and manage to struggle out of the seatbelt but my fingers refuse to move properly and I lose my knife in the foot-well. There's shouting and the sound of running feet but it doesn't sound like concerned citizens. Those are heavy boots, military. Which means this isn't an accident. This is something else.

My door is pulled open and I let myself go limp, trying to figure out what's going on. My head is spinning and someone punches the airbags so they go down completely and I'm pulled out of the passenger seat. It's hard for them to manipulate someone who's swooning and loose-limbed. I'm dropped unceremoniously in the middle of the road; I close my eyes and play unconscious.

'She's out of it,' a gruff voice says. 'Get the others. Caleb wants them alive.'

There's the sound of punches landing and my world comes sharply back into focus. There are six of them and they're all big meaty guys and look the business. Two large SUVs are parked near the Cayenne and one has an incriminatingly crushed front-end. No one is paying me any attention and I get my legs under me slowly, until the earth is solid below my booted feet. The Cayenne is between me and the fight but I can just see three guys trying to contain Aiden, who's fighting and snarling savagely – more wolf than boy. Dante has one of his opponents mewling and crawling on the floor and the other guy looks wary as he moves around him, staying out of range of those long legs and hard fists. The guy that's been set to look after me is just watching his mates fighting. I feel offended. I hate not being considered a threat, even when I'm technically out of a fight.

My watcher doesn't see me coming at all, his attention absolutely elsewhere. I waste no time being smooth or fair in my attack. I stamp down on the back of his left knee and, as his balance shifts backwards, I grab his hair and pull him further towards me. I punch him on the side of the throat as there's a tiny set of nerves clustered there. If punched hard enough it causes the attackee to pass out. I've practised the move with Jamie enough times to be pretty sure my aim's right and, even as I strike, I hold my breath. He makes a soft surprised noise and then he's gone, legs buckling beneath him. I help him to the ground, grunting against his weight.

I find zip ties in his back pocket and quickly tie him up before I duck back into the foot-well of the car and find my knife. It's faster to climb through the car and out of the driver's side and I prepare to do that, just as Aiden physically picks up one of his attackers and hurls him a few metres through the air. He crashes into the side of one of their parked SUVs, grunts and slides bonelessly to the ground.

Aiden lets out a snarl as the second of his attackers gets a lucky slice in at his ribs. The smell of blood is heavy in the air and Aiden flashes his teeth in pain.

Aiden's two attackers haven't seen me and I slide quietly out of the car. I tap the nearest guy on the shoulder and when he swings around, I punch him hard with the pommel of the knife on the nose and he goes down. Just to make sure, when I move past, I step on the hand that holds his knife. There's the distinct pop of bone snapping and he lets out a loud scream before passing out. I retrieve his knife, which is black steel, military grade – they're clearly well-supplied by someone.

Dante's guy looks worried, because now he only has one team-mate left. And after a few rounds with Dante, the guy's face is already one big bruise with an ugly cut just below the eye. Dante seems happy to just keep hitting him, evading badly aimed punches and keeping a wary eye on any sweeping legs. In the end the guy just throws his hands up after a particularly hard rabbit-punch from Dante which jerks his head back with a snap. The attacker curls into a ball at Dante's feet, sobs escaping from his heaving chest.

Dante crouches down at his side and, as I did, easily finds the zip tie handcuffs in his pockets and slides them on.

Aiden's guy makes one last effort to throw a punch but even as he's swinging he's already decided that running is a better option. Aiden gives him no chance at all and brings him down a few paces away with both boots to the small of his back. The guy face-plants in the street and even from a distance, I can hear the wind knocked out of him and possibly some teeth breaking as Aiden lands on him with a little too much force.

Aiden shakes his hair out of his face and stands up, hauling his attacker upright and marching him back. The guy looks badly dazed and he's not at all steady on his feet, sinking to the ground in a heap when he reaches us.

I kneel down next to the guy who I busted. It looks like he's struggling to breathe through his bleeding nose so I prop him up against the wheel of the car and manhandle him so his head is upright. Aiden shoves his guy next to his unconscious buddy, leaning him up against the car, and wastes no time tying him up too, his movements rough.

'This is getting damn annoying,' he mutters as he glares at our attackers. We were set upon on a relatively isolated stretch of road bordering a park – I guess the best they could manage for an unobserved London ambush. No cars or early morning dog-walkers are out yet, but our luck might not hold. Aiden sits back on his heels and stares at me and Dante. 'But it could have been worse.'

'I'm calling the SDI,' Dante says, holding his phone in a bit of a daze. Then he thumbs a number and rubs a shaking hand over his face. I vaguely listen to him as he gives details of our attack to the Spook operator on the other end of the line. 'I think it's best if you merely call this in to the local cops on patrol,' he advises. 'We definitely don't want to be involved and the less . . . Yes. Exactly. We suspect an attempted kidnapping. I'm with Aiden Garrett and Kit Black-hart.' The level of noise on the other end of the line becomes loud and Dante grimaces, pulling the phone away from his ear slightly. Aiden's murderous expression lessens a bit and he grins when he hears what they're yelling at Dante. I doubt they are extolling our virtues. 'No, neither of them had anything to do with the attack. We think it's connected to a case we're working on. We think the guys have ties to the Jericho Gang. Call it a hunch.' He rolls his eyes but then nods. 'As soon as you can, yes. Thank you, Zoe. I owe you.' He pockets his phone. 'We're leaving as soon as we hear the sirens. Make sure they're all tied up.'

I leave that to the guys and instead check to make sure all knives and whatever weapons they used are tucked away in the Cayenne. It's icy cold out and, combined with the come-down from the adrenalin of the car crash and the fight, I've started shaking badly.

Dante pulls me close and rubs my arms in an effort to warm me up. Aiden hauls the six guys around and dumps them in the road by their two cars. Then we climb into the Cayenne to get out of the cold and Aiden grimaces at the state of his car.

'Let's see if we can drive away from here. Otherwise, we walk.'

The Cayenne gives a sour cough but the engine ticks over and somewhere in the distance there's the sound of sirens. Aiden doesn't wait. He throws the car into gear and we're moving. He spins the wheel, makes an illegal U-turn and heads away from the two SUVs and the six men. We don't look great, but they are much the worse for wear.

Chapter Twenty-Five

As he drives, Aiden rummages and finds both Dante and me a chocolate bar to help with the shakes. He uncaps the energy drink he has stored in the side pocket and drinks it all in one eye-watering go. I silently eat the chocolate and stare out of the window, feeling decidedly numb and displaced. It's usually like this after an unexpected fight. It feels as if I'm retreating into myself – until I'm no more than a tiny dot of light in a large black abyss where all sound is muted.

Aiden's turned the music on. I think he's talking to Dante, but I can't lever myself out of my bubble of silence.

'. . . not hearing a word.'

'Sorry, what?' I blink and frown at the hand on my forearm – Dante's hand.

'Call Kyle and Marc,' he repeats. 'Make sure they're safe.' He watches me until I nod and fish around for my phone.

'How did they know where to find us?' Aiden mutters to no one in particular, his fingers drumming on the steering wheel. 'They must have followed us from the house. They must have known they wouldn't be able to get to us otherwise.'

'It felt like an opportunistic attack, for sure,' Dante said. 'They weren't prepared. No weapons, apart from the knives.'

'Maybe they thought it would be easy to take us. A girl and two young guys. Didn't think we'd put up a fight.'

I snort. 'They left me unguarded. Shows how little they know about us.'

I find Kyle's number and wait for the call to connect. It rings for far too long and my heartbeat kicks up a notch. Aiden tilts his head towards me and frowns.

'Kit?' His voice holds a note of alarm, but then there's a fumbling noise on the other side of the line followed by muttered swearing and then Kyle's voice: 'Ohmygodwhaddayawant? This better be serious.'

I sag in relief. 'Kyle. It's Kit.'

'It's a terrible name, for a terrible girl,' he groans out loud. 'A girl who should be tucked up in bed somewhere, safe and sound and *not at all* calling me. At all.' There are noises in the background and I imagine him pushing himself up. 'Kit, seriously though, what the hell? It's stupid o'clock. I think there are laws against being phoned this time of the morning. And if there aren't any laws, I'm going to petition the government to introduce it as a law.'

I let him ramble because this is how he wakes up. But eventually the tirade stills.

'Kyle, is Marc with you?'

'Yes, why? He's next door. Sleeping like all normal people should be doing.'

'I need to talk to you both. Wake him up.'

Something about the ridiculous time and my tone of voice must worry him, because he just says, 'Hold on.'

Then Marc's there, sounding sleep deprived but awake.

'Kit, what's going on? Are you okay? You're in a car, I can hear the engine.'

'I'm with Aiden and Dante. We've just been attacked. We think it's because of the Glow case. They were trying to kidnap us and they already have Connor and Shaun. Aiden's dad was sent a picture of the guys tied up in a warehouse.'

'The picture could be fake –' this from Kyle – 'send it on to me and I can see if there's anything else in there.'

'We're pretty sure it's real, Kyle,' Aiden says. 'But I'll get Kit to send it anyway. You've got the software to analyse this type of thing. My dad has someone working on it too. He's not heard from my brothers for two days now, so we're pretty sure the Jericho Gang's had them for that long at least.'

There's absolute silence on the phone and for a second I worry that the phone's cut out, but no.

'The Jericho Gang has your brothers?' There is zero trace of drowsiness in Marc's voice now. 'Aide, do you guys know who these guys *are*? The stuff they've been doing . . . a mate of my dad's is on the drug enforcement squad and they are literally chomping at the bit for an excuse to go in hard.'

'We know,' Aiden answers. 'Marc, listen. They've got my brothers tied up in a way that tells me someone's told them how to incapacitate werewolves. And it's not just the crap you see in *The Wolfman* either.'

'Okay, we're both up now. I'm calling Dad. Kit, have you spoken to him at all?'

'No, I wanted to make sure you guys were okay first. They've been watching us and tried to take us when we left the Garretts' – around an hour ago. It makes me think they've found out who we all are. And as you guys are in the middle of nowhere – in a field, basically – I wanted to make sure you were okay.'

'Hey, the house is practically done. We just need you to finish a few more spells over Christmas, then we'll be moving in.' Marc sounds inordinately proud. 'We're okay. Kyle's installed cameras and alarms all over the place too so if anyone comes snooping, we'll be alerted.'

'What about the Spook?' Kyle asks suddenly. 'Is he, you know, okay?'

'I'm fine, thanks for asking, Kyle,' Dante mutters and ducks his head in a smile: both of us know what Kyle really means. As the only person in my family who actually knows Dante is Fae, Kyle was trying to check nothing weird had happened with Dante. 'We kicked ass. They didn't expect that.' There's appreciative laughter from Kyle, and I suddenly miss my family very much.

'Where are you guys right now?' Marc asks. 'What's your plan?'

'Just heading back home where we can regroup and wait to get instructions from my dad,' Aiden replies.

'Okay, listen. I'm going to call my dad too. Keep your phones charged, don't do anything stupid. Don't try to fix this by yourselves. You need back-up. Let's see what we can do to help.'

We say our goodbyes and hang up. I slump in my seat and look at my watch. It's nearer to five than four. Looking back on the past few days, it feels as if we've hardly managed to catch our breath, as if events have been gathering momentum. It suits me fine, to be honest. I don't have the patience to pore over books, and action is better than inaction.

We get to the Garretts' Kensington mansion; the place looks untouched. Aiden sets the door alarm and passes Dante a cricket bat from the stash of sports gear near the door. I get the metal baseball bat that I used last summer during a game in Hyde Park. It's nicely balanced. With my sword upstairs this will do nicely.

We check the rooms, working as a team. All four floors. I swap the bat for my sword in my room and immediately feel a hundred per cent better. Nothing is out of place and there's no sign of any intruders. I go back to my room and change into track pants, sleep socks and a baggy long-sleeved T-shirt. I scrub my hands and face and vow to shower before bed. Right now there was thinking to do and things to be puzzled out.

Back in the kitchen I start the coffee machine and put the kettle on for Dante's tea. I rummage around and find the box of Cheerios Dante thinks he's managed to hide away, but my search and destroy skills are impressive. I'm munching on a bowl of them by the time they're both back downstairs.

We settle down to watch the news. There are power outages in Scotland and along the east coast, with power companies unable to give any explanation. Not even the increased demand for heating could be blamed. Tied with this is a warning of heavy snow hitting the British Isles in the next week. The news and weather reports show thick cloud and dropping temperatures across Eastern Europe, the rest of Europe and our set of islands. There are low temperatures recorded in the southern hemisphere too, where it's supposedly summer. There are photos of Canada, Alaska and parts of North America already swathed in several feet of snow. Not that unusual, to be sure, but even the locals seem alarmed by the amount of snow that's been falling. There are reports of similar power outages along the eastern seaboard in the States.

'Remember when we discussed the idea of Fimbulvinter last year when we were trying to sort out Thorn and the mess in Alba?' Aiden asks. 'What if Olga's appearance as a dragon had a knock-on effect? And what if the weather we're seeing now is all still a cumulative result of everything that happened last year?'

Chapter Twenty-Six

'Wait a minute.' Dante holds up a hand and scowls at us both. 'It's funny because I think you mentioned Fimbulvinter and you were serious about it. You do know it's just a . . .' Dante's brain catches up with what he's saying and the implication makes his voice drift off. 'It's not just myth and legend, is it?'

'Werewolf,' Aiden says, indicating himself, 'creature from mythology.'

'Human monster-hunter who uses magic,' I say, and then, pointing at Dante, I declaim, 'Faerie changeling left behind in the human world and glamoured to look human. Oh, who also has horns – and magic when he remembers to use it.'

Dante's eyes close and he exhales heavily. 'Okay, so we are talking about the *actual* winter that precedes the *actual* end of the world – which could be a real thing that's happening right now?'

'Ragnarok, baby. Bring your weapons.' Aiden's smile doesn't meet his eyes and he looks sombre as he stares up at the TV screen showing the ominously shifting weather patterns. 'If the Veil really is as frayed as Thorn thinks it is, then anything is possible.'

'But don't the legends say that the Fimbulvinter is about three consecutive winters, with no summer?' I respond. 'Our last summer was really hot – so it can't be related to what we went through last year.' I push my cereal bowl away. 'I can't shake the feeling that we're missing something.'

'Explain.'

'Okay. There's all this disjointed stuff going on. It started off with the kids being stolen.'

'No, it didn't. It started when you met Thorn in the forest.'

I blink at Aiden in surprise and nod, because he's right. 'It started when I met a faerie prince in the forest. And it went sideways from there, I think. There were monstrous Elder Gods two siblings tried to bring back with the help of the High King of Alba's banished brother, Eadric. But we stopped them. We saved the prince and stopped an attempted coup. And instead of being used to break the world, the prince becomes the guardian of the realms. For months things tick over, and we hear nothing from him. I have some weird dreams but, you know, that's just me. Then I meet Dante and we're asked to help figure out who is snatching children from a Brixton estate.'

'We then find the child thief . . .' Dante supplies.

'And we meet his boss, who is . . .'

I nod at Aiden and continue, 'A person whose family worked for the Elder Gods back in the day, and is still looking after one of them; a goddess who lives off the energy from stolen human children. And because of her, the mystical Veil that separates the human world from faerie is still intact. But she's dying, we've been told. Her grasp on holding the Veil together is slipping and we don't know how to stop it.'

'Then we have the faerie drug, Glow, that's cropped up out of the blue,' Aiden adds.

'Is the Glow involved in all of this? With the Veil, with the goddess, with Thorn?' I wonder.

'Or is it a distraction, maybe? A move by the enemy to divert us from what's really going on?'

'Like what?' I question Aiden and then suddenly I go ice cold. *What is their endgame for the Glow?* Mar had said. And why indeed would someone want to get humans addicted to faerie drugs?

'The incident in Hyde Park,' Dante offers. 'Was it Glow-related? Our attackers were Fae . . .'

'What if they're trying to remove us? What if they're planning something really big and they want us out of the way?'

'Also consider the attack this morning. With no other players, we can be pretty sure they're guys from the Jericho Gang. And why have the gang taken the wolves? It's all points to Glow and *yet* . . .'

We stare at one another. 'Look, I'd *love* to be this vainglorious and think the scariest drug lord in the UK is trying to take us all out, as we may be an obstacle to him and his dastardly ways. But no, I don't *think* so.' I grin but neither of the two guys is smiling. In fact, they're both looking far too serious, as if I'd hit some serious nerve. 'Come on. That's the stupidest thing I've heard. Really? We worry this guy so much he's sending his bullyboys after us? Shouldn't he be worried about spies and cops trying to arrest him?'

'They definitely weren't there to invite us to tea with the queen,' Aiden points out and he looks a little flushed. 'And they *do* have my brothers. Why else would they kidnap them? And send photos to my dad if they're not asking for a ransom? They're definitely making a move against us.'

'But are we sure the guys who came after us were part of the Jericho Gang?' I counter. 'We didn't stick around to chat to them.'

'Those guys were with my brothers.'

My eyes widen. Aiden's voice has taken on the low rumble I recognize only too well. That's the sound of him working himself up into punching things. I've been with him in the past, at a nightclub, when a guy slapped his girlfriend for accidentally spilling his drink. Aiden had sounded exactly like this, talking to the guy, telling him to back off.

'I could smell Connor and Shaun on them.'

'We should have brought them back with us,' Dante said, 'asked them.'

'Tortured them, you mean,' I say, and I frown, my gaze drifting to Aiden. He's looking progressively tenser.

'No, he's right. We should have stayed, talked to them, maybe brought them here instead. They would have given up what they knew.'

'Leo said that none of them ever spoke to the cops. Why would you think they'd come clean to you?'

'I would have made them.' The way he says it makes my heart race – so matter-of-fact, but with a fixed stare and eyes that seem to almost spark, appearing unnaturally blue around the iris.

'Aide, come on. Now's not the best time to freak out, okay?' I hunker down in front of him. 'Come on, show me your eyes. Snap out of this weirdness.'

Dante watches, worried. He must feel the low sounds coming out of Aiden as they're sitting so close. I admire

Dante's projected calm because I can practically feel my heart thundering against my ribs.

'Kit . . .' Aiden puts his hands on mine and they're trembling slightly, but he keeps his eyes downcast. 'I think I need to be alone right now.'

'Aide. Your eyes. Show them to me.'

His hands flex above mine and I swallow audibly in the very quiet room. If he decides to go feral, there is no way I can stop him. Dante maybe can, if he completely drops his glamour and goes full-on siren on Aiden, but it isn't a scenario I'd like to be around to witness.

'Kit, please. Go. Take Dante with you.'

'I can't. You'll freak out and do something dumb.' And the words sound harsh even to me, and I grimace. 'It's best if you . . . just try to calm down, okay?' I say. 'We're going to get Shaun and Connor back. There's something these guys want from your family, and we just have to wait for them to tell us what that is.'

'Kit, stop talking.' Aiden hunches forward so that he's almost completely bent over. His voice is agonized, as if he's in real pain, and I know he must be fighting his shift with everything in him. 'Just *go* . . .' The growl reverberates through me.

I stand slowly and stare at Dante, who's deep in thought. Everything in me tells me I should turn around and walk out of that room and take Dante with me. But then I also know how much Aiden must be hurting. How scared he is. I just can't leave my best friend and make a run for it. This is not how we do things.

'I'm sorry.' Dante's words take us both by surprise and we turn to look at him. For that brief second I see the very ice blue of Aiden's eyes, and those are the eyes I was scared of seeing. Those are the eyes of someone who's barely holding on to themselves.

'What for?' Aiden rasps.

'For this.' As he speaks, Dante leans into Aiden's personal space, pressing a soft slow kiss onto Aiden's mouth. It's like time slows down as they kiss, then speeds up again when Dante cocks his arm back and punches Aiden on the arm. His fist hits Aiden's bicep and it sounds painful and sharp. Aiden manages a shocked gasp before pulling away abruptly, looking as if he's not sure if he wants to clutch his arm, rub his lips or punch Dante back.

'What the *hell*, Dante?' he gasps, leaning away from the older boy. I've never seen Aiden this badly shaken up and right now he looks like he's been pole-axed. But the electric-blue eyes are gone and he looks far less feral than before; merely stunned.

'And he's back.' Dante grins in shocked triumph. 'Well, that worked in unexpected ways.'

I turn back to Aiden, who's glaring at us.

'You almost wolved out, Aide,' I said. 'Wouldn't want that, right?'

'Yeah, but I didn't. Instead I'm the one who got mauled.'

'Be glad it was Dante who distracted you and not me. I would've hit harder.'

'Yeah, but would you have kissed me?' he shoots back, looking annoyed.

'I dunno. Would you have *let me*?' The question comes out fast and without much thought. Aiden's eyes go very wide and he shoots a look at Dante, who's smiling quietly to himself, staring back with a raised eyebrow.

'Oh, go ahead and answer,' Dante says, waving a hand,

his smile stretching wider. 'I'm interested in hearing the answer too.'

'You really are the worst, Kit,' Aiden manages, avoiding Dante's eyes completely. 'I need coffee. Excuse me.'

He walks off and I turn to Dante. We got Aiden back but we didn't do it in a good way. I can sense his confusion and turmoil at what Dante had done and it makes me feel bad. 'Maybe you need to go and talk to him.'

'Yeah.' Dante pushes his fingers through his hair. 'I think I just screwed that up. It was our first kiss.'

'Go and make it up to him,' I tell him. 'I'm going upstairs to call my uncle.'

'And sleep? How about some sleep.'

'Yeah, I'll give that a try too. I hear all the cool kids do it,' I respond sarcastically. 'See what happens.'

'I don't know how you guys survive on no sleep,' he says, giving me a quick hug. 'Go on. We'll no doubt be fighting for our lives again in about two hours or something.'

I waggle my eyebrows at him and mouth, 'or something', while making kissing faces; he just shakes his head at me.

'You are an actual eight-year-old sometimes. Go.'

I go.

Chapter Twenty-Seven

Crow is seated against a large oak tree in the garden, his hands sunk deep into the grass. I only know he's aware of me because the tall trees in the garden seem to sway towards me and I hear my name whispered on the air as the leaves rustle.

I inhale the scent of Crow's magic and open my sight to it. The colours are all hues of green and it tints my vision. It reminds me of the magic that held the Manor safe, before Olga tore it down and destroyed the only real permanent home I'd ever known.

The magic in the garden feels thick, like tree sap, and I sense myself buzzing with it. Crow looks as if he's completely under, swept away by the leyline that runs at the back of the Garrett house, through the carefully landscaped garden and disappearing towards Kensington and Hyde Park.

'Why are you here?' he asks me and his voice is so unexpected in the quiet of the garden that I jerk with surprise.

'Ah,' I breathe a little laugh to try to cover how much of a fright he gave me. 'The question is, what are you doing here, Sir Crow?'

He opens his eyes and they glow a soft verdant green;

even as I watch the colour fades and his eyes return to their normal grey colour.

'You're the one that fell into the songlines, Blackhart. You followed me here.'

Around me the trees sway and move and the familiar garden slowly recedes. Instead, I find I'm standing before the largest tree I've ever seen, not just in girth, but in height too. Above me is a thick canopy of branches and leaves that lets in hardly any light at all. Crow stands before me now and he watches me curiously.

'How did you get here?' he asks me and I shake my head because I have no idea at all.

'Is this a dream?' I ask.

'No. You are awake.'

I look around and peer up into the recesses of the tree. 'It's like the world tree from mythology,' I say. 'May I touch it?'

In answer, Crow moves aside and I walk forwards, and after a moment's hesitation I press my hand against the bark, lightly scraping my fingers against the rough texture.

'She's beautiful. How old is she?'

'As old as time itself.' Crow smiles then. 'That is to say that she's never told me. She's quite private.'

I smile and duck my head, leaning against the tree completely. It feels good and I feel safe and calmer than I've felt in ages.

'Why am I here, Crow?' I ask. 'And I really didn't mean to come here. I don't know how it happened.'

'I'm not sure why . . .'

I have no idea where the bow comes from, but it's unexpectedly in his hand, drawn and nocked in a move I'd have assumed was CGI if I wasn't seeing it for real. I step away from him, giving him room to move. At the same time I cast around and pick out the barely audible noises of movement in the undergrowth. I lean down carefully and pull my knife from my boot just as Crow glances at me enquiringly and I give him a nod to let him know I'm ready.

'It is not polite to sneak around *my* forest,' he says, and his voice holds a mild reprimand. 'These are dangerous times and you should show yourself now – before we decide to shoot first and ask questions later.'

There's a snort of laughter as the Sidhe pushes through the undergrowth. She's not very tall and she's dressed in soft furs. Her hair is a rich auburn and her eyes are a wide moss green set in a neat kittenish face. She looks harmless, but the fact that Crow hasn't put down his bow worries me a little.

'Forester Crow, I mean neither of you harm.' She inclines her head in greeting. 'Lady Blackhart. My name is Yukiko.' She pronounces it Yoo-kee-koo and it sounds musical and beautiful.

Crow lowers the bow after a few more seconds and it's weird how it just *goes away*, but then he's bowing and I'm a little shocked, because I've never seen him show deference to anyone before. His hand tugs mine. 'Curtsy,' he hisses at me from the corner of his mouth.

'Why?' I whisper back.

'She's a Japanese deity.'

My gaze goes back to the Sidhe, and although she seems pretty she's not what I would call deity-like. I mean, although they aren't deities as such, I've been face to face with Dina, Thorn's mum, who's the High Queen of Alba. Also, I've encountered Suola, the Queen of Air and Darkness *and* survived to tell the tale. This young Fae woman, who looks barely older than me, doesn't strike me as someone to whom I needed to curtsy.

'He's right, Lady Blackhart. But as I am an intruder, and I worked magic to bring you both here, I do not expect you to show me deference.'

Crow straightens and if I didn't know any better I'd say he looks annoyed.

'If you would explain yourself, Lady Yukiko?'

'I am here to ensure the safety of my nephew.' We both just stare at her, then she makes an impatient gesture. 'The boy. The changeling boy? You have him.' She looks at me pointedly.

'Dante! You're talking about Dante?' When she nods it's my turn to look impatient. 'Listen, we sent word ages ago that he wanted to meet his family. If you do represent them, why haven't you made a move to come and find him? And what did you mean when you said you *brought* me here? How is that even possible? Crow?'

Yukiko has the grace to look abashed, but only slightly.

'We have not been allowed to make contact. But we know he is safe. We watch from afar – know that, Lady Blackhart. But we are unable to claim him as one of ours. Not yet.' She moves forward slowly and I'm struck by her grace. 'As for bringing you here, a small cantrip only. You really should learn to protect yourselves better.'

'What!' I move towards her and impatiently shake off Crow's restraining hand. 'You realize that what you've done is illegal. But that's beside the point. This is about Dante and I have to say this: what you're doing is completely unfair, okay? He's alone in this mess right now. His magic is growing. He has *horns* that he has to glamour away every day. And because of who his father is, he can't show his face in the Otherwhere. If he did, someone might identify him to the High King, as the son of the man who tried to usurp his throne. He's not doing well. We've not heard from any of you and he's already worried that you've rejected him before you've even *met* him. And now here you are talking to *me* instead of *him*.' I point my finger and jab it a little in her direction. 'That is not nice at all.'

Yukiko blinks a little at my outburst, but then starts laughing. It's not an ugly laugh, as such, yet it annoys me.

'It's not funny,' I say, grimly carrying on regardless, 'and I'm being serious. Dante is so worried. Dammit, you guys have to do something.'

'We have been,' Yukiko says, trying to appease me. 'I am so pleased he has you for a friend, Lady Blackhart. I do not think he can ask for a fiercer defender and for that we are truly grateful.' She holds out her hand but I ignore the gesture. She drops it and continues smoothly, as if I've not offended her at all. 'I wanted to meet you both to apologize for the delay in coming for him. There has been some infighting amongst the kami. But I volunteered to meet with you, to ask you to guard him a little while longer only. We *are* preparing a place for him.'

I glance helplessly at Crow because I have no idea what she's talking about.

'When you say "prepare a place for him",' Crow says cautiously, 'what do you mean, exactly?'

Yukiko looks surprised. 'Well, he is our crown prince.'

Chapter Twenty-Eight

'Your what now?' The words are out before I can stop them.

'Eadric married my sister. She was next in line to become the ruler of our people, but she died within days of her son's birth. While we were still mourning, Eadric stole the child. He hid him, fearing for his safety. It took us a very long time to find the boy. But soon he will return and rule our people, as is his birthright.'

Next to me Crow mutters 'our people' to himself and he sounds a little shocked. I feel like pushing him into the trees because what isn't he telling me? I take a breath and frown at Yukiko. 'Look, I'm not sure why you're talking to *me* about this. If you can bring me here, then you can bring Dante here too. Dante needs to know he's not been cast aside by his real family.' Then, because it doesn't look as if she understands, I continue. 'Dante is going through hell. He discovered that he's Fae over a month ago. He has no one to guide him, to teach him how to control his powers. He wouldn't be safe here by himself. You need to sort yourselves out and come and fetch him, treat him like someone real. Don't talk to him about birthright or destiny or being a crown prince. Talk to him about being family, about making him part of yours. And you need to do this sooner rather than later. We've already been attacked by Fae and they tried killing us both.'

'We know of the attack.'

And the way she says this makes me practically blind with rage. She almost sounds bored, but then I notice how her hands tremble and I wonder what kind of strain she's under. And what is the real reason that brought her here, to talk to me in Crow's endless forest? 'Yukiko, if Dante is so important to you and your people, you have to show that you claim him as family. If Eadric's enemies are hunting him, then they need to know he's not a wild Fae living by himself in the Frontier. It would mean open season on him. You *know* that.'

There's a flash of anger in Yukiko's green eyes now and the wind's picked up a little, stirring the leaves.

'I can't,' Yukiko says, her voice faint. 'I'm just here to talk to you about protecting him.'

Crow closes his eyes in a way that makes me think he's just done with all of this and, to be honest, so am I.

'Look, Yukiko. Dante is my friend, a very good friend, and I will always watch out for him. You are the ones who need to get your house in order and fix this bloody mess his father made – by taking him away. Sooner, rather than later.' She opens her mouth to speak but I hold up my hand. 'I'm done. You brought me here against my will. I can judge you for breaking a ton of your laws and ours, but I won't. Just send me back to the Garretts' house where you found me. I'm busy and don't have time for Fae dramatics.'

I glance at Crow, but he's already moving towards me. By my side he sketches a polite, if stiff bow that holds nothing of the grace of his earlier abeyance towards Yukiko.

She, in turn, looks very much as if she would like to punch us both. Then he turns to me and holds out his hand.

'My lady, it would do me a great honour to escort you home.'

I blink rapidly and nod, giving him my hand. I let him lead me out of the clearing towards one of the larger trees and we step right into it. There's a moment of disorientation and, like all the times before, a vivid sense of life and energy rushes through me. In Crow's wake, I pass through what feels like a hundred clearings and trees, following a pattern only he can determine. What seems only moments later, but is in reality probably a lot longer, we walk out into the garden behind the Garrett mansion.

My stomach lurches and I have to inhale deeply to prevent myself from falling over. Crow peers back over his shoulder into the darkness behind us.

'What's wrong?' I ask him when I get my voice back.

'I'm not sure. For a moment it felt as if we were being followed.'

I become aware of the knife I'm still holding and say, 'It's okay, I'll protect you from wild things.'

He smiles then and shakes his head. 'Do you ever not cause trouble when you're in the Otherwhere, Lady Black-hart?'

'Hey, I'm pretty sure that's victim blaming. I never end up in the Otherwhere by choice. And that woman, that Yukiko, she used magic to kidnap me from the safety of the Garretts' garden without even asking permission. She can be glad I didn't punch her.' Crow is laughing now and I scowl at him. 'I totally could have beaten her up.'

'I don't doubt it, but I think you fundamentally missed who she is.'

'Please enlighten me then, oh superior magical being.'

'She is a nature spirit. She is what you might call an avatar of Gaia.'

I close one eye and stare blearily up at Crow. 'She looked very real to me, very corporeal and not spirit-like at all.'

'That is because she is as real as you. Or me. Her people, the kami, are difficult to describe. They are also what our friend Dante is . . . They are the nature gods and spirits that both humans and Fae have prayed to since even before the Elder Gods. It is they who make the crops grow, the rains fall, the winds that stir the trees, the clouds flow across the skies.'

'No.' I laugh a little. 'Come on, Crow, that's just . . . no. Remember science, okay? Magic, possibly, can do these things too, but people can't. Come now, you sound . . .'

'Like a creature from another world?' Aiden supplies as he jogs down the back stairs towards us. 'Kit? Forester! What are you doing here?'

They grip each other's forearms in a manly greeting and I can practically hear them try to out-macho one another. Then Crow says, 'Wolf,' and Aiden says, 'Crow' – and they give one another a brief hard hug before separating.

'I've brought the Blackhart home. She took an unexpected detour to the Otherwhere and found me.'

Aiden looks surprised at Crow's words but then he lifts his head and stares into the garden intently. 'Have you come alone?'

'Why?' I turn to follow his gaze, feeling that itch between my shoulder blades. The shadows in the garden feel thick and cloying.

'It feels . . . like there's someone else here.' But he shakes his head after another searing look around the dark garden.

'Maybe it's just the magic dripping off you both. It almost always messes with my head. Never mind.'

'Perhaps we can go inside?' Crow suggests and I realize I'm shivering because it's freezing out here. The temperature seems to have dropped another few degrees since I'd been taken.

With a regal nod, Aiden leads the way into the mansion and I attach myself to the nearest radiator like a limpet, clinging to it in an attempt to warm my cold fingers. Both Crow and Aiden stare at me curiously but continue into the lounge, where I hear Dante greet Crow. I press my legs against the radiator and close my eyes. The Yukiko thing was weird. It felt off and strangely fake. I reacted really badly but, even so, she just stood there, barely spoke and let me rail at her. And then let me go.

I'm halfway down the passage to the lounge when the house shakes. I stand for a second, almost too surprised to move, but then I rush down the passage.

'I promise you that's not me,' I shout as I hustle into the lounge. The house shudders again and there's a groan from somewhere that sounds disturbingly familiar.

'No . . .' My gasp is barely audible but my mind flashes back to the memory of the Blackhart Mansion under attack by Istvan and his sorcerers. Ultimately Olga tore down the wardings and spells that kept the house safe and the house disappeared completely, as if it had never existed. 'We have to go,' I tell Aiden and there's no way I can keep the panic out of my voice. 'Get your stuff. Put on shoes.' I'm running for the stairs and my room when it feels as if a giant hand's taken hold of the house and shaken it. I give a startled yell and tumble forwards but Crow is there to prevent me from braining myself against the banister.

'Where are your weapons?' he asks us and I sprint up the stairs to my room. I pull on my jacket, grab my sword and cast a quick look around the room. My Blackhart antler lies on the bedside table so I grab that too and slip it around my neck. It settles beside the obsidian mirror Thorn gave me.

I hear Dante and Aiden in their rooms and beat them back down the stairs.

'We have to get out of here,' I shout at Crow, but he just shakes his head and his gaze moves to the stairs, where Dante and Aiden come clattering down in a rush of bristling weapons and coats. Aiden's carrying a sword I only vaguely remember seeing him use before. Dante sword looks like a Japanese wakazashi, and the way he holds onto it tells me it's a weapon he's used before.

'What do we do?' Dante asks me. 'Do we run or fight?'

'Depends on who we're fighting.' Aiden heads for the lounge so he can peer onto the street. 'Nothing . . . oh, here we go. Redcaps out front. At least fifteen of them. I count two Sidhe.'

I twitch the curtain and spot them too. They're not doing anything, though, yet. Crow is standing with his head bowed, concentrating on something, but when he looks up his eyes are the same colour they were in the forest – that unearthly glowing green.

'Let me,' he says, and before either Aiden or I can stop him, he pulls open the front door and walks out onto the steps. Like the majority of homes along the road, there are neatly trimmed hedges in front of the house. Crow looks down at them for a second, spreads his arms wide and then when he looks up at the redcaps moving closer, he jerks both his arms up sharply. The hedges, mature hawthorn shrubs, quiver for a moment – and then they start growing up and outward at an alarming rate. I move back, and watch in shocked silence as the branches interlock and weave together and within moments the hip-high hedge has grown to six foot, then seven. And it just keeps on growing, forming an impenetrable defensive shield around the front of the house.

'That is not what I expected,' Aiden says quietly in my ear and all I can do is nod. 'Wait – does this make me Sleeping Beauty, with a forest of thorns surrounding my castle? Am I going to prick my finger and fall into a swoon? Who will give me love's true kiss?'

I nudge him with my elbow but his words relieve some of the tension. A boom shudders through the house and we all turn to look at towards the back door.

'I locked up,' I tell Aiden and suddenly I doubt myself. 'I'm pretty sure I did . . .'

We watch the back of the house as Crow steps in through the front door, closing and locking it securely. He presses both hands to the door and *grows* the wood into what looks like a massive railway sleeper. He looks satisfied with his impromptu fortifications.

'Unless they have a druid with them, the front of the house should hold.' He brushes past me and heads for the back door. 'Now, let's see what else is going on.'

Chapter Twenty-Nine

Werewolves hold territories, and these territories are where they are strongest. You want to fight a werewolf? You lure him away from where he has the home advantage. You throw him off balance and you take the opportunity to hurt him as much as you can. You don't attack him in his own lair. That's just stupidity.

We're arrayed on the back porch, staring into the darkness. Even with my enhanced sight, I don't see anything and apparently neither does Aiden. He growls low in his chest, a questioning sound that trembles through the unexpected quiet of the garden. He cocks his head and steps off the stairs and into the garden, scenting the air. An answering sound comes from the garden's far side. Something moves there and I get the impression of limbs, long and bone-white; limbs ending with glinting claws. I glimpse a bony face with elongated teeth, but then it's gone.

By my side Crow's posture goes hyperalert.

Sluagh.

Maybe he says the word at the same time as I think it, but it's as if acknowledging the creature gives it shape and form. It lurches from the shadows, gangly limbed, almost laughably unbalanced on backwards bending knees. It has four arms, two of which are actually tentacles, and an awkward hunch. Aiden is fast, but even as he launches into an attack, the sluagh slaps him backwards with a taloned hand, steps towards him and wraps one of its tentacles around his neck. It lifts him high and proceeds to try to squeeze the life out of him.

I ready myself to run towards him but turn my head just in time to see someone in those ridiculous robes Fae sorcerers favour, like Gandalf-rejects, move towards the house. He gestures at the house and a blast of energy thunders into it. This was not happening, I decide. Not again. Not to my friends' house. I snarl something but Crow's hand stills me. He smiles grimly at the sorcerer.

'Two can play at this game. You and the kami go and help the wolf. I've got the little magician. We need to shut the gateway before more come through.'

'More?' My eyes widen as two large armoured Sidhe warriors step from behind the sorcerer. The garden is still too dark and I wonder if they've created a cloaking spell to prevent us from seeing them properly. 'Crow?' I say over my shoulder, already moving. 'I've plans for my life. I can't die today.'

His laughter follows me as I sprint towards Aiden. Behind me Crow leaps off the side of the steps, longbow held in his hands like a staff and he's swinging it in an elegant arc.

The sluagh is one thing I've never wanted to face. It's big, ridiculously agile and, once kindled, its appetite for destruction is legendary. I don't think even the Fae are entirely sure what the sluagh is; they just try to keep it sated and direct it at their enemies until they're destroyed. Then they clean up the aftermath.

And right now, it's in the Garretts' garden and it's making a mess of Aiden.

Dante's a few steps ahead of me. He has his sword drawn and he looks savage and possibly too excited about getting into a fight. We both run towards the sluagh, which is now bent over a thrashing Aiden, one of its tentacles keeping the boy pushed against the ground, whilst the other tentacle has crept up beneath his shirt and – oh God, it looks like it's pulsing with something. Aiden's partially shifted too, fighting hard against the limb choking him. His eyes are a wild electric blue and his hands have warped – I can see the tips of almost-claws curving downwards. He uses these to swipe at the sluagh, but the creature seems unconcerned at coming close to having its throat ripped out.

The sluagh has its back turned, its limbs moving as it bats at Aiden. I propel myself forward as I leap into the air, kicking myself off one of the decorative rocks that dot the garden. I launch myself at its wide back but, impossibly, it moves, turning to face me. As I'm mid-air, like some scrappy Superman-wannabe, I can't redirect myself, and it obviously knows that. One of its arms flashes towards me, grabs me around my throat and yanks me forwards – towards its bony face with its flat features and extended teeth. Its eyes are huge and flat, like a shark's, and within them I read a deep dark satisfaction that chills me completely. It opens its mouth wide and hisses at me. I scream back in defiance. In response, I'm flung to the side and hit one of those damn decorative rocks hard enough to stun me for a few seconds.

Dante wastes no time in attacking the sluagh. His movements are graceful and considered as he harries the sluagh whilst keeping an eye on Aiden, whose own attacks are becoming weaker by the second. Dante fakes with his blade and ducks beneath that awful arm tipped with black talons. He comes up beneath the sluagh's guard but, before he can land a blow, the sluagh whips around, twisting its body sideways and out of the way. It wrenches Aiden with it, holds him up with both tentacles now. As I stagger upright, he throws Aiden at Dante and both boys go down hard.

I run at the monster, ignoring the voice in my head that sounds like Jamie's, telling me I need strategy, a plan. I've never been a strategy girl. I'm all about full-frontal attack and stabbing – until the thing goes down either dead or dying.

The sluagh straightens and I almost fall back because that hunch is just more spine that's somehow scrunched up and the thing is at least nine feet tall. As it stretches its neck – which bends impossibly backwards – it lets out the weirdest sound I've ever heard. It's not even audible; it's more like a wave of sub-sonic energy.

I can actually feel the wave rush past me before the creature turns to me. Its mouth – *maw* – opens and I register the rows upon rows of teeth. It *grins* at me. As if it's happy to see me. Which is when I hit it with my sword. I flow into a series of strikes and parries of which Jamie would be proud. It feels good being able to use my sword for more than just practice. I lose myself in the movements, trying to anticipate how to get inside the creature's guard so I can kill it outright.

There's a startled scream from near the doors to the house, and horrible cracking noises that sound very much like bones breaking into pieces. But I keep my eyes on the sluagh, which looks as if it might be a little bored. It keeps looking over my shoulder to where Dante's trying to get Aiden upright.

The thought that my friend may be hurt or even dying fuels my anger. I fake a thrust, the sluagh twists, I do another fake thrust, diverting my blade-tip at the very last moment – then I drive it up beneath its guard. But it's just not there any more. At all. I spin in alarm, right into its attack. It drives a huge fist into my stomach and as I double forward, it's right there, getting a hand around my neck and lifting me off the ground. The hand squeezes experimentally and I gasp for air, trying to hook my nails into its wrist but it shakes me hard whilst tightening its grip.

I really hate being thrown around by things bigger than me. I shift the grip on my sword, drive it upwards into the sluagh's arm and twist the handle. The sluagh blinks confusedly when the blade punctures muscle. It cocks its head, like a dog would when it's trying to understand something, then blinks at me. It almost looks offended that I've managed to land a hit but doesn't drop me.

Dante whistles soft and low to attract its attention, and when it turns to look at him, Dante gives an ugly grin. He then punches the monster – the monster even monsters are scared of – in the face. If I had strength left in me I'd laugh, because Dante's wearing his knuckleduster covered in angelic script.

The sluagh lets out a shriek and Dante lands another punch, this time using a reverse cut with the blade of his sword to the sluagh's exposed chest. It's a risky move, because he could easily have hit me at the same time. But the sluagh keeps me away and slightly to the side, whilst squeezing the life out of me, which ironically keeps me safe from Dante's attack.

The sluagh moves, batting at him irritably, and I use the opportunity to lash out with my legs, hoping to hit something, *anything*, but no such luck. I'm starting to have real problems now with breathing and my vision is going fuzzy at the edges.

Danger. I'm not sure if I'm the one thinking the word or if someone else in the garden says it – but I can't help but agree. Yes, danger, so much danger and pain.

I shake out my fingers, grip my sword again, and with my remaining energy I plunge the blade back into its arm, closer to the wrist this time. I *twist* hard, feeling bone grate against the blade. Shockingly, the sluagh's adjusts its grip on me slightly, so it's even tighter than before. I give up pretending I know how to get myself out of this, because my life is being choked from me.

Blackness creeps into my vision and it's a struggle even to breathe through my nose. And God, my nose has started bleeding again! If I don't die from being choked to death by the sluagh, I'm going to choke to death on my own blood filling my mouth and lungs.

Dying.

There's a vicious snarling noise from close by and I attempt to focus on Aiden, who's swaying on his feet whilst foolishly trying to get a grip on the sluagh, but the creature is ridiculously agile as it switches and moves in random patterns, evading both him and Dante.

My oxygen-starved limbs are lethargic as I claw ineffectually at the grip around my neck. I have to do something, anything, or I won't get out of this alive. A shudder passes through me and I reach desperately for my magic. It hums happily at my summons.

I make a pathetic noise as I drag my magic forth. The ball of light that forms in the palm of my hand isn't big but it is bright, neon bright, and I pack my angry intent and desperation into it.

I pull the sword from the sluagh's wrist and try to remember how I killed Olga in dragon form. I somehow, impossibly, remember how I stretched my magic and light across the sickle's blade before lodging it into Olga's muscular draconic neck. And as my breath runs out, I try to layer my magic onto the blade in my hand.

I can't see if it's worked and I don't care because I'm so near to blacking out that this will be my last attempt. Gripping the blade in my stronger right hand, I don't plunge into the sluagh's arm this time. No, I thrust it forward, sharp point held out front, and drive it towards what I assume is the soft flesh of its flanks and up, hoping to strike a vital organ.

The blade slides beautifully through the air, it's a graceful strike and even though I can't see it, I can feel it's perfect. And it does nothing. Nothing at all. It somehow misses its mark entirely and I lose all feeling in my hand. I drop the sword just as the sluagh twists, jerking me with him. I can sense him attacking someone in the bunch of his muscles and the way he gracefully moves aside, away from the counter-attack.

There's a gasp and groan of pain. The sluagh's turned enough so that I catch sight of Dante, a hand clasped to his throat and a look of astonishment on his face. The air is thick with the smell of iron and magic as blood spills between his fingers, before his knees give way.

I futilely reach for him, and the sluagh lets out an exasperated hiss. Another of its hands wraps around my throat and I open my mouth to scream but I've got nothing, no air, no energy, nothing.

My vision's almost gone completely but I keep focused on Dante, willing him to stand up, to heal, to fight harder.

My mind feels cast adrift and I blink slowly. Each blink lasts a hundred years as consciousness starts to leave me.

Kit. Stay with me. I'm almost there.

Thorn's voice thunders through me and I jerk, giving a relieved sob and lick my bloody lips. I muster my last resources and force my heavy eyes open to stare down into the strangely calm face of the sluagh. 'You'd better watch out. My boyfriend's coming to kick your ass.' My voice is a dry rasp, but I hope my words are loud enough for Aiden and Dante to hear.

My vision fades and I drift into unconsciousness, and it is warm and welcoming.

A thick billow of magic buffets me and the sluagh moves fast and hard, tucking me tighter against its undulating form.

The garden fills with a bestial roar that shakes me to my bones. Try as I might, my eyes refuse to open, not even when hands pull me from that darkness, lifting me clear. I curl against the person holding me, struggling to find breath when it feels as if my throat's never going to work properly ever again.

Another roar rips through the night, a jagged red slash against the darkness. And as the sound escalates, I feel the undeniable pulse of Thorn's magic soak the air all around us.

I've lost track of the sluagh because there's too much movement around me, but nothing prepares me for the whistling note of pure fear that must come from its throat. The sound climbs high until it's piercing my brain and then all sound just stops. For the longest beat. The crack and snap of lightning hitting flesh and bone that follows isn't as loud – but it is a sound I'll never forget, not ever.

The stench of ozone burning, along with the smell of scorched hair and skin, fills my nose. I lean forward and spit blood into the grass at my feet before I throw up.

'I've got him. See to Kit,' Crow's voice floats towards me. Thorn's pale face hovers over mine and I force a smile onto my lips.

'Hey,' I rasp, swallowing with difficulty. 'You're here. How did you . . . ?'

'Shhh. Are you hurt?' From somewhere he produces a cloth and wipes my face. 'Kit? Can you hear me?'

I nod and wince because my head is pounding. 'Yes. I'm okay, I think. How's Dante?'

I struggle upright and for a second I think Thorn's going to push me back down, but instead he's helping me upright with careful hands. It feels good to be this close to him, in the aftermath of almost dying. Crow has Dante propped up on a bench against the wall. Dante's pale and shaking and there's a vivid diagonal slash across his throat. His ripped shirt shows that the cut ends just below his clavicle. It was a killing slash delivered with intent.

Crow has both his hands on Dante, one resting against the back of his neck, the other pressed high against his chest, just beneath the cut. Even in the grey darkness, it's easy to see Dante's tattoo shifting and reaching for the smooth edges of the wound. The smell of their combined magic is an intoxicating mix of fresh clean air, meadows and sun-drenched forests underpinned by the heavier cinnamon and nutmeg scents I've come to associate with Dante dropping his glamour. Thorn's arm tightens around me and

I lean my head on his shoulder for a second, just appreciating being alive.

Dante's eyes find mine and I give him a small smile that he returns. Then Aiden brushes past me to kneel beside Crow in front of Dante.

Amidst the mess of blood and gore in the garden, in the aftermath of the fight, it feels as if we've won. But there's no doubt in my mind that this was only a skirmish and that bigger things are to come.

Chapter Thirty

The Otherwhere, Borderlands of Alba

The High King of Alba's left-hand man was worried.

Oswald paced. He was a man of action and disliked inactivity. Inactivity meant that he had too much time to contemplate failure. He did not appreciate being let down and yet something told him that his men had once again failed in their task. Not one of them had checked in, suggesting they had not succeeded in their attempt to kill the Blackhart and the boy. For the second time.

The attack in the park had been badly planned. It was an unexpected opportunity, but they hadn't been ready.

Convincing the female kami to betray her nephew had not been too difficult. The boy was an unknown quantity and a risk to the stability of the kami as a whole. Being half kami and half Sidhe meant that he could have inherited a vast array of potential problems from either of his parents. And with no training to speak of, his magic could be unstable. Dante could even destroy the kami and all they stood for. Naturally, the bait that she could ascend the throne as the rightful ruler of the kami had swayed her. It would be easy enough to remove the current steward in a clever bit of sleight of hand and install her as the queen.

Occasionally things went too well. He'd brushed aside her fears and had given her the reassurances she so obviously needed. He merely needed a safe way to get to the girl and the changeling. Arranging for the girl to be taken from the Garretts' garden and then following the forester's pathways when he took her back was one of Oswald's better ideas. The sluagh practically guaranteed a nice bit of mess and death for all concerned. And, to be on the safe side, he'd dispatched one of Aelfric's sorcerers, two of his trusted Sidhe warriors and a handful of redcaps as back-up. Even if all the wolves had been at home, which he knew they weren't, these would be enough to demolish the targets.

A chime from his mirror brought his pacing to an end and he turned towards it.

'Report,' he instructed, triggering the mirror's communication spell.

The kami, Yukiko, was a small shadow in the garden and her face was pale. 'All your forces are dead, Oswald.'

'Impossible. What of the sluagh?'

'Dead. They are *all dead*.'

Oswald sighed. She sounded terrified. He had no time to deal with the hysteria he suspected was coming. 'How did this happen?'

'The forester was with them. He killed the sorcerer and . . .'

'How?'

'The sorcerer? The forester trapped him amongst the roots of an old oak. The roots pulled him under.'

Oswald grimaced. 'That's certainly . . . unique. What of the soldiers?'

'The forester stabbed them to death. It was savage.'

'The sluagh?'

'The guardian killed him.'

'I'm sorry, did you say *the guardian*?'

He could see her face clearer now as she leaned closer to the mirror. Her pupils were dilated and she was so pale in the shadows that she looked like an apparition. '*The prince*, Oswald. Aelfric's son appeared out of nowhere and he just took the girl from the sluagh. And –' her voice wavered – 'he tore it apart with his bare hands. I have never heard of anyone killing a sluagh.'

'That is because it can't be done. Sluagh do not die . . . they regenerate if close enough to a leyline . . .'

'No, Oswald. He burned the sluagh. As he touched it, flames engulfed it and it burned to ash. The guardian has abilities no Fae has had in a thousand years. *Please*, Oswald. I must come back. This place is not safe.'

'Very well. Join me here. We need to report to Aelfric and explain to him how you failed him.'

'*I didn't* . . .'

'Make haste, Yukiko. The high king is not a man who likes waiting.'

She scrubbed at her face but gave a brief nod before the mirror went dark. Oswald stared at his own reflection for a long few moments before turning away. First, he had an audience to prepare for and a traitor to present to the king. He'd only just sat at his desk when there was a knock at the door. It swung open and a young Sidhe warrior walked in.

'Feran,' he said mildly, 'this is *not* a good time.'

'Sir, Lady Firesky sent me on an errand.' The man's mouth twisted, apparently seeing himself above such things. 'I thought it was a good opportunity to bring you some paper-work we found in the princeling's room.'

Oswald accepted the notebook with a raised brow. 'Is it significant?'

'Sir, he had the scrolls glamoured to resemble alchemy tracts.'

'Well then, let's see what we can see.'

Oswald skimmed the pages of careful writing and, as he read, a growing sense of unease stole over him. 'This is rather remarkable, Feran. Have you told anyone else?'

'Of course not, sir.' Feran looked offended at the thought and Oswald nodded. He was right to trust the young man. Middle son of a large, minor noble family with no career prospects. He'd joined the King's Army but had excelled in languages and strategy. Oswald had hand-picked him for his elite squad of spies and assassins, and the boy flourished.

'Good. I am pleased. The *king* will be pleased. Go and run the errands Lady Firesky demands of you and make sure you get back to the tower in a timely fashion. She must not suspect you of dawdling.'

'Yes, sir. Of course.' Feran was almost to the door when Oswald called his name.

'Feran? Good job. You've done well.'

A look of pleasure flashed across the warrior's features. He gave a brief nod before ducking his head and pulling the door shut behind hm.

Oswald sat back and traced the words on the page with a callused finger. *So it goes*, he thought. *One door closes and another opens.*

Chapter Thirty-One

Thorn looks a little lost standing in the middle of my room. He is more unkempt than I've ever seen him and he's thinner too, as if he's been so busy running that he's not stopped for long enough to eat a decent meal. He looks around the room, cataloguing my few possessions. His gaze lingers on the pendant I placed back on the mirror, and when his gaze eventually settles on me, it's almost a physical thing. It carries weight and an intent that's not lost on me.

'Kit.'

I feel strange, so just give him a tired look.

'Thorn.'

'I told you to be *careful*.'

'I was. The sluagh attacked the house and almost killed Dante and Aiden. What did you expect me to do? Stand by and watch my friends get slaughtered?'

'Aiden is a wolf, he's almost healed anyway.' The statement is baldly factual, and it shocks me. I gape at him, feeling anger uncoiling inside me.

'That's a horrible thing to say. He *can die*, Thorn. He's tough to kill, but it's possible. And what of Dante? He was almost killed too. We all almost died.'

'Dante has protection like none I've ever seen. They are

both fine, but what about you?' He gestures at me and it looks as if he wants to move towards me but he stops himself. His voice is soft and sounds raw. 'I thought I was going to lose you.'

My heart flutters at that and I swallow with difficulty. The bruises around my neck are painful. 'I'm tougher than you think. You should remember that.'

There's a heavy silence for a few moments. He looks up at me from beneath his lashes and gives a small smile. 'Let's not fight.'

'No, let's not. I have to clean up, wash the blood off my face and get changed. We have to regroup and figure out what we're doing next.'

'Someone is trying to *kill* you. You should stay safe and not put yourself in harm's way.'

'Really? You expect me to just nod quietly, embroider you a pennant and wait for you to go and have adventures all by yourself?'

He looks miserable for a second but then sighs. 'I had to try, at least.' He closes the gap between us and picks up my hand. 'Do you know how to embroider?'

'I know how to stitch wounds together, remember?' I tell him. 'That's the extent of my domestic skills.'

He nods. 'I remember.' He kisses the tips of my fingers and I try to pull away, feeling oddly vulnerable at the touch of his lips on my hand. 'I'm alive because of you. I can't bear the thought of anything happening to you, Kit.'

I drag my eyes away from him with difficulty. 'Is that why you came today?'

'I sensed you were in danger.' His other hand drifts to the small of my back and he pulls me a little closer. 'I felt your pain and knew that if I didn't intervene you'd be lost to me. I had to do something.'

'That's a very big gesture, Thorn. A little reckless, even for the guardian of the realms.'

He nods, and we're so close now that our mouths are millimetres apart. 'I don't care. I saved you. I killed the sluagh and I would do it again in a heartbeat.'

When his lips meet mine it's for the softest sweetest kiss we've ever shared. I close my eyes and let it carry me away. For a moment it's just the two of us, in my room, with all the world shut out. We're just a boy and a girl kissing. And for a handful of seconds it's exactly the right thing.

Chapter Thirty-Two

We're all cleaned up, sitting downstairs drinking tea and trying to make sense of the attacks. Crow's broken down the heavy spell he cast on the front hedges, but the door is still solid. No one is getting in. Dante is restless, moving to the window to check outside and then returning to sit next to Aiden.

Crow and Thorn are taking turns explaining their findings and the more I hear, the more concerned I'm becoming. Aiden's subdued. He's pressed tightly up against me with Dante on his other side. It's as if he feels proximity to us will anchor him and keep him safe. I link my fingers with his and gradually become aware of him relaxing against me. Dante has an arm wrapped around Aiden's shoulders and occasionally Dante's fingers would brush against my shoulder too. We make a pitiful trio of less than badass fighters.

'The goddess is dying,' Thorn is saying. 'She should have been banished with her brothers. And her hold on the Veil's growing weaker because she's growing weaker, and nothing Brixi or any of the Faceless are doing will stop that from happening.'

'So the kids? They're dying because she's using them up faster?' Dante asks Crow, who looks bleak.

'In a way. The older the children are, the more likely they are to survive.'

'We should go and fetch them, bring them back to their parents.'

'If we do that, the goddess will wake and the Veil will tear. It would be disastrous for your world.' Thorn looks at me and sighs; it's a sound too close to defeat.

I frown a little at that. 'It would be worse for yours.'

'It would be bad in general, for both our worlds.'

'What has this to do with the attacks on us?' Aiden asks. 'Why would they come here? How did they even know *how* to get here?'

'I think we were followed. When I brought Kit back from the Otherwhere, they must have tracked the route I took, forced the gateway to stay open and brought the sluagh through.'

Thorn frowns at Crow in confusion. 'Why were you with Kit in the Otherwhere?'

'Oh.' I start slightly and when I open my mouth to talk my throat closes up and I have to take a sip of tea to ease the ache. 'That was a very unexpected visit, sort of against my will.' I lean forward so I can catch Dante's eye. 'Dante's aunt brought me to the Otherwhere, before the attack. She wanted to make sure I would look after Dante until they were ready to reach out to him officially.'

'*What?*'

Crow holds up his hands as both Dante and Thorn start talking at once. 'It's true.' Crow explains far more swiftly than I would have been able to. Aiden is so out of it, he doesn't even make fun of Dante being an actual prince who may end up with his own kingdom to rule.

Thorn listens all the way through without interrupting,

but once Crow's done he's the first to speak. 'Do you think Yukiko is the one who followed you?'

'She would have had the skill to control the sluagh and there was no one else there. I would definitely have sensed them,' Crow says. 'I should have been far more careful. I knew something was off.'

Thorn clasps a hand to the forester's shoulder. 'Don't do this, my friend. You're all here, we're safe. And that is what matters ultimately.'

'The boy could have been killed. It would have been my fault.'

'But the boy is safe.' Dante's holds out a hand to Crow and Crow shakes it. 'You saved me. From my own family. Thank you for that.'

Aiden sighs softly and his grip flexes on my hand.

'Hey, you okay?' I whisper so only he can hear.

'Exhausted.'

I rub his hand and listen to his breathing. When I look up, I find Thorn's gaze on me and I give him a small smile.

'So, Yukiko is behind these attacks? And you think she wants to *kill Dante*?'

'It would appear so. And it would make sense. If she wanted the throne for herself, and Dante stands in the way.'

'What if I don't want their stupid throne? What if I just want them to acknowledge my existence and maybe teach me how to control my weird abilities? Maybe explain to me who I am and who my mother was? And why they let me go in the first instance and never thought to look for me?' Dante's scowl is dark as he jumps up to walk to the window once more. 'So now what do I do? Carry weapons with me at all times and watch out for assassins?'

'No, wait, before we get talking about that. How do the

attacks on Dante tie in with the goddess and the Veil?' I ask Thorn. 'You made it sound earlier as if these could also be linked.'

Thorn looks away from his cousin's pacing and grimaces. 'I fear if I talk of yet more prophecies Kit may stab me.'

I groan and lean back against the couch. 'You cannot be serious. What *is* it with your people and prophecies?'

Three pairs of eyes watch me warily and Aiden pushes away from me. 'You're twitchy,' he complains, moving to take up the seat Dante has vacated. His eyes start drifting shut immediately and I stare worriedly at him.

'Okay, shoot, tell us about the prophecy,' Dante says, sounding as tired as I look. 'I'm sure it's going to be great.'

'You remember the prophecy?' Thorn asks, looking at me. 'You remember how it goes?'

'The one about the Elder Gods?'

When he nods, I close my eyes, digging for it. '*Woe to the prophesied son as the Elder Gods await his coming. Upon his decision to cast aside* . . . uhm, what? Oh yes. Hold on, I've got it. *Upon his decision to cast aside what has gone before rests the fate of the world and the Elder Gods' return.*'

'*They will remake the world as it once was, bringing with them the destruction of fire and water and all will be as new.*' Thorn's voice rings beautifully in the quiet of the room and I stare at him a little.

Dante closes an eye and squints at us. 'Seriously?'

Thorn has the grace to look embarrassed. 'Well, yes. Prophecies don't have to be pretty or eloquent, do they?'

'And this is about you?'

Thorn nods silently, looking tense. 'I've found that there

is more to the prophecy and more of the prophecy. I think it's about Dante.'

'Hell, no. You're joking right?'

Aiden snorts his laughter from the far side of the couch where he's slouching, chin on his chest and eyes closed. 'Oh, this is gonna be good.'

'I approached Em.' At the name of Olga's adopted grand-father, I sit up and scowl at Thorn but he holds his hand out to me to placate me. 'No, listen to me. He has been keen to make amends after what Olga did. You should know he never had any idea of what she'd been planning with Istvan. Anyway, Em has a great many contacts, who in turn have access to stores of knowledge. We've been talking on and off for a few months now and I trust him. All the information he's shared with me in the past has proven to be accurate. I spoke to him about the rest of the prophecy because it felt incomplete and he's come up with something that I think is relevant.'

'You *trust* him?' Aiden's the one to ask the question. 'Olga was his granddaughter. She almost *killed* you. She almost killed Kit. She –' he waves his hand around irritably – 'and her brother tried to bring around the end of the world, Thorn. And you trust someone else from her family?'

'I trust Em. He's been around far longer than Olga or Istvan were. He adopted them as a favour to a friend. He had no idea what they were planning. Besides, Em thinks Olga did what she did out of loyalty to her brother. They were deluded and their actions were misplaced and it had nothing to do with Em. He hadn't seen Olga in over a century and had no idea what she'd been up to.'

'And you believe him?' Again this came from Aiden.

Thorn nods, his gaze firm. 'I do. I know she betrayed

you most of all, Aiden. You were friends, from what I remember, but Em had no part in that.'

'Okay, let's move on. Tell us about the prophecy you've found about our boy Dante here.' Aiden's lips twist when he says the word 'prophecy' and I sense that his anger is bubbling very near the surface. I wonder if focusing on Olga and her betrayal of us both is helping him come back to himself. He certainly seems more awake than before.

'It speaks of a vessel, of a person – either Fae or human – who can take the power from the Elder Gods. The vessel will then become the repository of all their magic.'

A long silence follows these words.

'And this is about me how?' Dante asks eventually.

'*One will come. Unwished for and cast aside by those who do not see his true value. He will be a vessel and take into himself the power of the Elder Gods. In him lies the ability to change the worlds.*'

If the silence before was resounding, now it echoes. I repeat the words to myself and frown.

'Okay, so *maybe*, if you squinted really hard, this could relate to Dante. Possibly.'

'Maybe.' Aiden's voice is soft and slurred.

Thorn looks so uncomfortable that I just know he's hiding something.

'There's more, isn't there?'

'*The vessel is marked by nature. He will be hunted for his abilities and by his side he will have steadfast companions, a warrior and a wolf. They will see to it that he succeeds in all things.*' Thorn frowns and looks unhappy. 'I'm translating this from our language, of course, and so it sounds stilted and odd, but that's the essence of it.'

Dante looks as if he wants to be sick. I stare at Thorn because I can't really form words right now.

'You're kidding me, right?' Aiden, once again, is the voice of reason and sass, even if he sounds half asleep. 'Again, that can be you, Thorn. You've been marked by nature – you're a bloody *dragon* – and by your side stand a warrior and a wolf.' He points at me then at himself. 'It's easy enough to make these prophecies fit whoever you want them to fit.'

'The markings,' Thorn says, gesturing at Dante's tattoo, visible above the curve of his shirt. '*The vessel is marked by nature.*'

'Do I have a say in this?' Dante asks. 'I don't want to be a vessel. I don't want to be whatever this alludes to me being.'

'What do you want, cousin?' Thorn makes a small helpless gesture. 'I'd like nothing more than for you to get what you want. To walk away from this prophecy before it binds you and traps you in its web.'

'I want to be free. I want to know who I *am*.' He turns to stand in front of Thorn. 'I want to know you. I want the chance to get to know your brothers and my other family too. I don't *want* to hide.' He looks over at me and Aiden. 'I want to be able to go out with my friends and know we won't be attacked. I want to continue working for the Spook Squad because I'm good at it. I want to make a difference.' His voice sounds raw and he puts a hand to his throat and swallows. The cut has mostly healed, but it's still red and raised. 'I just would like the chance to have things go my way for once.'

Thorn's arms go around his cousin and I have to look away as they hug. It feels too much. The memories of what that prophecy I recited did to Thorn are too raw – and now there's this new information that pulls Dante into the mix. Thorn's prophecy took away his chance to have a normal life, which hit him hard. I remember how I screamed at Dina when she came to me. How I called her a traitor because she forced her son to fulfil that prophecy. Mostly I remember what she told me before she left, when she closed my hand over the ring I now wear: that sometimes choices are taken from us and that fighting against them only leaves us bruised and battered.

I stand and leave the room, sensing Aiden doing the same, leaving the two Fae cousins to talk. Crow still looks out of it, as if he's communing with spirits beyond our realm. He stands, a silent sentinel in the lounge, watching over the sons of Alba.

Chapter Thirty-Three

'Aide,' I say when he boosts himself onto the kitchen counter, swinging his legs like a child. 'What are we doing?'

'Keeping sane?' he suggests and he looks so weary. 'You need to put ice on your neck, Kit. Those bruises are going to look really bad in the morning.'

'It's already morning,' I point out but touch the skin around my neck and wince. 'Shit. That hurts.'

'Let me help.' He jumps down and puts together a wrap of ice in a well-folded dishcloth. 'Even if you do it for a little while only, it should help keep the bruising down. Why don't you go and let the leyline help you heal?'

I tilt my head back and hiss between my teeth when he presses the icepack to my skin. 'Because I really don't want to be outside at the moment. Not with bodies in your back garden.'

'Oh yeah, that makes sense.' He grimaces. 'What do you think of the new prophecy?'

'It sucks.'

He snorts at my eloquence. 'Yes, it does. But do you think it's real?'

'Thorn seems to think it is.'

'Yeah.' His voice peters out and I glance at him. His face look drawn and I nudge him with my boot.

'What's going on with you? What did that thing do to you?'

In answer Aiden shrugs out of his shirt and I actually stop breathing for a moment. The tentacle had made a mess of him. There were cuts and bruises all over his chest and they covered his back too. He turns to show me.

'Aide, these look really bad.'

'They're better than they were.' He watches me with a wary expression as I smooth a careful thumb over what looks like a circular bruise the size of a shot glass. In the middle of the bruise is a deep cut. I lean closer and squint at it. 'What are you *doing*?' He exclaims.

'Looking. This thing tore you up. Did it suck blood out of you or did it pump something into you?'

'Both, I think. When it had its tentacles around me, I felt myself getting slower and heavier. It must use a toxin to paralyse its victims.'

I look up at him and his eyes are wide and a little wild.

'Aide, do you need to shift to heal?'

'Yeah, I think so. Will that be okay? I just need maybe an hour to get this out of my system.'

'You idiot, of course it's okay. Bloody hell. Come on, where do you want to do this?'

'My room.'

I help him up the stairs and wince when he leans on me. He's a big guy and after too little sleep, a handful of insane fights and a car crash, I'm not strong enough to bear his weight. We eventually get into his room and he shifts between one step and the next. There's this weird sense of disorientation as I see my best friend change from human to wolf.

He leaps onto the bed, circles a few times, lets out a sigh and curls up on himself. I sit next to him and sink my hands deep into his fur. He makes contented noises and I lean close and press a kiss between his eyes.

'I'll come for you in an hour. Sleep tight, wolf boy.' I stay until his eyes drift shut.

I walk back downstairs into the kitchen and reclaim the melting icepack, pushing it against my neck in the places where it hurts the most.

Dante and Thorn are talking in the lounge; they both look up, but Dante's eyes move past me, looking for Aiden.

'He shifted. Whatever the sluagh did to him really screwed him over. I took him upstairs so he can get an hour's rest.'

'We could all do with some sleep,' Dante points out and I nod in agreement, but it doesn't seem likely at all.

'Dante has been telling us about the Glow and Antone's involvement. I can't believe *Zane* is behind this.' Thorn moves up a little so I can sit next to him. I press close to him and he gives me a smile that makes my heart ache because that's the smile I miss most when he's not around. He laces his fingers with mine and I definitely don't blush at the gesture either, or so I tell myself. 'Everything that we're facing both here and in the Otherwhere makes me wonder if it's all linked. The Glow, the children not being sufficient to feed the goddess, the Veil tearing, the wolves being taken. It all feels like a strategy game.'

'It does. But how do we even play the game, if we don't know who all the players are?'

Dante looks at me in surprise. 'We know who the players are. We know Zane is involved. We know about Merrick and the Jericho Gang.'

'I think what Kit means,' Crow says, and I startle because

he's been so quiet that I forgot he was even present, 'is that as strong as Zane is, he doesn't fit as the head of this sprawling plot. He has connections in both the Sun King and Suola's Courts, as well as having access to the High King's Court, but it's not enough.'

'Who then? The Sun King himself? Queen Suola?' I stare at them. 'Any of the other foreign Fae courts?'

'How about your father?' Dante says, jerking his chin in Thorn's direction.

Thorn's expression freezes and he looks grim. For a second I think he's going to pull the *my father is the king, and you do not question the king* line, but then he just nods and something inside me shifts.

'You can't be *serious*?' I say. 'You actually suspect your father could be behind this?'

'It is not something I would put past him.'

'He's your *father*.'

'Who does whatever he likes,' Thorn says quietly, 'and says it is for the good of Alba. And no one at his Court or in any of the other Courts thinks to move against him.'

I want to question him further but I see a flash of warning in Crow's eyes and realize now isn't perhaps the best time to do that. Something must have happened between Thorn and his father for him even to react this way and I'm hesitant to push the matter further.

'So we have to find out who's behind this. And tie it all together.' Dante's not oblivious to the undercurrents in the room, but as usual he brings our attention back to the matter at hand. 'How do we do that?'

'I go back with Crow,' Thorn says. 'I take the bodies of the fallen Sidhe to Court and tell the story of how a sluagh came to the Frontier and was set to attack the wolves and the Lady Blackhart. I make a scene and see who runs for cover.' He smiles wryly. 'I can do that now, you know. I *am* the guardian of the realms. People have to answer to me.'

'Don't go crazy with all that power,' I joke back but it's strained. 'We don't want anyone coming after you to shut you up.'

'Let them come. I have a few tricks up my sleeve I'd like to show them.'

He stands and we all follow suit. His arm settles around my waist and the move is so natural that I don't even notice it, until I see Dante's pointed glance in my direction. I feel like pushing him into the wall, but Thorn tightens his grip slightly and he must think I'm trying to move away from him. So I ignore Dante and follow Crow as he leads us to the back door, stepping outside onto the small patio that overlooks the garden.

'What about the –' I jerk a thumb back towards the front door – 'slab of wood that used to be their door?'

'The spell will wear off in about an hour,' Crow says, as if it's no big deal. 'You can still leave through the basement, correct?'

'It's not the most convenient way, but it will do,' Dante says, and Crow regards him with affection.

'You're doing remarkably well, boy. Your glamour holds even when you fight and that is truly impressive. I have seen older, trained Fae, unable to control themselves the way you do. I believe that Yukiko does not speak for all your family. I will do my utmost to speak to someone else – your grandmother, perhaps – and see if they sanction Yukiko's behaviour. I very much doubt it. The kami are not devious. They are creatures and spirits of great compassion and beauty, but sometimes they are too naive for their own good.'

Dante doesn't say anything. Instead he grips Crow's arm and submits to being drawn into a hug. My hip buzzes and I pull my phone out, seeing Jamie's name lit up on the screen. I ignore the call and turn in Thorn's arms. I stand on tiptoes and brush my lips against his, placing a kiss on the corner of his mouth.

'Don't be a stranger, Thorn.' I step back and away from the hand that reaches for me and I immediately feel a bit lost. But then he smiles and blushes slightly, and I feel a giddy rush of pleasure knowing that it's for me.

'Don't get into more trouble without me, Kit Blackhart,' he replies softly, before turning towards Dante to hug his cousin. 'Be careful, all of you. I'll be in touch as soon as we know more about everything, including the prophecy.'

Dante and I watch Crow and Thorn drag the three Sidhe bodies and the charred remains of the sluagh to the side. There's a dizzying sense of Crow and Thorn's magic as they open a gateway and then they're both stepping sideways, and the garden returns to normal.

'Our lives are far too exciting,' Dante says heavily and I nod, unable to deny it. 'But, you know, I think we have some good people watching our backs.'

I grin. 'I need more coffee and must call my uncle Jamie – to tell him how we fought a monster in the Garretts' garden and survived.'

'Yes, let's not forget that part. Will you mention your boyfriend to him?'

I open my mouth to deny that Thorn's my boyfriend, but then Dante holds up a finger and I close my mouth with a snap.

'You realize Thorn possibly bent time and space to get to you as fast as he did? He sensed you were dying, Kit, and he came to save you.' Dante's gaze is intense as he stares at me. 'Saving me and Aiden was just an added bonus.'

I wrinkle my nose. Dammit, he was right. Thorn did in fact save my life. I'm not sure how I feel about that, as I'm used to fighting my own battles, but somewhere inside me something warm and fuzzy grows a little bit warmer and fuzzier.

Chapter Thirty-Four

'Jamie, will you just stop shouting for a *minute*?'

I try to hold the phone far enough away from my ear so I'm not assaulted by Jamie's parade-ground voice, which alternates between swearing in Russian, possibly French and Italian, and definitely English. To say that my uncle is angry is to put it mildly. That he's angry with me is a given. I grimace in apology to Dante, who looks more and more alarmed the longer Jamie's speaker-phone tirade lasts.

'He'll run out of steam in a second,' I tell Dante, putting my hand over the speaker. 'I think we've gone through most of the swearwords he knows now.'

Dante's look is pained but he keeps quiet until Jamie's voice peters out – more because he has to take a breath than because he's finished with me.

'Jamie?'

'You've been irresponsible. You've been stupid and reckless.' Jamie's voice echoes through the room again and I stare at the wooden slab that is the front door. 'Everything I've taught you, Kit. Everything, and you just . . . you ignore it all because . . . I don't even know why. What were you *thinking*?'

'Dante's a good guy, Jamie.'

'He is *Fae*, Kit. And he was abandoned by his family in the human world. Do you have any idea how that can fu— screw someone up? Someone who obviously has a lot of magic potential? I *knew* something was going on when you called me the other month, asking me about changelings. God, I have been so stupid. You've put our family in jeopardy. Do you realize that you've compromised our standing with the Courts by hiding this kid? Everything we've done since can be called into question. We do *not* take sides, Kit. We work for the Courts and keep the balance on their behalf. Hiding this changeling could be our *undoing*. And to make things worse, he's the son of a traitor.' Jamie snorts and I can practically hear him scrub at his face, the way he does when he's had enough of me and the trouble I get myself into. 'Andrew is going to be so pissed off.'

'You think keeping a kid no older than Marc and Megan alive is a bad idea, Jamie?' I counter. 'You've not even *met* Dante. How can you stand there and judge him? He is a good guy. He's saved my life a number of times and I've saved his. It's what friends do, Jamie. It's what *family* does, right? Isn't that what you've taught me since I became a Blackhart?'

'You never *became* a Blackhart, Kit. You were a Blackhart since the day you were born.'

'Lucky me,' I shoot back. 'Lucky me to be dumped in this world where practically every day I have to fight for my life against monsters that no one else can see. Lucky me that I've been left to my own devices by uncles and cousins who are moving on with their lives, leaving me to deal with all of this *by myself*.'

Dante opens his mouth to say something, but I give him

a short sharp shake of the head and he just leans back against the chair, spinning his empty mug between his fingers.

'Kit, you know that's not true. We're all here for you if you need us.'

'Really? And where are you now, Jamie? Hawaii? India?'

'The Philippines, actually.'

'So not a five-minute journey away, then. Jamie, I am doing my best here with what I've been taught. By you and Uncle Andrew. And if I tell you guys that Dante is a good guy and that we have to help him and that we have to stand with him against whatever trouble's coming our way, you need to agree with me.'

'You have had a sluagh sent against you. Assassins tried to kill you when you went jogging, Kit. For God's sake. He is the son of a traitor to the High King of Alba. That is huge. If Aelfric finds out we've been harbouring someone who has the potential to try to overthrow him, the Blackharts could be brought in on charges of treason and conspiracy to commit regicide against Alba's crown.'

'Hi, excuse me.' Dante clears his throat and it sounds like it hurts. 'For the record, that's definitely not something I want to do, okay? I don't want to be a prince or a king or, uh, anything like that. I just want to know who my family is so I can meet them. And have someone tell me what I am. And to train me how to use whatever powers I have.' He looks so tense I worry he's going to just explode. 'And I want to continue working as a Spook. I belong here, in the human world. It's what I've known all my life and I'd like to keep working with Kit. She's been my partner on the Child Thief case and we work well together. I am not going to steal Aelfric's crown or become the ruler of a bunch of nature spirits or whatever my family's supposed to be. I just want a normal life.'

The silence from Jamie is heavy and I close my eyes, waiting for the blast of angry words, but they don't come. Then Jamie speaks up again.

'I need to talk to Andrew. We've got to sort this out. I need to make calls about Connor and Shaun. We're helping the wolves, so I need you and Aiden to be ready to go when I call you with any information.' He hesitates. 'Is that clear?'

'Yes.' I look at Dante. 'All three of us will be ready.'

'Kit . . .' his warning tone makes me flinch.

'Either Dante does this with us, or I sit it out with him.'

I close my eyes against the sound of something smashing into the wall in the background at the other end of the line, followed by some startled yelling. 'Don't do anything stupid,' Jamie says, and his tone is clipped as he ends the call. And if anyone can end a mobile phone call aggressively, then Jamie manages to do it.

I turn to look at Dante but it's Aiden who catches my eyes. He pushes away from the door behind us and walks into the lounge looking rumpled but far better than he did just under an hour ago.

'That went about as well as I expected it to go,' he says, and he looks at both Dante and me with frustrated affection. 'You guys are impossible together. What did you *think* would happen?'

'That Jamie would listen to reason, maybe,' I say, and grin at him as I take a seat.

'Yeah, that was never gonna happen, Blackhart – you know that.'

I shrug and spin my phone on the table. 'Kyle sent me a text before I rang Jamie. The tracker on the Jericho Gang guys stopped working, so we don't know where they've gone either.'

'Did Kyle say why the tracker stopped?'

'The signal disappeared. So they either found the tracker in the jewellery box or the thing just stopped working. I'm surprised it worked as long as it did. Electronics and magic just don't mix very well. And listen, let's not ever mention that Kyle actually knows about Dante being Fae. He's scared his dad's going to have a fit about it. Only you, me and Kyle know about Dante being, you know, a sexy siren Fae in training.'

Dante snorts at my description and shoves Aiden when he gives the older boy a knowing glance in response.

'I don't think getting sexy is part of the training, though, right?' Aiden opines and I start laughing because his flirting is awful and it makes me happy.

'You're terrible,' I tell him and he nods, looking smug.

'I know, and you love me for it.'

'I do not, stupid werewolf.'

'Stupid human.'

'I have magic.'

'I have claws. And fangs.'

I scowl at him. 'You're ugly.'

He sags dramatically and clutches at his heart.

'Babe, you gonna defend my honour?' he demands of Dante, who just shakes his head and gets up from the couch.

'You called me *babe*. No one calls me *babe*.' Dante's look is arrogant as he sweeps from the room and Aiden just stares after him in shock.

'Babe is a great nickname,' he tells me, looking solemn.

'No, Aide, not really.'

Dante walks back in with my laptop and shoves it at

Aiden. 'Make the tracker work. We've wasted enough time being distracted.'

'We were attacked. By monsters. And sorcerers.'

'Still, wasting time. Come on. Let's figure out where your brothers are being kept so we can clear this mess up. I need to sleep.'

Aiden gets to it pretty fast. 'Did Kyle say anything else?' he asks me after about ten minutes of doing mysterious stuff in a software program that looks both archaic and futuristic.

In answer I pass my phone to him. 'Talk geek to my cousin. He mentioned tracking them to a certain point and then something blah blah, electronics, sunspots, I don't know.'

He grabs my phone and hits Kyle's number and I wander into the lounge to turn on the TV. There are three channels off the air but I keep pressing buttons until I find one of the big international news channels. They seem to be talking almost exclusively about the weather. There's concern about massive weather fronts moving in and terms like weather bombs were being thrown about. I watch in shock as they show footage of the sea striking the north-western shores of Scotland and Ireland, with up to forty-five-foot swells battering the coast.

Unprecedented storms also meant lightning strikes had cut power across areas of Scotland, the Western Isles and parts of Northern Ireland.

The screen switches to footage of Iceland and huge drifts of snow. And, although it's a country known for its harsh winters and snowfall, it's struggling to cope. Emergency services and the army have been called in to try to reach remote communities to bring people to safety. There's more, and after about half an hour of this my mind is reeling with the enormity of the problem. It's completely out of hand.

'Okay, listen, we've got a route,' Aiden calls out and I jerk with surprise, noticing that Dante's come to sit next to me and I didn't even see. 'The tracker headed towards Welwyn Garden City, past that, along the motorway and then we lost them. But then it shows up near Coventry again, and since then, there's nothing.'

'Do you think they found the device?'

Aiden shrugs. 'It's possible.' He rummages around in one of the large drawers in the kitchen and comes back carrying a large AA map book. 'Let's map this out.'

'Let me call Leo and check something with him,' I say. Aiden waves at me to go ahead as he leans over the map looking at the tracker info, tracing the roads with his finger.

Leo answers on the third ring. 'Hello, pretty girl,' he breezes and I laugh because he sounds delighted that I've called.

'Hello, hipster boy. Why are you out of breath?'

'I'm running,' he says, a little breathlessly. 'To keep in shape. It's all for you, of course.'

'That's so sweet, but so unnecessary.'

'I know, but I can dream. So, why are you calling me?'

'I need to know where our friend Caleb lives,' I say.

'You can't be serious.'

'Like . . . deadly serious. There's also been kidnapping. Aiden's brothers have been taken.'

'Shit. Are they okay? Is there a ransom? How's Aide?'

'He's fine, but it's a close thing. Connor and Shaun, though . . . we don't know,' I trail off. 'But we really need more information to sort this out.'

'Write this down,' he says.

I grab my notebook and a pen, and cradle the phone while I write down the details he gives me. I frown at the string of numbers and repeat them back to make sure I have them right.

'Kyle will know what to do with it,' he tells me. 'I knew you'd phone me to get this. I argued with my dad about giving me the address. I hate passing it along because I know you guys are going to do something stupid, but, Kit, listen to me when I tell you to stay clear of this completely, as much as you can. These guys are not nice.'

'I can't promise anything, Leo. We have to do something. They already tried kidnapping us earlier. We got away, but Leo, if we don't act, they'll just keep coming.'

There's an unhappy silence on the line and I wait for him to process what I've just said. All I can hear is the sound of traffic in the background. 'Tell Aiden not to lose his head. Call me when you guys are done.'

'I will. And thanks, Leo.'

'You're not welcome. Just stay as safe as you can.'

He rings off and I wordlessly hand Kyle the string of numbers and go to make coffee.

Chapter Thirty-Five

Aiden grins at the note and shakes it like it's his 'eureka' moment. 'I love that guy. He's made it so easy. This is how we passed notes at school. It's a cipher.'

I prod his shoulder as I pass him his coffee. 'Get to work.'

He sets to work on the code and five minutes later he holds up an actual address. 'It's about an hour away from where the tracker stopped working. Do I get a cookie now?'

'Go get changed. We're dressing for a long ride.' Dante taps Aiden's shoulder as he continues talking. 'Ring your dad too. Let him know we've got info and have him get in touch with Kit's uncle. We need everyone to know what's happening and where we're going.'

We split up and head to our rooms. I layer up, shoving my gloves and beanie into my backpack, along with my notepad and iPod. It is going to be a long drive.

When I pull open my door, Aiden's standing there, holding his own backpack and a jacket. He looks at me and behind those pretty eyes of his I see the fear he's been trying to hide from both me and Dante. I reach up and give him a brief hug.

'Your brothers are gonna be okay. We're going to go in

and get them out. Even if we tear down the entire world around them. Connor and Shaun are like family to me too.'

He nods and holds out the jacket to me. 'Here, it's warmer than that leather jacket.'

I lean my backpack and sword against the wall and take it from him. Although it's a bit too big for me in the arms, it fits well enough, giving me space for more layers beneath. 'Thanks. Whose is it?'

'Mine. When I was like twelve.' Then he's laughing and I consider pushing him down the stairs.

Dante joins us with his own go-bag and we head to the basement garage. Aiden stops short, staring at the handful of cars. 'I forgot the Cayenne's all screwed up because of the accident.'

'Any of these would do,' I tell him but he shakes his head.

'No, Dante struggles with the iron and steel.' He looks thoughtful. 'I had the Cayenne fitted out so that the iron and steel wouldn't bother him so much.' He points to the Audi. 'How about Kit rides shotgun and you sit in the back, Dante?'

Dante blinks, seemingly touched by Aiden's consideration. 'Yeah, that's fine. I get to catch some sleep then.'

Aiden grabs the keys to the powerful Audi I drove to the North London Hold and we settle ourselves in. As I pull my seatbelt on I look at him.

'What's our plan, by the way?'

He starts the engine and frowns at me. 'I thought you had a plan.'

'My plan was just . . . you know –' I motion vaguely with my hands – 'go to that address, kick ass and take your brothers back.'

'How are you two still alive?' Dante asks from the back seat. He's settled himself as far away from the doors as he can get and is dressed warmly in a thick black jacket and roll-neck jumper. The way Aiden looks at him I wonder if I'll have to take over driving so he can climb all over Dante halfway through the drive. 'I spoke to my boss at the SDI. He's going to speak to your uncle Andrew. They know what we want to do and I'm hoping they'll come in with back-up. We're not giving them a lot of time to act, but it means they can't really stop us.'

'Excellent. Let's get this show on the road.'

I fall asleep somewhere after Welwyn Garden City. It's thankfully dreamless and I wake up an hour and a half later to the buzzing of my phone in my pocket.

'Ngggh.' My eloquence is staggering and I scowl at the screen blearily. 'Un'le Andrew?'

'We've booked flights to the UK. We'll be there tomorrow,' he says without preamble. 'Both Megan and I are coming. Your aunt Jennifer is still in China, but she'll be flying in in the next few days.'

'Okay.'

'Why do you sound awful?'

'I've just woken up from falling asleep for the first time in maybe twenty-four hours,' I say, gratefully taking an energy drink from Dante. 'Why are you all coming to England?'

'Because things are getting out of hand. I'm calling a family meeting.'

'Oh.'

'Keeping the fact that you've been working with a Fae

and hiding his real identity from the family is not the way to endear yourself to me, Kit.'

'I know. Jamie already threw his tantrum at me. I feel crappy.'

'Language.' But there's no real censure there, just tiredness. 'Jamie's been working his contacts in Special Branch and it sounds as if he's managed to get them very interested in the Garretts' kidnapping. Aiden's dad has given us all the information he has on this too, so you guys won't be going in alone.'

'We're *not?*' At the shocked tone in my voice Aiden turns to look at me, tapping his ear. I fumble the phone and find the speaker. 'I'm putting you on speakerphone, Uncle Andrew, so the boys can hear you too.'

'Who'll be meeting us, sir?' Aiden asks, never taking his eyes off the road. It's been raining on and off the entire time we've been driving and the traffic heading out of London was heavy, as usual.

'Friends of Jamie's. They're *aware* of a couple of things, supernaturally, but even so don't push your luck and wolf out on them when you get angry. You might get shot.'

Aiden snorts. 'I'll remember that.'

'I'm sure this will go okay. These guys have been after the Jericho Gang for a long time.'

'How does Jamie know them?' I ask but Andrew makes a noncommittal noise in the back of his throat.

'There are some things I don't need to know. I think probably from his Forces days. For now, just get to the services. I'm texting you which one it is as soon as it's confirmed. Wait there for the team to show up. They're solid guys, apparently. Jamie's trusting them with your safety and vice versa. *Don't* screw up.'

'We'll try,' I promise, trying to sound solemn but then Aiden spoils it by unexpectedly laughing.

'But you never know,' he says. 'We're like the start of a bad joke: a human, a faerie and a werewolf walk into a bar . . .'

Andrew mutters something beneath his breath, but then he says, 'Not until you can all legally drink, I hope. It's a good one, though. What's the punch line?'

'I'm not sure yet. They all walk out alive afterwards?'

'That works,' he agrees. 'Kit, please be careful. All three of you. Don't take unnecessary risks.'

'We'll do our best, Uncle Andrew. We'll see you guys tomorrow.'

I have never felt more disreputable in my life. We meet a group of six people – four guys and two women – in the parking area of a large service station off the motorway to Birmingham. They look as if they're heading out for a big hike somewhere. They're all dressed in warm clothes and hiking boots that look military issue. The two girls have hair shorter than mine. One of the guys, no older than twenty-five, has long blond hair and looks as if he'd be more at home on a beach somewhere with a surfboard under his arm. Everyone else looks *military* somehow, despite outward appearances, and I blame this thought on Jamie. Two of the guys have ugly beards and look civilian enough – given the way they dress and stand around drinking from take-away cups of coffee. But they don't fool me and they're all sporting ink of some sort, even the girls. I struggle to pinpoint what's off and it comes to me – they move as a team, and a disciplined one at that. There's an awareness of their surroundings about them that I've not really seen in others outside my family and the Garrett pack.

I'm aware that Aiden, Dante and I don't look like much, but then sometimes it's a good idea to be underestimated. I stand tall and lift my chin a little, pulling my shoulders back even though all of me aches from too many bruises and fights over the past few days.

The leader of the six, Hawke, has piercing grey eyes in a craggy face and he's one of the beard-wearers. I can't figure out how old he is. When his eyes rest on me I have the urge to snap to attention and call him 'sir' in an un-ironic way. But no one else calls him anything apart from Hawke. The girls, we learn, are sisters. Emily and Jane look alike enough to be twins, and they don't look older than their mid-twenties. The guy with the long blond hair is Rocco, and when he speaks it's with a Californian accent. The last two guys (Johann and Rick) don't say much and they remind me even more of Jamie, in the way they hold themselves and subtly watch everything that's going on.

'Jamie tells us it's your brothers who've been taken,' Hawke says, staring at Aiden. 'I think I've worked with one of them in the past. Connor: about six-three, two-forty, has the sense of humour of a MAC truck?'

'Yeah, that sounds like my big brother.' Aiden nods and grins. 'Sorry if he made a bad impression. He's not the best with people.'

'Cillian thinks very highly of him,' Jane says.

Aiden's chin jerks up and he stares at her in surprise. 'Cillian?' he repeats and she nods, seemingly oblivious to his reaction. Hawke, though, watches Aiden with interest.

'Yeah, he's the one who teamed us up with Connor the first time. We took out a nest of . . .' Jane's voice trails off and she grimaces. 'Ah, I can't tell you about that because officially it didn't happen. Sorry.'

'No, it's okay.' Aiden's expression is tight and controlled and I step forward to draw Hawke's attention.

'We've got the location,' I tell him. 'If you have a map we can show you.'

For the next few minutes, we pore over the maps. Listening to Hawke and his guys talk about entry points and perimeters relaxes me with its familiarity. This is the kind of talk I can handle.

In the end it's simple enough: Aiden, Dante and I will be Team B. We go in once Team A (Hawke, Johann and Jane) have secured the outside. Emily and Rick will cover us as our snipers and I'm not sure what Rocco will be doing, but he just grins crazily at us.

'We hit fast and we extract your brothers. We'll have a helicopter on standby two farms over, so all we have to do is get them that far,' Hawke says. 'The heli belongs to your family, I think?' He nods to me and I shrug.

'If you say so.'

'The pilot is called Isak?'

'Yeah, it's my great-aunt's helicopter. Isak is in her employ.'

'If we pull this off and we get Aiden's brothers away safely, remind me to send her a fruit basket.'

'Oh, I think she'd prefer a bottle of whisky,' I say, and Hawke looks surprised for a moment.

'I like her more already,' he says, and claps his hands. 'All right then, folks. Move out.'

We head back to the cars after a quick refreshment break and a frantic round of coffee, tea and sandwich purchases. We pull out ahead of the black van onto the motorway.

Dante's the first to speak. 'Things are moving faster than I anticipated.'

'If Cillian's involved, this is going to be over before we know it,' Aiden says. 'He runs a tight ship.'

'Who's Cillian?' Dante demands.

I try to catch his eye, but he ignores me and sits forward in his seat so he can stare at Aiden.

'He's my brother,' Aiden says moodily, staring at the road.

'You don't like him?'

'He doesn't really like us,' Aiden clarifies but his voice is flat. 'Cillian was born human. It happens, sometimes, and when he turned eighteen he just upped and left, saying he doesn't want anything to do with the pack, with us, any more.'

'And yet he suggested Connor work with Hawke and his team.'

'Cillian is a contractor. He's ex-military. He does stuff for governments most governments would deny completely. He uses people as tools. Connor obviously was the best fit for whatever needed to be done so he got him working with Rocco. Trust me when I say Cillian isn't the sentimental kind.' Aiden shrugs and overtakes a slow-moving car in the middle lane. 'It's weird. Sometimes I miss him, other times I remember how much he disliked being at home and the fights he got into with my parents and other pack members. It's better if he's not around.'

'I'm sorry.' Dante sits back after gripping Aiden's shoulder sympathetically. 'That sucks.'

'Family, right? Can't live with them and can't actually live with them.'

'Family's not just about blood,' I say into the silence. He

glances at me questioningly so I continue, 'It's who we choose to spend time with. It's about people who have each other's backs in bad times and not just good times. That's what family's all about. It's a Hawaiian concept Nan taught me. Family can mean blood relatives or adopted relatives or friends. A unit against the world. The Hawaiian word is *ohana* and I really like the idea of it.'

'I like it too.' Dante's smile swings from my face to Aiden's and settles there briefly.

'*Ohana*. Yeah, I like that, Blackhart. It's like being part of a pack,' Aiden says.

'I'd rather be *ohana* than pack,' I say, grinning. 'Less hair-shedding to deal with.'

Without taking his eyes off the road, he reaches out and tries to pinch my leg and mock-fights with me as I try to get away. It's only after Dante demands we behave that we settle down again, the air lighter. I pass around the food and we listen to the news. Yet again, it warns of unseasonably heavy storms for early December in the UK, plummeting temperatures and snow across the mainland – all being driven by the so-called weather bomb.

Chapter Thirty-Six

We stop once more, near Walsall. Rocco brings out the kind of equipment that would make Kyle geek-freak out and I take a step back from it. Dante does the same and Hawke gives us each a searching look.

'Electronics,' I say. 'They don't like us. I don't want to be liable for screwing up whatever the big guy's trying to do there.'

'I built this baby myself,' Rocco assures me, running a hand over the keyboard. 'She can withstand a nuclear blast and still be up and running in less than five minutes.'

Hawke turns back to Rocco and I'm interested to see what they're doing. I edge closer and peer over their shoulders. The laptop, if we can call it that, is small and compact, no bigger than a tablet. However, it looks sturdy, encased in a solid-looking rubber housing. It definitely looks home-made. Rocco sees me leaning in and beckons me closer.

'I've piggy-backed onto a satellite,' he says. 'We'll be able to see the entire compound soon, but I estimate that we'll have about ten minutes before we lose the satellite once we get there.' He looks at Hawke, who nods. 'That means we have to be fast, otherwise we're going in blind and you guys don't want that.'

'No, you definitely don't want to go in blind. Rocco will be our eyes.' Hawke turns away and takes a small black case from Jane. He opens it to reveal comms equipment. 'Put these on now so we can check them before we get to the compound. Keep talking to a minimum once we get there.'

Jane helps us secure the ear- and mouthpieces. They're small and don't seem particularly robust. My earpiece fits neatly and the mouthpiece disappears beneath my scarf against the skin of my throat. There is no way, dressed like this with my beanie on, that anyone would remotely suspect I'm microphoned up.

'Rocco built these too, so they should be okay for you to use. Please don't lose them or break them,' Jane says, adjusting Aiden's. 'Because he will cry like a girl over his first break-up if you do. I've seen it happen.'

In answer Rocco flips her off but then he taps his watch. 'Fifteen minutes till we're ready. Let's go.'

We head to the Audi and they all climb back into the van. We follow their vehicle this time. We each get to check our comms too and listen to the others do the same. I make sure mine's turned off and then sag back against the passenger seat, breathing shakily. Both Aiden and Dante look tense and Dante glances at me as I bite my lip.

'There's going to be shooting,' I say. 'I'm not sure how I feel about that.'

'The Jericho Gang aren't good guys,' Dante points out. 'Drugs, guns, and we've been told they kill people – so they've most likely done a lot of other very unpleasant stuff.'

'They have Connor and Shaun. And they tried to take all three of us hostage.' Aiden glances at me. 'We're going to be okay. These guys seem pretty together.'

'But there are nine of us and who knows how many of the Jericho Gang,' I say, feeling panic rising. 'I'm less concerned about the gangsters and I'm more worried about Hawke and his team. I mean, they all look so *nice*.'

The boys stare at me and then they start laughing. I blink in confusion because I'm pretty sure I've not said anything funny at all.

'Kit, Hawke and his team? They've probably done very bad things for our government. Deniable things in countries we can't even pronounce, so I'm pretty sure they can handle a handful of gangsters.'

I slump further. 'That still doesn't matter. I don't like putting good people in danger.'

Dante pats my shoulder. Sooner than I like, we've turned off an A-road and we're shooting along a narrow country road and I turn my comms back on and so do the boys.

'This is Alpha Team,' Hawke rumbles in my ear. 'ETA: five minutes.'

Johann is driving the van and he doesn't indicate when he turns, just ahead of us. Aiden swears, swinging the Audi's nose behind the van, up a narrow rutted dirt track. We travel fast and it's getting dark, with the clouds lying thick and heavy on the horizon.

Johann parks near some trees and we all clamber out of our vehicles. I grab my sword, check the baton strapped to my wrist and make sure it flicks out fast and controlled. I secure my knives and check that they slide out easily. I look up when I feel eyes on me; Hawke's watching me with an expression close to admiration.

'What?' I ask him, wondering if there's something wrong with the way I've adjusted my knives, but he just shakes his head.

'To be honest, you Blackharts are the only people I know who take blades into a gunfight.'

I grimace at him. 'Guns – I don't like them. They don't like me.'

He holds up a small compact pistol. I know I should know what it's called because Jamie's trained me to recognize the most common weapons on sight. 'You sure I can't convince you to use one of these?'

I pat my sword. 'No, my blade doesn't run out of ammo,' I tell him and he grins and, when I look round, I see his team shares his amusement.

Rocco soon has his laptop out again and Hawke points at the compound, outlined on the screen via satellite imagery. Hawke hustles us close. 'Game plan is this: snipers take out the guards here and here. I lead Team A in and we take out as many as we can. Team B, you guys follow once we've secured the area and you get the Garrett brothers out. Clear?'

'Roger that.' Hawke's team splits in two. Rick and Emily disappear into the trees and I watch as they appear on the satellite image as two dots outlined in green. They move incredibly fast in the dark. Even with my sight, I tend to take things slower at night but neither of them hesitates. 'In position,' Emily murmurs in my ear. Next is Rick. 'Got you. We're ready, Team Leader.'

Hawke gestures and we follow him into the darkness. He uses hand signals to direct Jane and Johann and they spread out in a sweeping motion towards the large compound. He points to Aiden next, then towards what looks like a shed. Aiden nods and moves off stealthily. Hawke pushes his fist down towards me and Dante and we stay put.

'I can see four guards on the far perimeter. Now three.

Two.' Rocco's voice is a soft murmur in my ear. 'Now, one. And we're clear. Good shooting, Emily.'

'Thanks, Roc.'

'I've got movement at my nine,' Rick says. 'I can't see. What's going on, Roc?'

'A deer. Just pushing through the undergrowth. You'll be fine.'

For a few seconds there's silence, then Rick breathes, 'It's gone. Bloody wildlife.'

It carries on like this as we move steadily closer to the compound, Emily and Rick sniping and covering us. Aiden ghosts back to us in the darkness and my hand tightens on the fighting knife in my hand when I see his dark shape come running.

'There's someone in the shed,' he says, low and clear, not using the comms. His eyes meet mine in the near dark. 'I can hear four heartbeats. Two of them I know as well as my own. The other two . . . I can't tell who they are.'

I frown at him because he is staring at me very intently and then he deliberately makes an explosion gesture with his fingers, keeping his back to Hawke.

I close my eyes because I get it. Magic. Someone in the shed with Connor and Shaun is a sorcerer.

'Hawke,' I say into the comms. 'How much do you know about us?'

'Here we go,' someone says, and I'm not sure if it's Rocco or Johann. 'Here's the stuff they didn't want to tell us.'

'I know some things, Blackhart. What's going on?'

'The shed. That's where they're keeping Shaun and Connor. But they're not alone.'

'We didn't think that they would be. How many more are there?'

'Two. Which shouldn't be a problem – except that one of them is a sorcerer.'

The silence on the comms is deafening.

'When you say sorcerer, you're not using it as some kind of *code* are you?'

'No, sir. I mean a sorcerer that taps into the magic of the energy lines that criss-cross the earth and then bends that energy to their will.'

'I suddenly wish I'd taken the R&R I was signed up for,' Rick gripes in my ear, but I hear him adjust his weapon. 'If you can get the sorcerer into the wide open, I can take him down.'

'They have magic,' I point out.

'And I've got high-velocity armour-piercing rounds. I don't see any of this as an issue.'

I roll my eyes but Aiden grins at me. 'Come on. Let's give it a try.'

We move through the night, changing our trajectory. Hawke sticks close to Aiden, weapon up, flanking him. Dante's even quieter than Aiden and he brings up the other side, sticking close to me.

'Plan?' I whisper, knowing Aiden would hear me.

'I howl. They come out. We take them out.'

'That's a terrible plan.'

'But it will work.'

'Wait. I have a plan. Give me five minutes,' I say, sliding past him. Hawke makes an abortive grab for my arm but I sidestep him and move into the cold night. My hand closes over the ever-present chalk in my pocket and I kneel down on the ground and sketch a circle in front of me. By my estimate we're about fifteen metres from the door of the shed. All Aiden has to do is get the sorcerer into the circle and I can do the rest.

The chalk glides over the ground, skimming leaves, and I close my eyes, opening myself up to my magic. It rushes out of me in a flood and I sway as it hits me full on. It feels fantastic and the lethargy I've been suffering is wiped away. I anchor myself and cast the circle, using a binding spell I taught myself and altered to fit my needs (usually speed and accuracy). I embed the spell as firmly as I can. I next step out of the circle and walk it three times in the right direction, or deosil, keeping my hand out to ensure the lines I've drawn and cast meet and match. As I do, I will energy into the lines and speak the spell over and over. I repeat it nine times, the Latin tripping off my tongue faster than I would ever have imagined months ago. I kneel down and quickly sketch two Norse binding runes on opposite sides of the circle too, just in case. I walk the circle three more times, binding the runes together and linking them with the initial spell.

I step back and give Aiden a thumbs-up. We all melt into the darkness and Dante pulls me towards him so we can stand in the shadows of the dark undergrowth.

If I wasn't expecting the sound it would have made me sob. A wolf's howl is a personal thing and I've never heard Aiden's before. It starts low and seems to tremble in the cold air around me. There's a muttered 'Jesus' in my ear from someone over the comms. The sound is long and raw and beautiful. Dante's fingers flex on my arm and I grip him back, because, yes, the sound tears at me too. Aiden is calling to his brothers, to his pack-mates, and the sound holds all the worry he's been trying to deflect since he heard they were taken. The sound swells, becoming louder, and in the timbre I hear a snarl of anger but he tempers it back as the howl fades away.

For a few seconds there's nothing, no sound and no movement in the all-encompassing darkness. Then the sound of wood shattering rends the air. It's coming from the shed, followed by another cry that sounds very human. It's cut off with a garbled yelp and I straighten, gripping my sword tightly. Aiden moves towards the door and he's doing the *I'm bigger now* stance that intimidates people so much. The way he moves tells me he's listening to what's going on inside the shed. He looks over at where I'm hidden in the shadows with Dante.

'The sorcerer killed the human,' Aiden's voice says in my ear. 'He's got the area and the door warded, so I can't get in there.'

'Your brothers?'

'I can hear them. Their heartbeats are slow.'

'They are drugged.'

He nods at my words and somewhere Hawke swears.

'Kid, if we blow up that shed, will your brothers make it?'

'Yes, but I'm not keen to blow up my family. I mean, they annoy me sometimes, but no one deserves to be blown up.'

Hawke snorts. 'Rocco. How much time?'

'Three minutes, then we lose the satellite.'

'Emily, get ready with that weapon of yours.'

'Roger that, H.'

Chapter Thirty-Seven

'Here's what I want you to do, kid,' Hawke says to Aiden. 'I want you to make a hell of a racket outside that shed. Can you do that?'

Aiden nods and within seconds it sounds as if the forest itself has come alive and is trying to implode. Aiden howls and snarls around the shed, lunging at the walls a few times. I can only imagine what it must sound like from the inside of the shed itself. Hawke watches for a few seconds before he lifts his gun and fires two shots into the nearest tree. The noise startles us all and Aiden ducks low but doesn't stop his noise-making.

As bold as brass, Hawke walks up to the shed door, puts a finger to his lips and gestures for Aiden to stay down. Then he leans forward and uses the butt of his gun to knock on the door.

'Sir?' he calls softly. 'Sir, the wolf has been contained.'

For too long there's silence from the shed and then the door cracks open slightly.

'Who're you?' The man's voice is suspicious.

'Caleb sent me, sir. My name is Caine. The compound's been attacked and we followed one of the rogue wolves here. The others have been taken care of.'

'Caleb is here?'

'He arrived about an hour ago.'

'Good. Have you got men to guard the shed?'

'They are in position, sir.' Hawke's voice sounds authoritative but not arrogant and the man, who must be the sorcerer, seems placated. 'I need to speak with Caleb. We need to move. If the wolves could find us, others can too.'

'I can escort you, sir.'

The man looks over his shoulder into the shed but then nods and pulls the door shut behind him. Hawke turns around and starts leading the man away from the shed. I hold my breath as he angles his body and brushes just past the circle I'd drawn with the chalk. The sorcerer, oblivious to anything but his need to speak to Caleb Jericho, steps into the circle, triggering the spell, and the wards slam shut with a *whump*.

'Holy Batman's utility belt,' Rick's voice mutters in my ear. 'The chick did the magic and it's real.'

Dante and I sprint towards the circle and my heart thunders in relief that I've managed to pull this off. The sorcerer, and I have no idea who he is, stares at me in real shock and then his gaze moves to Hawke, who looks a little smug and surprised that I've done this.

'A little help here?' Aiden calls from the front of the shed, where he's braced against the open doorway. He's straining his body to try to peer in, but an invisible barrier prevents him.

'Watch him,' I tell Hawke and Dante, gesturing to the Fae. 'If he does anything like escape, put bullets in him.'

I jog over to front of the shed, seeing magic sigils carved into the doorjamb. They look simple and designed specifically for wolves. Not just to keep other wolves out, but to keep the captured wolves *in*.

'Can you smell something weird?' I ask, and turn to look at Aiden, whose eyes have taken on a faraway expression. 'Aide?'

He jerks his attention back to me and just drops, as if he's a puppet and someone's cut his strings. My fingers find his pulse and it's steady but slow. I chance to look into the shed and spot two slumped figures in the semi-darkness, sacks over their heads. There's no sign of the other person Aiden mentioned initially, and I wonder exactly what the sorcerer did to him.

'Oh shit,' I mutter and turn back to the shed's wards. I grab the chalk and start writing my own counter-spell. I trace the carvings in the door and rely on instinct to change them. I have no idea how long I am working there, but at some stage someone says, *We've lost the satellite*, and then, *More guards are coming*. Someone replies, *Not any more*, and when I look up into Dante's concerned eyes, he's holding out something in a mug to me. I drink it and grimace because it's foul coffee and exactly what I need. He kneels next to Aiden and wrinkles his nose.

'What *is* that smell?' he mutters and I shake my head.

'I don't know? Aconite – wolfsbane? Other stuff that smells a little familiar, I can't be sure. Whatever it is, it dropped Aiden unconscious after he'd only inhaled a bit. It's what they're using to keep Connor and Shaun sedated in there, for sure.'

Dante peers into the shed before hunkering down next to Aiden again. 'Get them out, Kit.'

'I'm trying.'

'We could always just blow the shed up,' Hawke says

again, and when I glare up at him he's smiling. 'It's a joke. You're doing well, kid. I don't know what exactly you're doing, but you're doing good. Your uncle will be proud.'

'Jamie's pissed at me,' I tell him as I go back to the carved spell. I'm two-thirds of the way through and I'm exhausted. 'He thinks I betrayed the family.'

'Sometimes he's a bit of an idiot,' Hawke tells me and he sounds resigned. 'Whenever we ran any ops together things always went sideways. It was a guarantee.'

'How long have you known Jamie?'

Hawke talks and I listen. His voice helps me work. I don't know why, but having him at my back steadies my hands. Dante's moved Aiden a few paces away and I glance over my shoulder to see the sorcerer sitting in the middle of my circle. The guy looks annoyed and defeated. And the fact that Johann is standing over him with a gun the size of a small child doesn't seem to help his demeanour either.

'Okay,' I say, interrupting Hawke telling me about a job he'd been on with Jamie and Connor in the jungles of Peru. 'I think I'm done.'

'Now what do we do?' he asks me as I wipe my hands to get rid of the chalk and sweat.

'Now, you step aside. If this backfires on me, you blow this shed up and get the wolves home.' I glance at him. 'Promise you'll get the Garrett boys to safety?'

'You have my word.' Hawke's hand rests on my shoulder for a moment and then it's gone.

'Dante, I need your help,' I say but he's already there, anticipating me in a way that makes me proud.

'What do you need me to do?'

'I'm going to push and I need you to do the same.'

'Kit, my magic is unstable. I'm not sure . . .'

'Listen, we need to get them out of there and I'd rather risk blowing them up with magic, than blowing them up with whatever Emily's got aimed at this shed.'

He grins then. 'Okay. Since you put it that way.'

'Here we go.'

I close my eyes and concentrate on my magic. I pull a strand of it out and cup it in my hands. The light is bright and small, but as I stare at it, I will it larger, into a ball the size of a football. There's no heat there, just the crackle of barely contained energy. By my side, Dante's worked his way through the opening moves of a martial arts kata that looks similar to tai chi and his breathing is deep and even, his expression serene. When he catches my eye, he gives me a nod, moving his hands so that it looks as if he's holding onto his own ball of energy – his being invisible – between his hands.

'On three,' I say, and it's a testament to how we've grown to know one another over the past few weeks that he doesn't quibble about which part of *on three* we're going to go on. 'One.' I inhale and anchor myself. 'Two.' I extend my arms towards the doorway. 'Three.' As I exhale, I will my ball of curling energy at the door I've spelled. And by my side, Dante does the same. Our magic hits the barrier at exactly the same time in an arc of light. It flattens out and there's that weird sub-audible *whump* I've grown accustomed to when magic does what it's supposed to do. I crouch low, turning my back and pulling Dante down to my level, in case there's a larger flash of light or, the gods forbid, an explosion.

'We're still standing,' Hawke mutters in my ear and I stand upright. The shed looks no different to before and I glance at the sorcerer sitting disconsolately in the middle of the circle I'd cast earlier. He's glaring at me and I can't help but feel a thrill creep down my spine at the intense look of dislike on his face.

Dante is at the door to the shed without hesitation and I step into the room with my scarf over my face and speak into my comms.

'We need to get them out. They've got a nebulizer in here polluting the air with aconite and something else. The wolves are down.'

There's a flurry of movement and I step out of the way as Hawke, Johann and Jane come in. Between us we get Connor and Shaun out and I try not to see how they've been torn up. Aiden staggers to his feet to crouch beside his oldest brother, touching Connor's face with trembling fingers.

'They're gonna be okay,' I tell him. 'They've been poisoned. Come on, you need to help. Aide, *hey*.' I snap my fingers in front of his face. 'Connor is too big for us to carry. Can you help? Can you do that?'

'What? Yes, of course.' He picks his brother up in a fireman's lift and blinks heavily at me. 'What now?'

'I've got your brother,' Hawke says, slinging Shaun over his own shoulder. 'Let's go.'

'What about this guy?' Johann asks motioning to the sorcerer in my magic circle. 'Do we take him out?'

'No.' I scowl at the Fae. 'No, he comes with me.'

'Kit, no.'

I shake off Dante's grip. 'Listen, he'll know stuff.'

'We won't have room on the heli,' Johann says mildly. 'And we've gotta go now. Someone's going to notice guards have gone missing. And I'd like to be away by then.'

'I'll drive back with him. In the Audi. We shove him in the boot.'

'You have *got* to be kidding me,' Dante mutters. 'Kit, we don't have time for this. Leave the guy.'

'He'll have information about Merrick, Dante.'

That brings him up short and he scowls at me. 'Dammit.' He glances at the sorcerer. 'Get the circle down, he's coming with us.'

I walk widdershins around the circle and ignore Hawke's voice in my headpiece as I mutter the reverse form of the spell. It goes faster than I would have liked, and as soon as the final ward disappears, the sorcerer lunges for me. But Johann is there with the muzzle of his gun and he presses it hard into the guy's throat. I can smell flesh singeing.

'Don't make me shoot you, mate.'

'You won't get away with this,' the sorcerer grates. 'They'll know who's taken the wolves.'

'Good,' I say. 'Let them come. We're ready. But in the meantime, you're coming with us.'

I prod him with my sword and he flinches. 'You can't make me.'

'Oh for heaven's sake.' Dante steps up and punches the guy in the side of throat. He drops like a tonne of bricks. 'Just stop arguing with idiots, Kit.'

'Good job,' Johann mutters and gestures with his gun. 'After you.'

Dante and I get the sorcerer lifted and carried between us. If he manages to fall a few times it's no real big deal. We rendezvous back at the cars and Hawke's face looks as pleased as a pit bull that's swallowed a wasp.

'*What?*'

'We're going to question him,' I say, swiping the beanie

off my head and wiping my face. Carrying an unconscious guy was hot and hard work.

'No place in the heli,' Hawke says evenly.

'I know. I'm driving back.'

'I'm going with her,' Dante offers, nudging the unconscious Fae on the ground with his toe. 'Someone has to keep an eye on this guy.'

'I'll play escort,' Johann says. 'I've got nothing better to do with the rest of my night.'

Hawke's glare is ominous but then he's shaking his head. He mutters something about Blackharts and Garretts and I'm sure it's not flattering, but it makes me grin anyway.

'There are manacles in the van,' he eventually says. 'That should keep him quiet.'

Emily and Rick materialize from the darkness and climb into the van with their rifles, just as I've finished tying up the sorcerer. Johann hands me a wadded-up piece of fabric and a roll of gaffer tape that he digs out of his Kevlar jacket. 'Never leave home without it,' he intones sagely. I'm not comfortable tying the Fae up this way but, as a sorcerer, he's more dangerous than most. Not only can he speak spells (making it necessary to keep his mouth shut), but his hands and feet have to be secured too, because he could cast spells by movement alone.

'Let's go,' Hawke instructs. Dante and Johann heft the Fae into the back of the Audi after I opt not to throw him in the boot after all. I take the passenger seat and Johann slides in behind the wheel. Dante arranges himself next to the Fae and keeps as far away from his steel chains as he can.

Everyone else piles into the van and Aiden blows us a kiss from the passenger seat as we leave the compound behind. We've been driving for about five minutes when the sky behind us lights up in a massive explosion. I twist around to see what's going on.

In the direction we've just come from, flames lick at the night sky.

'*What*?' I glance at Dante and find him watching Johann. 'What was *that*?'

'Probably Emily. She really doesn't like arms-dealers. Or gangs.'

'So she blew up the Jericho Gang's compound?'

Johann shrugs as he sinks lower into the Audi's seat. 'It's going to keep them off our backs.'

'It will also bring the police.' Dante nods. 'Clever. They'll find the weapons. Possibly drugs.'

'Exactly.' Johann smiles and I sit back in my seat. 'And everyone will forget about us being there. For a little while at least.'

Chapter Thirty-Eight

My great-aunt's man Isak is waiting for us in the middle of a field, the Blackhart helicopter crouched low against a row of trees. To my surprise, Dr Forster is there too, to take over Connor and Shaun's care. He puts Aiden on oxygen immediately, as he's still woozy, and goes about treating the other two wolves. Isak meets my gaze briefly before he turns to talk to Hawke. The way the two men interact makes me think they've met before. In fact, Johann greets Isak like a good friend, and both Emily and Jane get hugs. Isak's always been friendly towards me, but I realize I know nothing about him at all.

'So. Your family has their own helicopter,' Dante says from my side. 'With a crest and everything. I don't think I knew that.'

I bump my shoulder against his. 'What of it?'

'Are you telling me you're rich?'

I frown. 'I . . . I suppose so. I mean, I'm not rich. But the family? Andrew runs the family businesses so I assume there's money.'

'You know none of this is in the Spooks files about your family?'

'No?'

'And I won't be putting any of it in there, before you ask,' he supplies.

'I didn't think you would.' We share a smile before Johann comes walking back to us. 'We've gotta go. We've got a long drive ahead of us. Em is driving the van back to base, and the others are choppering out.'

'Okay, just give me a minute.' I move past him, towards where Aiden's sitting in the open door of the helicopter. He pulls the oxygen mask off his face and smiles wearily up at me.

'We got them back.'

'We did. Well done, wolf boy.' I lean over and ruffle his hair before kissing his cheek. 'Get some rest. I'll see you at home soon.'

I'm a few paces away when he calls out to me and when I turn he looks tired and vulnerable. 'Thank you. For saving them.'

'That's what family's for, Aide.' I bite my lip and shove my hands into my pockets as I walk towards the car. I pass Dante, who looks undecidedly between the car and Aiden.

'Go to him,' I say as I walk past. 'You'll regret it if you don't.'

Without a word he jogs towards Aiden. I slide behind the Audi's wheel, and when I look back, Dante's hugging Aiden hard. I grin and strap myself in. Johann gets in next to me, adjusting his weapon so it won't get tangled with the seatbelt if needed.

'Are you old enough to drive, Blackhart?' he asks me and I look at him incredulously.

'It's as if you don't know my family,' I point out. I start the car just as Dante flings himself into the back seat. He checks over his fellow passenger and gives me the thumbs up.

'Let's roll.'

I spin away from Hawke and his team and head back towards the rutted side road. We drive in silence until we hit the tarmac. Johann finds a music station and settles himself into his seat with a contented sigh. The familiar *whap-whap* of helicopter blades draws my attention and I lean forward a little just as Isak pilots the helicopter above us, keeping low over the fields before climbing away.

'I never knew quite how many empty warehouses there were in London,' Dante says as he crosses to stand next to me. We're on the roof, another one, overlooking a large lot of seven warehouses. 'I feel that we need to blow them all up as a matter of health and safety.'

I lift my eyebrows and grin at him. 'Really? You *feel* that?'

'This is where bad things happen. They're cooking Glow in there.' He points at the middle warehouse. 'This is the base for their operation.'

'Until they decide to move.' I stare out at the warehouses. 'Our good friend Obreht was very forthcoming yesterday, almost too forthcoming.' I let my doubt shine through. Obreht, the Fae sorcerer, quickly opted to talk once Hawke took over his questioning. I was assured by Johann that Hawke wouldn't use violence on him. When I asked how Hawke managed to interrogate people without hurting them, Johann had merely shrugged and said something about him being the scariest person in the room. After two hours we had a lot of information about Merrick and Glow distribution in both London and the Midlands. We weren't sure how they ran things in the States but, right now, dealing with things on our home-turf was most important.

'Yes. So we should blow them up.'

'I feel that you and Emily have maybe bonded too much over things exploding,' I tell him and he grins.

'She's cool. I like her. I like all of Hawke's people.'

There's no denying that Hawke and his crew are good people. They made themselves useful and slotted themselves in with us without any effort. I fully expected them to drop the wolves at home and then go on their merry way, but instead they'd stayed, made sure both Connor and Shaun were okay and fussed over Connor until he threatened to punch Rocco in the face.

The two wolves were in a bad state. Dr Forster set them up with oxygen in their rooms and instructed all of us how to bathe their wounds with cleansed spring water, blessed under the full moon. For humans who'd had little enough exposure to the weirdness of our lives, Hawke and his team took their instructions without question and set about helping in any way they could.

'They're planning on moving out,' Rocco says in my ear. 'They're talking about it now. They've heard about the attack on the compound and they're unsure if their location is safe here.'

He's stationed on the warehouse opposite ours, with listening devices set up all over the main warehouse we're watching.

'Merrick is arguing with Jericho himself on the phone, telling him that they can't just leave everything behind; it's a mobile set-up so things can be packed up fast and moved, but Jericho wants everything left and his people gone.'

'We should just blow it all up,' Dante mutters again and I have to stop myself from laughing.

'Stop it.' I nudge him and he pouts.

'They're arguing. Lots of swearing.' Rocco groans. 'I'm too young for this. Hawke, if you wanna go in, now's a good time to do it. They're distracted.'

'Agreed.' Hawke's voice is a low rumble. 'Are we ready?'

His team calls in, then he addresses me and Dante. 'You come in afterwards, once we're clear.'

'Don't forget your masks,' I say. 'Don't touch anything. That stuff will have you high in seconds.'

'Roger that. We go in in three.'

The sword in my hand feels heavy. I slide it home into the scabbard on my back and shrug my shoulders to settle the weight. 'Come on.'

Dante drops halfway down the building, finds purchase for his toes and fingers, kicks off and lands silently on the concrete. I brace myself, call my magic and drop silently to his side, crouching low.

It sounds like all hell breaks loose in the warehouse. There's shouting. Also muffled gunshots and the *whump* of magic – followed by silence before a loud, wild scream.

'What's going on?' I ask into my mouthpiece but there's no answer. I shoot a look at Dante and we run for the doorway, only to find Emily slumped against the side of the warehouse holding her bleeding arm. Her mask's been ripped off and her eyes are wide and staring but she waves me off when I lean over her.

'I'm fine, I'm fine, it's just a scratch, get in there.'

I shove my own mask onto my face and wait till Dante's done the same before we duck into the warehouse.

There are long tables that run the whole length of the

floor. Piled onto these tables are glass tubes, flasks and filters. I have a flashback to Istvan's lab, with its dried blood on the knives and scalpels amidst the scientific equipment. This place seems cleaner, but one of the tables has been overturned in the struggle and there's powdered Glow everywhere. Three Fae and two humans are lined up against the wall, guarded by Rick and Jane. Hawke's staring at the mess with an expression of distaste visible above his mask.

'Not quite what I expected,' he said. 'Cleaner, less chaos. No guards. Stupidly arrogant. And we got your boy Merrick, right here.' He points to one of the Fae and gets a snarl in response. Rick taps the muzzle of his gun against the man's face and he subsides. But if looks could kill, both Hawke and I would be melted skeletons.

'It seems small,' I say, looking around, but when I pay attention to the open shelving units against the far wall, my jaw drops. 'Actually, I take that back.'

There are bags upon bags containing hundreds of thousands of baggies stacked on the shelves. Jane straightens from where she'd been crouching to examine them.

'I reckon we're looking at just under a tonne of this stuff, boss,' she says to Hawke. 'I can't even begin to put a street value to it. But it's a lot. Like, a lot *a lot*. There's enough stuff here to get the whole of the British Isles addicted and keep everyone that way for a good few years.'

The Fae, Merrick, snorts and I look down at him. 'You have something to add?' I ask him. 'Alchemist?'

His gaze widens for a second and then he grimaces. 'An actual gods-cursed Blackhart – I should have known.' His gaze travels to Dante, who's standing a little behind me. 'Humans, and a kami. Where's your pet dog, Blackhart?

You seem to have a whole menagerie of unpleasant creatures with you today.'

Aiden strolls in from the open doorway with an exhausted-looking Fae gripped by the arm, dumping him unceremoniously on the ground beside Merrick.

'I was just running down your cowardly little assistant. But now I'm right here,' Aiden says, and gives Merrick a grin that shows too many teeth. 'My brothers tell me you helped concoct the drug that took them down. Is that true?'

'Vermin need to be exterminated.'

I grab Aiden's hand as it flashes past me; I shake my head.

'*No.* He's doing this on purpose.'

'I know. I want to smack him on purpose too,' he mutters and twists his wrist out of my grasp. 'What now? What do we do with all this?'

'You guys talk to your friend Merrick and we make a call to some friends in the SOCA. They're going to have a field day with this haul.' Hawke pats my shoulder. 'Get a move on. I'm tired and hungry and need sleep sometime this century.'

Dante and Aiden haul Merrick up and I follow close behind.

'What do we do with him?' Dante asks me as we walk out into the sunlight. 'Question him?'

'I think we send a message to Zane. Tell him we've got a friend of his.'

Merrick's head snaps up and he scowls at me. 'You know nothing, girl. Nothing.'

'I think we know enough, Merrick. You make the drugs and peddle them to Caleb Jericho, who then distributes them into the clubs. We know you're using Pensa's business contacts to store the drugs for you too. How many businesses is that throughout the UK, Merrick? Fifty? Seventy? A hundred? That means plenty of storage places, but it's fine. We've got a list. We'll hit them all.' I stare at him for a few seconds. 'Bring him. I've a circle prepared to take him back to the Otherwhere. It won't take long to sort out. I've one of the Stormborn meeting me.'

'No. Wait. There's so very much more to the story.' Merrick scowls and tries to shrug off both Aiden and Dante but it only makes them hold on tighter. 'Blackhart, you are in so much trouble, you honestly have no idea.'

'Why don't you tell us?' Dante stops and stares down at Merrick. 'You're dying to do just that, aren't you? Tell us your grand plan.'

Merrick tries to take a step back but Aiden's chest is blocking his escape. 'If you let me go, I'll do my best to keep your name out of all of this that's happened,' he says, his voice low, confident. 'Think about it, Blackhart.'

'I think not, Merrick. I know you're hardly the innocent pawn being manipulated into doing this.' I pull off my mask and let it dangle around my neck. 'You're not getting any kind of deal, but you are going to reveal the identity of Zane's boss, as Zane's definitely not the one running all of this.'

Merrick laughs then, and I resist the urge to hit him. 'You've not figured that out yet?'

'Can I hit him now, Kit?' Aiden asks me. 'Hawke will never know.'

'No,' Dante says, tugging Merrick away from Aiden. 'I think Merrick and I are going to chat privately about this.'

Merrick's eyes widen. 'I am not going anywhere with you, kami.'

Dante tightens his grip on Merrick's arm and I see the Fae blanch at his touch. A sudden sense of wrongness sweeps over me and I start towards them, but Dante gives me a shake of the head before addressing Merrick.

'It will be *fun*, I promise.'

'Dante, don't do anything stupid.' My voice, even to my ears, sounds flat and tired.

'I won't. We're just going to talk about what Merrick knows. And how he uses his glamour to charm young humans to come with him, when they really should know better.'

I suddenly remember Antone Pensa telling us of Merrick's predilection for young human girls and bile rises in my throat.

'Dante.'

'Kit. Trust me with this.'

I hear the quietness in his voice and notice how his grip on Merrick tightens a little. The Fae is so ordinary-looking, even without his glamour. I realize he's one of life's invisible people, with no charisma to speak of, so he must have some other kind of trick when approaching people.

'Whatever you're planning on doing, Alexander, hurry it up. SOCA's ETA is fifteen minutes,' Rocco's voice comes over the comms.

'Roger that,' I say. Dante takes advantage of my distraction to march Merrick away towards some crates. I don't expect to see the blue flames that drop from his outspread hands as he crowds Merrick into a corner, and I realize that the feeling of dread that stole over me previously was Dante drawing on his magic – not necessarily his siren magic, but something else, the stuff we've only lightly researched. The kami are heavily linked to the earth's leylines, being nature spirits. And the Fae get most of their magic from leylines – and the kami are rumoured to have the ability to snuff out another Fae's connection to that magic completely. Dante didn't even have to trot out his full repertoire to frighten the young female faerie at the Soho club. He merely lurked with intent and played with those blue flames, threatening to snuff her out. And it would seem that's what he's planning on doing now too, with Merrick.

I hesitate, uncertain whether to move closer to rein him in, when Aiden just shakes his head.

'You already freaked Merrick out, telling Dante to not to do anything stupid.'

'What?'

'You did what Dante wanted you to do. You panicked a little and Merrick picked up on that. I could hear his heartbeat escalate because there was a hint that *you*, Kit Blackhart, didn't trust Dante to behave himself.'

I still look at him uncomprehendingly.

'Kit, you have a reputation for doing dumb things. For you to tell someone else not to do a dumb thing is pretty bloody terrifying.'

'Oh.' I frown, trying to digest that. 'Oh, well, that's okay then, I think.' I look over to where they're standing. Dante's talking and Merrick looks as if he wants to be sick.

'What are they saying?'

Aiden tilts his head a little and closes his eyes. 'Merrick is giving Dante some attitude. Dante's not really saying much and it's freaking Merrick out. Oh – he's just done something and it smells like ozone burning.'

'Crap, he's messing with the leylines.' I start forward and Aiden's right behind me. I don't run but it's a near thing. By the time we get there, Merrick is sagging. Sweat has pooled on his upper lip and he looks about to cry. There's no sign of his previous bravado and he looks miserable. I spare him a glance but focus on Dante, who has the grace to look a little guilty.

'We okay here?'

'We are. Turns out Merrick will be more than happy to take us to Zane and clear up this whole mess for us.' Dante pats the Fae's shoulder.

As much as it pains me, I feel I have to check on the Fae, despite wanting to walk away. 'Merrick. Are you okay?'

In answer the Fae gives a shuddering breath and makes a valiant effort to wipe his face. 'I'm fine, truly, Blackhart. I have agreed to help you, now let's go.' With that he straightens and rolls his shoulders. 'Lead the way.'

I gesture for Dante to start walking. I fall in behind Merrick; he doesn't take his eyes off Dante. Dante's magic is still a grey area and we don't really know his full capabilities. He's been keeping a tight lid on them and I suspect that this has been a damaging experience for him.

Rocco looks up from where he's packing his equipment into the van.

'We're ready to go as soon as Hawke comes through those doors,' Rocco says, and nods at Dante. 'You okay, kid? You look a little . . . high?'

Dante runs an unsteady hand through his hair. 'I'm okay. Just a bit wired.'

Rocco grunts noncommittally and looks over as Hawke and his team exit the warehouse and pile into their van.

Aiden pulls up in the Audi and I help Merrick into the back seat. For a second I hesitate, staring at Dante over the roof of the car, but he gives me a questioning look.

'Front or back, Kit?'

'Back,' I say, sliding in behind Merrick. 'You go next to Aide.'

We leave the warehouses behind and, as we approach a large intersection, we pass an ominous-looking convoy of large black SUVs, driving at full speed. I wonder if they're bound for the warehouse complex.

'Where to?' I ask Merrick. 'Where do we go?'

The Fae tears his gaze from the road and, after shooting a brief look at Dante, stares at me, looking miserable.

'There's a gateway beneath Tower Bridge,' he says. 'We gain entrance there.'

Chapter Thirty-Nine

It starts snowing heavily halfway into central London, and the traffic is snarled up around the Houses of Parliament because of some protest. By the time we reach Tower Bridge, it's late afternoon and I'm tired, hungry and feel a little feverish. We radioed our thanks to Hawke and his team, before peeling away as soon as we hit London. They'd passed by us with cheery waves and promises to keep in touch.

Holding onto my sword, I cast a glamour over it so it looks like an umbrella, then pull Merrick out of the car. We head towards the nearest coffee shop to make use of the facilities and get something to eat and drink. The boys follow and place the drinks orders.

In the toilets, I splash water on my face and stare at myself in the mirror. I am pale and my eyes are massive in my face, which looks far too thin. All I needed to complete my take on emo goth-Kit was heavy eyeliner and black lipstick. Beneath my scarf, the bruises around my neck stand out horribly in the bad overhead lighting. I touch the largest and wince a little before readjusting the concealing scarf.

Back in the coffee shop, Merrick's very quiet and only sips half-heartedly at the god-awful camomile tea Aiden bought him. He barely looks away from Dante the whole time.

'My dad's home,' Aiden says, after I've demolished part of my toasted sandwich. I'm sure Aiden must have heard my stomach rumble, hence the food. 'So are Andrew and your aunt, and Megan.'

I stare at him in surprise. 'Why didn't you say anything before?'

'Because they called you too. But I don't think you have your phone with you.'

I dig in my pocket and hold up my phone. It's dead. 'I hate technology,' I tell no one in particular. 'So what do they want us to do? Get back there?'

'Yes. Andrew's annoyed we're not home.'

'They sent us with Hawke and his guys to take the Glow thing to the next stage,' I mutter. 'What do they expect us to do? Sit at home and wait for it all to happen while we watch remotely?'

'I get that impression sometimes.' Aiden's smile is strained. 'Anyway, at least with them home, I know that Connor and Shaun are being looked after.'

I throw back the rest of my hot chocolate and button up my coat. The guys do the same and when we exit the coffee shop, my breath plumes in the air.

'I swear it's colder than it was ten minutes ago,' I say, shivering and hunching my shoulders. I check for traffic and walk towards the Embankment. The Thames lies grey and sluggish beneath us and there are very few people in the area.

'Are we heading to the troll caves?' I ask Merrick, and don't miss how he blinks in surprise at the question. 'Let's go, time's wasting.'

We follow him along the Embankment until we can see the Tower of London across the water and, closer to hand, a flight of narrow stairs leading down to the river. There's a new gate there and I take a steadying breath. Then I push at the gate, at the same time as saying, 'I command thee, open.'

It swings open on silent hinges.

'Kit,' Dante says. 'There's a hell of lot of water at the bottom of these stairs. Are you going to do something about that?'

'Keep walking, Dante. Trust me.'

He utters a weary sigh but leads the way down, regardless. The water laps briefly at his feet but then, as I remember from almost a year ago, the illusion vanishes and we're standing on a muddy riverbank.

'That is so cool,' he mutters and stands there staring at the Thames that laps at the little beach as if it's the sea. Then he turns to look at me. 'Now what?'

'Now, Merrick is going to open a doorway for us.' I smile at Merrick. 'Aren't you?'

He shoots a glance at Dante, who doesn't seem to be paying him any attention and is instead staring up at the bridge almost directly above us.

'Yes, of course.' Merrick scrabbles in his pockets and brings out a bit of chalk. 'Can you just move . . . to the side? A bit more? Thank you.'

I try to keep track of the sigils he draws on the stone before they sink away. The door he sketches is large and I slide my fingers towards the button on my wrist that propels my baton forward. If this guy is messing us around, I won't hesitate to take him out.

Then, far sooner than I could have managed, Merrick

steps back, examines the door and gives a brief, satisfied nod. He holds a hand out to me.

'If you could cut my finger, Blackhart?'

I pull a small ring dagger from my hip pocket and, steadying his hand, I nick the skin just enough for blood to well up. He presses the blood to the top and both sides of the door as snow starts to fall.

'Now what?' Aiden asks us.

'We wait.'

A full minute passes before Aiden twitches. 'So, let me get this straight,' he says, looking at Merrick. 'You've just decided to help us. No questions asked.'

'I'm helping you because my I value my life and my abilities. Without them, I'm nothing. Worthless to friends and easy prey to a great many foes.' He shoots sour looks at Dante, who looks too innocent by far.

'Did you threaten him?' I demand of Dante. 'Or did you promise him something?'

'No. We just spoke.'

There's no lie there, I can sense it, and it only deepens Aiden's scowl.

'So what's the plan, anyway? We go through the gateway, enter the Otherwhere, and then what?'

'We get to Zane. We force him to tell us who's behind the Glow mess.'

'As easy as that?' Aiden's voice shows how unlikely he thinks that will be. 'No fighting, no almost dying?'

'Don't be an ass,' Dante says with a laugh, but he looks uncomfortable. 'No one is dying. Not now, anyway.'

Their banter is broken off by the doorway opening, only marginally. A pair of baleful white eyes squints out at us from the darkness behind it.

'Who calls?'

'It is me, old mother. Merrick. I have guests with me. We need access to the tunnels, to see Zane.'

There's a snort and I lift my scarf up to cover my nose at the foul smell of the air seeping out of the tunnels ahead.

'Come, then.'

There are shuffling noises as the creature moves off. Merrick looks over his shoulder at us, before gesturing feebly towards the doorway. I prod him in the back and we enter the passage. The smell is awful and I try not to see what I'm walking on. It feels squishy.

The tunnels here are completely different to those I entered with Thorn. They are dark, damp and smell horrible. The small hunched figure scuttling ahead of us is also not the guide I was expecting. Is this what happens to the trolls' tunnels when they vacate their lair? Or are we somewhere else entirely?

'I'd like to point out, once more, how much I hate being underground,' Aiden complains behind me. 'It smells bad and I can't stand upright. Also, why does this feel like a trap?'

'Stop it,' I hiss. 'It's not a trap. How can it be a trap?'

'Because this is *us*, Blackhart.'

I want nothing more than to reach back and slap him but there's a noise ahead. I stumble over absolutely nothing and fall against Merrick and he shoves me away from him. We emerge into a large cavern and, as I adjust my hold on the Fae's shoulder, I look up – and my jaw drops open.

It totally is a trap.

'I don't want to say it . . .' Aiden says, wiping a bloody hand across his shirt, before turning to kick a weird spindly creature made from sticks into a cage and slamming the door.

'So don't,' I huff as I parry a blow from a redcap who's doing his utmost to separate my head from my shoulders.

'More fighting, less talking,' Dante pants as he grabs one of the smaller goblins and punches it into the wall.

Merrick has disappeared in the confusion and I waste no time in taking out my frustration on the remaining redcaps that hurl themselves at us. As Merrick ran from the cavern, Dante shouted after him, which prompted a terrified look. But then he just pushed the largest redcap at us and ran for his life.

Since then we've been trying to fight our way through a crowd of creatures to follow him. But we are bogged down, and appear to have been doing this for the past million years now.

I have no idea how the fight is going because, really, there are so many redcaps and goblins that I've lost track of who I've punched, kicked and stabbed. And they just keep coming in a never-ending stream.

'We need,' Aiden huffs as he ducks an overhead swing, 'to get the hell out of here.' He grabs his opponent by the shirt and head-butts him hard, before lifting him and tossing him at a group of four advancing redcaps.

'I know,' I grind out, and pull my sword from a fallen goblin's ribs with some difficulty. 'I'd gladly follow any plan you might have.'

'Back the way we came, maybe,' Dante offers, clapping me on the shoulder as he surveys the mess of bodies and limbs strewn around us in the cave. 'You get us back out into the human world and we'll hold them off.'

'I like it,' I say, glancing over my shoulder at the passageway we left. 'But it means Merrick gets away.'

'It doesn't matter. We know Zane's the next step on the rung. We just need to get to him, that's all.'

'Guys? I think we need to go. Now.' Aiden lifts a kukri blade from the floor. 'Something's coming and it sounds big.'

I don't wait to see what he's heard. Instead I find the chalk in my pocket and run for the passage behind us. It's easy here to access my magic. I sketch a hasty spell of protection on the walls and ceiling and, praying it will hold, I whistle loudly to get attention.

They come running, Aiden first and Dante behind. They're both out of breath and covered in blood – and Dante's lip has split, making me wince. As soon as they're past me, I nick my finger and slam my hand into the wall, activating the spell. The soft *whump* makes me grin in triumph, but I don't wait to see how it affects our pursuers. I run up the tunnel with panic clawing at me, because it feels far longer than it did before. The smell is also worse.

I come to a stop and clamp down as much as I can on my growing worry. I don't recognize this part of the tunnel at all.

'I'm not sure how long my barrier will hold them,' I say, and rub my nose. It comes away bloody, because of course it does. *Avoid high-stress situations*: Dr Forster's voice echoes in my ear and I sag a little. 'Crap, I don't know where we are at all.'

'Kit, just breathe, okay. Just draw the doorway. It doesn't matter where we come out.'

'I can't,' I say, gripping Dante's wrist. 'Someone has to be on the other side to open it.'

'*What?*'

'Doorways work both ways. I can't just draw a door and open it myself. I'm not strong enough. Someone has to open it for me. From the other side.'

'Jimmy.' Aiden stares at me with an alarmed expression. 'You can ask Jimmy for help. His business is opening magical doors, right?'

'I don't know. I can't just impose on him, Aide. He's a busy guy. And then there's the thing with Megan . . .'

'Screw that, you're in danger of being eating by an ogre or something very big,' he says. And, as if on cue, there's a booming sound of something hitting the barrier further down the passage. 'And I reckon Jimmy would be delighted to save your ass.' Aide turns me around so I face the wall and prods my shoulder. 'Draw. Draw now. Call him.'

'Okay.' I'm reluctant to call Jimmy. Megan used the spell I'd taught her to call Jimmy, to help her get into a locked penthouse in New York last year. Things went south for them both, so I'm probably not in his good books.

Jimmy is unusual in that he works as a freelance doorway guardian. If you know how, you can call him and he can open doors for you. He isn't, to all intents and purposes, the most popular person in the Otherwhere either and I stumbled across him by accident on a job. We bonded over our mutual love for bladed weapons and deep house music. I tend not to ask him for favours because he is very pricey but, in this case, it seems worth it.

Chapter Forty

I sketch the doorway, made more on edge by Aiden's pacing. He keeps looking down the passage as if he expects someone to materialize from thin air at any moment. Dante's equally nervy, and one glance at his stony face is enough to make me hope the spell I'm using will work.

I eventually step back from the doorway. This was as good as I was going to get it. The runes were correct; the straight lines were less than perfect, admittedly – but the result holds all the intent and desperation I can muster. Then I lift my hand and knock. Three times. The door is pulled open so fast I actually step back in surprise and bump into Dante, who's crowded up behind me.

'Jimmy,' I say faintly. 'Hi. So, can you do us a favour and get us out of here?'

Very blue eyes regard me from beneath thick straight black eyebrows. 'Who's your friend, Blackhart? You breaking your boyfriend out of the Otherwhere?'

'Don't be an ass, Jimmy. This is Dante.'

He jerks his chin at Dante in greeting and then leans out of the door a little, bracing himself on the doorjamb, until he spots Aiden walking back towards us.

'And the wolf. Of course. Why aren't I surprised. What are you doing here?'

'Getting away from a trap.' Aiden's grin is wide as he rakes his eyes over Jimmy. And I don't blame him. Jimmy is sinfully pretty. 'Looking good, James. You gonna help us or are we all just going to die of stab wounds when a troop of redcaps and possibly an ogre break through the barrier spell Kit has set up back there?'

'Have you got payment? Or are you gonna owe me?'

'I have payment,' I say, and hold up a small velvet bag I remembered to grab from my backpack. 'I hope it's enough.'

Jimmy takes it from me and Dante mutters impatiently. Jimmy pauses and stares hard at Dante, who's scowling at him. The two of them are practically bristling at one another. 'Do you have a problem, mate?'

'My problem is that we need to get out of here. You can worry about payment later.'

'Patience is a virtue,' Jimmy replies, 'and I'm all about virtue. And payment.' He shakes the contents of the pouch out onto the palm of his hand and lets out a low whistle. 'Kit, these are exceptional. It's as if you know what I like.'

He trails a long finger over the glittering emeralds in his palm before sliding them back into the pouch. 'Come on in, then. Where do you need to go?'

Aiden steers Dante past Jimmy and I follow close behind. Jimmy swings the door shut behind us with an echoing boom and I relax marginally.

'Anywhere near my place would do,' Aiden says. 'You remember where that is, right?'

A soft light flickers on and Jimmy hands me a small ball of light, rolling it over my extended palm like a glowing marble. 'You take one too,' he says to Dante, and makes a little gesture with his hand as if he's grabbing the light from darkness. 'Don't drop these. The lights will keep you safe. Well, safe-ish. Just be ready to fight if need be.'

'What about me? Don't I get a light?' Aiden asks, and I swear I can hear a pout.

'You see better in the dark than I do, Aiden, and I was born to the darkness.' Jimmy doesn't smile often, but when he does it's remarkable. We all three stare at him a little open-mouthed. 'We're going to run, okay? If anything comes at you, you stab it or punch it and you do not stop, is that clear?'

We all three nod. 'Excellent. Let's go.'

He starts running and I hurry to keep up because I have no desire to be lost in this dark and shadowy world between the Veil and the human world. 'Where exactly are we?' Dante asks behind me. 'And who is this guy? And why is he so pretty?'

'Right,' Aiden says from the back of our small group. 'It's like darkness gave birth to the prettiest creature it could and made him promise never to leave.'

'That makes no sense,' Dante mutters.

'No, it totally does. Right, Kit?'

'It totally makes sense. But how about . . . ? Oh crap.' Talons slice past my face and I duck just in time to stab at their owner. There's a muted scuffle from behind me and the sound of bones cracking, but then Aiden's voice rings out.

'We're okay. *Keep running*.'

I look up to find Jimmy wiping his blade clean. His attacker lies still for only a moment before something grabs it and starts hauling it out of my circle of flickering light.

'You good?' he asks, and he gives me a quick once-over to make sure I'm not bleeding. When I nod, we start running again.

We get attacked twice more. I lose my sword in the second fight and almost pass out from a heavy blow to my solar plexus that knocks me flat on my back. But Dante's there, helping me up. Jimmy snarls something in a language that's all guttural growls and whatever attacked me makes a whining noise and retreats.

I don't know how long we're in there, but Jimmy suddenly stops dead in front of me and I have to take a step sideways so as not to run into his back. He exhales and the light from the small orbs intensifies.

The beast, monster or whatever, that brought Jimmy up short pads into the light and I scrabble back against Dante, because things like that should really not exist.

'*Chimera*,' I gasp and Dante holds me tight. Aiden's on my other side, surprisingly silent and possibly in awe of the sheer size of the creature bearing down on us.

'No,' Jimmy says, and frowns at the creature. 'It's a kirin.'

Jimmy keeps a hand on my arm as he speaks to it. His voice is lilting and it sounds like he's placating the creature. I have no idea what language he's speaking but it sounds almost Japanese. I watch as wide intelligent eyes track my movements and I try not to fidget against Dante's hold on me. Those eyes rake me over and then track the arm wrapped around me, to find Dante. When the kirin's gaze comes to rest on Dante, I swear I see a flash of recognition there for a second.

The kirin is beautiful, a part of me admits. It's massive – part ox, part something with multi-coloured fur. Its feet are clawed like a lion's and it has two huge, backward-sweeping horns growing from its head. Its eyes are a rich honey gold framed by curling dark lashes. And currently those eyes are staring hungrily at Dante.

It rumbles something low and throaty and I reach for my missing sword but Jimmy's hand on mine stops me.

'No. It's here to protect your friend. The kirin thought you were putting the kami in danger and came to help.'

'I. *What?*' I stare at Dante as he moves out from behind me.

The kirin takes a step back and I tense because the muscles in its shoulders bunch in a way that means either fight or flight. But Dante seems oblivious to the danger and stops just before the creature. And even with Dante topping six foot, he only reaches the beast's enormous chest. It peers down at him from its great height and for a second there is utter silence in this weird place between the worlds. Then the kirin somehow folds itself into a graceful sign of obeisance towards Dante, one clawed hoof extended, head lowered.

Dante looks unnerved by the bowing creature but sinks down before it, placing two hands on either side of its huge head. He says something soft and steady and the beast snorts and shakes its head in response, sending the ruff of fur around its neck rippling. Then the kirin moves backwards, and when it's swallowed by the darkness once more, Dante says, 'Let's go.'

'What just happened? Because I'm pretty sure that doesn't happen every day.' Aiden stares into the darkness, then at Dante, who looks a little shellshocked by the encounter.

'And running for your life through the shadowlands created by a magical barrier does?' Jimmy quips, and I wheeze a laugh because he's spot on.

'I'll tell you guys afterwards. Let's just get you home.'

Jimmy leads the way again and I can't help but feel that there's now a guardian in the darkness that keeps the other monsters from attacking. We're not assaulted again and, by the time Jimmy stops, I've lost track of how long we've been in here.

He wastes no time in taking a set of keys from his pockets. He flips through them before choosing a seemingly random key. He closes his eyes and exhales before sliding it into a lock that suddenly forms around the key's teeth. Then a door appears and he pulls it open.

'Get moving,' he says. 'We don't have much time.'

Aiden pats his shoulder in thanks as he squeezes through. Dante follows with a brief 'Thanks' and as I go to move past him, handing back the ball of light, Jimmy stops me.

'Kit, what are you doing running around with a kami? They hardly ever leave their homelands.' His voice drops very low. 'Do you know who that kid is?'

'A friend, a good friend.' At his thoughtful expression, I lift a chin in question. 'You got a problem?'

Jimmy's eyes seem to glow in the darkness as he leans against the door. 'Do you know the kirin only appear at the death or emergence of a new ruler or sage? And they're like unicorns in their rarity – except they're even more scarce.'

'Unicorns are *real*?'

'Kit.'

'I'm sorry. But unicorns?' I grin up at him and press a kiss to his cheek. 'Thanks for this, Jimmy. You're a real pal. I'll tell Dante he's destined to become the next ruler of Xanadu or something. I'm sure he'll be impressed.'

'Never joke about shit like this, Kit. You don't know

who's listening.' But his tone is teasing and he grins as he starts pushing the door shut. 'Tell Megan I say hi when you see her later. She needs some rest. She looks tired.'

Chapter Forty-One

The Otherwhere, Alba, the Citadel

'How sure are we that this is authentic?' Aelfric watched as Oswald examined the papers Feran had brought him once more, reading over the prophecy it revealed.

'Pretty sure, my liege. My man wouldn't have brought this to my attention if he thought it was a fake.'

Aelfric sighed. 'The day my lady wife told me she was pregnant with yet another boy, I knew he would be more trouble than he was worth. The fabled seventh son of the seventh son. I considered arranging for an accident to happen, thought about it for months. It would have been so easy, Oswald, so very easy. No one would have been any the wiser – but then my brother Eadric started bothering me with these stories about the Elder Gods and prophecies. I thought, perhaps I should let this run its course. See what comes of it, maybe there would be a way to work this to my advantage. And now look where we are.' He gestured grandly. 'My son, the bane of my existence, has become the guardian of the worlds. And yet he plays in the mud with a little human girl. He *defies* me at every turn. And his mother? She gathers with her Stormborn and has meetings with heads of state from across the Otherwhere – all under the guise of the upcoming Midwinter Ball. Does she think I'm stupid, Oswald?'

Oswald blinked at his king's question. 'No, I'm sure she's aware of your intelligence, sire.'

'Then why does she think talking insurrection and treason behind my back will go unnoticed?'

'I'm sure that is not the case, sire. The queen has ever been your greatest supporter in all things.'

Aelfric snorted and stood up. 'Once, perhaps. But no longer. She has her own spies, Oswald. She suspects something.'

'We have been very careful, your majesty. No one but your closest circle knows of our plans. And Zane, sire, he is happy to do whatever you wish of him. He is your most loyal supporter and wants humans back where they belong – cowering under the might of the Sidhe.'

'So he assures me every time we meet up. Tell me, Oswald. This prophecy you've brought me here. What if it is real? What if Eadric's kami spawn is indeed the vessel that can hold the Elder Gods' power?'

'Then I suggest we keep him alive, sire. I suggest we hunt him down and take him to the island. We already control the lake and surrounding area and no one would tell any tales of extra movements. Once we've performed the ritual to recall the Elder Gods, we bind them with the goddess and strip them of their combined powers. The boy can easily be manipulated into taking on their power. No one can stand the crush of that much magic, sire, and his mind would be yours. At your bidding he'd be able to tear the Veil entire and you would be able to send your amassed forces into the human world . . .' Oswald's voice hitched as he contemplated the wholesale destruction. 'The human world would once more be one with the Otherwhere. And a new age will dawn for the Sidhe.'

Aelfric smiled. 'You think it would be an easy victory?'

'With the help of the Glow, sire. Its spread is unprecedented and demand has tripled. Merrick's altered the compound and it's far more potent in its current form. Humanity never stood a chance against a drug this powerful. Those who withstand the drug may fight back. Humans are resilient and their weaponry would kill a great many of us, but with the Veil demolished, and with magic coursing through the Frontier once more, their weapons and technology would become next to useless.'

Aelfric considered Oswald's words. He'd known the boy all his life, had chosen him specifically for the role as his left-hand man. Very few people had met Oswald and knew the extent of his reach – Aelfric preferred it this way. As did Oswald. Oswald had a fast mind but sometimes his zeal and steadfast belief in Aelfric's numerous plans surprised even the High King.

'Very well. Change of plan.' Aelfric turned from the window where he stood regarding the vast forest. 'Bring me my nephew. Unharmed, if you can. Or rather, on the right side of alive. Let's see if this boy is really the one who will bring about all we desire.'

'How soon?'

'I'm surprised you're still here, to be honest.'

Oswald hid a smile at the petulant tone and quickly bowed himself out of the private chambers; exiting the Citadel via its labyrinthine secret tunnels.

Chapter Forty-Two

It's been two hours since we arrived back to find everyone crowded into the Garrett mansion. It's a huge shock to the system being surrounded by this many people, after the house has been quiet for some weeks, and to be hugged so much. Particularly by Megan.

I slip into the study where Andrew's been talking to Dante and listen to him question Dante about his upbringing, what he remembers about growing up and how he came to join the Spooks. Dante shows Uncle Andrew the ring he'd shown me during his fever and Andrew stops his pacing. He takes the box from Dante but doesn't touch the ring.

'They found this ring with you?'

'Yes. The brothers at the monastery kept it for me until I was sent to live with my foster parents.'

'The monastery you grew up in, was there anything strange about it?'

'Yes.' Dante grins. 'They kept awful hours and I think the only time I managed to get a full night's sleep was when I moved away.'

Andrew chuckles at that and hands the box back to him. 'This ring is not a common trinket, that's for sure. It's either a very clever fake or this is indeed Eadric's ring. I've never seen it myself, but all the sons of Alba carry the ring of their forefathers.'

'What's inscribed on Aelfric's ring?' I ask from where I'm stretched out on the couch by the window. 'I don't think I've ever seen it.'

'A griffin.' Andrew frowns at me as if he's just spotted me for the first time.

Before he can shout at me for asking dumb questions, I hold up a hand. 'You said you wanted to see me. I thought I'd wait in here until you were done because Megan was trying to strangle me, she was holding on so tight.'

I sit up and smile at him, glancing at Dante, who looks far more relaxed than I thought he'd be under the weight of Andrew's interrogation.

'I think we're done here. I don't *think* Andrew believes I've set you guys up in some way.'

'You really thought that of Dante?'

Andrew shrugs. 'I had to make sure for myself.'

I want to argue but Dante says, 'He's right, Kit. This could be bad for your family. If Aelfric chooses to see me as a threat, because of who my father was and what he did . . .'

'It's a possibility, but we'll cross that bridge when we come to it. My wife is currently working through some of the law books we keep in storage with Letitia at the fort. We'll find a way to introduce you to Alba in the least dramatic way possible.'

'Thank you, sir.' Dante shakes Andrew's hand and exits the study quietly, pulling the door shut behind him.

'That is a nice kid. I like him.'

'Told you so. Will you tell Jamie to calm down now?'

'You can tell him yourself. He'll be here in the next day

or so.' Andrew sits down in the large leather chair opposite me. 'I think now is as good a time to talk as any about a few things, Kit, don't you?'

I've faced monsters and fought nightmares. Seeing Uncle Andrew's serious expression makes my heart thunder and my hands sweat.

'You've promised, ages ago, to tell me about my parents. You kept mentioning Christmas and it's not quite Christmas yet . . .' I pull up a smile. 'Three weeks to go.'

'It's close enough and it's time you know what I know.'

Andrew's serious expression is disconcerting. I sit upright on the couch and cross my legs under me so I'm facing him properly.

'I don't know if I want to hear any of this,' I say, and I can't quite believe that I admitted that. 'I mean, obviously I want to know, but it's going to change my perception of them, isn't it? It could change how I see the family, and myself. Are you going to explain why my grandmother took me away?'

'It's time that you know, Kit. All of it – as much as I know to be true, anyway.'

I stare around the Garretts' library. It's a friendly room that invites conversation and study – but the mood is ominous in here now despite the welcoming fire in the grate.

'Okay.' I exhale through my nose and roll my shoulders as if I'm preparing for a fight. 'I'm ready.'

Andrew folds his hands on his lap and leans forward in the chair a little. He's a big, bearded guy in his fifties and still looks as if he could go a few rounds with the monster of the moment. But right now, he almost looks nervous.

'Your mother Sammy was always a little wild. But she had her head screwed on right. She hung out with Miron a lot when she was a teenager and she worried us with her wild partying but Mirabelle – your grandmother – just laughed and pointed out the stupid things we all did when we were younger. She knew her daughter and told us to stay out of her business. Sammy finished school, went to university and she met this guy there – he was German. His name was David Hoffman. We didn't think anything of it, at first. But then we found out that David was a Spook. He had been sent to make friends with Sam, to get her to give up as much about the Blackharts as she knew. Obviously things got out of hand and the family went crazy. My father wanted Mirabelle to order Sammy to come home, to break it off with this boy, but Mirabelle stood firm. She would not have her daughter's happiness jeopardized. We couldn't understand it. The guy was a Spook. They'd been trying to find a way into the family since the eighteen hundreds. And here he was, this threat to the family, and Mirabelle just told us to back off.' The silence in the library lay heavy and, as only a few lamps were lit, the room was swathed in shadows.

'Gran was so badass.'

'Yes, she was. My father, her brother, was head of the family back then. He threatened Mirabelle and she just ignored him and told him to mind his own business. He insisted Sammy *was* his business. Mirabelle wouldn't budge and she told him she would cut her ties with the family if he dared throw his weight around. She said that the family was a democracy and that she wouldn't stand by and see her child threatened. Anyway, my father cooled off after that. Mirabelle was an incredible asset to the family. She knew Fae lore like the back of her hand and he was reluctant to alienate her. She was working closely with your aunt

Letitia to expand our libraries at the time, so losing her would have been a terrible blow to the family. And she'd already lost her husband years before, when Sammy was about eight. My father knew that Mirabelle blamed him for her husband's death. Anyway, by this time Sammy knew that David was a Spook but she was okay with it. She finished her university degree and did jobs for the family when and where required, and she was good. Kit, your mother was one of the most talented strategists I've ever come across. She had a gift that would have made her a general in days of old. And obviously, she could fight. She had classical training in a variety of weapons but she could brawl with the best of the East End's bullyboys.'

'She sounds amazing.'

'She was. And David worshipped her. He proposed the day she got her degree and she said yes. She started doing jobs for the Spooks on a freelance basis. My father had died by then and I'd taken over running the family. And even though I wasn't happy with the way things were going, I'd have had to be blind not to see how much David loved her and that she loved him. I made them wait another year to get married, though, because I felt that they were both really young. But when that year was up, they set their wedding date and I've never seen the likes of it since. Imagine a wedding in the grounds of the Manor, Kit. With Miron and his ilk rubbing shoulders with full-blown Sidhe. Even Suola showed up. She was very fond of your mother. It was quite the party and it was easy enough for everyone to see that Sam and David were in love. A year and a half later you were conceived. And Samantha came to me one night, very late, very pregnant. She wanted out. She wanted to leave the family behind, take David and go and live somewhere quiet and away from the craziness that surrounds our family.'

'What did you say?'

'I agreed. The Blackhart family is large. Sam leaving was a blow to the family, but it was what she wanted. She had her studies she could fall back on. She'd been offered a job as an assistant professor at Oxford to teach theology, which was something she wanted to do. David would quit his job as a Spook and find something else too. His training was unique and he was sure he could get a job doing something for the government.'

'So they left?'

'They did. They moved to Oxford and Mirabelle couldn't have been more proud. They were so happy with the new life they'd made for themselves. We stayed in touch, of course, and you were just a few months old when they were on their way down to the Manor for Christmas, and their car was attacked.'

I gape at him. 'No. They died in a car crash. My nan told me. There was no –' my voice hitches – 'attack.'

'They were attacked by a group of redcaps. Their car was mutilated. Sammy died instantly. David wasn't so lucky. He . . .' Andrew swallows. 'He fought them off and was cut to shreds. When the rescue services found them, David had crawled halfway into the car to be with Sammy. He was holding her, and between the two of them, the firemen found you, fast asleep.'

Tears spill unchecked down my face. 'That's . . . awful.'

'I know. Jamie found traces of redcap interference at the crash site and he tracked them. But they disappeared into the Otherwhere and we never knew who'd sent them. At the funeral Mirabelle couldn't even look at me. She held you as we lowered your parents into their graves and then she just took you and walked away from the graveyard. And she kept on walking. Initially we thought she'd come back, but we lost all trace of her. For years and years we had no idea where she was. Jamie reluctantly admitted a few years ago that he'd been following your and Mirabelle's progress through Europe, China and Japan. He'd known where you were all along and he'd kept it from us. When you surfaced in the UK again, in that village, he'd reached out to Mirabelle and she'd asked him to stay away. Then, on the night of the fire, she'd called him, frantic. She'd been spotted by one of the Sidhe. Without the family's protection she knew that she was in danger, but more importantly, that you were in danger. She asked Jamie to come and fetch you. But by the time he arrived, he found the house in flames with firemen crawling over the place. Mirabelle was dead and you were in hospital with smoke inhalation.'

'And then he came to fetch me and we tracked the Sidhe and the redcaps . . .' I scrub at my face and sniff. 'I really wasn't ready to hear any of this, Andrew.'

'You needed to know, Kit.'

'My parents were murdered.' I gratefully accept the handkerchief he holds out to me and blow my nose. 'You've tried to figure out who did this?'

'We think the redcaps happened across them by accident. They saw the opportunity and took it. We've looked into the jobs your parents did prior to their death and there was nothing there out of the ordinary. Nothing at all. The cases were closed and that was it.'

'Someone hated my parents enough to kill them.' My brain can't seem to get past this. 'Why would anyone do this? They weren't bad people.'

'I can't say, Kit. But we've searched, trust me when I say this. Jamie's not left a stone unturned since that day. When he's not on jobs, he's following leads. And it all points directly to it being luck on the redcaps' part. Samantha and David were in the wrong place at the right time.'

I wipe my eyes again and stuff the handkerchief in my pocket. 'Thanks, Andrew . . . for telling me this. I need to be alone for a little while, I think.'

Andrew stands and walks me to the door. I slip out and take the servants' stairs at the back of the house. I start sobbing as soon as my door is locked behind me. I crawl onto my bed and pull my duvet over my head and cry. I cry for my parents and I cry for my nan, but mostly, I cry for myself – because, due to some random fluke, I never had the chance to know my mum and dad. I hold onto the small piece of antler around my neck that had been my mother's and I wish with all my heart that I'd never been born into this family. If it weren't for that, I'd have grown up with both my parents still alive.

Chapter Forty-Three

I don't make it down to dinner. I fall asleep, and when I wake up hours later, I'm a mess of swollen eyes and my nose has started bleeding again. I stumble into the shower and afterwards pull on yoga pants and one of Aiden's T-shirts and crawl back into bed. It's after midnight when someone scratches on my door.

'Kit? Hey, Kit. I've got hot chocolate. Let me in.'

'I'm not good company right now, Meg. Sorry.'

'If I wanted good company I'd be hanging out with Aiden and his boyfriend. But I can only stand so much existential angst as they stare at one another in this weird *I think I'm in love with you but I'm not sure you love me back* kind of way.'

I laugh. 'You're not going to go away, are you?'

'Nope.'

And God, when did she become this annoying? I shuffle over, unlock the door and shuffle back to the bed.

Megan is dressed in pyjamas and ridiculous knee socks with pompoms. Her hair's pulled back in a messy bun on the top of her head and she looks about nine.

'You are such a sucker for this stuff,' she says, and hands

me my hot chocolate. 'Shift up so I can get into bed. It's bloody freezing out.'

She squirms until she's comfortable and I smile at her.

'You look like you've been dragged backwards through a bush, girl,' she tells me seriously. 'But the hot choc will help. I even have cookies.'

'I'm not hungry,' I say, and see her jaw drop.

'Are you the real Kit Blackhart?' she demands, leaning close. She sticks her tongue out and actually licks my cheek. 'No, you still taste like her.'

'Uch, what the *hell*, Megan?' But she's made me laugh as I scrub my face with my sleeve. 'You've just become even weirder since I last saw you.'

'But you still love me,' she points out sagely.

'Sometimes. I love you sometimes.' I sigh. 'I have missed you, though. Are you only staying for Christmas?'

'Yeah, school starts again in the new year.'

We chat about her studies in New York and she looks so happy and relaxed that I envy her.

'But I miss you and Marc.' She closes her eyes for a moment. 'Seriously. My twin is giving me complete nightmares. He's become this complete bundle of stress lately – and even with Kyle there to help with the house, it's just got worse.'

'What's he worried about? School stuff?'

'Yes, but this past two weeks it's mostly the Glow thing. One of his college friends died from an overdose, like two days ago.'

I stare at her in shock. 'I didn't know. He never said anything. He should have *said* something. He knows we're handling the case.'

'You're doing really well, Kit, calm down.' Megan's

expression has turned very serious. 'You took out the main factory making this crap when you took down the Jericho Gang. My dad's been talking to the SOCA guys for most of the day and – thanks to you and the boys – they have a paper trail now. They're hitting all the businesses listed in this guy Pensa's files and raiding them. This stuff is being taken off the streets and no more kids will die.'

'But Merrick escaped,' I say. 'He led us straight into a trap and ran off.'

'Whatever your boy Dante threatened him with obviously didn't scare him enough.'

'You know about that?'

'Kit, you've been asleep for most of the day. We've been talking non-stop for hours and hours while you were up here.'

'Oh.' I take a sip of my hot chocolate and make happy noises. 'Well, I suppose that's okay then. When is Marc getting here with Kyle?'

'Tomorrow, I think. Looks like we're all camping out at the Garretts' for Christmas this year.'

'It doesn't bother you?' I stare into my mug. 'Blackhart Manor is almost rebuilt, and instead of celebrating Christmas there, we're all over here?'

'Christmas is about family and not where you spend it. Besides, the place has no furniture. And the Garretts have the best beds. My room here is on the far side, in the east wing. The bed is massive, it has a *canopy*, and the ceiling is painted.' She rolls her eyes. 'It will give me delusions of grandeur.'

We chat for another hour or so until she switches the light off and we curl up together and fall asleep.

I wake up before dawn and stumble out of bed, my heart thudding against my chest.

Something is wrong. I can feel the wrongness trembling through me. I grab for my sword but it's gone; missing after Jimmy brought us back. Instead I pluck my baton off the nightstand and yank the door open just as there's a muffled shout from Dante's room and a loud crashing noise. I don't hesitate. I shoulder his door open and take in the chaos of his room with a glance. Dante's grappling with a large Sidhe warrior in black armour.

The guy has him up against the wall and he's slamming Dante's head into it. He barely glances over his shoulder at me but Dante's eyes widen and he holds out a hand towards me as if he's trying to warn me off. The warrior takes Dante's lack of attention as an opportunity and just hefts Dante up and into the air with shocking ease and throws him across the room.

As the guy spins towards me I run at him with my baton, whipping my wrist forward so that it extends with a neat little *snikt* sound. He parries my attack with the back of his gauntlet and I let the baton slide down his arm as I step into his space. I grab the top of his cuirass and pull him towards me as I drop my head. Completely taken surprise by my utter lack of strategy, the guy is caught off guard. As my forehead crunches into his nose, he staggers back with a shout of pain.

There's movement and yelling behind me. The guy scrabbles to get away from me and runs towards Dante, who's woozily trying to get to his feet. The guy grabs hold of Dante, flings a last look at me as I move closer and then pulls a small token from around his neck.

I'm still in shock, remembering all too clearly how Istvan

took Thorn and disappeared with him while everyone else was too busy arguing.

No. This can't be happening again.

As he holds onto Dante, who's sagging heavily, the Sidhe snaps the token between his fingers and then they're gone.

Chapter Forty-Four

The noise is apocalyptic within Dante's room. There is a lot of shouting and people talking fast. I stay low, curling into myself because it's just too much to deal with on top of Dante's disappearance. I swallow my rising nausea as my head starts pounding and press my hand to my mouth. This is no time for histrionics, I tell myself. We have to get to Dante. He's been taken by the Sidhe to who knows where – I'm pretty sure it's not anywhere good, like the Maldives.

'Come with me.' Aiden pulls me up. He pushes me ahead of him and walks me out of the room, his broad back a barrier against the noise of his dad, Jonathan, and Andrew arguing about the best way to find out where Dante is now.

'We have to *find* him, Aide,' I mutter. 'They can't have him too.'

'I know, Kit, I know. Let's just get you sorted out. I need you thinking and on your feet. Right now you're freaking out.'

To my surprise he takes me outside and I shiver in my light clothes but he holds me close. The garden has been transformed by an overnight snowfall and is now a vision of white. It looks magical and beautiful.

'Just breathe for me, okay? Get some of the air into your lungs. Ground yourself.'

'It's *cold*, Aide,' I say, and point to my feet. 'I'm not wearing socks.'

'Kit.' Aiden points vehemently. 'Look at what I'm showing you.'

It takes me a few seconds to make out the figure in the cloak, as he comes walking out of the shadows. Thorn's wrapped against the cold and he holds another cloak in his hand.

'How did you know I was here?' Thorn's voice is pitched low so that it would only reach our ears. With the house behind us filled with angry wolves and shocked Blackharts, we didn't need an audience.

'You said he was *family*. That you would look out for him. You *knew* something like this would happen.' Aiden's hands curl into loose fists at his side. 'You *saw it in our future*, didn't you?'

Thorn's looks as if this is the very last place he wants to be, but he nods. 'I thought someone would find him and see his potential. I saw him being taken, in so many possible futures, but I just couldn't be sure . . . I'm sorry.'

'You actually saw it. You saw him being taken.'

'*I couldn't interfere.*'

Aiden's past me and in Thorn's face so fast I have no time to react.

'You're using him as bait.'

'No. You need to understand, Aiden, that what I saw . . . it's not always clear. I see the potential that something might happen. And even then there are always different possible outcomes.' His voice stays calm as he talks to Aiden. 'Do you think this is something I wanted to happen? To see my cousin dragged off in the middle of the night? For him to become yet another victim of someone's grandiose schemes?'

'You could have *warned* us. You could have told us to watch out.'

I put my hand on Aiden's shoulder and lean against his back. 'Aiden. He's here to help.' I don't say that he *did* tell us to be careful, but that as usual we decided how seriously we wanted to take it. Thorn is still gazing at Aiden, desperate for him to give some sign he understands. When Aiden's posture finally relaxes, Thorn pulls him into a hug.

'Go get dressed, both of you,' he says. 'Let's go and find Dante.'

'Do we tell the others?' I ask.

'It's up to you, but you need to decide fast. The longer you wait, the further away Dante and his kidnapper get.'

Aiden rubs at his face and considers Thorn's words before replying. 'I think we'll move faster if there are just the three of us.'

'You realize that whoever took him will probably have an army?' I say. I'm shivering now and hopping from foot to foot. It is *cold*. 'We're good, but we're not that good.'

'It's fine. I have people who are helping with this,' Thorn says, and he sounds offhand, as if he doesn't want to go into it. 'But we really need to hurry.'

'Are you just going to stay out here, while we get ready?'

Thorn makes an impatient noise and pushes Aiden towards the door. 'Yes, wolf, by the stars. I'm going to stay here and wait for you to sneak out of the house – better dressed and armed, I hope. Make haste.'

Aiden snorts and turns back to the house. I follow close behind and Aiden presses a finger to his lips as we close the back door behind us. We both sneak back upstairs without being spotted.

'This is dumb, you know that, right? Going after Dante by ourselves and not telling anyone.'

I lift my eyebrows in surprise, because I must have lost the memo where Aiden became the kid who played by the rules.

'Should we leave them a note?'

He looks relieved at my suggestion, despite its rather sarcastic delivery. 'Good plan.'

I watch him as he grabs some hiking boots.

'You don't have to do this, Aide. I can go with Thorn. You can stay behind and try to stop the lot downstairs from doing anything stupid.'

He makes a rude snorting noise. 'Yeah, not gonna happen, Kit. Dante's my friend too, even if you saw him first.' His hands still on his boot laces. 'I can't imagine what he must be . . . I have to help.'

I drop a hand to his shoulder.

'They'll be taking him to Lake Baikal.'

'Are you *serious*?'

'That would be my guess. You heard the prophecy – Dante also has the potential to be a vessel, to channel the Elder Gods' magic. And that's where the whole thing with the Elder Gods happened the first time round, when Istvan tried to bring them through. So, yes, we'll have to check it with Thorn, but I believe we get a repeat visit to our favourite island between the worlds.'

The enormity of what might be happening to Dante is hitting him now and he pales. 'We have to do something.'

I nod. 'I'll be back here in five minutes.' I hurry to my own room, keen to be as quiet as possible because the wolves

and their damned super-hearing make creeping around difficult. I strap the baton to my forearm before I change into
my jeans – and put on layers of tops before pulling on the
warm jacket Aiden gave me. I hesitate over my boots. They're
big and kick-ass but they are noisy. There's no way we'd
get out without being heard. So I decide I'll have to carry
them and Aiden will just have to carry me through the
garden till we get somewhere where I can put them on. The
logistics of sneaking around are far more difficult than I
imagined. I slip out of my room just as Aiden opens his
door. He holds up the note he's written.

> *Gone to Lake Baikal with Thorn and Kit. Come if
> you can. Sorry we ran off w/o telling you. No time to
> argue.*
> *You can be angry at us afterwards.*
> *Love*
> *A&K*

I nod in silence. Aiden looks nervous as he turns back to
his room to leave the note behind. When he comes out he's
carrying the Japanese sword I saw Dante use in the past.
He hands it to me without a word and I'm grateful to have
a weapon once more. I like my baton and my knives but
there's something comforting about having a decent-sized
stabbing and slicing sword on your hip.

Then we move swiftly along the passage and down the
back stairs. We slip out of the back door and I tense when
Aiden closes it behind us as softly as possible. Thorn stirs
from where he's taken up a place by the fountain. I know
this isn't exactly the moment, but I can't help noticing that

his eyes are incredibly blue against the white fur of his hood. I stay on the mat, so that my socks stay dry, and put down my boots to slip on the cloak Thorn offers me. He gently lifts the hood to cover my hair and touches a finger to my cheek. We stare at each other for a breathless moment. Then noise from inside the house breaks the tension. Thorn hands another cloak to Aiden, who looks uncertainly at it but flings it on anyway. I grab my boots just as Aiden lifts me in his arms, bridal-style, and follows Thorn to the edge of the garden where he disappeared last time with Crow.

I wonder vaguely why this corner makes such a good gateway, but as we walk into it, I realize that it's where the leylines are the strongest. I know that making this transition is not Aiden's favourite thing to do so I tighten my grip around his shoulders a little and tap my finger against his neck to distract him. He glances down and gives me a wink as we follow Thorn onwards.

It's different travelling with Thorn along the leylines. It's faster than with other people, for one. Unlike Crow, he doesn't use the trees to navigate his way from one place to the next. He merely walks into a racing stream of energy and, gripping Aiden's arm, he leads us along the leylines. He chooses paths and junctions at intervals, never hesitating once. The speed we're moving at is disconcerting and it feels as if we're on one of those moving walkways you find in airports – only a vastly speeded-up version. In fact, my head reels from how fast we're going and then Thorn starts moving faster still. Aiden just tightens his hold on me and starts sprinting after Thorn. I want to call out to Thorn and ask him to stop so Aiden can put me down – but then we're slowing down again and finally we come to a complete standstill.

I have no idea where we are. It feels as if I'm in the centre of the universe. There are explosions of colour and a cold icy wind buffets me, ruffling the fur of my hood and I duck my chin against the cold touch. Aiden lets me stand and I experience a moment of disorientation and cling to him pathetically before finding my balance. I sit down and pull my boots on, checking that both my knives are in their sheaths. When I stand, Thorn hands me my sword and I grip it tightly, suddenly feeling far better.

'Not much further now,' he says. His voice is comforting and vibrant in this strange place. 'You're both doing very well', he says, scrutinizing us. 'Keep close.'

And then we're off again. The journey is fast, colours streaking past at high speed; it's the equivalent of a CGI space shuttle hurtling through hyperspace at the movies. I wonder if I'm Starbuck or Luke Skywalker. The thought amuses me and then I'm being drawn to a halt by Thorn, with Aiden bringing up the rear.

'We're about to walk through a gateway. I don't know what to expect, so be ready to fight.'

I nod, unsheathe the wakazashi, practise a few cuts and slices with it and nod. It will do. It's not the sword I'm used to but beggars can't be choosers. Aiden rolls his shoulders, flicks his hand open and curves his fingers so that his claws curve outwards. He grins at Thorn.

'Ready.'

I anticipate a massive brawl, possibly being skewered, sliced to pieces and pierced by arrows. What I don't expect is to walk out of the gateway, my head still not quite with it, to see Thorn's mother and her full complement of Storm-born guards arrayed behind her. Behind them are ranks of around four hundred warriors and what look to be Sidhe nobles – representatives from all the major houses if their banners are anything to go by.

'Mother.' Thorn walks forwards and stops a few paces from her. 'I did not expect you to be here.'

Dina's expression gives nothing away, and her gaze sweeps over Thorn to notice Aiden and me. I stand my ground, tighten the grip on my sword and keep my chin up, refusing to be intimidated. Aiden lounges casually next to me, no doubt doing the bored, sullen face that gets under people's skin so much. It seems to works too, because just behind Dina one of the Stormborn shifts inside his armour, and a pair of hostile eyes fix themselves on Aiden.

'Looks as if I'm making friends,' Aiden mutters quietly enough for only me to hear. 'I should come here more often.'

'No, you really shouldn't.'

If Thorn or his mother hear our exchange they don't let on and Diana says, 'Of course I'm here. Where did you think I would be?'

I glance around at the assembled Sidhe warriors. The last time I saw this many of them together they were camped in a valley in Scotland. They were preparing to go through a gateway to fight the traitor Eadric. And now? What were they doing here now? Were they here to prevent us getting to Dante?

'I'm not entirely sure what's going on,' Thorn says, and his shoulders are tight with tension.

Above us the clouds hang low and dark, heavy with snow. The island I remember has changed completely. It no longer appears remotely tropical and instead feels strangely barren and desolate. The sandy bowl that baked beneath the sun when I was here last remains, but the soil generally is entirely lifeless.

A cold wind kicks up and I reflexively pull my cloak closer and take a step closer to Thorn. Aiden moves too until we're flanking him. He barely acknowledges our presence but I sense that he relaxes marginally.

'I think it's time that you and I spoke,' Thorn says at last. 'Mother to son. Guardian to his queen.'

Chapter Forty-Five

Dina walks towards a small pavilion they've erected. It's open to the elements and seems completely incongruous in this setting. Thorn follows, as do we. If Dina has any misgivings about us playing tagalong she gives no indication.

She stops at the table in the middle of the tent. It is covered in maps, one seemingly of the island. As she moves the papers, I see a detailed outline of the temple complex beneath it. That really would have made all the difference the last time I'd been here, trying to save Thorn. A good, hard look is enough for me to memorize most of it. I notice that the underground amphitheatre seems the same, but perhaps the stage area looks larger.

'What is this?' Thorn asks, pressing his fingers against the temple plan as he leans over it. The papers crackle under his touch and the air smells a little like fire as the atmosphere becomes even tenser. 'Where did you get these?' He lifts the maps and flicks through them.

'I had the complex mapped after the fiasco last year.' Dina says, looking angrily at her youngest son. 'But that is not what I want to talk about, Thorn. Did you think we wouldn't find out about Dante? Didn't you think we'd been looking for him for years?' Dina watches her son closely and when he doesn't say anything she looks exasperated. 'When you discovered him, why didn't you come to me with this and tell me?'

'You know why, Mother. Your loyalty is to Alba and to the king. Coming to you with the son of a traitor in tow, telling you that he is family and has a rightful place in the house of Alba, what would you have done?'.

The cold wind gusts through the valley and I shiver in my cloak and try not to fidget, taking my cue from Aiden, whom I've never seen so immobile. His gaze rests unwaveringly on Dina and I get the unwelcome impression that he won't hesitate to attack her – if she gives Thorn an answer he doesn't want to hear.

'My loyalty lies to Alba,' Dina says, her tone surprisingly mild given her son's question, 'but before that I am my father's daughter. And before that I'm the daughter of the dragon. Do you understand?'

I feel as confused as Thorn looks and when he shakes his head I'm relieved. Dina will have to explain herself better and I might have a chance to make sense of this.

'I too am kami. The dragon spirit that dwells within you and I is part of the kami pantheon. You and I are the last of our kind, as your brothers haven't manifested the talent.' Here she lifts her hands, and they're instantly wreathed in flame. Her eyes, the same changeable blue-green as her son's, watch us through the flames and she smiles, letting the fire die away. 'Dante's mother was my cousin and we were very close. I am the one who introduced her to Eadric. They fell in love at the wrong time. Had I not introduced them, they would never have met as their worlds – and personalities – were so far apart. Eadric the scholar and Haruku the child of spring. I heard that Eadric went insane after Haruku's death, after she'd given birth. He took the boy with him and disappeared and I've not stopped searching for Dante since.'

'You knew Eadric had a son? That I had a cousin? And you never *told* anyone – not even when we learned of Eadric's plans to usurp Father?' Thorn moves to tower over his mother. 'You kept that from all of us, including Father?'

'Yes,' she said quietly. 'The boy was blameless and hidden so well that none of my spies ever managed to find a trace of him. Until a few weeks ago –' her eyes find mine – 'when our little Blackhart took a job with Suola, and Suola took it upon herself to send me a message, that there was something strange about the human boy she'd employed to work with Kit.'

'And yet you *still* never said anything.' The silence at Thorn's statement hung heavy in the air. 'So have you decided that you'll stand against the king in this? You'll protect my cousin, despite his traitorous father?'

Her answer comes, grave but unwavering. 'Yes. He has my friendship and the swords of my Stormborn to command.'

Thorn seems to sag a little in relief, and Dina allows herself a small smile as she wraps her arms around him.

'I am so proud of you.' She cups his face and stares into his eyes. 'Your loyalty and honour cannot be questioned.'

Thorn pulls away, looking as if she's just delivered him a blow to the heart. 'How is that possible? I feel I am a traitor to Alba. I have gone behind my father's back and kept Dante a secret from him,' he says, his words heavy and holding none of the relief I thought I would hear. 'I dearly wish I could speak with him about this . . . but none of what I've seen in any of my visions shows me it would work to our advantage.'

'Your father . . . was a good man, once.' Dina's gaze as she stares past us to where the army is arrayed is melancholy. 'He held Alba dear, dearer even than he held his family, I would say. But he's changed, Thorn. We've all seen it. I have most certainly seen it and felt it. He no longer looks outward, to what he can gain for us and for Alba, for our future. Instead he looks inward, to what he can gain for himself, as Aelfric, the High King of Alba. He is no longer satisfied with what he has and his influence in the Otherwhere. He reaches for more.' Her eyes meets mine. 'Far more.'

'What are you saying?' It's testament to how shocked Thorn is by Dina's words that he doesn't address her as *mother* or *my queen* as he's done in the past. 'What do you know?'

'Your father is launching a full-scale invasion of the Frontier within a matter of weeks. He thinks he's kept this all a secret from me and he forgets I fought for him and I know him better than he knows himself.'

I close my jaw and clear my throat. 'Your majesty, can I just . . . ? He's planning an invasion of the Frontier? Have you alerted anyone – my uncles, maybe?'

Dina's full regard makes me want to cower but with Aiden pressing his shoulder against mine in support I don't waver under her gaze.

'You think, little Blackhart, that I will fail to stop my husband?' She nods to the Stormborn and the army before looking back at Thorn. 'These warriors are all at your side, ready to fight. They come from the twelve most prominent houses across the Seelie – and the Unseelie Court also supports *us*. They are all here to put a stop to Aelfric and his coterie of sycophants He is planning on performing the ritual to bring the Elder Gods back. He thinks he has the power to do so without rending our worlds apart. Your cousin has been brought here, drugged and insensible as their *vessel*.' Her scowl could flatten buildings. 'Their plan, according to my informants, is that Dante will absorb the goddess's power and that of the bound gods too. And that he will be fully under Aelfric's control at the time. With Dante by his side he could open a stable gateway between the worlds, flood the Frontier with thousands of goblins and Sidhe warriors and demand whatever he wants. If the humans do not comply, he will get Dante to use magic and destroy cities, bringing total chaos to the human world.'

'You've known about this? About the prophecy?' I can't help the anger in my voice. She meets my glare without so much as batting an eye.

'I found out when Aelfric did. Odalis's servants are very susceptible to bribes.'

'Mother, this . . .' Thorn's voice catches. 'It's too much. It is *exactly* what Eadric did, going against the crown in this way. And he started an insurrection that almost tore Alba apart. You cannot be involved in this. The king's retribution would be savage, to say the least. He would have you bound, locked away, my brothers . . . he would have my brothers murdered for this, even if they *are* all loyal to him . . . Let this be on my head alone. No one else needs to answer to him when this is done.'

For the first time Dina looks a little impatient at Thorn's words. 'But you won't be the only one to answer to him, Thorn. You have your friends with you. Do you think he wouldn't hunt them to the ends of all the worlds for as long as he is alive? They will not be safe, not ever, regardless of what you do.'

'We can take care of ourselves,' Aiden says, stepping

forward and sketching the most mocking bow I have ever seen. It was worthy of a slap. 'Thank you so much for your concern.'

Dina's mouth quirks and I see amusement in her eyes. 'And you, Blackhart? Are you capable of taking care of yourself? Of your family? You know Aelfric will come after all of you.'

'Not if we stop him.' My voice is almost too quiet and I clear my throat again. 'He shouldn't be able to play god with our lives in this way.'

'I agree,' Aiden says grimly, 'wholly and wholeheartedly. Thorn, mate, your dad's lost the plot. We have to stop him. I know you feel loyalty towards him because he's your dad and the king too, but what he's doing . . . it's not just Dante we're talking about – it's your world *and* my world and our futures he's messing around with here.'

Dina closes her eyes, pained, but she's nodding as Aiden speaks. When she looks at Thorn again her face is full of anguish. 'The wolf is right. Aelfric has to be stopped before he succeeds in any part of his plan.' She steps forward and captures Thorn's face between her hands. 'Thorn, you have seen all of this, I know you have. And you have seen the count-less outcomes, the repercussions our choices could forge. Even so, life doesn't always go to plan. In the end what matters is that we tried to leave behind a better world.'

Thorn bows his head to his mother and she smooths her fingers down his face before turning away abruptly, once more queen and commander of an army.

'We need to prepare.'

Thorn ignores her words and instead looks at me and Aiden in turn. 'You shouldn't be part of this, either. This is up to me to finish.'

For a second I just stare at him in disbelief, then I step closer and jab at his chest, making my point. 'Remember how I promised – no, *vowed* – to look after you when Scarlet lay dying? Do you think I give my word that easily?' I draw myself up to my full height and scowl at him. 'You go back in there and I will be right by your side. You try to leave me behind, I'll find a way to follow you. You brought us both here to rescue Dante. Nothing has changed. We're going. All three of us.'

'Yeah, and I go where she goes,' Aiden interjects. 'Sorry, mate. Besides, I've grown really *in like* with Dante. He makes excellent pancakes. You just can't let that kind of talent go to waste, you know?'

A smile stretches across Thorn's face and his attempt to glare us into submission fails badly. 'I don't deserve friends like you.'

'You're wrong,' says Aiden, grinning now too. 'You deserve a girlfriend like her *and* an awesome friend like me. Because, werewolves – you know? We're the accessory you can't live without.'

In answer Thorn just pulls us both into a warm hug. 'Fine. Let's try to save the world one more time.'

'It could be a hobby, don't you think?' Aiden says, and he winks at me but I can't wink back. Instead I nod and duck my head, desperately praying that we're not walking to our deaths.

Chapter Forty-Six

We wait until it is nearly dusk before we make our move. Thorn kisses his mother farewell. And after another scan of the maps showing the tunnels that run between the temples, we make our way to the larger of the buildings right on the edge of the complex. I just hope that we don't get spotted by Aelfric's scouts. Dina and her Stormborn will be bringing up the rear, moving in beneath three other temples. The rest of the massed army will stay behind, cover our backs and join the battle if required.

As we enter the first tunnel, the darkness stretches ahead – and even with my enhanced sight, things look positively Stygian. Thorn mutters softly and presses a hand against the carved stone wall on his left. A soft glow forms there and, as we move, the light moves with us, illuminating the striations in the stone and lighting our way just enough.

The tunnels are well kept and I wonder who maintains them. We don't speak at all but occasionally Thorn will look over his shoulder at me as if to ensure that Aiden and I are still hot on his heels.

'I hear something,' Aiden says after a while. 'Chanting. And drums, really big drums.'

A shiver passes over me and I close my eyes, fighting

against the memories. Last time I encountered this place, people had died and things had almost gone very badly wrong.

'We're close, then.' Thorn glances at me, then Aiden. 'It's not too late to turn back, if you'd prefer. I can do this by myself.'

'No.' My voice is firm. 'Stop trying to make us go back.'

'Yeah, it won't work,' Aiden agrees. 'Just lead the way, sweet baby dragon, and we'll back you up.'

I hide my grin behind my hand as Thorn scowls at Aiden. 'Sweet baby dragon?'

'I'm nervous, okay – it's the best I could come up with at short notice.'

'Wolf, you try my sanity.'

'What can I say? It's a gift.'

We've been hurrying down yet another passage as they quibble in low voices; just listening to them relaxes me. This I understand: it's a way for them to deal with the hot mess we're about to hit and it distracts me from my own growing anxiety.

Then Thorn pauses at an intersection and glances back at Aiden.

'I've got this,' Aiden says. 'Let me scout ahead. I'll be back before you can blink.' His hand brushes mine reassuringly as he ghosts into the darkness.

Thorn crouches, and I copy his movements, looking up to find him watching me closely.

'You're worried.'

I nod silently and lick my suddenly dry lips. 'Yes. I'm worried for Dante. I'm worried about us too, about what may happen if we don't stop them performing the ritual.'

'I need you to do me a favour, Kit.' Thorn pushes my

hood back and tilts my chin up so he can look at my face. 'When the time comes, you must ensure that Dante gets away, no matter the cost to me, or anyone else. Do you understand?'

'*No.*'

He jerks back at the force of my denial, and I put my sword down so I can rub at my face. My skin is cold and clammy and my hands are like ice, yet they're sweating. Explain that, science.

'We'll *all* come out of this,' I tell him. 'We have to. There is no other choice.'

'How are you *always* this stubborn, Blackhart?'

'You love me for it,' I say, trying for sass. But then realizing what I've just said out loud, I gape at him in dawning horror. 'Oh, wow, I don't actually . . . not, you know? Not *love* love, because that's just awkward. Holy hell, just let the earth swallow me now.'

I pull my hand away from my face in mortification and find that he's watching me even more intently than before.

'I do, Blackhart.'

'You do what?'

'Love you.'

I have the stupidest impulse to laugh right then, because this really isn't happening. Not now, not like this. But then he leans in and kisses me. It's not a big dramatic kiss, but a press of his lips to mine. It's soft, quiet and solemn – and filled with so much promise I can't help but lift my hand to the nape of his neck to steady myself because I feel as if I'm falling.

'Hey,' he says, resting his forehead against mine. He cups my face. 'I'm sorry, I shouldn't have said that. I don't expect you to say it back. We've not . . . this . . . ? This is not how I wanted to tell you.'

'It's fine.' My voice sounds so small. 'I, how about we do this again once we're back outside and not in fear of our lives?'

'Stubborn *and* clever.' His nose nudges mine in an Eskimo kiss and I grin because how is he this cute? 'It's a promise.'

He pulls me upright but doesn't stop staring at me, not even when Aiden silently appears out of the gloom.

'They have Dante on the stage in the main amphitheatre, tied to a huge black plinth. He looks drugged out of his mind. Aelfric is there too. And others I don't recognize – but they all look really pompous, swanning around in their black gowns like they're from Doctor Evil's School of Evil Wizardry or something.' He glares at nothing in particular as he gets his thoughts together. 'And there are around two hundred people in there, just chanting gibberish with those drums egging them on.'

'It's to help generate energy,' I say. 'It will help whoever has to perform the ritual, give them an extra push.'

'Well, the place reeks of magic. And it's not even a pleasant smell. Except when Dante uses his, then it's . . .' He grins at the distaste on my face. 'Why, hello there, Kit Blackhart. Are you about to call me out on being inappropriate when you've been making out with sweet baby dragon boy here?'

'Aiden.' But I'm laughing softly. 'Shut up.'

'Explain the layout ahead to me. Are there any guards posted?' Thorn asks.

'No guards now; the two I came across seemed very sleepy indeed. I helped them along nicely. But this tunnel basically opens out like this.' Aiden crouches down and draws the chamber in the dust, showing that we'll be coming through the main entrance centred at the back of the cavern. The passage turns into a clear walkway that leads straight down the middle of the amphitheatre, dividing the seating there in two, before it ends right before the large stage. 'And here, the stage area looks different to the rest of the place. Not as well made. I suspect you had something to do with that.'

'Yeah, we pulled the gateway stone down across the stage. It crashed and broke into pieces.' I try not to look smug.

'And then the ceiling collapsed, trapping Kit and she almost died.' Thorn's face is serious as he stares down at me. 'Let's not do that again.'

I roll my eyes at his dramatics but Aiden just grins. 'Your near-death in-jokes are hilarious. So, if I told you that there's a mirror up on that stage that's maybe fifteen feet tall and I don't know how many across. What would you say?'

'That we need to hurry.' Thorn takes a steadying breath and looks at both of us intently. 'I don't know what's going to happen in there but, thank you – for coming with me, for standing by me and for believing in me. I am very fortunate to have friends like you.'

'Uch, less drama, more slashing and fighting,' Aiden says, and then he's prodding Thorn but he looks really flattered at his words. 'Come on, before they make my almost-boyfriend do terrible things.'

The amphitheatre isn't as full as when I last saw it, but the magic in the air is thick and cloying. As we slip through the main doors, past the dozing guards that Aiden has so kindly put out of commission, we stay low in the shadows at the back as Thorn walks down the central aisle. I spot

Dante straight away, tied to the plinth as Aiden described, and my heart aches for him.

No one notices Thorn. He has the hood of his cloak up and I find it hard to concentrate on his figure as it moves down the aisle. Glamour, I realize, and wish I had the same level of talent to use on myself. Those who do seem to break from their chanting must assume he's one of the guards patrolling the amphitheatre and pay him no further attention.

He proceeds unmolested and it's not until one of the sorcerers on the stage glances towards the moving figure that there's any indication he's been spotted and recognized. The sorcerer speaks to his companion – a lean figure in light armour who's standing by the black plinth holding a book. Aelfric turns in surprise and stares at Thorn as he walks towards him.

'Son.' Aelfric's voice is amplified through the phenomenal acoustics in the amphitheatre.

Thorn stops at the bottom of the stage and looks up at him. 'Father.'

'I'm surprised to see you here. Have you come to join us?'

'I have come to stop you from making a mistake.'

'I think you are a little late for that, boy.' Aelfric waves nonchalantly off to one side. I stand on tiptoe, just within the tunnel's shadows, and I spot movement there.

A figure stumbles onto the stage and it takes me a moment to recognize him.

'Brixi,' I breathe in shock and press my hand to my mouth. 'He looks terrible.'

Two more people are shoved out onto the stage behind Brixi and they look vaguely familiar too, until I realize that they both resemble Brixi.

'They must be what's left of the Faceless clan,' Aiden offers softly. 'Let's move closer.'

As we move in the shadows, my eyes stray back to Dante, tied to the same plinth that held Thorn just over a year ago. Like Thorn, they have him tied with heavy iron chains and he looks dreadful, his expression dazed. One of the sorcerers lifts a bowl to Dante's face and, when he tries to pull his head back, the man grabs his jaw, forcing his mouth open. Dante seems to try to speak but the man just laughs and continues to angle the bowl towards his mouth. The liquid spills as Dante manages to jerk his face aside, the little he gets in his mouth, he spits out anyway.

The sorcerer gives a growl of frustration and brings his free hand down in a sharp striking movement. The metal binding Dante to the pillar tightens and he cries out in pain, straining against their hold.

'That guy is mine,' Aiden mutters. 'I'm going to enjoy feeding him his own entrails.'

Aelfric's talking more softly now and I strain to hear him clearly – although going by Thorn's rigid back, it's nothing pleasant.

'. . . you can do.' I make out as we shift ever closer along the wall, and Aelfric continues, 'The goddess is under my power, boy. As is my brother's whelp.' Aelfric tilts his head a little as he considers Dante's writhing figure. 'Just like his father, not quite aware of when he's beaten.'

'You will live to regret this,' Thorn says. The fact that the whole amphitheatre has fallen silent, watching father and son with burning intensity, does not pass me by. 'There is an *army* outside who will stop you in your tracks. You've worked for so much throughout your long reign. But instead, you'll be remembered as the man who killed his brother, imprisoned his nephew *and* tore down the Veil between the worlds in an act of hubris.'

'You have certainly taught my son to be eloquent, Lady Firesky.' Aelfric gestures to one of the robed figures. I realize now that she was the one who pushed the three Faceless onto the stage. 'I'm not sure if I should thank you for that.'

Odalis barely spares Thorn a look; instead she sighs and stares at Aelfric. 'My lord, the time draws near. We should start the ritual proper.'

Aelfric nods graciously. 'Very well. Bring the goddess.'

Brixi falls to his knees on the stage at the moment four Sidhe warriors bring out the sleeping goddess. Dante spots her too and struggles harder against his bindings, straining towards the unconscious figure with all his might.

Thorn leaps onto the stage and now has one of his long curved fighting knives in his hand. '*No*,' he shouts, pointing it at the Sidhe warriors. 'No, *you do not do this.*'

'It is already done, boy. She is dying anyway. It's a mercy.' Aelfric comes to stand by his side and peers down at the sleeping giant.

I don't miss Aelfric's nod to the sorcerers, but before I can scream a warning, they raise a wall of solid blue flame from the edge of the stage. It rises up, levelling off at a good twenty feet in the air at least. It seems to strain towards the open sky above the amphitheatre.

The drums and chanting start up once more and become an audible buzz that makes me itch beneath my skin.

'We have to get to Dante,' Aiden says, slowly straightening up. Everyone is far too focused on other things to pay us any attention now. 'How do we do that? I don't think we'll get through those flames by ourselves.'

'No, but there is another way onto that stage,' I say, and

I grin, because this I can do. 'Unless they've completely remodelled it, the tunnel to the left of the stage opens into a little antechamber. There's another passage from there that leads onto the stage.'

'Let's do this.'

I throw caution to the winds and run between the cavern wall and the assembled seats. An armoured guard appears from nowhere and aims a blow to my head. Before I can react, other than ducking, Aiden grabs the guy's head, twists it sharply to the side and lets him fall. The guard drops and we keep running.

Then we're past and move down the small passage into the room beyond. This is where Thorn, Kieran and I were held captive and it's not changed much – except for its new occupants: two large Fae standing guard over the unconscious bodies of several children. We last saw them connected to the goddess, fuelling her as she lay in her own deep sleep. I wonder briefly how she's managing without them. The guards seem as surprised to see us as we are to see them. But I react first, going to strike the guy nearest to me with my sword. He parries and we engage. I have no focus left for Aiden, but I hear him let out a snarl and then there's ripping noises. My opponent is good, really good – but he's probably used to fighting honourable fights with little to no underhandedness. When I switch sword hands he frowns but adjusts his response. He doesn't see me flick my iron baton from my forearm. He feels it, though. I whip it across his face once, and as he staggers back I follow up the blow with another. He drops his sword and grabs for his face with a howl of pain.

Aiden's there to slam the guard's head into the table. We watch the guy bounce once and then lie still. I remind myself that there's more at stake here than a Fae's possibly broken nose.

Without needing to communicate, we tie up both soldiers with their own belts and I waste no time quickly gagging them with strips torn from their shirts. Then I lean over the sleeping forms of the children. They're laid out on the wooden tables Istvan once used for his experiments, and it is so creepy staring down at their sleeping faces. But apart from looking too thin, they all seem fine.

A burst of noise comes from the amphitheatre and we sprint towards the stage. I round the corner and skid to a halt, because in the very short space of time we've been sorting out the guards, things have escalated dramatically in here.

Chapter Forty-Seven

Given how quickly things have moved on, I can only assume that Aelfric's sorcerers have a far better idea of how to summon the Elder Gods than Istvan and Olga. This in itself is a terrifying thought.

Dante is still bound, but is now looking more awake and also more horrified than before. Aelfric is holding a sword in one hand and gripping Thorn tightly around the shoulders with the other – effectively using him as a barrier between himself and the huge creature currently crawling through the ensorcelled mirror.

All six sorcerers are firmly focused on the heavy rune-inscribed mirror. And I don't blame them, because the creature following its brother looks even more terrifying. I clearly remember him picking me up and throwing me the length of the amphitheatre last time. Muscular, huge and horned, with an angular demonic face, he's a nightmare made flesh.

The god keeps straightening upright for what seems an age – and as he reaches his full height he lets out a bellow that makes my hair stand on end. The sound is raw and primal.

'*How many more?*' Aiden asks me. 'How many more of them?'

'Two more.'

As if my words bring them into being, two more creatures step from the mirror. They are lithe and beautiful until they turn to look at their welcoming party, and then their glamour fades and my brain struggles to comprehend the decaying horrors staring back at us. Taller than the Sidhe on the stage, they're smaller than their horned brother, and there's something even more *other* about them. I tear my gaze away from them reluctantly to try to make sense of what else is happening.

The sorcerer Aelfric named Lady Firesky moves towards the four gods, and says something rapidly in a high, lilting language. The way the four gods pause and swing their attention to the sorceress is terrifying. Four heads tilt in exactly the same alien way that gives me the creeps. She next uses a language that sounds guttural and harsh.

She gestures behind her and the gods' eyes flick to the prone body of the sleeping goddess. She then makes a sweeping gesture taking in the three kneeling Faceless and I watch, horrified, as the gods focus on their erstwhile servants. Each has a Sidhe warrior standing behind him and, as Lady Firesky gives a sign, the warriors slit their throats and they crumple to the stage. A dramatic offering to the Elder Gods, removing the servants who helped send them into exile.

The Sidhe warriors beside the goddess step away as the gods approach their sleeping sister. The guards look remarkably calm and their movements are almost lethargic. I realize then that they too have been drugged.

'What's going on?' I whisper to Aiden. 'Those warriors look high.'

'They are. Faeries are usually graceful, but those guys are practically falling over their feet.'

'Do you think they've been given Glow?'

'They . . . I mean? If they were guards you'd want them alert, why give them drugs? Do you think it's something else?'

I frown and shiver at the heavy magic in the air. 'I don't know. All I know is that we *have* to get Thorn and Dante away from Aelfric.'

'How?'

'I have no idea,' I hiss, feeling helpless and not a little lost.

Lady Firesky is now having an intense discussion with the four gods before her – she must have found a language that works. And she keeps pointing to the body of the sleeping goddess. The creature that first crawled from the mirror looks half-formed, and as Firesky speaks he drags himself nearer to the goddess. He leaves streaks of mud and slime behind as he moves, and it's a slow and torturous process as he crawls on his belly and elbows. He grabs the edge of the goddess's pallet and lifts himself upwards. He stares down at the sister who betrayed them at the dawn of time and – faster than I've ever seen anything move in my life – he lunges at her, his jaws wide.

That one movement seems to trigger something. The twins rush forward in their tattered rags, their gaping maws ringed with shark-like teeth. Their large black eyes shine with bloodlust as they reach for her over their brother.

I make to run forward, but as Aiden pulls me back the movement attracts the attention of the large horned demon. His eyes narrow and he takes a ponderous step towards us. Thorn is struggling against his father's grip and I hear Aelfric's surprised grunt when Thorn wrenches himself free. But he doesn't stay free for long, because Aelfric shoves him back with the blade of his massive sword, which rests heavily against Thorn's chest. I can see the lights gleaming off the blade and wince when I realize the blade is probably an unholy concoction of silver, iron and other metals. It must hold enough magic to actually burn through Thorn's clothing, as I can see rips in his clothing, and red welts beneath.

Lady Firesky, ignoring the commotion around the goddess, stalks towards Dante and grabs his hair to pull his head back. She says something to him, and her expression is vicious.

'*I won't do it*,' Dante thunders at her and we can all hear him. He manages to pull his head from her grip and stares down at her with loathing. '*Nothing* will make me agree to this.'

'It's interesting you think you have a choice.' She looks at Aelfric over her shoulder. '*Do it now.*'

Aelfric shoves Thorn towards the horned god with a savage push before turning on the three gods devouring their sister. Aelfric plunges the sword through the back of the first twin, before withdrawing it and doing the same to the other. He retrieves the blade in one elegant move, takes a two-handed grip and strikes off both their heads in rapid succession. The final god is bent over his sister, intent on devouring her, the mud on him shudders as his brothers' blood spills over him; the sound manages to be somehow both rich and gluttonous.

Aelfric doesn't pause and he flows from the two-handed strike into a graceful turn. Then, with a backward swipe of the blade, he severs the head of the mud creature. It's all over so fast that when the magic explodes from the bodies of the felled gods it flattens me completely.

I let out a startled gasp and strain against the wild power running rampant within the enclosed stage, the blue flames still cutting us off from the rest of the amphitheatre.

Thorn has staggered and dropped to one knee before the horned god and I see the creature bend down to try to grab him. Finding strength from somewhere, I push upright and run at the creature. I'm peripherally aware of the sorcerers harnessing the wild magic surrounding us in a way I've never seen before.

They are working in concert, performing a complicated ritual which resembles nothing so much as a particularly difficult dance. The magic levels in the air dip only slightly, but it's all I need to reach the horned god before he can grab for Thorn, who looks as if he's been wiped out by the wild magic coursing from the bodies of the fallen gods and goddess.

Because the god's angled away from me, I'm presented with his side, which is not the best target. I analyse the amount of damage I can do, even as I launch myself towards him. I ram my sword into the side of his neck with all my strength, and just keep thrusting the weapon upwards until it's up to its hilt behind the creature's jaw. It's a difficult move and I pray it will pay off. He sways towards me but I leave my sword in his neck and drop away. He claws at the blade as I reach down and help Thorn upright. He's heavier than I remember and feels burning hot to the touch – I pull my hand away when he's standing as his skin has actually singed my hand. I notice how his eyes seem far too shiny, and the pupils seem enlarged.

'*Run*,' he rasps. 'Kit. You must *run*.' But as he speaks his skin ripples and there's a definite scale pattern visible.

He's shaking as if he's coming apart and I don't know what to do.

Aiden's now by my side, and he's found a sword from somewhere. 'Guys, less swooning and more killing. Aelfric's having a fit and Dante's in a bad way. We have to get him untied.'

'*He's going dragon*,' is all I manage to say to Aiden before Thorn twists in front of us.

The movement looks terrifyingly alien, as his bones stretch and muscles change right before our eyes. Aiden catches him as he topples, and lies Thorn down on the floor. Thorn lets out a wild moan and his body arches as violent spasms shake him. When the moans transition into a full-on scream, I clap both hands over my ears as the sound reverberates right through me.

Behind us, Aelfric shouts a challenge and the horned god turns towards him; his hand finally getting a grip around the hilt of my sword that he's been pawing at in a dazed way. He starts pulling it out and the sound it makes as it frees is a horrible sucking noise.

Aelfric, the complete idiot, seems to think he's invincible, as he brandishes his own massive sword in his hand.

His sorcerers are now arrayed behind him in a semicircle. And as the creature lumbers towards Aelfric, they move to close the circle behind the god, leaving him facing the High King of Alba. Aelfric's attack is instantly fatal. There is no opening parry, no finesse.

He just delivers one straight thrust of that very large blade below the creature's ribs, aiming upwards into the chest cavity. The horned god bats Aelfric away with one huge hand and the high king of all of Alba staggers a few paces, wiping at the blood on his face. The blow does nothing to keep the look of triumph from his face.

The creature falls to his knees, still holding onto my blade. His other hand reaches for the sword thrust into his heart and as he withdraws the blade, an arc of thick red heart's blood gushes forth and the sorcerers move reflexively away from it.

I crouch low beside Thorn and try to get him to focus on my face. 'Thorn, you *need* to get up. You need to control this shift. *We need you.*' My voice catches and I glance wildly over my shoulder towards the Fae king, who looks manic now, almost berserk, partially covered in blood and gore from his killing spree. '*I* need you.'

Aelfric's gaze flickers to his son and he snarls. 'He's never been much use and now, when he's needed the most, he can't even get up and fight. It's better if I just end him now.'

'You have no idea who he even *is*!' I yell. 'Or what he's capable of. You never cared. How *dare* you talk about him like this?' I jump up and shove him with all my might and I don't know if it's because I've dared to lay hands on his royal personage, or if I actually have some strength left in me, but he takes a step back, registering surprise. 'We are all going to die if you continue with the ritual,' I gasp out and my voice is a raw sob of fear. 'Don't you *understand*? You're making a mistake.'

'Why do you think it's gone wrong?' Aelfric motions to the dying horned god behind him. 'That last god's death means I get exactly what I want, Blackhart.'

I glance over my shoulder and I'm not surprised to see Aiden trying to help free Dante. Lady Firesky is doubled over and looks to be trying to hold her lacerated stomach in place with trembling hands.

'I don't care about what you want, you evil egomaniac. Your kind should never be allowed to rule.' I stalk closer and flick my wrist so that the baton extends into my palm. 'You have used your son for your own gain. You've had your own nephew kidnapped, so he may become a vessel for the gods' power. And you think this is *normal*? Do you think that you've won, now you've ruined yet another person's life by forcing a prophecy upon them?' I draw a ragged breath. 'You are contemptible. Nothing you've done has been for the good of Alba or the Otherwhere. Do you think everyone around you is *stupid*? That no one has noticed and decided to stop you? If that's the case, you are even more deluded than I'd thought.'

'*You dare question me?*' Aelfric's voice rattles with anger. He's gone pale as he paces around the slowly dying god. '*You?* A human girl who runs after my son like a lapdog? You think you can judge *me*? You are nothing, girl, in the great scheme of things. Your existence is a mere blip on the scale of the life I've led. Once I've killed you, your family will be hunted for as long as I am alive. Not a single Blackhart will live to meddle in the affairs of the Fae. I am sick of their interference. I am sick of pandering to laws created in a time when people thought it wise to curb the Fae. Things will be changing, and I will lead that change.'

I want to tell him his reasoning is crazy. But as I move, the horned god reaches out a large hand, tipped with curved stained talons. He closes his hand around Aelfric's ankle and yanks hard. Aelfric lets out a yelp of shock as his leg gives way and he tumbles to the ground.

Forgetting my horror at the king's delusions, I run towards the god, who's now partially slumped over Aelfric. He is still gripping my sword in one hand and has nearly

356

pulled Aelfric's weapon from his body. His blood, where it hits the stage, sizzles violently and the smell of the iron-rich liquid hangs heavy in the air. I leap towards them both in a desperate attempt to stop what's coming next. I'm not fast enough, and skid over the mix of blood and viscera on the floor as the ancient god leans over Aelfric. With the weight of his sagging body behind the thrust, he drives the length of the blade right through Aelfric's neck.

I gasp and flinch when the god sees me stumbling towards them. He fixes me with one awful eye, which blinks before closing completely. The god's massive form sags forwards, covering Aelfric entirely. I can't slow my momentum and I crash to my knees, skid-sliding towards them both, crashing into their lifeless bodies. My hands scrabble frantically and I try to push the horned god off Aelfric but he's too heavy. I get my hands between them somehow and find Aelfric's neck. There is no pulse, no sign of life at all. I sit upright and lift my head to the dark expanse of the sky visible above and let out a shocked sob.

There's a moment of complete silence when those assembled on stage realize that Aelfric is dead.

He's succeeded in killing all the Elder Gods and, perhaps most importantly, the goddess is now dead at the hands of her brothers. The Veil is surely gone.

I cover my face with bloody hands and cry. It was all for nothing. Everything we tried to stop is happening. I look up to find Aiden desperately shoving aside one of the Sidhe warriors in an attempt to get to Dante – but they hold him fast. I try to stand in a vain effort to help him but my knees aren't moving the way they should.

A wild wind whips through the cavern and a blast of uncontained magic hits me full-force. I struggle upright, my feet finding purchase under me, and I stare around, trying to find the source of the magic. My gaze lands on the prone figure of the goddess. As I watch, I see *something* lift from her and it looks like her ethereal form but it's richly colourful and I'm reminded of what the leylines looked like when I travelled with Thorn. A wave of magic pulses from her form and lifts me at least three feet into the air before slamming me back down.

I give a startled scream and drop backwards, landing badly and hitting my head hard.

Lady Firesky's voice penetrates the throbbing in my skull and I force my eyes open. She's standing in front of Dante, who looks as if he's busy dying – pale and quivering from pain and fatigue. She has both her hands on her bloody and torn dress and I recognize those marks as produced by Aiden's claws.

The sorcerers have all moved to surround Lady Firesky, and she's become the focus of the magical energy they've gathered up from the fallen gods. As I watch, too dazed and nauseous to move, I sense the sorcerers gathering up the magic from the goddess too. Their gestures are no longer light or easy; instead they move as if under great pressure.

The entire amphitheatre now pulses with magic. I focus on Lady Firesky and, even using my normal sight, I can see her starting to shine with a dark pulsating light.

A soft sound and a far gentler brush of magic startles me and I'm relieved to see Thorn rising slowly to his feet from where I'd left him in the throes of an almost-shift.

He looks tense and his breathing is a little fast, but he seems in control of himself now. I must breathe out his name or make some kind of noise to attract his attention because when he glances at me, his eyes are a kaleidoscope of jewelled colours.

As if sensing my decision to try to get up and help Dante and Aiden, he gives me the slightest shake of his head and starts forward.

Thorn strides up to the Lady Firesky unchallenged and puts himself between her and Dante. This is just as she raises both hands to become the conduit of the gods' power, ready to feed it into the tightly bound boy. No one stops Thorn when he puts his hands on her shoulders and the lady's eyes open wide in shock but he doesn't let her move an inch.

His hands flame bright orange and within moments she's a writhing mass of flames in his arms. The coils of magic that the sorcerers had been channelling tear from her body in a kind of frenzied desperation.

This all happens so fast, it's as if time has speeded up. And I can only stare as Thorn drops the charred body of his tutor. He squares his shoulders as if bracing himself for an attack and as I watch in shock as he widens his stance and *inhales*.

'Oh my God, *no*,' Aiden whispers in horror and I don't even know when he got to my side. 'He *can't* do this.'

But he is. The power floods into Thorn, suffusing him, lighting him up from the inside. He's drawing all the energy from the Elder Gods into himself and it goes on for what seems an eternity – the light bright and violently active as it courses through him.

Aelfric's sorcerers start to panic as Thorn makes a move towards the closest one of their circle. He reaches out and at a touch the Fae crumples at his feet, unconscious. I jerk with fright because this I do not expect. As the thought crosses my mind, it seems to also dawn on the sorcerers that Thorn's not only drawing down the power of the Elder Gods, but he's draining the sorcerers of their power too. This, then, is Thorn's kami heritage on full display: the ability to drain Fae of their power and cut them off from the songlines. As the fifth sorcerer collapses, I pull Aiden towards Dante.

'Let's get him free,' I whisper. 'I have no idea what's going to happen next.'

We get to Dante and I worry at the chains holding him bound. They're thick and we don't have the keys to unlock the padlocks holding them in place.

Dante's face is a mess of bruises and cuts, and he can barely see us as his one eye is swollen shut and he's sagging heavily against the chains.

'Hey, we've got you,' I tell him and he tries to nod but gasps. His lips are raw from where he's bitten them. 'Just hold out a few seconds longer.'

Aiden mutters something about *focus* and then he's slashing at the chains with huge claws and full-on werewolf strength. One of the iron and steel cables gives way and he grips it between his hands and just keeps pulling and straining until it breaks completely. Then it's easy enough to pull the chains through the loops set into the stone and unwind them from Dante's body.

Chapter Forty-Eight

Dante sags against me but his eyes are on Thorn, who's bent over the last surviving sorcerer.

'He took my place,' he rasps in disbelief. 'Why would he do that?'

Aiden drops the heavy chains with a look of distaste and props up Dante on his other side, mindful of the ugly cuts lacerating his body.

'You can ask him, when we get out of here.' Aiden then looks at me saying, 'How about we do just that? I've got Dante, why don't you get Thorn?'

I hesitate, then carefully pass Dante on to Aiden, who holds him as if he's something precious.

At the death of the final sorcerer the blue flames ringing the stage flutter and die away completely. Sound rushes in and there's chaos in the amphitheatre. I barely spare a glance at the Fae climbing over one another in a desperate bid to get away from what is happening on the stage.

I run across the stage and stop a few paces from Thorn. He's cradling the final sorcerer's hand in his and he looks sad. I can't see any discernible movement of the sorcerer's chest and he certainly looks as if he's left this mortal coil.

Thorn becomes aware of me and looks confused to see me standing over him.

'Kit.'

'We have to go,' I say. 'Dante needs help.'

'Is he alive?'

'He is, thanks to you.'

He nods, looking thoughtful. 'It was a close thing.'

'I know. You . . . you were supposed to be the vessel all along, weren't you? Even though it really sounded as if it was meant for Dante?'

He tilts his head to the side as he considers my words and the gesture is so unfamiliar on him. It echoes the way the gods stared at Lady Firesky. 'Yes. Prophecies never mean what you think they do. I've seen this happen countless times in dreams and visions. Every time I don't interfere we all die and Dante becomes the monster that tears all our worlds apart.' His gaze, still a jumble of jewelled colours, finds mine. 'I had to do it. To save us all.'

From behind us, Aiden grumbles, 'The cavalry's just showed up, late as usual.'

I look up and find Dina half striding, half running down the centre aisle towards the stage. The Stormborn sweep into the amphitheatre behind her, and the Fae who haven't made their escape as soon as things went pear-shaped on stage are being rounded up.

She notes the carnage on stage but strides up to Thorn, taking his face between both her hands so that she can stare into his eyes. 'Oh, Thorn, what have you done, you stupid boy?'

'I stopped it,' he replies and his voice sounds far away, 'all of it. Now we have a chance to start anew.'

'The goddess . . . ?'

'I have taken on her power.' His gaze rakes the bodies of the fallen gods. 'I have taken all their power.'

'Your father?' She follows my gesture to where Aelfric's body lies half-buried beneath the horned god. She moves towards them but hesitates, her face expressionless as she stares at the body of her husband before turning back to Thorn.

I stand a little closer to him because he looks exhausted. The golden sheen of his skin is fading and he's starting to look more like the boy I've come to know. Dina blinks at me and in her eyes I see regret and a world's sadness banked into a slow-burning fire.

One of the Stormborn, whom I recognize as Korash, her second-in-command, moves onto the stage.

'Your majesty?' he says, and perhaps the intensity of his regard grounds the High Queen of Alba. I see her visibly get a grip on her herself before she turns to look at him. 'We have secured the complex and await your orders.'

'Clean this up,' she says. 'Bring the king's body to the Citadel. No one will speak of what happened here.'

Korash bows smartly and leaves to do her bidding.

Aiden and Dante start down the stairs, with Dante leaning heavily on the younger boy. I watch them to make sure they've got it under control before I head to check on the children we left behind. The room is as we left it, with the two unconscious guards still tied up.

I drop to my knees beside the first sleeping child and, as I do, I put a name to the face, something I didn't dare do the first time I saw them bundled together – here in their little cocoon nests of blankets and wrappings.

I check them all, looking for their pulses. Faint but steady. Roberto Santos. Joanie Powell. Christopher Singh. Jerome

King. Rachel Mitchell. All accounted for, all alive. Except for Tia.

I swallow heavily but it doesn't help. The tears just spill silently as I hunch over their sleeping bodies and I let sobs rack my body. This then is the end. I've found the children and, assuming we can wake them, they will be able to go back to their parents. I can't even begin to fathom what their lives will be like as they readjust to being awake and present in the human world once more. Roberto and Rachel have been gone for over two years and the psychological effects of their return on their respective families will be massive.

I look up when someone enters and I sit back on my heels. The Stormborn warrior takes one look at my tear-stained face before he crouches down next to me.

'Lady Blackhart, you have done your duty. Let us take the children to safety. The queen and guardian await you, so you may all return to the Citadel. Her majesty fears for your safety, should any of the dissenters escape the army.'

I wipe my face but I'm really just too tired to form words. He helps me stand and walks me over to the door. I look over my shoulder at the tiny forms.

'Promise me you'll keep them safe?' I say to him. 'Find me when you've got them safely settled?'

His look is as solemn as the small formal bow he gives me. 'I am Elof – at your command, Lady Blackhart.'

I let Elof lead me to where Dina and Thorn are standing amidst a small cadre of Stormborn. Their cloaks are vivid splashes of colour in the darkening amphitheatre. Thorn takes my hand as we move up the central aisle to the main tunnel out of here.

We're joined by Dante and Aiden at the start of the

passage and one Stormborn helps Aiden support Dante's weight as we leave the complex.

As we near the end of the tunnels, Dina beckons Korash closer.

'Tear it all down. This is never happening again. This island presents too much of a temptation to any who wish to bring ancient gods forth or ban any –' she stares hard at Thorn – 'newly made gods. I will not stand by and see a repeat of this. Bring sorcerers who are loyal to us, gather them from across the Otherwhere and sink this island into the depths of the lake. But only after you burn it down.'

'Your will, your majesty.'

'See it done. Set guards. No one goes in or comes out without my permission.'

Korash salutes and hurries away to carry out her wishes. I watch him go and struggle to feel any relief at her instruction. Instead I look up at Thorn, who's staring thoughtfully at me as if he's not entirely sure why I've not run from him yet.

I'm given the same suite of rooms I had when I stayed at the Citadel in the past. The main room overlooks extensive gardens, and the sound of hundreds of fountains fills the air with a soothing music. I sit out on the chamber's balcony, feeling more wrung out than I've been in a long time. It's only a few hours after we left the amphitheatre and I'm unable to sleep – even though I feel as if I should be curled up in the middle of the giant bed, dead to the world.

Instead, my mind is in turmoil, replaying over and over again the scenes I witnessed. A gamut of emotions rages within me. I'm relieved we've seen the end of all of this for now. I also feel sorry for Dina and the responsibilities that she's about to shoulder. I can't begin to imagine the impact Aelfric's death will have on Alba. I'm not even sure if any of Thorn's brothers are fully aware of the deadly game Dina and Aelfric have played behind their backs. Petur, the eldest, will be crowned as high king in the next few weeks – Dina said that much on our journey back to the Citadel. She went into full planning mode once we reached the forest. I watched in awe as she set about laying plans to handle damage control after what had just happened.

In the end I just trudged along, part of the group, barely listening as she spoke to Thorn and gave instructions covering every eventuality.

Messengers were dispatched to inform the other rulers of the Otherwhere of the passing of Aelfric, High King of Alba. Logistically speaking, she had a nightmare on her hands in terms of keeping everything under control. And yet I fully expect that she is capable of handling the situation.

There's a soft knock on my door, and it's pushed open on silent hinges. Aiden finds me sitting in the shadows of the balcony.

'Lady Blackhart, may I enter your chambers?' he asks with a cheeky grin and an eyebrow wiggle that I've seen him use to devastating effect in clubs.

'Are you here to steal me away?' I ask him as he drops into the other chair with a sigh and props his feet up on the railing beside mine.

'I can if you like. Do you *want* to run away?'

'I'm not sure any more. I don't think anywhere I run to will be far enough away.'

'Wow, that's pretty extreme.'

I flick a finger at him and get lightly shoved in return.

We sit in silence and stare over the gardens. The distant forest glowers beneath a night sky thick and heavy with snow clouds.

'They're not letting me see Dante,' Aiden says after a few minutes. 'I got sent away.'

'As in, he's under heavy guard and is deemed a threat, or . . . ?'

'No, the healers. They don't want me near him. They say I'm a disruptive influence while they're trying to help him.'

'Oh, that's okay then.' I lift the corner of my mouth in a grin when he lets out a frustrated groan. 'He's going to be fine. Just let them do their magic.'

He grumbles and crosses his arms over his chest and scowls out into the night. 'It's going to snow,' he tells me. 'You can feel it in the air.'

It feels good to sit here, in the growing dark, with Aiden by my side. I empty my mind and breathe the cold air. It starts snowing some time later and the world takes on a monochrome tinge. Aiden dozes off, and I watch the shadows darken around us. It's cold but not wholly unpleasant. Then there's a noise behind me and I glance up to see a young page lighting the fire in my room.

'Laurent?'

The young faerie jerks in fright.

'Lady Blackhart, you gave me a shock. I didn't think anyone was in here.'

I walk into the room, leaving Aiden sleeping in the chair.

'Sorry, just sitting outside for a little bit. How are you? How is your grandmother?'

Laurent smiles politely and answers my questions as he moves around the rooms lighting candles and lamps. He moves with a Sidhe's innate grace and he talks quietly about his grandmother and the North Hold in London, not wanting to wake Aiden.

'Is he one of the wolves, my lady?' Lauren asks, lifting his chin towards Aiden's sleeping form.

'He is. His name's Aiden Garrett.'

The page smiles. 'The rest of his pack arrived about half an hour ago. They were very noisy.'

'They're wolves,' I say. 'They're only ever quiet when they're eating.'

This startles a shocked little laugh from him. 'I'll be sure to watch at dinner tonight. I'll be serving in the main dining hall.'

'How is everyone, with the high king . . . ?'

The way he stills makes me think he's weighing his words carefully. 'Tense. The princes and the king's advisers have all been in conference with the queen since she returned with the king's body.'

'What are people saying?'

'That the king was killed while attempting to put an end to another coup threatening the House of Alba. That those present at the ritual had all been imprisoned and will be charged with sedition and plotting to overthrow the House of Alba.'

I blink rapidly. 'Yes. That is exactly what happened.'

Laurent looks at me with large blue eyes and his expression is open and guileless. 'I am glad you were there, helping put a stop to it all.'

I can only nod and have to walk away, back towards the balcony. 'Yes, me too. We're all very lucky to have come away safely.' I lean over Aiden and shake his shoulder lightly.

'Wake up, sunshine. Your pack's here. Laurent will show you where they are.'

Aiden sits up with a groan and scrubs at his face. 'What? Oh.' He nods at the young page. 'Okay, I'll see you later, Blackhart. Dinner, I guess?' He kisses the top of my head and follows Laurent out of the room. Dinner's going to be a late, informal affair, he tells me over his shoulder as he guides Aiden out – served in the smaller great hall.

As they leave I can hear Laurent's high voice, edged with obvious awe, ask Aiden if he can turn into a wolf at will or if he could only do it at full moon. I don't hear Aiden's reply but his voice is a low rumbling growl and I grin, imagining poor Laurent's face at the sound of it.

I rummage around the large wardrobe and am pleased to find one of the soft white cotton sleeping gowns I remember from my last stay. I strip off my dirty clothes and put that on before I get beneath the crisp covers on the bed, deciding that I would do my utmost to get a few hours' sleep before dinner.

Chapter Forty-Nine

The dinner is tense and there are far too many people for a small gathering. But I know Dina needs to make a show of presenting a united front to certain Sidhe nobles, with her sons at by her side.

Uncle Andrew and Jonathan Garrett are also present. The moment I walk in with Aiden and a very pale but much-recovered Dante flanking me, Andrew hurries over and pulls me into a long, hard hug.

'You and I, young lady, are going to have words. A great many of them.'

'I know. I'm sorry.'

He sighs heavily and glances at the boys with a scowl. 'And the two of you.'

Dante's the one who speaks. 'Sir, if you're going to blame anyone, you should blame me. I'm the one that was kidnapped. I should have been better prepared, sir. I put everyone at risk by not being alert to the dangers that faced us.'

Andrew lets go of me and walks up to Dante, gripping both his shoulders hard. 'That is the stupidest thing I have heard you say since we met, Dante. You are not to blame here, at all. Unless, of course, you're going to tell me that you worked with the kidnappers. Then you and I would need to have a little more of a chat. So, were you in cahoots with the guy that came into your room and took you away?'

'Well, no.' Dante frowns at him. 'But I should have been able to stop him.'

'He drugged you.' Andrew grips him tighter and gives him a little shake. 'We found the syringe. This isn't on you, boy.'

'But Kit and Aiden . . .'

'What they did was dumb and reckless.'

'That was my fault.' Thorn clears his throat as he walks up to us. He looks far better than earlier today and, like all of us he's had a bit of a wash and cleaned up. 'I invited them along. I knew the three of us would move faster as a team, to track Dante. And if I'd left them behind, they could have easily become targets themselves. I couldn't risk it.'

Andrew's face tells me he doesn't quite buy Thorn's explanation but he inclines his head.

'The matter isn't settled, but I understand what was at stake. And, I think, so did you. You did what you thought was best at the time, but it was still dumb. And reckless. You could have been killed. All of you.'

Silence falls as Andrew stares at each of us in turn. 'I just hope this will not happen again. None of our families would ever be the same if the worst happened, so next time, *think*. Speak to us and let's come up with a solution that isn't charging headfirst into danger.'

He gets muttered agreements from us all and, as he moves away from us, we share a combined look of relief. Then a page calls us to take our places. Dante, Aiden and I are seated close together whilst Thorn takes his place at the top table at one end of the hall. Aelfric's chair is empty and

Dina presides over the table. To her right is her oldest son, Petur.

As I watch the brothers and their families arrange themselves at the table I realize that they're doing it almost too obviously, making a show to those present that the House of Alba stands together. Kieran, the brother closest to Thorn in age, catches my eye and gives me an exaggerated wink.

Once Dina is seated, we are all free to sit down. The pages bring in the food, the musicians start up, and soon the hall is abuzz with the sound of cutlery and conversation. But the atmosphere is muted.

The official declaration of Aelfric's death won't happen until the morning. This will give everyone the chance to express their sadness at his heroic death. All three Courts will sit in judgement on those who plotted the failed coup and they will be sentenced to death.

Laurent, when he brought me a pretty blue tunic and trousers to wear, confessed he'd overheard that Petur will become the High King at the Midwinter Ball. In the meantime Aelfric will lie in state in his throne room for a week, so that his subjects will have the opportunity to pay their respects. His funeral will take place on the day of the Midwinter Ball, culminating in the ball itself, which will then end with Petur being crowned as the High King of Alba.

Anticipating the pomp and ceremony of the day takes my breath away and I wonder how exactly I'll be able to get away with not attending any of it. But then I remember Strachan's words, when he delivered my invitation to the ball. Though it's impossible to believe that was only about a week ago. Apparently no one turns down an invitation to the Midwinter Ball.

I sigh into my fizzy apple juice and get a look of sympathy from Aiden. He drops an arm around my shoulders and hugs me lightly.

'Just keep smiling,' he murmurs. 'We're outta here tomorrow.'

'Then a week of shouting and anger, then a party. Yay,' I say, and he grins.

'You've got it easy. My grandmother wants to meet me,' Dante says as he leans across the table towards us. 'Dina's set it up. I had to tell Dina about Yukiko's visit when she started questioning me about the sluagh attack.'

'Dude, that's brilliant news. You get to meet your fami— No? You don't want to meet them?' Aiden trails off. 'I'm confused.'

'I'm just nervous.'

'It's important, Dante.' I shuffle closer and keep my voice low so that our table companions can't hear us. 'If your grandmother accepts you as her grandchild you'll be safe. You will be claimed as kami. It means protection and safety in the Fae world. It also means that if any of Aelfric's cronies decide to come after you, for whatever it is that Eadric's done in the past, they'll be facing an entire race of pissed-off nature spirits.'

'I get all of that, Kit. But what if they don't want me? They didn't even bother trying to find me all those years ago. Why would they care now?'

'Just. Dante.' I grab hold of his wrist and force his eyes to meet mine. 'Stop this, okay? Give them a chance to talk to you. Take Uncle Andrew with you if you want to. He'll be on your side and act as an arbitrator if you're uncomfortable about any of this. Let him help. Let us help. You're not alone.'

Dante drops his eyes to his plate of half-eaten roasted game before nodding.

'Fine, just stop shouting at me with your eyes.'

I open my mouth to retaliate, but he grins and I start laughing because this is a conversation we've had in the past.

'No one can shout with their eyes,' Aiden points out. 'That's just weird.'

And it just makes us both laugh harder while he ducks his head in annoyance at our shared amusement.

'I can't do this.'

I meet Megan's frustrated gaze in the mirror as she wrangles my hair into some kind of weird up-do that makes me look both older and more elegant and ridiculously harmless. I mean, who wants to look harmless?

'Kit Blackhart, I will stab you to death with all these pins I've sorted through if you don't shut the hell up.'

I eye the pins she's holding. They're diamond-encrusted combs and are possibly worth the combined GDP of several European countries. They also look lethally sharp.

'Fine, I'm shutting up.'

'That counts for fidgeting too.'

I growl at her and she actually laughs. 'You must stop spending so much time with Aiden, you're getting worse than him.'

'I've always been this bad. I've just disguised it better in the past.'

She pats my shoulder and turns my chair around so she can inspect her handiwork.

'Why can't you just grow your hair out like a normal girl, Kit?'

'Not everyone is cut out to have Rapunzel hair, Megan.' I barely refrain from pulling at her own elegant up-do that looks effortlessly incredible. I have no idea how she manages it. My cousin is stunning and no matter what she wears, she looks like a dream. Me, on the other hand? Not so much.

'Okay, I'm going to my room to change into my dress. Are you sure you're going to be okay getting into yours?'

'No, but I'm a fully grown young woman and I'm sure I can manage this by myself.'

Megan looks at me with amusement. 'Okay, grumpy. I'll be back in five minutes. Try not to hurt yourself.'

I put my tongue out at her back as she leaves for her own room.

The week after Aelfric died and Thorn saved Dante has been a busy one for everyone. The news of Aelfric's death spread like wildfire. We kept a careful ear out and heard nothing but the official version of the story: that the beloved High King of Alba, Aelfric the Wise, had given his life to prevent the return of the Elder Gods. He'd fought the gods in single combat as his sorcerers kept them trapped, preventing them from rampaging across the realms once more.

The human children had all been returned to their parents after a brief stay in hospital. We called Detective Shen in to deal with that. Jamie'd turned up to help with this and he worked hard at coming up with plausible explanations for the children's reappearance.

The newspapers had a field day and ran the carefully constructed story of the children being discovered in an abandoned home, where they'd been kept prisoner. Apparently the man who'd taken them suffered from various personality disorders – chief among these being the fact that he thought he was the Pied Piper from the Andrew Lang fairy tales. As such, he thought he was keeping the children safe from the terrors of the real world.

The kids soon left the hospital and, although they were a little undernourished, ultimately they were physically unharmed.

The morning after the news story broke, I received a text on my phone from a blocked number. All it said was: *You kept your word. Thanks, Chem.*

I showed Dante the text from our young contact on the kid's estate and we hugged it out, biting back tears. We did it. We fixed things a little.

Later that same day Antone Pensa came to the Garretts' house. He didn't stay long at all. He just thanked us for arranging his wife and son's escape from Zane. It turns out that Zane had been in the amphitheatre when everything went down, along with Merrick. Dina's Stormborn had gathered them all up in a sweep, and they were awaiting judgement and sentencing along with everyone else who'd taken part in the ritual. With Aelfric, Merrick and Zane tidied away, new incidents involving Glow in the Frontier went right down.

And we'd effectively cracked the case, once we'd passed Antone's business contacts onto the SOCA guys. They were now having fun investigating all those involved.

As Antone was about to leave he slipped me a slender black box and told me he'd be honoured if I wore the contents to the ball. When I went to open it, he shook his head and told me to open it only on the night of the ball.

I walk over to the carefully wrapped dress hanging against the wardrobe door, pull the cover off and stand back to look at what I'm expected to wear.

'You have *got to be* kidding me.'

It wasn't a dress; it was far more than that. It was a thing with a tight bodice, cut low at the front and even lower at the back and the skirt was huge and pouffy and basically it was a meringue in black and silver. I move closer. No, not silver. Diamonds. Actual diamonds. Hundreds of them. I pass my hand over the fabric to check for glamour but no – no glamour. It was the real deal.

'How?' I pick the creation off the door and hold it up. 'How do you even get into this?'

I stare at the bodice and the back and eventually find what look like hundreds of tiny buttons along the side. I put it back against the door and groan.

There was no way this was happening. Not ever. I turn away feeling panic rising in my chest but then my door opens again and Megan's back.

'You haven't changed.'

She glides towards me, taller than me for once, in high heels and a dress that looks as sheer as mine does not. I gape at her. It basically looks as if she's not wearing anything, except for swirls of lace encrusted with diamonds and pearls. I touch her shoulder just to make sure there's a bit of fabric there – it's almost invisible.

'You look . . . wow,' I manage and she preens a little.

'I know. I know. I can't believe they sent me this to wear.' She steps back and spreads the skirt a little so I can see the full effect of the dress. Whoever created it had spring in mind, not winter. 'Your turn though, Kit. Come on.'

I slump my shoulders and shake my head. 'I'm never going to fit in that. Have you seen how tiny it is? How do I get into it?' I point at my chest. 'It looks like a torture device.'

'That dress was made for you by Dina's seamstress. Come now, you're going to be the most gorgeous thing at this ball. And I've seen Dante in his suit. That boy is stunning.'

She takes the dress off the hanger and inspects it. 'Okay, this is actually easier than you think. Strip.' She snaps her fingers at me in annoyance. 'Come on, you're already late.'

Chapter Fifty

It really is easy to hide knives in a ball-gown. Especially if that ball-gown was designed specifically for you and the designer knew you had a fondness for bladed weapons. The skirts are less of a problem than I'd anticipated because of the underskirt. There are layers that keep most of it from twisting between my legs when I walk but the train is a definite issue. How would I run with it?

I grumble under my breath and fluff the skirt a little. My hands disappear into the lush fabric and I try to smooth it out before I wrinkle it, but the movement makes me smile because it just feels *so nice*.

I look at myself in the mirror and honestly don't recognize the girl I see there. I look like me, but different. Older, perhaps, and far more graceful than I've ever looked in all my life. Megan's done magic where my hair and make-up are concerned. My eyes are massive with subtle shading. She's given me real cheekbones and a strong mouth.

'Okay, someone told me you need to wear this.'

Megan pops back from the dresser with Antone's slender box in her hand. I open it and stare in awe at the large teardrop diamond suspended from a gossamer-thin necklace.

The glimmering stone is the length of my thumb and shines so fiercely it hurts my eyes a little.

'Kit . . .' Megan takes it out of the box and dangles it in front of me. 'This is stunning. Who gave you this?'

'Antone Pensa,' I say, turning around so she can put it on. 'He helped us with the Glow case. He's a jeweller.'

'You are a lucky girl,' she says quietly, fastening it around my neck. 'Turn around.'

The front of the dress is not as low as I'd feared and the diamond drop comes to rest in the hollow of my throat, somehow gently illuminating my skin.

'This is insane,' I say, as I look at myself in the mirror, catching Megan's own wide-eyed stare. 'This isn't me.'

'No. This *is* you tonight. Accept it. Mostly we run around and fight monsters who're trying to kill us, but occasionally nice things come our way.' She hands me my wrap and it's even softer than the dress I'm wearing. 'You have your knife to hand so you've nothing to worry about. Come on, let's go crown a king.'

I press a shaking hand to my stomach and Megan takes hold of it.

'This is meant to be fun. Just breathe with me, like we've practised with Dr Forster and his witch. Come on.' Megan puts my hand on her diaphragm and breathes. 'Come on, Kit. This is meant to be fun. You have an actual god waiting to dance with you.' Then she grins at my bleak look. 'Fine, *Thorn's* waiting down there for you. You're going to dance and have a good time.'

We breathe together. I centre myself and after a few minutes the rising panic's evened out and Megan gives me a gentle hug.

'You look amazing. I look amazing. We're going to go have a great time. Let's go.'

We leave my rooms and four Stormborn in dress armour form up around us. Megan and I share a look and start grinning at one another. I lose track of the route to the ballroom but we start passing more and more Sidhe and various lesser Fae in elegant evening and party wear. They come in all shapes, all kinds and all sizes. The Stormborn keep close and we're escorted to the main doors of the ballroom, where we're made to wait for our turn to be introduced to the room by the major-domo.

I stand at the top of the stairs beside Megan and stare down at the gathered throng spread out below. I've never experienced anything like this before and all eyes turn to us as our names are announced. A page leads us down the stairs and I'm tempted to just turn around, pick up my skirts and leg it back to my rooms. But as I'm about to just do that, Dante's right there, taking my hand in his and bowing over it in a very formal way.

'No running away, Kit,' he says, voice low and teasing. 'Not unless you take us with you.'

Aiden bends over Megan's hand and smiles at me. 'You both look incredible. It's going to be hell tonight, Dante, keeping the girls safe.'

Megan laughs at that and points a beringed finger at Dante. 'Aide, he's the one you should be keeping an eye on. I've seen a few mamas eyeing him up for their daughters and granddaughters and I've not even been here five minutes.'

Aiden straightens and scowls at the offending mothers, who are not paying us any attention at all.

'I'll have to graciously rip them apart if they even think

about that,' he says through a tight smile, and Dante chokes on air, making me laugh.

'You both look very handsome too. How about we go and find a corner and hide until the coronation starts?'

I let Dante guide me through the assembled masses. If I thought the dress I'm wearing is over the top it doesn't hold a candle to some of the gowns present. We blend in perfectly, for which I am suddenly very grateful.

Aiden snags glasses of something fizzy for us all from a passing page and hands them to us. We make conversation and attract some attention, but it's due to our novelty rather than our outfits, being two Blackharts, a kami and a were-wolf attending the biggest event in the Fae world's social calendar.

'Kit, heads-up. You've a godling prince heading your way. And he looks yummy.' Megan lets a hand drift to her neck and she glances at me. 'I am just a little jealous. But only a little.'

I look over my shoulder and turn to find Thorn striding towards us. He's dressed to complement my dress, I realize, and for some reason this makes me shake a little. He wears a black heavily embroidered double-breasted waistcoat beneath a plain black coat cut in a military style. Unlike the boys and many of the men present, his shirt collar's open and he's not wearing a necktie of any sort. The embroidery on the waistcoat echoes the style of embroidery on my dress.

'You look incredible,' he says, and if he acknowledges the others I'm not even aware of it, just as I'm not even aware of him moving us away from Megan and the boys. But suddenly we're alone near the windows, which open out onto a large balcony. 'I'm glad you decided to come.'

'Hey,' I breathe and I wonder how to be polite about wanting to just rub my face against his, because he smells fantastic. 'I, yeah, it was a close thing. I got to the bottom of those stairs and almost ran back up them. But Dante got to me first.'

'I'll have to thank him for that.' He smiles softly. 'My, what large eyes you have, Lady Blackhart.'

I laugh a little, feeling myself colour. 'Fairy tales now? Seriously?'

'It seems to fit, don't you think?' With his back to the ballroom he's shielding me from curious eyes. Over his shoulder I spot Megan giving me a grin and a thumbs-up.

'I suppose.' I tilt my head up a little so we're eye to eye. 'I missed you. This has been the longest week of my life.'

'I know. I've hardly had any time to myself. My new duties . . . the new role,' he trails off and shakes his head. 'No, tonight is not about that. Tonight is my chance to spend time with you. I get to dance with you and there will be no blood or gore and we will converse like civilized beings. You'll stand with me as we crown Petur as the new high king and then we'll have dinner and dance some more.'

'Really? No one else to dance with?' I tease and desperately try to still the wild fluttering of my heart when his gaze lingers on my mouth for that fraction too long.

'None that I care for.'

I swallow with difficulty when he lifts my hand to his mouth, kissing my knuckles. 'None? Not even Aiden?'

'I saw him having a dancing lesson earlier today. I would not wish that on anyone.'

I lean into him and laugh because he's not wrong. 'Poor Megan. Poor Dante. They will have to dance with him.'

'They'll be fine,' he says, and he sounds so dismissive of

their potential pain that I laugh harder, but I become sober when he links his hand with mine, ducking his head lower.

'Kit?'

'Thorn?'

'I don't want to wait until things are bad again.'

'Neither do I.'

I look over my shoulder at the empty balcony and the flickering lights out there. It's been snowing non-stop and no one seems to have been out there for hours. I raise myself on tiptoes and glance over his shoulder at the milling Fae in the ballroom behind him before I pull him behind me, out of the doors and onto the balcony.

He reaches for my wrap before it can fall in the snow and drapes it around me, using it to pull me closer to him so I'm pressed up against his chest.

'You were saying?' he says, dropping a kiss on my temple.

'Bad things.' I swallow and stare at the hollow of his throat. 'We mustn't wait for bad things to happen again, to say what we mean to each other.'

'I agree.' He peers down at me. 'Kit, I have fallen very much in love with you. I think it happened in the forest, that first day, when you fought off the redcaps, then curtsied and told me that you were my rescuer. I have never in my life seen anything as bright – or as brave or beautiful – in my life.'

'You were barely conscious and possibly delirious,' I point out because I can't help it and he shakes with laughter against me.

'Even so. You made an impression. I wanted to get to know you, and everything I tried to keep you safe, you just ignored. And then you argued with me all the time, you never listened and then you just did whatever you wanted.'

'Hence making myself irresistible?'

'Maddening.' His lips brush mine. 'Frustrating.' A further kiss. 'Impossible.'

'Lovable?'

'Yes.'

I tilt my head a little bit further towards his and move that tiny fraction closer so he can kiss me properly. It feels as if I'm on fire. My heart races so fast that I'm sure he can feel it, where he's wrapped his arm around my waist so his hand rests below my ribs.

'I've been in love with you too,' I say when he lifts his head reluctantly so we can breathe. 'For a long time. And it's scared me so much because I don't know if we can have this. We never spend time together – apart from when we're running and fighting. I'm worried that things won't change, that we'll never have a normal relationship like other people do.' I look into his eyes and notice that they're no longer the blue I remember. There's gold in there now too and flashes of green. I'm distracted for a moment only, but then I'm talking again. 'I want to watch movies with you. I want to go to restaurants with you. I want to take you dancing. I want you to meet all my family and go on holiday with me. I want to walk the forests of the Otherwhere, with you showing me the places you've discovered. I want you to show me the places you see when you travel the songlines. I'd like to spend time with you and I don't know if we can do that. Or have that.' I close my eyes against the stark expression in his eyes. 'You made it clear when we first met, that humans and Fae can't be together. That the Fae are not allowed to mingle or marry or have relationships with humans. Has any of this changed?'

'No.'

I pull away slightly. 'Then what are we doing here?

Talking about being in love if we can't take it further than stolen kisses? If I can't be with you, or if you are ashamed of me, then there's no *us*, Thorn. Do you understand what I'm saying? I'm not going to be your guilty secret. I'll leave here now, because it will be better for us both. I don't want our relationship to be built on deception and I'd rather have a broken heart now than months down the line, because I don't think I'm strong enough to cope.'

Thorn's eyes are intense as he stares down at me. 'You are incredible.' The grip he has on my waist tightens slightly and I'm momentarily distracted by the heat I can feel from his palm through the fabric of my dress. 'I spent most of the day with my mother, Petur and the high council. With Petur's ascension to the throne, they feel it should herald the start of a new era. Many ancient laws that have little to no bearing on how we live now will be reviewed and changed. My mother suggested revoking the law preventing Fae and humans from being together. They want to review the case law and my mother is very vocal about her support. She argued that if the Fae are to survive the upcoming changes Petur's reign will herald, then the relationships between Fae and humans need to be reconsidered. Naturally safeguards will be put in place, and it will have to be proved that a human has willingly entered into a relationship with a Fae, but the law *will* be changing.'

'Your mother did this?'

'She did. I think she's grown tired of me watching you with heavy sighs and a pining expression.'

'There was that to consider. But she also did it because it's a law made by ancient old men, bent on keeping the race of the Fae pure. They never stopped to think that before they'd created this rule, thousands of Fae already had husbands, wives and children spread across the Frontier. Fae had been marrying into the human race for centuries – living among them, becoming more and more human with each generation.' Dina surprises me as she steps out onto the balcony. She is a vision in a slim-fitting gown that flares around her slender hips into a full skirt. The colour is so darkly deep red, it is almost black. She wears the Stormborn colours and she is as fierce as any of her warriors as she moves to stand with us. 'I am truly sorry for interrupting you,' she says, 'but I need to crown my oldest son as the new High King of Alba and I need Thorn to fulfil his role as guardian of the realms.'

I smile at her and nod. 'I'll entrust him to you, as long as you promise to return him at the end of the ceremony.'

'On my word,' Dina says, her expression unexpectedly solemn. She takes both our hands and we move back through the doors. 'Come, the ministers are waiting to get this over with. They've heard what's being served at dinner and seem keen to install Petur as high king so they can celebrate and eat me out of house and home.'

Thorn gives me an apologetic look and I can't help but laugh at his put-upon expression as we follow Dina into the ballroom.

Chapter Fifty-One

Six months later
The Caribbean, Buck Island, East of Tortola

If anyone ever promises you a relaxing day on a privately owned island in the Caribbean, stop to ask why. And definitely consider the life choices you've made up to that point and maybe give yourself a stern talking to.

I repeat *why why why* in my head as I run in a dead sprint along the pristine white beach. Behind me the undergrowth explodes as a monster the size of a bus comes charging out at me. The thing is all thick black fur, bunched chest muscles and long arms à-la-gorilla. It already almost took my head off further inland and I only managed to get away because I squeezed through a crevice in a small rock outcrop and it had to scramble around.

Dante's lounging on the jetty in the distance and I'm too exhausted even to shout at him. Instead I just feebly wave my arm in an attempt to get his attention as I run. He eventually glances up when I'm about a hundred metres away. The smile on his face freezes and he brings his hand to his mouth.

'Kit, run faster! He's right behind you!'

As if I didn't know that. I can feel the creature's breath at the nape of my neck. Dante jumps off the side of the jetty and starts towards me.

'Run back!' I gasp-yell. 'Just keep running. Away from here.'

He doesn't listen and we almost plough into each another. I sidestep Dante as he barrels past me and I pivot, spraying sand as I spin back, ready to back him up in a brawl with this hairy long-armed creature from someone's nightmares. I have no idea what to call it and I'm pretty sure my Giant Book of Monsters That Try to Eat my Face Off has no entry on this one. Dante trips up and almost face-plants in the sand but he stops, hands up, and starts talking rapidly in the kami language he's been studying.

The creature drops to all fours after a very frustrated-sounding grunt. It then stares at us, scenting the air with a wide flat nose, before it starts pacing in front of us, blocking our way up the beach. But at least it makes no move to come closer or attack us.

'What's it doing?' I gasp at Dante, hands on my knees as I struggle for breath. Running on the beach is a completely different kettle of fish to running on the street or on a treadmill. My calves are burning and I'm so out of breath I can barely speak.

I know I'm fit but this, fleeing for your life, tends to take things to another level entirely. Adrenalin courses through me and I wish I had my knife with me. Or a sword.

'We're fine, it's just posturing. Where on earth did you find it?'

I wave a trembling hand in the general direction of the island's interior. 'I was just, like, hiking. Thought I'd get some photos to send back to Megan and then I look around and there's this thing charging towards me.'

'Did you do anything to antagonize it?'

'I was standing on a little hill taking photos of the sea.' I bite the words out and straighten. I push my hair out of my face, as it's fallen out of its loose knot. 'Unless it was – I don't know – heavily objecting to the filter I was using on my phone, then no. I wasn't doing anything to antagonize it.'

'Actually,' a familiar voice calls from a distance. 'You were near her nest. She has babies. That's why she chased you.'

I look up to see Thorn striding towards us from the undergrowth. He's dressed in a scruffy white T-shirt and a pair of cut-off jeans that leave his legs bare from the knees down.

He's not wearing any shoes and he looks suntanned and relaxed. His hair has grown even longer than the last time I saw him, and he looks so different from the put-together young prince I'd left behind six months ago that my jaw drops open.

The creature ignores Thorn's presence entirely and instead settles down into a weird approximation of a human sitting with their legs outstretched as he walks past. I get ready to run towards him if she grabs at him but she seems more intent on trailing her fingers through the white sand. It looks to all the world as if she's sulking.

'Thorn, what are you *doing* here?' I move towards him once he's past the creature and throw my arms around his neck. Words rush out of me and I don't even pretend to play it cool. 'I thought I wouldn't see you for *at least* another three months, until they've passed the new law and—' I stare at him in dawning shock. 'Oh my God, they passed it already, didn't they?' I squash his face between my hands and stand on my toes to peer into his eyes. 'Yes?'

He wraps his arms around me in a hug and lifts me off my feet. 'I missed you so much. I may have caused several scenes and threatened a few people to pass the law faster. But yes, it's done. We're allowed to see one another without fear of breaking any ancient laws.'

I kiss him hard and fast and he hugs me tight before dropping me back to the ground. He frees an arm and reaches out to shake Dante's hand. 'You're looking better, cousin.'

'You're not looking too bad yourself.' Dante gestures to his hair and clothes. 'It looks as if you've made yourself at home on the island. Are you're staying here?'

'I've been here a few months, actually, getting to grips with some things. It was deemed safer for me to be separated from society where I could do little harm to others if my new powers didn't settle.' He looks completely at ease saying this and I ache for him. 'And although I appreciate solitude, it was getting a bit much. Although –' he glances at the creature – 'Erica and I have come to a mutual understanding: if we happen to spend maybe five minutes a day in one another's company we agree not to see one another for at least a further twenty-four hours. It keeps our relationship fresh.' Thorn gives me a little shake without removing his arm from my waist. 'And why didn't you read the instructions that were left in your cabin, by the way? It said not to go out into the island until someone came to fetch you.'

'I got bored,' I admit, feeling only slightly abashed. 'Besides, it's an island the size of a postage stamp. I mean, I didn't expect Godzilla's bride to be out here.'

Thorn manages a long-suffering sigh but he's definitely not looking grumpy. 'Where's the other troublemaker?'

'Aiden's out diving.' Dante closes his eyes to concentrate for a second before unerringly pointing off the beach, towards the sea. A dark head pops up as if summoned and Aiden whips his mask and snorkel off to wave at us. We wave back and, as we wait for him to reach us, I stare up at Thorn. His eyes are exactly the same colour as the sea. It is both remarkable and stupidly, distractingly, pretty.

'Why are we here?' I ask him. 'And why are you dressed like a surf bum?'

'Remember the night of the Midwinter Ball? Do you remember everything you said you'd like us to do together?'

I nod, remembering the words all too well. I'd felt raw and exposed, not quite believing I was putting everything I felt out there in the way I did. He could so easily have walked away, said that I was expecting too much, but instead he'd listened and brought us closer still.

In my mind I run over what I'd said and when Thorn lifts his eyebrows at me meaningfully, I grab his arm in shock.

'Wait. This is a holiday? You've arranged this? For us?' His acknowledging smirk is cute. I turn to Dante. 'Did you know about this?'

'Nope. Aiden just said he was coming to the Caribbean for a few weeks as his dad wanted him here on business, and that you were coming along so . . .' He shrugs lightly. 'Who'd say no to some sun and sea when we're riding out the tail-end of a really rubbish winter in the UK?'

'Exactly.' I scowl at Aiden as he comes out of the water like a Bond girl, shaking water from his hair and face. He catches my scowl and stops mid-step, his expression immediately going sheepish. '*You knew!*' I said accusingly. 'And you never said a thing.'

'Hey, don't hate me cos I did something nice for you,' he retorts. 'It took ages to set this up, okay? Just enjoy it.' He gets an arm around Thorn and gives him a hug. 'Dude, you've gone surfer on us. It's a good look on you. Is this what living gods look like these days? Because, let me tell you, I totally await my own godhood.' He poses dramatically as if waiting for a light to shine from above and when it doesn't happen, he just laughs. 'Do you have food? I'm starving and – holy hell what is that?' Aiden stops to stare at Erica, where she's drawing in the sand. He glances at us. 'No one mentioned the furry monster to me when I got involved in planning this.'

'That's Erica, and she's fine. Just don't go near her nest or her babies or she'll chase and probably try to kill you.' I peer at the creature and she peers back, looking moody.

Aiden drags his eyes away from her and nods slowly. 'Okay, yeah, I'll do my best *not* to do that.'

Thorn points to a rooftop that's just visible above the treeline ahead. 'The house is that way. Everything is at your disposal. If you don't want to stay in the main house, there are two villas on the other side, on the cliff overlooking the sea. Just, wherever you want to stay is fine. The island is my mother's, so we're safe here.'

Dante pushes Aiden ahead of him and they start chasing one another up the beach towards the house. The wind kicks up and I push my hair out of my face and smile at Thorn.

I've missed him so much these past few months. After the Midwinter Ball and Petur's coronation, we all returned to the Frontier, back to our normal lives. I threw myself into helping Kyle do research for a trickster case Marc was

LIZ DE JAGER

handling in Exeter. I'd spent more time with Dr Forster and his colleague Elki, working on heavy meditation and yoga techniques. These not only helped my migraines and nosebleeds enormously but also stabilized my magic further. The nosebleeds have stopped but the migraines have not. However, at least they don't strike as often and they're also less intense. I am still a work-in-progress but it's only been six, going on seven months. There is time. The family keeps me busy but I still have a lot of down-time.

After talking to Andrew, I have now opted to go to university. Classes start in September, after my birthday, and it feels massive, knowing that I'll be entering a new phase of my life. Andrew insists I take a break from family jobs during the first year at uni, because he wants me to pay attention to my studies. I agreed readily enough, but don't think I'll be able to stay out of trouble for more than a week. I don't think he thinks I can either, but the fact that he wants to give me at least a year of being a normal student is sweet.

'Hey, you're deep in thought.' Thorn peers down at me. 'Already bored of your holiday?'

I give him my sweetest smile and a quick peck on the lips. 'No, not at all. This is really nice of you, thank you.'

'I hear this is what normal couples do. Go on holidays together. Relax. Spend time together. Read. Sleep. Watch the sun rise together. Kiss.'

He takes my hand in his and links our fingers together. We follow the boys up the beach at a slower pace. Erica lumbers to her feet and passes behind us, moving back into the interior of the island. The undergrowth is so thick that she's gone from our view within seconds.

'What about the monsters?' I ask him. 'What do we do about them when they come for us?'

'The island is monster-free; I've made sure of that. You have nothing to worry about, at all.' He nods out to the sea and does a complicated gesture with his free hand. A wall of magic shoots up with a *whump* sound and a dome slides shut over the island above our heads. 'Being magically stronger has been a revelation.' He waves his hand and the dome disappears, but not the sense of being safe.

'No monsters? What will we do if we aren't fighting any?' I stare out at the ocean, then look back at him. 'Won't we get bored?'

He shakes his head and tugs me towards him. I stand on my toes a little so we fit together better and kiss him slowly. His lips are warm beneath mine and I let myself melt into him. He worries my lower lip between his teeth and when I laugh he kisses me harder and I revel in it. By the time we pull apart I'm shaking from the intensity of the kiss and he looks a little dazed and no less affected.

'For the next few weeks it's just us. Will that suit the Lady Blackhart?'

'No idea who she is, but this suits me perfectly.'

He nods thoughtfully. 'Does that mean the new sword I had made for my Lady Blackhart wouldn't interest you?'

My feet still and he walks on a few paces more before turning to stare at me.

'You had someone make me a sword?' I squeak out.

'Yes. I know you lost yours.' His expression goes from teasing to worried within seconds. 'Is that a problem? Do you not want it? I can have it destroyed . . .'

'No – what? Why would that be a problem? Thorn, that's the sweetest thing anyone's ever done for me.'

'You've not even seen the sword. You may hate it.'

'Shut up, I'll love it. Show it to me immediately.'

He laughs at my pout and yanks me faster along the beach. 'I hope you do. Come on, we've only got a month. We've a lot of relaxing to do.'

I let him tow me towards some stone stairs that I missed during my initial exploration. He turns to look at me and I grin at him.

'What?' I ask him.

'You. I never thought we'd have this. Us. I'd hoped and dreamed and now . . .'

'It's a new world,' I say, and he nods solemnly. 'With a lot of things to figure out.'

'You're right, but at least we'll have the choice to do it together. And we know my mother approves, at least.'

'Well, that's half the battle won, then,' I say, feeling myself blushing and then because things feel a bit too intense I hop onto the stairs next to him. 'Come on, take me to your lair, dragon boy. And I really do hope you've enough food to feed everyone because I am starving.'

'The island comes with its own brownie. None of us will starve with her helping out.'

We jog up the stairs side by side and as we reach the top, we look out over the picturesque bay, where the sailing boat we arrived on bobs. I don't think I've ever seen a place more tranquil and soothing.

I lean against Thorn, tilt my head towards the sun and breathe in the smell of the sea.

Standing here, like this, nestled against the boy I've come to love, everything is just perfect. I don't know how long it will stay perfect, but I'm prepared to fight to keep it.

Maybe being a named and claimed Blackhart isn't so bad after all.